# THE CASE OF THE
# HOOK-BILLED
# KITES

# THE CASE OF THE
# HOOK-BILLED
# KITES

## J. S. BORTHWICK

ST. MARTIN'S PRESS
NEW YORK

The Doña Clara National Wildlife Refuge,
the city of Boyden,
and all the characters in this book are fictitious.

Design by Laura Hammond

Library of Congress Cataloging in Publication Data

Borthwick, J. S.
  The case of the hook-billed kites.

  I. Title.
PS3552.0756C3        813'.54        82-5617
ISBN 0-312-12335-3                  AACR2

First Edition
10 9 8 7 6 5 4 3 2 1

*To Jim and Peg and Rob*
*along the Rio Grande*

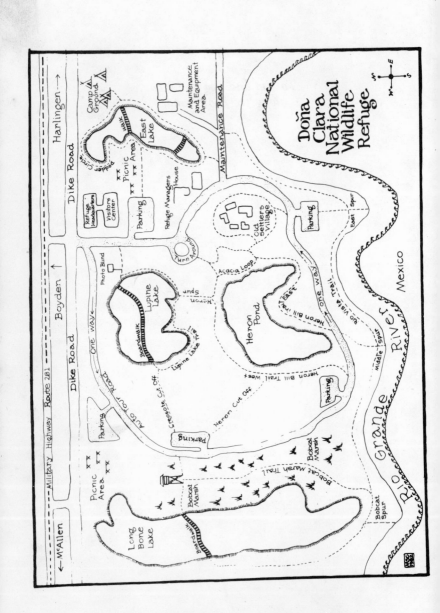

# CAST OF CHARACTERS

Sarah Deane—teacher, graduate student from Boston
Alex McKenzie, M.D.—physician from Boston

Waldo Plummer—captain of the Hamburg
                Bird Club
Enid Plummer—his wife
Lois Bailey
Constance Goldsmith
Nina Goldsmith  niece and nephew to Lois
Jeff Goldsmith  and Constance
Mrs. Milton van Hoek

} Hamburg Bird Club on tour

Major George "Big" Foster—Ready Tour leader
Eduardo—driver of the Ready Tour bus
Arthur Ready—president of Ready Tours, Inc.

Mrs. Orwell Meyer, Iris—sister to Major Foster

Leo and Janice Axminster—lepidopterists

Philip Lentz—instructor, Miss Morton's Academy
Eleanor Lucas—instructor, Miss Morton's Academy

Kate McMillan, Honoria Epstein, Dory Williams, Susan
Gorham, Nancy Gorham—students at Miss Morton's
Academy

Mrs. Addie Brent
Miss Margaret Fellows

} Cactus Wren Tours

Carlos Allen—manager, Vacation Villa motel
Cheryl Cabot—desk clerk

Sam Hernández—manager, Doña Clara National Wildlife Refuge

Bud Wojak—assistant to Sam

Tomás Pérez—lieutenant, Homicide Division, Boyden Police Department

Theodore "Tiger" Cotton—sergeant, Homicide Division

Earl "Pork" Nordstrom—captain, Homicide Division

Johnny Shapiro—clerk, Homicide Division

Sergeant Gleason—detective, Homicide Division

# THE CASE OF THE
# HOOK-BILLED
# KITES

# FRIDAY, MARCH 15

The mid-March day that closed with a corpse imperfectly hidden by the chaparral growing near the trail began in an ordinary way for a certain number of people making their way toward Doña Clara, the new National Wildlife Refuge that lay along the Rio Grande some twelve miles south of Boyden, Texas. The travelers came from Massachusetts and Maryland, from Idaho and Connecticut, from New York State, and from Texas itself. They were, all of them, moved by a variety of interests having to do with the flora and fauna of the Texas border, but what would bring them together was murder.

## I

Those who hate to fly find it necessary to keep a wary eye on the plane's equipment. Now it was time for another engine check. Sarah Deane, from her aisle seat, leaned past the bulk of her seat companion and peered through the window. Yes, the engine was still there, fastened to the underside of the wing and seeming altogether too ponderous an object to be held in place by a few bolts and rivets. Sarah frowned at the wing. Was metal fatigue visible at this distance? Or did everything just give way all at once? She leaned back once more in her seat and considered the life expectancy of a rivet—a rivet under stress.

A disembodied voice sounded from somewhere in the middle of the plane. "This is Captain Barnes. Ah hope y'all are enjoyin' your trip on Texair Flight 53. Right now, folks, we're flyin' at twenty-one thousand feet over Anderson County. It's a little dusty down there, but we ought to get us some rain tonight."

Reminded again that she was a considerable distance above the ground, Sarah swallowed hard and tried to breathe deeply as she had once been told to do when coming out from an anesthetic, but now some unhappy process in her stomach demanded attention. Fourteen inches from her nose sat the remains of a Reuben sandwich on its plastic plate, strings of sauerkraut draped over its curling crusts. This object had mismated with an unaccustomed piña colada taken at the Dallas airport to quiet jitters. The whole, working in synergism with a central emotional lump, had assumed a life of its own underneath Sarah's ribs and seemed uncertain whether to participate in its own digestion or to take the return route.

Trying not to hear the rattle and tap of other passengers' knives and forks, Sarah closed her eyes. Vertigo. She opened them and, sighing, reached for a small knapsack at her feet and lifted out the top member of a pile of books, all field guides from Philip. A book mailer had arrived two weeks ago, together with a note: "Dear Sarah. Looking forward to Texas. Be sure to go through the description of those species of birds common to the Gulf coast and the Rio Grande Valley. Take notes on the characteristics of each. Bring insect repellent. All my love, Philip."

Well, she certainly didn't feel up to taking notes on a bunch of strange birds, but Philip had been very kind, taken care of everything. She opened her book, *Roger Tory Peterson's A Dozen Birding Hot Spots.* Even she, indifferent birder that she was, had heard of Mr. Peterson. A hot spot, it seemed, had nothing to do with the tropics or a fungus infection; it was just a good place in which to see a lot of birds. Sarah swallowed again, turned a page, and stopped at a paragraph headed "Worth It All." Apparently anyone could bird-watch anywhere, anytime . . . on the job as governor, telephone lineman, or dentist. Sarah paused, and the picture of a bird-watching dentist halting in the middle of a cavity to spot a blue jay presented itself unpleasantly. But it certainly was a compulsive activity. She remembered Philip, the most serious of tennis players, once dropping his racket at set point and shouting, "A goshawk!" They lost the set.

Sarah yawned, replaced the book in her knapsack, and drew out another. Mr. Peterson again. *A Field Guide to the Birds of Texas.* She turned at random to a plate entitled "Heads of Terns" and confronted row on row of bodiless unsmiling birds. Sarah glared at the picture. They were all exactly alike. She closed the book.

A flight attendant gathered in her tray, a gong sounded, a voice urged passengers to return to their seats and promised turbulence.

Sarah's window-seat companion, a vast lady of middle years packed into a pink pantsuit, tugged at her seat belt and then produced a length of crochet work from a cloth bag. Her face was that of an unbaked muffin, her hair a variation on the beehive, and her eyes decorated by slanted silver-rimmed glasses with a feather motif.

"Visiting southern Texas?" Pink suit swung her wool smartly around the hook. Turbulence manifested itself in a sudden drop and bump.

Sarah blew through her teeth. Perhaps conversation was better than huddling in misery. "I'm meeting a friend down in Boyden," she said. "We're going to visit some of the wildlife sanctuaries."

"Now isn't that nice." Sarah's companion beamed. "I'll bet it's a special sort of friend, you traveling all the way from Dallas."

"My friend is a former colleague of mine," said Sarah with dignity. "We taught at the same school in Maryland last year. But I'm not from Dallas. I just changed planes there. I'm teaching in Boston this year."

"And your friend is still in Maryland without you? But, dear, you have such a young face, much too young to be a teacher. You look like a student yourself."

Oh God, thought Sarah. Why did I get into this?

"And do you have a special interest in wildlife, dear?" Sarah's companion executed a series of loops and spins with her crochet hook.

Sarah sighed. This woman could never be snubbed into silence. Better behave and be polite. "We're going bird-watching," she replied. "My friend will be leading a school group on field trips, and in his free time we'll visit some of the refuges."

Pink suit nodded and smiled. "Well, now! I look at birds myself. Cardinals and those cute chickadees, my favorites, come right up to the feeder. It's by the kitchen window. And the titmice with that tiny crest and lots of others. There are so many names I just don't know, and the price of sunflower seeds . . ."

Sarah, an English teacher by trade, shuddered. Aloud she said, "I'm a beginner, too. We're going to Doña Clara and to Aransas to see the whooping cranes."

"You couldn't do better, dear. I know that." The woman began to fold up her crochet work, and Sarah saw that yellow daisies alternated with what seemed to be chocolate kisses.

"What's your name, dear? Sarah? That's a real nice old-fashioned name. I'm Iris. I'm meeting my brother down in Boyden. He just loves to bird-watch, and he's almost a professional. I mean he gets paid to do it. I'm coming down to see him because Orwell passed away a year ago February, and I just have to get out of the house."

Sarah was too enfeebled by indigestion to pursue Orwell's widow through her bereavement. Wearily she returned to her field guide. The wretched birds were blurring into masses of speckles, stripes, spots, and wing bars. At the end of the book, Sarah found an account of "Extinct and Unsuccessful Birds." Perhaps, she thought, I can become a specialist in those. She closed her eyes and pictured herself standing in the center of an admiring group of ornithologists, Philip, silent for once, listening while she conversed knowledgeably on vanished birds. "*Francolinus pondicerianus,*" she would say, "was really a brown partridge, thickly barred above and below, with a rufous tail and . . ." The gong sounded again, and a voice began its ritual reminders about seats and belts and no smoking. "We will be landing," it concluded, "in four minutes, one-ten Central Time."

"There it is, Sarah. Corpus Christi." Sarah's seat companion patted her shoulder. "Remember, I'm Iris. Maybe we'll bump into each other somewhere looking at birds."

Sarah wiped her perspiring hands on the knees of her new safari-cloth pants, pressed her elbows against her ribs, and jammed her head against the seat back. Corpus Christi rose around her . . . bump, thump, whirr, bump. Down on dear old lovely ground again. "Thank you," said Sarah aloud.

The plane rumbled with decreasing speed toward the terminal and stopped. Sarah grabbed her knapsack, her camera, her handbag, and shoved herself into the aisle behind Iris, relict of Orwell. From somewhere on that ample person a narrow yellow folder drifted down into the tangle of legs.

"Hey," Sarah called, "did you drop this?" But Iris, in the short interval of Sarah's bending down, had pressed ahead and become lost in the forward-moving crowd of passengers.

"Y'all have a nice day," said the flight attendant at the door.

Sarah peered from the top of the boarding ladder for Iris, but the pink suit had vanished, so, bag, pack, camera case slapping at her side, she made her way down the metal stairs and into the hazy air.

## II

Alex McKenzie finished his glass of beer, rose to his feet, and reached for the check. The plane was coming in. Again he wondered why, in the middle of what was a part-time holiday, he had offered to make a detour to the Corpus Christi airport to pick up and drive Sarah Deane to the Texas border. There were shuttle planes, weren't there? But he had promised Philip, and, of course, given more favorable omens, he might have welcomed her. But Sarah seemed not much aware of his existence, and now she would be hastening with his help into the arms (clutches? sleeping bag?) of his old friend Philip Lentz.

Alex shouldered his way to the top of the entrance ramp. There was Sarah now, hastening forward, her face flushed, her dark hair in damp wisps against the sides of her face. Even with her long legs and the almost defiant tilt of her chin, she looked to Alex more like a cross child after too long a trip than a purposeful adult. Alex fought an irrational surge of annoyance and smiled at her.

"Sarah, hello. Good flight? Right on time. It's great to see you. Let me take that." Alex reached for the knapsack, but Sarah snatched it away from his outstretched hand.

"I'll keep that. Thanks, it was a hellish flight. I hate flying. Is there something to drink here? I've got a sandwich stuck halfway down."

"Not right here, there isn't." Alex, his role as porter rejected, turned and walked away.

Sarah knew she wasn't being friendly; after all, here he was ready to drive her all the way to Boyden. She trotted after him.

"Have you seen any birds yet?" This question proved irresistible. Alex's face lightened.

"Matter of fact," he said, pushing his way toward the luggage-claim counter, "there are three long-billed curlews by the airport fence."

Sarah tried to sound delighted. "Curlews? How great."

Alex looked down at Sarah from the advantage of seven inches. "Have you ever heard of a curlew? Well, you'll have to hold on because the luggage isn't in yet. Go and get a drink from the water fountain, and I'll buy you something cool when we get out of here."

Sarah departed and returned with water dripping from her forehead and the tip of her nose. She looks fourteen, thought Alex.

"That should fix the sandwich," said Sarah. "The curlew would be, what do you call it, a life bird? Philip is trying to make me keep a life list, but he wouldn't let me count a dead owl we found last week."

"Philip is very strict. After all, there are rules."

"And the rules are stupid. I mean it was a perfectly good owl. I picked him up, and he was so beautiful. I saw him a lot better than I ever do those warblers bouncing around in the leaves."

They stood together and watched the luggage trundle into sight. Alex allowed Sarah to wrestle a lumpy green duffle off onto the floor. "I won't ask to help you and insult an emerging woman," he said.

Sarah frowned. "Give me a break. I'm so tired. You can carry any damn thing you want. I had to leave Logan at seven and then had a long wait in Dallas. Don't ever drink a piña colada before flying."

"I'd as soon drink crème de hemlock," said Alex, picking up the duffle. "So let's get the show moving."

They made their way outside to the parking lot, and Sarah watched as Alex rummaged about making space in his elderly red Volvo, finally settling her duffle beside a small battered black bag.

Sarah eyed this object dubiously. "Do you always travel with that thing? Isn't it almost asking for trouble?"

Alex slammed the back door. "I always take it . . . feel unfinished without it. Where are your binoculars? You can't see a curlew properly without them."

"Back in Boston, all out of whack. Philip is bringing me his father's old ones. He's had them fixed up for me."

"Philip is always thoughtful. But in the meantime we have miles of birds to go before we sleep, and I've got an extra pair too —from an uncle. For emergencies like this. There, put the strap under your collar. It's a single-wheel adjustment. The curlews are over there. We'll move up quietly. This curlew has a sickle bill twice as long as the whimbrel's, no striped crown, and when it flies look for the cinnamon underwing."

"Cinnamon, yet. You don't say." Sarah lifted her binoculars, and together they moved slowly and discreetly toward the fence.

# III

At one-twenty-five, a green minibus pulled into the parking area of the Doña Clara National Wildlife Refuge and rolled to a stop. The air in the refuge, in common with most of southeast Texas, was on the opaque side, owing to unfavorable western winds. But the thickness of atmosphere did not prevent a listener from hearing the calling and screeching of birds, for here along the road's edge, in the brush and in the tree canopy, was the treasure that drew bird-watchers from all over the world to Doña Clara.

The green bus, door open, was disgorging the twelve members of the Hamburg, New York, Bird Club. Despite the blowing dust, the legend on the side panel of the bus was still clear: "READY TO TOUR—Ready Tours, Inc., Boyden, Texas." For a good round sum, the members of the tour had been promised "exciting birding, first-class accommodations, well-chosen meals, and experienced leadership." The prospectus had also assured them that Arthur H. Ready himself, "well-known ornithologist, author of the monograph *Migratory Patterns along the Rio Grande*, and his assistant, Major George Foster, of the Boyden Bird Club, will be your guides through selected refuges and parks."

The fortunate members of the Hamburg Club, now free of the western New York snow belt for two weeks, and hatched from their bus, stood about blinking in the hazy sun, grateful to be warm. They clutched binoculars, cameras, hats, telescopes, and field guides. Some raised their binoculars in a tentative way in the direction of the bird calls. Several began to sidle quietly in the direction of the rest-room sign.

Waldo Plummer, president emeritus of the club and trip captain, began waving a map over his head and making little glottal noises. White-haired, angular, with ears suggesting flight, he was a bottomless source of information on the world's flora and fauna and had strong opinions about everything else. He now rapped loudly on the side of the bus. The driver, Eduardo, slumberous after the drive from Dallas, sat up.

"Welcome to Doña Clara. I have a few ideas to share with you about the remnants of the subtropical forest in which we find . . ."

Only a faint shuffling of feet on the gravel could be heard, for Mr. Plummer, although long retired from teaching, still had the power to command.

"Good Lord, I've got to get to the john," whispered Mrs. Bailey to her sister-in-law Mrs. Goldsmith.

Ostentatiously apart from the group, Jeff Goldsmith, thirteen-year-old bird-wunderkind and nephew to the two women, stood at the perimeter of the parking lot and fixed his binoculars on the center of an ebony tree. His younger sister Nina, shaped like a basketball in shorts, wandered up to him, jaws moving, and blew slowly and with intense concentration a large bubble. It collapsed over her round face like a discarded skin.

"Nina . . . God," Jeff snarled from the side of his mouth. How could a person look like a professional with this creep around?

"Screw you," said Nina.

Mr. Plummer raised his voice. "If the two children in our party would like to run down the road for a distance, they may."

Jeff moved away toward the ebony tree.

"Shit head," yelled Nina.

Mr. Plummer arranged his face in an expression well known to old students. He peered at his flock and resumed in a threatening tone, "Doña Clara is home to the black-spotted newt, the giant toad, the ocelot, and the jaguarundi. The eastern coral snake is rarely seen." Here his audience began to look at its feet and uncertainly at the nearby undergrowth. Mr. Plummer paused, struggling in advance with the problem of publicly enunciating the names of such flora as tepeguaje, guayacan, and huisache.

Lois Bailey and Constance Goldsmith slipped quietly away.


Waldo Plummer, having wound up his résumé of the wonders of Doña Clara, held up his hand. "Major Foster, our guide for the first week, will bring our lunch. Now we must all wear our name tags." Mr. Plummer indicated a label stuck to his jacket that announced "Hi! I'm Waldo Plummer—Ready to Tour." "Now, we all know each other, but to Major Foster we are unidentified species." Here Mr. Plummer beamed at his group, and Mrs. Plummer laughed obediently.

Suddenly from the fringe came a cry, "It's a golden-fronted!"

"Where?" Binoculars were raised, fingers pointed.

"On that branch. But it looks like a red-bellied."

"No. Zebra back, white rump. See that orange patch?"

A tan Dodge van turned in to the parking lot and stopped next to Mr. Plummer, who waved a knotted hand in welcome. "Major Foster, well met!"

Major George Foster, known in the Valley as "Big," wore

two hats. After pulling his van to one side of the Dike Road, which lies north of Doña Clara, he had done his quick-change act. The friendly salesman of hotel glass and china had shed his outer skin of business attire and changed into the khaki costume of the field leader. The patch of the National Audubon Society decorated the major's right sleeve, the triangular emblem of the Boyden Bird Club his left, and the effect, borrowing as it did from the Boy Scout uniform, was altogether reassuring. Big Foster, now arrived before his troops, squared his shoulders, inflated his chest, pulled at his belt, opened the door of his van, and heaved himself out.

"Yessiree. Y'all got yourselves a golden-fronted woodpecker. Hope that's a life bird for some of you." Several hands were raised. "Now here's an oriole comin' in. Anyone know what kind of orioles we have in the Valley? Young fellow, do you know an oriole when you see one?" Big Foster, who liked to include the children in his discussions, now pointed at Jeff, who skulked at the edge of the group.

Jeff, thus addressed, came forward, looked directly at the major, and announced in a hoarse voice that threatened to crack, "That's the Altamira oriole. It used to be called Lichtenstein's oriole. *Icterus gularis.* It's listed as common here and at Santa Ana. Then maybe we'll see the hooded oriole and the black-headed oriole, though they're both listed as uncommon to rare. That's *Icterus cucullatus* and *Icterus graduacauda,*" he added.

There was a moment of silence while Major Foster considered what fortune had allotted him in the guise of a thirteen-year-old boy. Then club members, long inured to Jeff Goldsmith, began to talk and move about. It was well past lunchtime, a fact not lost upon the major. He called them to order.

"Okay, folks, the picnic is all packed in the van. When you finish washin' up and visitin' the rest rooms, I want everyone back in the bus. Eduardo will follow me, and we'll go over to Long Bone Lake where there's a picnic ground." His tone became serious, fatherly. "After lunch I'll talk about a few little old rules we have. Don't want to lose anyone—these trails can be mighty confusin' at times—so we ask the group to stay together." The major looked at Jeff and Nina Goldsmith and smiled. "No solos. Okay? Up and at 'em. Chowtime."

# IV

By two o'clock in the afternoon, the parking space behind the Casa Queen Diner in Raymondville was almost empty. Only a vintage Buick shared the space with a new blue Club Wagon. This latter vehicle, like that used by the Ready Tour, announced that it, too, was in the bird business; the inscription on each flank read: "Cactus Wren Tours—Madison, Connecticut."

Across the booth table inside the diner, Mrs. Addie Brent put down her fork and confronted her associate and co-director of the Cactus Wren enterprise. "Now, Midge, stop it. You have been in the dumps since we left home. You didn't get out of the car at Antietam, you stayed in the motel at Natchez, and I don't think you even looked at the whooping cranes yesterday at Aransas."

"Yes, I did, Addie. I don't neglect my birds." Margaret Fellows poked in a moody way at the limp body of a burrito. "And I've seen battlefields before. They're depressing. As for Natchez, it was raining."

Mrs. Brent pushed her plate aside and peered at her companion over the tops of her glasses. They were a curious couple. Mrs. Brent was a small square woman with a small square face framed in swatches of brindle hair, the effect being rather that of a miniature schnauzer. And, like that breed, she could be both fierce and combative, a fact she had impressed on successive classes of the girls of Miss Morton's Academy in Butler, Maryland, over which she had reigned for thirty-three years. Miss Fellows, however, was tall, large-boned, and large-featured. Her hair, still almost entirely brown, was looped around her head and into a bun at the rear. She had the countenance of an elderly and troubled ruminant; her top lip protruded slightly, and nature, in an act of balance, had caused her chin to recede.

Margaret Fellows, intelligent without being clever, had been labeled almost from birth as one of those girls who had best be given strong academic training with a minor in field hockey and fitted for pedagogy. When, however, she found herself unequal to the stress of doctoral orals, fate arrived in the person of her old college classmate Addie Brent, who flushed Miss Fellows from the university backwaters and gave her the vacant post of history chairman at the academy. There, as teacher, leader of field trips (she was an informed amateur naturalist), and field hockey coach, she had rested content until the past year. Academy girls of the past decade, alert for signs of aberration, had given Miss Fellows a nickname: "the Great Gelding."

Addie Brent, spared such by the facts of marriage and early widowhood, had long recognized the sensitivity of her old friend and her need for a strenuous occupation in a safe place. She also knew that her colleague required careful handling in moments of distress. There had been many since last June.

Miss Fellows, head down, regarded her burrito.

"Midge, look at me," commanded Addie. "That's it. It's not your fault that we lost the Hamburg Club. My dear old Margaret, you are letting your resentment run away with your sense. We are business people now. A fine business . . . as good a way to teach conservation as any there is. But we have no time for temperament."

Miss Fellows's eyes were moist. Her large hands pulled and shredded her paper napkin. "I said it wouldn't work, Addie. I'm a fish out of water. I can't handle men, especially when they're being difficult. As the girls would say, I'm just a drag."

"A drag? Nonsense! I never want to hear you use that word again." Mrs. Brent beckoned to a waitress. "We'll have some of that nice-looking cheesecake with the strawberries."

Miss Fellows looked up and addressed the waitress. "*Por favor,*" she said distinctly.

Mrs. Brent, unrebuked, continued. "You have cold feet, Midge. We will be a success. Tours are big business in Texas, and we will have our tiny share. Now use that good head of yours. When you heard that Mr. Plummer dithering, you should have called me. Never mind. We start anew. This is excellent cheesecake."

"But I'm not hungry, Addie."

"Of course you are. That Mexican food was not edible. Eat the cake and keep up your strength. I'm quite glad, really, not to have the Hamburg group. Mr. Plummer talked too much, you said."

"He did seem to be an expert on Texas birds."

"So we are well rid of him. After all, it's our first time on the Texas circuit, so we must learn the territory in a hurry and be ready when a group comes along. In the meantime, we can register at the motel and see if we can pick up one or two tourists."

"At least we have the Morton girls next week." Miss Fellows's voice had more vigor, and she cut a piece from her cheesecake.

"Yes, indeed. Quite providential . . . like being in harness again. I've had a note saying that Miss Lucas will be at the motel with four or five girls, and we are to work out a schedule with her."

"Will Mr. Lentz be there?" The question was barely audible.

"You know he will be. He's the only decent birder they have now." Mrs. Brent removed a small notebook from her handbag. "Here's the plan. Philip Lentz will take the girls for morning field trips, Miss Lucas will do botany in the afternoons, and we will be fitted in as substitutes. The last week is ours entirely when we drive the girls to Big Bend National Park. It's just as well to get Philip Lentz over with. Don't let him know that you feel a thing. Forward march. Remember, 'How dull it is to pause, to make an end . . .' "

"I knew you were going to say that, Addie. I just knew you were going to throw Tennyson at my head."

" 'To rust unburnished, not to shine in use'!" continued Mrs. Brent firmly. "So we must . . . if things as old as we are can shine. For heaven's sake, Midge, don't droop. Big people should never droop. You knew we would see Philip Lentz again; we've both been invited back to graduation. Finish your cake. It's time we got out into the world. Perhaps he did us a favor, after all."

But Miss Fellows shook her head and then struck her fork savagely into her cheesecake, impaling a strawberry en route.

"No, Addie," she said.

# V

Philip Lentz pulled his car off to the side of the road and cut the motor. He was pleased. Everything on schedule. Because, really, it was just a matter of planning. Field trips needn't turn into a shambles—lost trails, forgotten maps, missed birds. This year he had taken the Saturday-morning bird walks at the academy and wrought order. He had turned those rambles, formerly conducted by Miss Fellows, into disciplined investigations of the world of ornithology. Of course, on this trip he would ease up on the girls—perhaps tennis at the motel. He hoped Eleanor Lucas wasn't going to be difficult; she certainly had a talent for it. But they were adults, weren't they, responsible adults.

Philip ran his pencil down his Laguna Atascosa Refuge checklist. Satisfying, with a fine view of a least grebe in the pond at the end of the Paisano Trail. He hummed softly to himself as he entered the details of time and place in his field notebook.

Starting his car, a blue rental Escort, Philip saw with annoyance that a film of dust had coated the hood. He would have to see about a car wash tomorrow. Which thought brought his attention around to Sarah. He swung the car back on the road and considered her. Yes, Sarah, too, had to be attended to. Some gentle management. This Philip was ready to provide. Physically, she had everything going for her—on the thin side, but good bones, tall, and with roundness where necessary. Intelligent, perceptive. But an odd sense of humor. Sometimes she laughed when he saw absolutely nothing funny. All in all, though, she was everything he wanted in a woman. He'd made mistakes with females before, but now, with Sarah, this was it.

Even with all that mess. Bags, notebooks, trivia, lost and found objects unraveled and swirled about her. But this was going to be a good trip, without all the bother of school pressure and those hurried trips to Boston. He would help her find out what a joy it was to have life running smoothly; for a start, he would put her bird list in order, help her make coherent notes. It shouldn't be difficult. Sarah was a responsive person. And, although he didn't want to rush her, if all went well, he hoped they would be sharing a bed at the end of the two weeks. What could be more natural? She probably expected it, and he certainly wanted it.

Philip suddenly slowed and pulled again to the side of the road. Was that a swallow-tailed kite? Yes, the black-and-white pattern, the wide split tail. There it was, balancing in the air just beyond that fence. Philip leaned out of the car window, raised his binoculars, and adjusted the focus. The swallow-tailed kite skimmed close over the ground and then rose into the air. It arched and dipped and soared low again over the furrows of a distant field. Philip, unmoving, watched the bird until at last it vanished over the rim of the field. For a moment he sat smiling and then looked at his watch. Almost three, but still time for another stop, and then an hour or so left for a sortie to Doña Clara. After that, Sarah.

## VI

Sarah had expected Texas to surprise her, to bare its chest and say "I am the Lone Star State." She had hummed the "Streets of Laredo" while packing back in Boston, but as Alex turned the car south onto U.S. 77 and the landscape began unrolling, she felt let down. It seemed quite ordinary, farm country on a wide scale. Here and there a windmill stood by a water trough, cattle dotted a grazing stretch, a cluster of farm buildings broke the expanse, and now and then a line of pumping jacks appeared, moving up and down like hammerheaded robots.

Even with the car window open, the air was stifling, and Sarah felt heavy-eyed and sleepy. She tried to count the tank cars on a siding and then to read the message on a historical marker, but she could only make out the first line before they drove past. Something about Zachary Taylor and a march to the Rio Grande. He was the one, she remembered, who wore old straw hats and died after drinking cold milk and eating raspberries—or was it cherries? What was he doing marching to the border? It was all a long time ago. Sarah yawned. Even Philip seemed a long time ago. And far away. Not a real person, just a commitment of time and place. That's what flying did to you; it cut connections.

Sarah tried to conjure up Philip as she had last seen him, standing in the drive next to her apartment in Boston. It had snowed hard all that Sunday morning, and Philip was brushing the snow from his car before the drive back to Maryland. She had stood at the door and watched because she had a cold and Philip had ordered her not to come out. He had kissed her goodbye cautiously, just a light touch of a mustache across her forehead. Sarah closed her eyes and blotted out Texas. She could see Philip in his new tan coat pulling up the alpaca-lined hood over his fair hair. She saw him brushing the snow, working methodically with the wind from the rear to the front of the car, and then waving to her with a flourish of the long-handled brush. She remembered thinking that, even with the snow blowing puffs around him, he seemed competent, decisive. His car started at once. It always did. Philip saw to things like carburetors and batteries, and he spoke seriously to Sarah on the subject of "proper maintenance" because her old VW never started without a struggle.

"We're making progress," said Alex. "Three towns gone through while you were daydreaming. Clarkswood, Driscoll, and Bishop."

Sarah looked over at Alex and nodded. She had forgotten all about him in researching Philip. At the airport, Alex had seemed almost a stranger, although she had known him about ten months. But in Boston she had always seen him in the insulating presence of friends, of Philip. She studied his face. Older than she remembered. From the side view it seemed to be all corners and planes, no curves, and the dark hair was cut shorter than was fashionable with Sarah's male friends. The eyes were set deep under heavy brows. Genus Heathcliff, she decided. But she saw that the long uncompromising mouth was relieved by a humorous lift at the corners, and one thing about Heathcliff, as far as humor went, he was a dead loss. She suspected that Alex could be sardonic. Genus Mr. Rochester, perhaps. Not, said Sarah severely to herself, types that interest me. Thank heavens she had gotten over that Byronic nonsense long ago. In a mood of clinical detachment, Sarah shifted her attention to Alex's hands—square, nails short, scrubbed, a mark of his profession.

"Look," said Alex, pointing ahead to a huge sign reading "WELCOME TO KINGSVILLE," over which was suspended the bleached skull of a cow. "You're in Texas, Sarah. Now, shall we hit the side roads for variety? Look for some birds. What's your schedule?"

"I'm not meeting Philip at any particular time. He said that he might not even make it for dinner—he's checking out a couple of refuges for the students' trips. But I'd like to make it by five-thirty . . . to clean up, take a swim."

"Fine. After we get through the King Ranch, we'll turn off and wander around and still have you in the swimming pool before dark."

Alex was aware of Sarah sitting next to him, her left knee, her shoulder, only eight inches away. But, he thought, she might as well be in a glass case. I could be any taxi driver that happened along, while she hangs in waiting for Philip. With an effort, Alex turned his attention back to the road and silently pointed out to Sarah the wildflowers showing by the side of the road: clusters of cream, lemon, blue, wine, coral—phlox, storksbill, bluebonnets, star violets, scarlet paintbrush. Sarah smiled and turned her thoughts again to Philip.

# VII

Back home in Idaho, Janice Axminster found little room for her artistic inclinations, and her job as secretary at the Amber Park Methodist Church was a penance for a free spirit. However, loose on vacation as an assistant to her husband, Professor Leo

Axminster, she could let go. Despite the discomforts of brush, thicket, and insect life, Janice chose for a field costume a printed dirndl as an outward and visible sign of a sensitive and girlish nature. This dress she enhanced by open-toed sandals, ankle socks in a pastel shade, and a series of beads and chains that tinkled and clicked as she moved. Janice's hair, confined by a net in her church persona, was now released aft in a gray ponytail that bobbed behind her when, plump and uncorseted, she moved and bounced. Her husband's profession—he was a lepidopterist—was her delight. Each butterfly espied, each one netted, each thorax pinched brought excitement.

Today Janice and Leo were headed southeast on their tenth trip to the Rio Grande Valley to augment what was known as the Axminster Collection at Middle Moscow College. They had not found the number of specimens hoped for on their sweep through western Texas but the promise of the Mexican border kept their interest at pitch.

"Motel first, sweetheart?" asked the professor, turning to his wife and so guiding the Land-Rover into a pothole with enough of a jolt to cause his wife's cheeks to joggle.

Janice, recovering stability, shook her head. Her features, which for a time in her late teens might have been thought pert, were now blurred into a series of soft rises and hollows from which an upturned nose emerged looking unrelated. As a faculty wife she was, however, among the more presentable, particularly on the arm of her mate. Professor Axminster, with the return to favor of the beard, had rescued a nondescript face with a gray Vandyke. This change in appearance, plus a natural indecisiveness that alternated with spasms of irritability, was put down now to character by those students who had not known the professor earlier.

"Almost three-fifteen," persisted the professor, "and we're coming up to Boyden now. Shall we stop?"

"No, Leo. Straight to the refuge," said Janice. "After those ridiculous letters from the people here, we shouldn't waste time. We can call the motel from the Visitors Center."

"But which refuge? Santa Ana, do you think?"

"No. Doña Clara. A smaller staff and not so tourist-conscious. We can park away from headquarters."

"Janice, you're absolutely right. Have you got a list of the species we're still missing?"

"Yes, and the ones for which we need replacements. This should be our year. Five weeks. The grant came through just in time."

"Amen, sweetheart." The professor accelerated and shot the gray Land-Rover into the passing lane. "I think we'd better run over our *modus operandi,*" he said. "More problems this year."

"Piddle," said Janice with scorn as she tossed her ponytail. "Nothing we can't handle with a little imagination."

# VIII

Sarah and Alex had stopped once for an iced tea (Sarah) and a Dr. Pepper (Alex), and now a second time to examine a light-colored hawk that obligingly stayed for several minutes on the branch of a dead tree next to the road. Back in the car, Sarah shook her head and made a face.

"Hawks are worse than sparrows. All those spots and stripes, only bigger ones. I suppose I'll have to write it up in my logbook. Philip wants to put my bird-watching habits in order . . . and the rest of me too, I guess."

"Is this a vacation or an overhaul job?"

"That doesn't sound friendly. I thought you two were good friends. Philip said you were. You were roommates at college, weren't you?"

"For the last two years. You got to know him at Morton's Academy for gracious girls, didn't you?"

"Not always gracious, but yes, we both taught there. Philip did wonders for the place. He reorganized all the departments and cleared out some of the faculty deadwood."

Alex looked over at Sarah. High cheekbones, strong chin, wide mouth, eyebrows set well over dark-rimmed eyes. It was the sort of face that Hollywood used to cast in those aloof spinster roles: high-collared lace dresses, unworldly, then suddenly passionate. Was she as unforgiving as she sounded when she spoke of "faculty deadwood"?

"That sounds a little brutal," said Alex quietly.

"But Miss Morton's was stuck in about the 1890s—especially the history department."

"In terms of literacy that might be an advantage."

"Alex, you can't sit back and let an all-female school sink into the genteel mud of good manners and getting ready for marriage and the azalea festival—no, let me finish. Now at least the girls have a modern curriculum and a faculty that doesn't hobble on canes."

"Sarah, you sound like—"

"I know. Like a real bitch, and I do think Philip came down pretty hard, but that's what he was hired for. It wasn't a solo; he headed a committee for the trustees. Pensions were paid, proper notice given, silver trays handed out. Everything in order."

" 'How thoroughly departmental.' "

"Are you in a Robert Frost phase? The well-read man. But yes, you're right. I was only in my second year of teaching, so I didn't get too involved, but most of the younger faculty felt that the senior citizens should move on. And I did enjoy the old ladies. Honestly. Old pros, interesting, intelligent, but they'd been there since I was a student. And hung up—you wouldn't believe. Most of them resigned without a fuss; only the head of the history department had to be pushed. And Philip tells me that she and the headmistress have started a bird-tour business and will be down in Boyden helping out on some of the school field trips. So you see, a happy ending."

"I doubt that. But why did you leave? Not old age anyway."

"A chance at an M.A. I got a job teaching at a day school that left time for grad classes at B.U. Maybe I'll go back to Morton's someday. Philip tells me that all the dust has settled, wounds are healing, and some of the beheaded faculty have been invited back for graduation. We'll all sing school songs and talk about what it was like in 1923 or 1937. Sometimes the whole scene gives me the creeps."

"Tough Ms. Deane."

"Not so tough. I start giggling when we sing 'How Firm a Foundation,' because it makes me think of those girdle ads, but by the time we've worked up to the school hymn, a tear is brimming."

"Nostalgia is a powerhouse. It'll get you every time. How about one more bird stop and then motel land?"

And the Volvo sped over a rise and pointed south.

# IX

Old Settlers Village squats near the center of the Doña Clara. The broken-down buildings, crumbled walls, and rusted iron railings are of negligible interest to the historical archaeologist; the village dates only from the 1870s and was abandoned in the 1950s. A condominium scheme was defeated by a conservation bloc, which subsequently established the refuge itself, and now the village is one of the favorite stopping places, perhaps because there is always something to sit on.

"Thank God," said Constance Goldsmith, collapsing on what was either a step or an overturned gravestone. "I've had it."

"I see an eastern yellow coral snake," said Nina Goldsmith, hopping in a circle around her aunt.

"That's the fifth coral snake you've seen," said Mrs. Goldsmith without moving. "See if you can find a python."

"This heat is murder," said Lois Bailey, sitting down next to her sister-in-law. "Major Foster's still looking for those groove-billed things."

"Anis. Groove-billed anis. Here's the picture." Mrs. Goldsmith opened her guide. "Ugly, aren't they? I hope," she added wearily, "he doesn't find them. My feet are going to explode."

It was past four, the temperature had gone to 88 degrees, the dust had settled, and the air was heavy. The Hamburg Club had hiked long and hard, sighting birds and swatting bugs. Bird lists had lengthened, necks were stiff with craning, and hiking boots pinched. Enthusiasm had quieted, and most were grateful for a respite.

Two college students sat on a brick wall and puzzled over their lists; next to them sat Mrs. Milton van Hoek, who for her first birding trip wore an Inverness cape and was bitterly regretting it. She was now slumped like a collapsed tweed mushroom on the edge of a ruined well. Nearby was Mrs. Enid Plummer, consort of Waldo, who called Mrs. van Hoek "dearie," and was placidly readjusting a strap on her husband's pith helmet. Others sat, leaned, looked for ticks.

A kiskadee flycatcher swooped from a branch and disappeared, rattling his noisy "kiss-kee-dee," but only two heads turned. Everyone was an old Texas birder now, and this was the sixth kiskadee. The tour members chattered: "How can you tell if you've got chiggers?" "Are you using the new Peterson?" "You can just unscrew a tick. Counterclockwise." "It's the same bird, but one has a black crest—you can't count two. They're both tits." (Here Nina Goldsmith giggled and poked her elbow into the rib of an aunt.)

"Now, people," interrupted Waldo Plummer, who in his reclaimed pith helmet looked like someone pausing in his search for the source of the Nile, "we must trust the A.O.U. for species nomenclature."

"Goodness, what's an A.O.U.?" asked Mrs. van Hoek in a stifled voice from around her cape.

"That's the American Ornithologists Union. They settle species debates," said Jeff Goldsmith with the air of a tenured professor informing a freshman. "The black-crested titmouse and the tufted titmouse hybridize, so they're the same species."

"Jeffrey is correct," said Mr. Plummer, "but now we must all be silent. Major Foster is trying to find an ani for us."

"He moves quietly for such a big man," observed Lois Bailey.

Jeff rounded on his aunt. "Any good ornithologist moves quietly. Only stupid people make a lot of noise and talk all the time."

Lois Bailey and Constance Goldsmith sighed in concert. Not for the first time did they regret their invitation to take their niece and nephew on the Texas tour. Jeff, of course, was an avid birder, but an impatient one. Thirteen was an uneasy age, and the difference in years and what Miss Austen might have called "habits of address" made social moments distinctly sticky. As for nine-year-old Nina, she was overheated and bored stiff.

"It's time for the motel and the swimming pool," said Mrs. Bailey, and she wiped her forehead, leaving a wide streak of dirt.

Major Foster reappeared on the brink of the group and held up a hand for attention. "Can't see hide nor hair of those anis, but we'll try again tomorrow. Now, folks, it's after four, and I'm goin' to check out some other trails for new arrivals. Eduardo will drive you to Lupine Lake where there's a photo blind. Then he'll take those folks dyin' of heat to Progreso for a milk shake or a cone. For those that stay, I suggest goin' around Lupine Lake or Dodder Circle over by East Lake—they're both close to the Visitors Center. Don't go off'n your own. We've been havin' a mite of trouble here on the border. Be at the parkin' lot by six and I'll meet you there. Then we'll drive up on the Dike Road and try and get ourselves a pauraque just when it's turnin' dark. That's a bird'll tickle you. It sits sideways on the road with eyes that look like little red taillights."

"Isn't it sort of a whip-poor-will?" asked Lois Bailey.

"Yes, ma'am," said Big Foster. He looked squarely at Jeff. "Order Caprimulgiformes; family Caprimulgidae. The pauraque is *Nyctidromus albicollis*. All right, folks, into the bus. Left foot, right foot, hay foot, straw foot."

"He's certainly a dynamo," said Constance Goldsmith. "Well, I'm ready for a change. Jeff and Nina, how about something cold?"

Jeff looked up from his study of the refuge map. "I'm not going to waste time with ice cream. The birding just gets good now."

"All right, Jeff. Nina and Aunt Lois and I are going with Eduardo. You stick with the tour group, understand?"

Jeff did not answer.

"Did you hear me, Jeff Goldsmith?"

"Yes, Aunt Connie." Jeff aimed a short kick at his sister's shins, looked at his watch, and then resumed his inspection of the trails of Doña Clara.

# X

Cheryl Cabot had one simple policy regarding dress: if it fit, it was too big. As a consequence, Cheryl always appeared as a sort of sausage forced into too small a casing. Now the last thing that Carlos Allen, the manager of Vacation Villa, wanted on the desk was a sexpot, but clerks who could type, keep accounts, and speak English and Spanish were valuable, so, for the time, he held his tongue.

It was almost five o'clock, and the telephone at the reservation desk had not rung for at least twelve minutes. The lobby was empty, and Mr. Allen had seen fit to improve a dull hour by quizzing Cheryl. She was bent low over the reservation charts and was concentrating on keeping a wad of gum secure in the cheek away from Mr. Allen. To anyone within a hundred yards, it was obvious that the motel's strictures on modest necklines had been ignored. Mr. Allen, however, was all business.

"Good. We're almost booked except for the rooms behind the Rotary Room and the Annex. Now where are our bird groups going? Let me see. We have the Cactus Wren leaders for tonight and on through next Friday. Then we have the Morton Academy students with two instructors and an adult guest, a Miss Deane. Then there's the new Ready Tour group, also for one week. The Hamburg Bird Club this time. Someone has put them off on the second floor. That won't do."

Mr. Allen shuffled sets of floor plans. He was stout, under five foot six, and his hair was sparse and combed across a bald spot. But under the exterior of a mouse lurked a motel lion. He had been with the Vacation Villa chain only a few years but had risen like a rocket. Mr. Allen's gimmick was the care and feeding of the nature-lover. He made a point to gather the tired, the hot, the bug-bitten into a better trap, and by dint of this single vision the Boyden Villa had gone from a mediocre tourist bin to a refuge for those weary of the refuge. Guests dined in the Avocet Room, were quartered on the likes of Warbler Walk, raised their spirits in the Roadrunner Bar, and were catered to by the Grackle Gift Shop. In short, Mr. Allen had wrought a nature-lover's Xanadu.

He now spoke sharply to Miss Cabot. "Get rid of that gum." Cheryl sulked.

"In the wastebasket, Cheryl. It makes a bad impression. Now look at these charts. We always give our tour groups the best. Tour groups are our bread and butter, Cheryl."

"So how can I fix it up?" Cheryl yawned. Birds were for the birds. All this jazz about tours was a pain in the ass.

"I will do this over now, Cheryl, but I want you to make yourself familiar with our reservation priorities. And it wouldn't hurt you one bit to go out to one of the refuges on your day off."

Mr. Allen, ignoring the look of horror on his clerk's face, bent to work with his eraser. He lifted the Cactus Wren ladies from Kingfisher Row and slipped them into safe nesting on Warbler Walk. He took the members of the Texas Gay Alliance Directors' Conference, operating under the name of Alternates, Inc., out of their slot next to the girls of Miss Morton's, and, humming softly, wrote them into a series of ill-lit chambers behind the Rotary Room. The Ready Tour people he tenderly rubbed out from the second floor and replaced them in units on the Oriole Hall, which gave out on the garden and pool. Miss Eleanor Lucas and Mr. Philip Lentz, he separated and placed on the starboard and port flanks of their students, who remained on Caspian Turn. Miss Sarah Deane, whose reservation had been made by Mr. Lentz, he moved to Warbler Walk, which should make a stiff hike for Mr. Lentz were he amorously inclined. Mr. Allen was old-fashioned when it came to children being proximate to cohabiting adults. An apparent stranger to all these, an A. McKenzie, M.D., was left on Warbler. Mr. Allen smiled and pushed the charts under the desk counter. The telephone rang, and he snatched it from Cheryl's hand.

"Vacation Villa. Yes. Indeed, yes. A nice room in the annex. All just finished. So good to hear from you again." Mr. Allen turned to Cheryl with satisfaction. "That's Professor Axminster and his wife. Here every year. They're butterflies."

"What's butterflies?"

"Professor Axminster is. A lepidopterist. A new word for you, Cheryl. As a matter of fact, I'm thinking of using butterfly names for the corridors in the annex. Swallowtail, monarch . . . something like that. There's a butterfly called sleepy orange."

Cheryl was bored with the Axminsters. One hand quietly sought the open pack of gum cached under the counter.

The glass door of the lobby glided open, and two persons came over the threshold, stepping warily as people do when not sure about self-opening entryways. They were each hung about with leather cases and canvas baggage. Cheryl Cabot thought they looked like a couple of tramps who had wandered in by mistake—those dusty boots, crumpled hats, and bandannas. But Mr. Allen always kept a weather eye for expensive optical equipment and the safari look; such promised cash flow, grist to the motel mill.

"Good afternoon." Mr. Allen nodded and rubbed his hands.

The tall man dropped a knapsack at his feet and lowered a green duffel. "Hello," he said. "I'm Dr. McKenzie, and this is Miss Deane. We both have reservations."

Mr. Allen smiled a tight little smile. "Welcome to Boyden. Now let me see." Mr. Allen slid his chart a small way into the open. "Here we are. You have a nice corner room on Warbler Walk, Doctor. And you, Miss Deane . . ."

"Philip Lentz made the reservation for me," said Sarah.

A faint shadow settled on Mr. Allen's face. He frowned at his room chart, but, eraser artist that he was, he could not, having once lifted Miss Deane from the purview of Mr. Lentz, now keep her out of the sphere of Dr. McKenzie. He shrugged. At least the Morton girls were at a discreet distance. Perhaps Miss Deane was sharing her favors in one of those threesomes he had heard so much about. And Miss Lucas? Was it a four-way affair? Well, as long as everyone was quiet about any bedtime frolic, he was not one to object.

"Ah, yes, Miss Deane. I have your room. Warbler Walk, number seventeen, with a nice view of our patio."

Alex turned to Sarah. "I'll leave you now. I've an appointment in Boyden. This was fun. Hope the birds didn't bore you to death."

Sarah looked up at Alex, then let her glance slide toward a

sign reading "POOL AND GARDEN." "Yes—oh, thanks, Alex. For meeting me and everything . . . the iced tea and all. And the birds were great. I hope we'll see you around . . . birding somewhere or maybe dinner tonight."

"No, not tonight. I'm going over to the station to see Tom Pérez about that drug project I'll be working on, and then going back to his house for dinner. But keep in touch. If Philip can get loose, perhaps we can make a day of it later on."

"Maybe we can." Sarah smiled a bit vaguely, reached out, and shook his hand. Alex was already a little out of focus. She thought of a shower, a swim, and a cool drink. Then, perhaps, Philip and dinner. She turned back to the desk. "Has Mr. Lentz checked in?"

Mr. Allen consulted his file. "No, we haven't heard from Mr. Lentz yet, but we have his deposit and will hold his room."

"He'll be here," said Sarah, "but maybe not until much later. Please tell him to call my room when he comes."

"Certainly, Miss Deane." Mr. Allen indicated the binoculars hanging around Sarah's neck. "I hope you have rewarding birding during your stay, Miss Deane."

"Oh Lord," said Sarah. "I forgot to give Alex back his binoculars." She ran to the door, but the Volvo was just turning out of the drive. Never mind, she thought, he has his own; I'll give these back later. And she moved to follow a small person in a blue uniform, who, encumbered with her duffel, was vanishing down the hall.

# XI

Eleanor Lucas, present colleague of Philip Lentz's at Miss Morton's Academy and instructor in botany, tennis, and fencing, had been hiking since three o'clock in the Doña Clara Refuge. In this activity she had been joined by her traveling companion and most promising pupil, Dory Williams, but at four o'clock they split up after making plans to meet in the parking lot and return to the motel in time to meet the small clutch of Morton students who would be arriving from the airport.

Cactus Wren Tours, in the persons of Mrs. Brent and Miss Fellows, arrived just before five o'clock and launched themselves onto the maze of paths that wound through Doña Clara. Shortly afterward, Professor and Mrs. Axminster, now assured of a motel room, plunged into the thicket south of Heron Pond laden with nets and bottles. By five-thirty, Philip Lentz had put up his telescope, opened his notebook, and settled himself on a folding stool in the part of Bobcat Marsh that he believed favored the appearance of wildlife.

By five-fifty, those members of the Hamburg Bird Club who had voted to skip the ice-cream trip had begun to emerge in wilted condition from the nearby trails and to make for the parking lot and the six-o'clock rendezvous. On the returned bus, Nina Goldsmith, victim of heat, boredom, and a strawberry soda, was asleep on a rear seat. Her two aunts, sticky and numb, sat next to her, beguiled by visions of showers and tall frosted drinks.

Jeff Goldsmith, after the departure of the bus, had immediately asserted his independence from the tour, and at six o'clock was running hard across the Lupine Lake boardwalk leading to the Auto Tour Road. He arrived more than ten minutes late, to face the ire of Major Foster, who had just pulled up his van ready to lead the group across to the Dike Road.

By six-thirty, cumulus clouds that had begun to form earlier in the east Texas sky appeared, the edges luminous in the fast-departing light. The heat had lessened, thunder was grumbling somewhere in the direction of Brownsville, and a northeast wind was rising. As if nudged by the change in the weather, most of the remaining visitors to the refuge converged in the parking lot, climbed into their cars, and left.

At six-fifty, dusk had almost changed to dark, and the wind moved forcefully through the brush and rattled the tops of the trees beside refuge headquarters. Inside his office, refuge manager Sam Hernández walked to a side window and heaved it open. The wind hit the screen furred by the day's dust and sent a storm of dirty air into the room. Sam sneezed, closed the window, sat down heavily at his desk, and collected the papers scattered by the wind, then opened a field guide and bent over it. Assistant refuge manager Bud Wojak was balanced atilt a wooden chair, his legs resting on a low file cabinet. Holding a flyswatter ready, he was watching a spider move across a large wall map of the refuge.

"That clinches it." Sam slapped his field guide on the desk top.

"Clinches what, Sam?"

"Clinches the kites, old buddy Bud. Hook-billed kites! Two of the devils. Male and female—first time in the refuge. Hot damn! *Chondrohierax uncinatus.* That'll keep Santa Ana in its place. They've had kind of a monopoly on hook-bills along with Bentsen State Park."

"Where d'ya see 'em?" Bud took aim with his flyswatter.

"South end of Bobcat Marsh, just before five. I'd stopped the Jeep, and, goddamn, there they were. Two on the big dead oak near the edge of the road. Light wasn't great, but okay for coloration. I had time to check the field marks, but wouldn't you know, a family came along asking about the rest rooms—nobody reads signs—and by the time I looked again they'd gone to a tree up the marsh. So what d'ya say?"

Bud Wojak brought the flyswatter down hard on the map, and the spider disappeared hastily behind the wooden frame.

"Bud, if you'd spend more time on your field I.D. work you'd get a real buzz from this. God, hook-billed kites at Doña Clara."

"You said that, Sam."

"They've only been seen at Santa Ana and Bentsen in the last few years. First reported in Hidalgo County in 1967."

"So now you can write 'em up, Sam. Me, I like trees and plants. They don't fly off on you."

Sam snapped off the lamp at the edge of his desk. "Let's close her up, Bud. Only six cars left in the parking lot, and I guess they belong to the Kansas biology team. I gave 'em permission to stay in the campground and park in the lot. Trails were almost empty when I went through just after five. Think the weather's scarin' 'em."

Bud lowered his legs, keeping his chair on point until the last possible moment. He was young and unruffled by the trials of a refuge manager's life. "Where's Art Ready's bus?" he asked.

"Probably still out on the Dike Road. Big will try and find some night birds if the weather lets him. A helluva hot day for that bunch. From somewhere near Buffalo . . . you know, that snow belt. I saw 'em in the Settlers Village and they were shot."

Bud stood up and stretched. "I got me a girl waitin' in Boyden. You goin' sweep the trails, Sam?"

"You got too many girls in Boyden. Yeah, I'll sweep early tonight. Hell, anyone in here after seven is probably making damn sure he isn't found. Well, one thing for sure, anyone hidin' out is goin' get a good soaking. Looks like a helluva storm comin' in."

# XII

Sarah woke to a siren screaming somewhere beyond the motel encampment. Confused with sleep, she pulled her pillow back over her head. The siren faded, and a heavy machine rumbled past. Suddenly she was completely awake. She groped for her bedside light and held up her watch. Almost midnight. She had slept through dinner, through the whole evening. Exhausted by the long day, she had, after her swim, put on an old kimono, flung herself on one of the beds, stuffed the telephone under one pillow, pulled another over her head, and, like a stone dropped in deep water, fallen asleep. Damn, now she had missed Philip. She'd only meant to take a short nap. If he'd come by dinnertime, he'd be furious. With the pillow over her head she wouldn't have heard him knock. But no, he wouldn't be furious—he'd be kind and talk about taking responsibility for a relationship, and smile and say let's start from here. Well, it was too late to call now; he'd be long in bed.

Sarah sat up and pulled the flowered counterpane around her shoulders—it had turned quite cool. Vacation with Philip. What was he like on the loose? A freewheeling Philip was almost a contradiction. Were they going to sleep together? Did he think so? Did she? But here Sarah reached a block. She couldn't even picture Philip in what the previous century had called a "state of undress." The clearest image that Sarah could muster was of Philip in pajamas. Then a pair of slippers covered his feet and a dressing gown, neatly tied, closed around his figure. Sarah tried again and placed Philip next to the motel swimming pool, but she had never seen him in a bathing suit, and a picture rose irresistibly of Philip in a swimming costume of the 1920s—the Jay Gatsby look—dark trunks, white webbing belt, striped top; then a towel appeared across his shoulders and high white sneakers on his feet. By the time Philip was in a terry-cloth robe and holding a beach umbrella, she saw that rather than disrobing Philip in the usual sexual fantasy, she was smothering him in garments. A case for Dr. Freud, she thought, and chuckled. There's something wrong with you, Sarah, my girl; you can never imagine Philip mussed up. She unwound the bedding, rose, and shuffled to the bathroom. Coming back, in an afterthought, she went to the door to see if any friendly note from Philip had been pushed into her room. Yes, there it was—a small card folded in half. Opening it, Sarah read with a slight sense of irritation: "Hi. Think you said Philip would be tied up with the girls at Doña Clara in the A.M. Glad to drive you to refuge for hike and lunch. Will then turn you over to P. Lentz. Breakfast at 7:00. Will knock. Alex."

I might as well, thought Sarah. I don't want to sit around the motel all morning. She walked over to the half-open window and saw that the rug under the sill was wet and the window streaked with rain. Across the motel garden the light from the terrace lamps was reflected in standing puddles of water on the flagstones. An extra puff of wind blew suddenly into the courtyard and sent a garden chair spinning. Thunder cannoned somewhere to the east, and a burst of lightning lit the tops of trees and the roof of the motel. Sarah winced, pulled the window down, and climbed back into bed and replaced the pillow over her head.

# SATURDAY, MARCH 16

## XIII

Birders are notorious for ungodly morning hours. They are up and off betimes, their persons enlarged and hampered by field equipment. Off they go into the dawn, muffled with bandannas, hats, long sleeves, and high boots, redolent with insect repellent and sulfur powder, hopeful always of the never-before-seen bird, the rare, the accidental species just over by the next swamp.

Vacation Villa's happiest feature was its Early Bird Breakfast Buffet, served from five o'clock on in the Wake Robin Room. It was now six-fifteen, and droves of bird-watchers had come, breakfasted, and gone fortified into the field. Birders from several less accommodating motels were taking their places at four long tables, and Mr. Allen, seeing future guests in embryo, rubbed his hands.

The Hamburg Club, having pushed its way out of the dining room, was now lining up for a last-minute visit to the lavatories off the lobby while Big Foster was helping a sleepy Eduardo load the lunch baskets into the bus. Mr. Plummer called for attention.

"Quiet, everyone. Major Foster wants to tell us about today's program. Jeffrey, do not play with the cigarette machine."

Major Foster, moving in a cloud of aftershave lotion, freshly minted and immaculate in his tan field costume and oiled boots, placed himself on the bottom step of the lobby staircase. "Got something extra special for y'all today. Last night when I was scouting around, I had a pretty good view of two mighty special birds. Anyone want to guess?" Here Big smiled indulgently and allowed a few cries of "Bachman's warbler" and "ivory-billed woodpecker," and then shook his head. "They're not in most guidebooks except as accidentals. Hook-billed kites. Yessir. A

Mexican species. First time ever at Doña Clara." And here the major began a detailed exposition of kites, plumage, underparts, and sex differences.

Jeff stopped fingering the cigarette machine and raised a hand.

Major Foster, under full steam, continued: "Cross your fingers that they're still hangin' around. Saw 'em right in the Settlers Village, so we'll go there first . . . and keep tryin' for those anis, too. Yes, son. Speak up."

"Major Foster," said Jeff, "When did you see those kites . . . sir?"

"Well, boy, I saw 'em pretty near to six o'clock. Say about five-fifty. Watched 'em for about five minutes or so. That answer your question, son?"

Jeff opened his mouth as if to speak and then closed it. He nodded slowly and looked at his feet.

"I don't have to remind y'all," said the major, raising his voice, "to keep together. Jeffrey, that goes for you double. Now before we hit Doña Clara, we'll make a stop down along the Military Highway and see if we can spot us some ducks and shore birds. Bring your scopes. Up and at 'em. Mr. Plummer, after you, sir."

The Hamburg Bird Club pressed forward, binoculars at the ready. Jeff Goldsmith followed them at a safe distance, his yellow baseball cap pulled low over his forehead, a map of Doña Clara in his hand.

# XIV

"You haven't done justice to the Early Bird Buffet, Sarah." Alex McKenzie poured himself a second cup of coffee and smiled at his breakfast companion, who was pushing scrambled eggs about on her plate. "Try something else. You've worried those eggs long enough."

"I'm not really hungry, but I suppose I'd better have something." Sarah broke off part of a muffin and eyed it doubtfully.

"Have some marmalade. The muffins taste homemade." Alex helped himself to another and spread butter over its warm surface. "Don't be upset about Philip. He'll be there with bells on."

"I didn't say I was upset," said Sarah through her muffin.

"You didn't have to. Never mind. We'll go right over to Doña Clara and catch up with Philip and his harem."

"If there really is a Philip."

"Of course there is. He just couldn't get through to sleeping beauty last night any more than I could."

"There wasn't anyone at the desk this early, so I couldn't ask," pursued Sarah. "But why didn't he leave a note under my door? You did. Or this morning? He didn't call."

"Probably took off at dawn . . . didn't want to wake you up. As for a note, maybe he didn't want to mess up the rug. Oh, come on, Sarah, smile. I won't have you going about like a maiden in distress."

"I'm nothing of the sort, Dr. McKenzie. It's just that Philip always . . . oh, skip it. Besides, don't you have a job you're supposed to be doing in Boyden? How can you go fooling around at Doña Clara with any maiden?"

"It's only a part-time thing. The Public Health people in the Northeast are very interested in a drug that's turned up there—apparently coming from the Texas border area, near Boyden."

"What sort of a drug? Heroin? Cocaine?"

"Something new, called Celluwell."

"That sounds like a cure for wrinkles . . . or acne."

"I wish it were. But Celluwell is supposed to be a new version of Laetrile. It hit the States last year and took off. All you have to do is say 'cancer cure' and you've got customers. But it's untried, untested, and so far untrue—and, I think, damn unhealthy."

"You're an internist, aren't you, Alex? Does that mean cancer, too?"

"Yes, though oncology is really a sub-specialty. I want to find some patients who've been dosing themselves with Celluwell, run some clinical studies, and see what the stuff's doing to them. We're afraid it's going to louse up a safer treatment. The Texas border has got enough poverty and health problems without a fake cancer cure messing them up. Anyway, enough of that. This morning is made for getting out in it. That storm last night really cleared the air."

Sarah rolled her napkin in a ball and dropped it on the table. "Okay, let's get on out to the refuge and track Philip and those girls down. This is ridiculous. I could have gone skiing in Vermont with my brother Tony instead of trailing around through swamps and bushes. If Philip is too busy to remember that he asked me to spend my spring vacation . . ."

Alex rose and pushed in his chair. "Philip hasn't forgotten, but his car may have broken down, a family emergency . . . anything."

Sarah stood up, a smile flickering over her face. "Do you know what my Grandmother Douglas says when someone doesn't show up? She says, 'Oh dear, I hope it isn't an appendix.' She and her friends still live in dread of appendicitis." Sarah walked ahead and turned to Alex at the door of the breakfast room. "I don't believe in appendicitis."

# XV

Sarah and Alex, in their pursuit of Philip Lentz and the academy students, had, by their choice of a side motel door for their departure, entirely missed these same students, who now languished on the front steps of Vacation Villa.

"We've been abandoned," said Kate McMillan, a senior given to sarcasm. "We've been lured here to begin a life of crime."

"Or we're going to be sold or traded for oil." Honoria Epstein, known as "Pogo" by her classmates, opened the top button of her shorts and wiggled them down her hips. "Anyway," she continued, elevating a sun reflector over her face, "it's peaceful without them."

Four of the five students were present in Texas less by virtue of any interest in biology than by a geographical distance or family situation that prevented their spending spring vacation at home. Only Dory Williams, advanced botany student and one of the eight black girls at the school, was there by choice and did not take part in the general discontent. Dory remained aloof, an open textbook across her knees, studying a diagram of the Berlandier nettlespurge.

"But I'm serious," continued Kate. "Where the hell are they? Miss Lucas is never late, and Mr. Lentz is never, never late."

"Something's up," said Susan Gorham, another senior. "They weren't down for dinner last night or for breakfast. I haven't even seen Mr. Lentz, but, Dory, you were with Miss Lucas yesterday at the refuge. Did she say anything about a day off?"

Dory put a careful finger in her text. "No way. It's supposed to be a meeting at breakfast, birding in the morning, and botany in the afternoon."

"Maybe it's a suicide pact," said Nancy Gorham; she was Susan's younger sister. "Like Mayerling. Their bodies are lying—"

"Oh, shut up, Nancy," said Kate. She continued in a thoughtful voice, "Miss Lucas isn't so bad, just repressed."

Pogo Epstein put down her sun reflector and rolled her shirt to expose her midriff. "Repression," she said, "eats you alive. It eats through your vital balances so that one day you just go 'snap.' "

Nancy Gorham shook her head. "It's because she's jealous. Lucas wants Philip Lentz's job, and she wants his body, too, I'll bet, but she's not subtle about it. It's a love-hate thing. Jealousy is so gross."

"They're both obsessive," said Pogo. "You know, obsessive-compulsive. You can't do anything wrong. The day before vacation, Mr. Lentz made me do three pages of optional questions on the United Nations, and I was only a few minutes late for class."

"Yeah," said Kate. "Old Philip Magnesia. His toilet training must have been really rough. But I like him. He's handsome and he's in good shape, and when he smiles . . ."

"You can forget it," said Susan, "and so Lucas can too. P. Lentz loves S. Deane. Squeaky clean Sarah. Don't you remember how he used to look at her last year? And guess what? She's going to be down here with him and Lucas. Real-life drama."

"In French we say *ménage à trois,*" said Kate. "But I haven't seen Sarah Deane either. Where have they all gone? Who's going to hold our hands and show us the birds?"

"Oh, to hell with it," said Susan. "Let's play tennis."

And in general agreement with this idea, the students ambled in a ragged line toward the tennis courts, Dory Williams in the rear, her botany textbook tucked under one arm.

# XVI

"The refuge manager here is an old friend of mine," said Alex as he and Sarah made their way south along the Auto Tour Road. "A great guy and a top ornithologist. I want you to meet him."

"Fine," said Sarah in a noncommittal voice.

"And speak of the devil," Alex pointed at a Jeep coming down on them.

Sam Hernández stamped on the brake and jerked the Jeep to a stop, causing his assistant to clutch at the windscreen.

"Son of a bitch. Alex McKenzie! What are you doing? Not looking for birds? None here. We've shipped 'em all back to Brazil."

"This is Sarah Deane, Sam. A bird fanatic."

"Don't listen to him," said Sarah. "I'm along for the air."

"Great air here at Doña Clara," said Sam. "This is my assistant, Bud Wojak. The terror of Boyden. Women double-lock when he's around."

Bud rolled his eyes, but looked pleased.

"Okay, Doc." Sam shifted into first gear. "I've gotta finish checking the trails. And hey, Alex, keep an eye out for a pair of hook-billed kites down the way you're heading. Special for you. Then come back to the office around noon, d'ya hear?"

Sarah and Alex watched the Jeep go down the rain-soaked road toward the observation tower, little spurts of water shooting out from the tires, and then continued their leisured walk in the wake of the manager. Sarah inspected an Inca dove, acknowledged the presence of yet another Harris's hawk, and dutifully read a sign proclaiming the site of *Bromus unioloides*, better known as rescuegrass.

"What a funny name," she said.

"It's also called self-heal. A sort of do-it-yourself plant."

"I'd rather be rescued without having to do the work. Self-healing is such a bother, don't you think?"

"What I think is that your mind isn't on this expedition of ours." Alex looked down at Sarah, who remained staring at the fuzzy panicles of rescuegrass, and then, hearing an approaching motor, he looked up. "Hello. Here's Sam again. That was a quick trip."

The Jeep pulled over, and Sam hauled himself out from behind the wheel. In Bud Wojak's place a thin, wide-eyed boy sat hunched and still.

"Alex, can I have your private ear for a minute? Excuse us, Miss Deane." Sam turned aside with Alex, spoke in a lowered voice, gesturing down the road, and then spoke across to Sarah. "Miss Deane, I'm going to borrow your friend for a little while. We've got a problem back near Long Bone Lake."

Sarah nodded without speaking.

"And," continued Sam, "will you hike this young fellow back to refuge headquarters and give this note to Otto at the desk?" He handed her a piece of paper. "Hop down, Jeff. Stick with Miss Dean and don't discuss our problem with anyone, understand? Just stay put in the office. You're with the Ready Tour, aren't you? I'll see that word gets back that you're okay. Miss Deane, will you wait with Jeff until we get back?"

Sarah watched the Jeep accelerate down the road and then looked at the boy beside her. She saw that there was a suggestion of pallor under the baseball cap, emphasized by a sunburned nose. He was standing awkwardly, hugging binoculars to his chest.

"Okay, Jeff, let's go. You've been bird-watching?" she asked.

The boy nodded. "Yeah, I'm pretty good at bird identification . . . at least, I'm a lot better than some people. Do you know what I found back there?" Jeff's voice came in short gasps.

"No. You heard what the refuge manager said. I don't want to know." Sarah crushed a sickening and rising curiosity. "Come on."

"Don't go so fast. I've been running, and I don't feel very good. I ran from Settlers Village to the Bobcat Marsh and then back after . . ."

But Sarah had started off, and even though she set a moderate pace, she too was panting by the time they reached headquarters. She gave Jeff a little push into the outer office, marched up to the desk, and confronted a man in uniform. "Excuse me, but if you're Otto, I have a note from Mr. Hernández. He said it was important."

The man opened the note, scowled, and disappeared through a door marked "Refuge Manager." Sarah heard the mutter of a deep voice, and then the man returned and faced Sarah and Jeff.

"Ma'am, please stay here with the boy, and I'll try and locate the Ready Tour people and tell 'em he's here."

The door slammed and Sarah turned to Jeff. She saw that his bare legs showed several long, ragged scratches and his hiking boots were coated with mud. He seemed ill at ease, twisting his shoulders and wiping his hands along the sides of his shorts. Sarah, searching for distraction, pointed out one of the display cases that alternated with chairs along the walls, and together she and Jeff inspected a remarkably well-preserved specimen resting on a papier-mâché log. A label below the case announced, "Meet the Red-eared Turtle."

Sarah backed away from the case and sat down on one of the chrome-and-plastic chairs. She picked up a brochure from a table at her elbow and studied a photograph of the Rio Grande at sunset and felt the skin on the back of her thighs below her shorts sticking to the tacky surface of the chair. She began to have that special sense of being in a doctor's waiting room that prevents even the most compelling reading matter from competing with the coming event.

Jeff slowly made the rounds of the cases of stuffed birds and animals, and then planted himself in front of Sarah.

"Have you ever seen a hook-billed kite?"

"No," said Sarah, startled. "I don't think so."

"You'd know if you had . . . anyone would. That's what it looks like." Jeff unfolded a pamphlet and pointed with a dirty finger at a malevolent-looking bird with a bent bill. "That's at Santa Ana, but I guess they can turn up anywhere. You really have to check them out because they're rare."

Sarah nodded and was beginning painfully to loosen the skin of one leg from the plastic seat when the outside screen door opened and a woman's face appeared around the edge. Sarah thought, hysterically, she's going to say, "Doctor will see you now." Instead, the woman stepped inside, saw Jeff, and came to a halt.

"Jeff Goldsmith! Where have you been? We got a message you were here. Aunt Lois and I have been having fits, and Major Foster is off checking the trails. This is the second time you've pulled this."

Jeff turned his head away from his aunt and swung one foot back and forth, balancing on the other.

"All right, Jeff. On your way. We're all down at the Visitors Center. You'll be lucky if you're not shipped home tonight."

"I can't come, Aunt Connie." Jeff's husky voice trembled.

"It's true," said Sarah, freeing both legs and standing up. "The refuge manager asked Jeff to stay here until he gets back."

"Well," said Mrs. Goldsmith doubtfully. She hesitated and then said sharply, "Jeff, what on earth have you done?"

As if on cue, the screen door was thrust open again, and Big Foster blocked the light of the opening. "Jeff Goldsmith! What'n hell do you—" Major Foster stopped and took in Mrs. Goldsmith and Sarah. "Jeff, I've been all over the refuge lookin' for you. Thought you were a topnotch birder, not just a punk runaway kid."

Sarah stepped forward and again defended Jeff's presence. Big Foster listened and then nodded. "If Sam Hernández says so, it's gotta be that way. But, Jeff, you watch it. Your aunts are real nice ladies, and they don't need any more trouble from you. I'll come by at lunch and pick you up. Mrs. Goldsmith, after you, ma'am." The screen door snapped shut behind them.

Sarah saw that Jeff was perspiring. "Jeff, you take it easy," she said. "I'll do the talking. Anyway, here comes Mr. Hernández now."

But it was Alex McKenzie who came through the door and walked directly up to Jeff. "Would you be a good guy and let me talk to Miss Deane alone? You can sit on the porch but stay in sight of the office window."

When the door closed on Jeff, Alex turned to Sarah and reached for her hands. "Sarah, let's sit down."

Sarah disengaged herself from Alex's grasp and backed toward the chairs. Her brain repeated: Doctor will see you now, bad news, I'm afraid, Doctor will see you now. She sat down suddenly and Alex folded his length in the seat beside her.

"Sarah, it's bad news, I'm afraid."

"Yes, I know." Sarah placed one hand on top of the other and examined the pattern made by her fingers.

"What do you know?"

"Bad news about Philip."

"Yes, I'm afraid that's it."

"He's been hurt?"

"Worse. Philip's had an accident. Out by Bobcat Marsh."

Sarah's hands took the binocular straps and twisted them tight around her fingers. She watched two fingers turn white. She loosened the straps and saw the color come back.

Alex said quietly, "Philip is dead. He was found in the brush off a trail. I think it was very quick."

Sarah practiced breathing. In and out, in and out.

"Put your head down, Sarah. There. Right between your knees. No, keep it down." Alex cradled Sarah's forehead, supporting its weight with one hand, while with the other he smoothed the hair away from her face and then unwound the binocular straps from her fingers. "I can't tell you much about it yet. We'll just stay here until Sam gets back. Okay, try and sit up now. Easy does it. You see, Jeff found Philip. That's why he has to stay here."

"Yes," said Sarah. She felt as if she had stepped out of her skin and now sat across the room listening to this dull sad conversation.

"This is going to be rough, Sarah. I haven't any urgent plans, so I'll stay here with you and then get you back to the motel."

"Yes," said Sarah. "I see." From across the room she watched her seated figure—red shirt, blue shorts, feet square on the floor.

"Has Philip any of his family living nearby?" Alex asked this in a slightly louder voice and frowned at Sarah in concern.

"Oh," said Sarah, "I don't know."

"Sarah, look at me."

Sarah saw her seated self lift its head and look at and entirely through Alex and then come back and examine his face. Funny, she'd never noticed that one of his eyebrows was higher than the other. A little higher. And the cuffs of his khaki pants were wet and streaked with dirt, and look at his boots—muddy with clots of earth wedged into the lugs of the soles. She looked at the floor and saw that the linoleum was made up of green and black squares. My doctor has brown and black squares, said Sarah to herself. And a braided rug. She looked past Alex at a map of the refuge, its frame made of twisted rope with knots at each corner. What kind of knots? And her brain responded, "For they're hangin' Danny Deever, you can 'ear the Dead March play . . . the regiment's in 'ollow square—they're hangin' him today. . . ."

"Sarah, come to. Look at me."

"Your pants are all muddy and so are your boots. I woke up last night and it was raining."

"Yes, the ground is wet." Alex stood up and, taking Sarah's forearm in a firm grip, pulled her unresisting to her feet. "Let's look and see if Jeff's all right."

Sarah's separated self reluctantly centered itself in her numb miserable person. They walked to the door and saw Jeff sitting on a bench bent over his field guide.

"Sarah, listen." Alex spoke urgently. "I know Philip's parents are dead, but there was a sister. We've got to reach her, and, I think, we've got to reach you. You're going to have to function. Just a little. Sam has called the police. You and Jeff are going to have to help them."

Sarah looked at Philip with opened eyes. "Help them? The police? Why?"

"I'm sorry. I guess I haven't explained, but it wasn't an accident. Someone got hold of Philip. Perhaps it was robbery, or maybe someone thought he was someone else. We'll know more later."

Sarah, followed by Alex, walked over to a case containing a small gray bird with a yellow glass eye sitting on a glass pond. It was, she read, a gift from the Boyden Boys' Club. She ran her finger up and down the case, following the outline of implanted cattails. "What was Philip doing in that marsh?" she whispered.

"We don't know yet. Now we must get in touch with his sister."

Sarah sighed and tried to focus on this single problem. "I think she lives in Oregon. She's married. Her name's probably in Philip's address book because he usually has it with him. He's very good about postcards."

"All right, then. The police will find the address. Let's go out. Jeff's been alone long enough."

The air seemed fresh on the porch, with a soft wind shuffling through an overhanging persimmon tree.

"There's a rose-throated becard over there by that bush," said Jeff in a listless voice. He was now sitting on the porch steps. "That's a good bird to see," he added, "but I still feel sort of sick."

Sarah frowned. "I don't think I ever want to see another bird."

"No, perhaps not," said Alex, "but you will forgive Jeff if he does. We have some time to get through."

Sarah didn't answer, but sat down on the steps next to Jeff, drew up her knees, wrapped her arms about them, and put her chin down. She watched the leaves of the tree turning over in the breeze.

"That's the Texas persimmon," said Jeff. "The leaves are round on the end."

"Yes," said Sarah, and she peered down the gravel path and tried to see Philip walking toward them, Philip who was meeting her after lunch.

# XVII

Eleanor Lucas was the sort of teacher whose arrival in the classroom caused students to stop shuffling their feet and bend quickly over their textbooks. She was a tense-faced young woman with almost colorless blonde hair that she pulled tightly back into a braided knot. This, and her fair skin and blue eyes, suggested fiords and snow-covered slopes, and only a slash of color across her cheeks and the occasional lift of her sandy eyebrows gave promise of a possible thaw. Although slim and of only medium height, her upright posture, her springing step, and her decisive gestures gave the effect of a larger woman.

Now, rounding the corner of the tennis-court backstop, Eleanor Lucas came down on her students like an angry warrior maiden. The tennis players stopped in mid-volley, and the girl sunbathing scrambled to her feet. Miss Lucas halted and took in the general dishevelment, the transitor radio cleaving the air with hard rock, the scattered candy wrappers, and Pogo Epstein, who, in the interest of a more complete tan, had achieved almost total nudity. Only Dory Williams, in the school sports uniform of navy shorts and light gray shirt, managed by her conformity to regulation dress to mark a distance between herself and the others.

Miss Lucas attacked. "Pogo, pull down your bra, pull up your pants. Give me that sun reflector, you'll end up in the hospital. Nancy, go and put on a school uniform shirt with a bra under it."

"Oh, Miss Lucas, uniforms are so gross," protested Nancy.

Miss Lucas brushed a loose strand of pale hair behind her ear and leaned forward. 'We are down in Texas as a school. At home you may ride around topless in a pimp-mobile for all I care, but right now my job and the college recommendations which I will be writing for you depend on your behaving yourself . . . and you will."

"But, Miss Lucas," said Susan sweetly, "you weren't here this morning, or last night, and Mr. Lentz wasn't either. We didn't know what we should be doing."

"What you should not have been doing was making great howling nuisances of yourself. I'm sorry that I'm late and that I missed dinner. I had a very bad headache. However, I thought I could trust you not to act like three-year-olds."

"But where's Mr. Lentz?" persisted Susan. "We need him so we can get on with the all these dumb Texas birds."

Miss Lucas looked annoyed. "He hasn't arrived yet, so instead of going to Doña Clara—I can't fit all of you in my car— we will work here, in the motel garden. Tomorrow I want to see in each notebook a list of ten plants found in the Rio Grande Valley—family, genus, and species characteristics. We will have a quiz on Monday."

# XVIII

Alex watched Sarah while apparently listening to Jeff explain how he wrote up his bird sightings.

"First I do my own identification work, and then I put down the time and place and stuff like that in my field notebook." Here Jeff reached into a pocket and handed a curled and greasy object to Alex. "I make a sketch, and later on I transfer everything to my logbook. But what I really need is a good scope; not having one is a real handicap to a good birder."

Alex put one hand on Sarah's shoulder. "Okay?"

"Yes . . . no. I'm just a blank."

"Well, go blank for a while, but not too blank." Alex turned back to Jeff. "You've got a good start on your Texas list."

But Jeff's mind was now elsewhere. "Dr. McKenzie, if someone finds a valuable object that's sort of abandoned, could the person finding it claim it? I mean would there be salvage rights?"

Alex returned Jeff's notebook and settled himself sideways on the lowest step. "Report whatever you've found to the manager's office, and if this object isn't against the law—like, say, a machine gun—then you might be able to keep it. I gather you are the person."

"Yeah, I found it," admitted Jeff. "It still works. I sort of forgot about it because of finding . . . you know . . . the other thing."

Sarah drew herself up in a sudden shiver. Philip as a "thing" had intruded rudely on the image she was constructing of Philip, who would shortly swing up the path toward them, his light hair ruffled in the breeze, his binoculars slung to one side, waving a hand and then taking a quick look at his watch to see if they were both on schedule.

"Hang in there, Sarah," said Alex, leaning forward to block out her view of the road, for at the edge of his vision he had seen a sequence of squad car, black van, police ambulance, and two unmarked sedans, all moving at a sedate pace, turning west toward Bobcat Marsh. Then, from the opposite direction, the refuge Jeep reappeared and halted by the end of the path. Alex rose and walked down to meet Sam Hernández.

"Alex, Tom Pérez wants you to stick around. He's coming back here to talk to the boy and to Miss Deane after he gets the lab and photo guys squared away. As you said, it's sure enough a homicide. Christ, the border is turning into a real no-man's-land. Those g.d. teenagers, junkies, the whole lousy drug scene, and those poor damn illegal aliens crossing over. Now it's a refuge visitor. Hell."

Alex nodded. "I agree, Sam. Philip Lentz was an old friend, and Sarah has almost gone into shock. Have you closed the refuge?"

"Closed to all visitors. For today anyway. Everyone we could round up has been corralled in the Visitors Center picnic area. Police are taking statements, and the Ready Tour people have sent out for sandwiches all round because this thing may take all day." Sam took off his brown uniform hat, mopped his grimy face, and climbed back into the Jeep. "Hell," he repeated.

Alex returned to Sarah, still rigid on the steps, her arms around her knees, her lips colorless, her face pale, her eyes staring.

"Sarah, I think you'd do better if you moved around."

She looked up. "I can handle this. You don't have to play doctor."

"Sarah," returned Alex evenly, "I'm not playing, and I am a doctor. And I'm in this with you. Now stand up and move. Walk with Jeff around the building; you've both been sitting down too long. Would you like something to make you less tense?"

"No dope," said Sarah. "I'll take care of myself." However, she got to her feet. "Come on, Jeff. Doctor's orders. Let's go, and you can tell me about Hamburg, New York."

Jeff stood up and started down the path. "Hamburg's south of Buffalo, and we get a lot of snow. Blizzards blow in off the lake, and then, pow. I'm in a special step-up class, and we do a lot of science on the college level. I can't decide between microbiology or ornithology, but now I'm into subatomic particles—you know, quarks."

"That's great, Jeff," said Sarah bleakly. She quickened her pace and rounded toward the Visitors Center.

"So maybe nuclear physics," gasped Jeff, trotting to keep up with her. "Wait a minute, my stomach still feels kind of funny."

# XIX

The professionals had spread like a platoon of well-trained carpenter ants over the trampled chaparral off the Bobcat Marsh Trail. They photographed, measured, took samples, made casts, all the while depressing an even wider swath of vegetation as they accorded to the body of Philip Lentz the deference and care that a modern forensic laboratory demands. Tom Pérez left them at it and returned to refuge headquarters braced for an afternoon of questioning, juggling telephone calls, orders, and counterorders

—all the tedious scut work that is part of a homicide investigation.

Deciding, on consultation with Alex, that Sarah would need further time for recovery, Tom left her in the waiting room and asked Alex to join him for a session with Jeff in Sam Hernández's office. However, after settling in with a police stenographer and getting Jeff's age and address on record, Tom ran into resistance.

"Come on, Jeff. Dr. McKenzie tells me you've got a good brain, and I need someone like that to help us out."

Jeff, unmoved by flattery, shifted his feet back and forth on the floor. Tom studied the boy. He saw almost a cartoon of the boy-egghead—a mop of red hair tumbled over his face and tufted over his ears, so that the thin triangular face had an overgrown look and the glasses with their dark wire rims suggested a disguise. But Tom, as far as experience with the young was concerned, was long in the tooth. He tried again.

"Jeff, we need a sharp observer. You're not being charged with anything, and your aunts have indicated that they want you to cooperate. After all, you found the body, we didn't. It might have been there for quite a spell if you hadn't come along."

Jeff moved his boots together so that the leather gave out high-pitched squeaks, and then let his back curve down into its natural slump. He began to see himself, as Pérez had intended, as a sort of man on the spot whose intelligence was indispensable to the police. The body moved back somewhat from its awful prominence and became only a large piece of a greater puzzle.

"Well, okay, I guess," he said.

"All right," said Tom briskly. "Let's begin with this morning at Doña Clara."

"Well, I was with the Hamburg Club. It's got some good birders, but a lot of them goof around and get in the way of serious people, serious ornithologists, and, of course, my sister had to come along because my aunts thought she might get interested in nature, which is a big laugh because Nina is a real nerd."

It was one of those times when Alex, sitting in the shadow by the side of the desk, was glad that he hadn't gone into pediatrics.

"And this morning at Doña Clara?" prompted Tom.

"This morning we were supposed to be looking for groove-billed anis and trying to find two hook-billed kites and—"

"Hold on," said Tom. "Alex, you'll have to help me out with this bird stuff."

"The anis are related to the cuckoo and should be around here, but the kites are Mexican birds, unusual. They're a kind of hawk."

"It's all new to me. Okay, Jeff, did you see these birds?"

"Not in the Settlers Village. You see, I split."

"You took off?" said Tom, making a note.

"Yeah, I got out and even Nina didn't catch me, which is lucky because she'd have yelled her head off."

"Stop a minute," said Tom. "Why this compulsion to leave your group? I've heard that you tried this last night and were warned not to pull the same trick again. What gives? Are you allergic to groups or are you trying to get sent home?"

Jeff moved his boots back and forth; he frowned and rubbed his nose. Tom could almost hear little wheels and pistons turning in his head, adjusting his reply.

"I guess maybe I'm allergic to groups," said Jeff. "Like I always want to make the identifications myself. I mean it's a real pain and—" Jeff stopped and looked intently at a framed photograph of Sam Hernández's wife that stood on the desk. "I guess I just went, that's all."

"For no reason except that you can't stand groups?"

"I bird a lot better on my own. I can maintain a scientific procedure, and no one needs all those people tramping around like a herd of cows. You don't get good sightings with a herd of cows."

"All right, Jeff," said Tom. "We'll let it go for now. But what took you all the way to Bobcat Marsh?"

Jeff just shook his head, not looking at Pérez. "It's just a good habitat, that's all."

Tom finally prodded Jeff into revealing that, by running most of the way, he had arrived at the Bobcat Marsh Trail entrance at about nine-fifteen. Yes, he had a watch, and no, he had not seen many people on his way. "Only two old ladies near the village and a man with a butterfly net near the Observation Tower."

"Jeff," broke in Alex, "you mentioned a valuable object—something you found that might have been lost."

"Now's the time to speak up, Jeff," said Tom in an encouraging voice. "Look, no thumbscrews, nothing up my sleeve."

"I just checked the optics. It was lying down in the marsh. I guess the wind blew it over in that storm."

"Optics on what?" asked Alex.

"A telescope. With a tripod. I set it up and wiped it off. There was a stool, too. I just sat down and tried out the zoom. It worked okay. I thought the rain might have wrecked it."

"Fine, Jeff," said Tom. "The police are going over the area now. I'll make a note that your prints will be on the telescope."

"Tell me, Jeff," persisted Alex, "was the reason that you went to the marsh today because you'd spotted the scope there yesterday?"

"I wasn't near the marsh yesterday," said Jeff, his voice truculent.

"But did you see the telescope, with or without a person near it, Friday night?"

"No. I just fooled around last night. You know—near that boardwalk. Lupine Lake and around there. I didn't go into the marsh. Like I said, I just want to bird by myself."

"See here, Jeff," said Tom. "Did you see anyone at any time, yesterday or today, who attracted your attention. Anything unusual? A car going too fast, someone running? Someone who didn't look like a bird-watcher? Hear anyone calling out?"

Jeff, his face flushed, shook his head. "No, I didn't."

"Until you found the telescope this morning, and then the body?"

"Yeah, that's right."

"But the body was almost thirty feet into the brush. Why did you leave the trail?"

Jeff fidgeted in obvious embarrassment.

"Looking for the men's room?" said Alex, who knew something of the problems of early-morning bird-watching.

Jeff relaxed. "Yeah, I saw the bushes were pushed down, and so I went in, and then I found a sneaker, and I went further in and saw a leg sticking out, and then the whole body."

It was all coming in a rush. Tom nodded encouragement.

"I kicked some of the leaves away, and I saw it was a man

with his face down, and he wasn't moving at all, and I got out fast."

"Best thing to do. Thanks, Jeff. You've been very helpful. I'll have this typed up, and then you can add or change anything. Now, how about a Coke? You've had quite a morning." Tom walked Jeff out of the room, pointed out the Coke machine, spoke a few words to the man at the desk, and returned. Tilting back in Sam Hernández's chair, he said. "We're sending for Jeff's aunts, because, like it or not, he's going to rejoin that herd of cows. A bit shifty, isn't he?"

"Maybe that telescope really was the attraction. He spotted it yesterday and came back. Won't admit it."

"I'll be seeing him again. Now, how about Sarah Deane?"

"Make it short, Tom. I want to get her back to the motel."

"How well did she know this Lentz? Love him? Sleep with him?"

"Damned if I know. She and Philip got to know each other at Morton's Academy last year. Perhaps this trip was a trial run."


Sarah painfully, hesitantly considered the problem of Philip, Philip who should have been part of this week in Texas . . . else why in God's name was she here? And that poem kept banging in her head. A curse of the teacher of literature was that so many errant shreds and patches floated without control through one's head, and right now it was that awful "Danny Deever" with its pounding ballad meter. She couldn't get rid of it.

What's that so black agin the sun? said Files-on-Parade.
It's Danny fightin' 'ard for life, said Files-on-Parade.

Alex opened the office door and saw Sarah, her eyes staring, her lips partly open. He returned to Tom. "Sarah's in no shape to answer questions now. I'll take her to the motel now and come back later and see if I can fill in some gaps for you."

When Alex had departed, Tom turned to the police stenographer sitting in the back of the room and said testily, "Some gaps, hell. It's all one big lousy gap, and all I've got to fill it so far is one wise-ass thirteen-year-old kid who says he's allergic to groups."

# XX

The Visitors Center picnic area is a tree-sheltered square bordered by post-and-rail fencing. Sam Hernández, observing the aimless grouping and regrouping of the people therein, was strongly reminded of recently penned cattle, restless in their unexpected confinement.

In the far corner of the corral, Professor Axminster had Mrs. van Hoek of the Hamburg group cornered and was describing to her the genesis of the Axminster Collection. Mrs. van Hoek, who didn't know a hummingbird from a handsaw, let alone a butterfly, was nevertheless pleased at the attention. Adjusting to the heat in Texas, she had shed her tweed cape and was dressed in tan linen, with the thinnest of jade-green scarves tied about her head. She was looking forward to making a statement to the police.

The Boyden Police Department (Crime Against Persons Division) had set up an informal inquiry station at one of the picnic tables, and here was much business in the matter of taking names and asking questions. Sergeant Gleason of Homicide had just signaled to Mrs. van Hoek, who twitched the back of her skirt, lifted her head, and went forth, if not to glory, at least to an improved prominence.

Addie Brent, standing apart with Miss Fellows, had now raised her binoculars in the direction of a sugar hackberry and edged closer to her friend. "Pretend to look at something, Midge."

Miss Fellows, obedient, put up her glasses. "What is it, Addie?"

"That is what I wish to know. Why are we being kept here? Obviously it has to do with the police, but what is it?"

"I'm not sure," said Miss Fellows. "I think it's connected

with that tour group, the one that got the Hamburg Club away from us."

"I believe you're right, Midge. I just overheard their leader, that Mr. Plummer, talking. It seems there's been an accident. Someone injured or dead. The police are asking what everyone was doing this morning and yesterday afternoon."

"Oh dear, I hope not, Addie." Miss Fellows's face creased with worry, and the hands that held the binoculars trembled.

"I'm sure it's one of those border things. One would have hoped that a wildlife sanctuary would be free of such problems."

"I'm quite tired, Addie. I think I had a touch of sun yesterday."

"Nonsense, Midge. Pull yourself together. We must sit down and make sure we have a coherent idea of our whereabouts last evening. I will put together a joint statement. It will save the police trouble."

Lois Bailey moved crablike away from Mr. Plummer's explication of variations in that rare tufted annual, Mediterranean lovegrass, sidled up to Constance Goldsmith, and pointed at Jeff sitting at a picnic table writing in his notebook.

"They really worked Jeff over," she whispered. "He was in the office being questioned for ages. One of the police said that Jeff was the one who found the body on some trail. The poor boy."

"Poor nothing," said Mrs. Goldsmith. "He'll recover. Finding a body will give him status. Jeff loves to be noticed."

"Connie!"

"It's true. Oh, sure, part of Jeff has had a real jolt, but the other part is probably trying to get some mileage out of murder."

"You don't know if it's murder."

"Then why are all these policemen creeping around, and why all this statement-taking? Well, I have my alibi ready."

"Stop it, Connie. I don't think anyone says 'alibi' in real life. Look, they're waving at you. It's your turn."

A blue-uniformed arm lifted, a hand beckoned, and Mrs. Goldsmith scuttled over, clutching her binoculars, and rummaging anxiously around in her youth for acts of dishonesty.

A balding head raised itself. "Please sit down. I'm Sergeant

Gleason, and that's Sergeant Cotton. We just need a few details."

Mrs. Goldsmith sat down submissively and plunged in. "I'm Constance Goldsmith, and I'm with the Ready Tour Group."

"Yes, ma'am. Arthur Ready is pretty well known here in the Valley. Now when did you leave the motel this morning?"

"About six-thirty. Major Foster met us and then we went out in the bus looking for water birds and ducks."

Sergeant Gleason sidestepped the water birds and ducks. "And when did you get to Doña Clara, ma'am?"

"It must have been almost eight-thirty by the time we signed in."

"Signed in?"

"Registered. We all signed the registration sheet for visitors. It's a paper with the date and a place for your name and address, and a line for 'remarks and sightings.' "

Sergeant Gleason turned to Sergeant Cotton, a giant in plainclothes who was making hard work of copying statistics onto a pack of file cards. "Cotton, can you get over to the refuge office and see what's happened to the registration sheet and give it to Pérez? He'll probably want them for at least a week back."

With a grin of relief, Sergeant Cotton set off with a long stride.

"Now, Mrs. Goldsmith," continued Sergeant Gleason, "after you registered, did you drive to Settlers Village?"

"No, we hiked down the Auto Tour Road. It's not far. Major Foster was going to try and find the anis and two hook-billed kites."

"Those are birds? And me right here in Boyden and never heard of them."

Mrs. Goldsmith wondered how to explain to a hard-working policeman this compulsion to travel hundreds of miles and pay hundreds of dollars, in order to stand in a thicket being eaten by bugs, hoping to catch a glimpse of two of the homeliest species in North America.

The sergeant recalled her to business. "Did anything attract your attention on the way to Settlers Village?"

"I suppose there were other people, but I didn't notice. You see, Sergeant, bird-watchers are kept pretty busy just looking for birds. You know, I think if King Kong showed up, no one would notice him unless he flew."

"King Kong?" said the sergeant warily. "A bird called King Kong?"

"Oh, no, Sergeant, it's just that we all have birds on the brain."

Sergeant Gleason shook his head. As he said to his wife that evening, "If they'd been a softball team or a bowling league, I might've made sense out of it. But they're just a bunch of loonies." To Mrs. Goldsmith, he said, "That's fine, ma'am. Now, did anyone join or leave your group this morning?"

"You must mean my nephew Jeff. He's so interested in birds."

"Did you see your nephew Jeff," continued the sergeant heavily, "leave Settlers Village?"

"I'm afraid not." Mrs. Goldsmith ruffled her already confused hair. "We were all busy, as I've said, and I never thought Jeff would leave again because he'd gone off yesterday. Against orders."

"He went off without permission yesterday, too?"

"I'm sure he will tell the lieutenant all about it. I'm afraid he left after the major asked everyone to stay together. We were to meet together back at the parking lot at six."

"Was everyone on time?" pursued the sergeant doggedly.

"More or less. The bus group which went for ice cream was back early, and then the rest came, and Major Foster a few minutes after that. I didn't pay much attention because I was looking for Jeff, who was more than ten minutes late. Major Foster chewed him out, and so did we. Then we all got on the bus and followed Major Foster in his van to the Dike Road to look for pauraques."

"I won't ask if that's a bird. Anything else, Mrs. Goldsmith?"

"Well, I did see some Boy Scouts in the picnic area yesterday, and later two people with butterfly nets. I noticed them because they were right in the middle of some bushes where we'd heard a vireo. The woman was wearing a dress, which is a terrible idea with all those thorns and ticks. Some women have this thing about being feminine. . . . Oh, you don't want me going on, Sergeant. That's all, I'm afraid."

Sergeant Gleason thought if some women could see their behinds, they'd stay out of the bushes and out of pants. Aloud, he said, "Thank you, Mrs. Goldsmith, you've sure been helpful."

"And thank you, Sergeant," said Mrs. Goldsmith, not to be outdone in constabulary courtesy. "It's been very interesting."

Sergeant Gleason nodded his dismissal and beckoned to Waldo Plummer, little suspecting that he was in for a lecture on the gradual corruption of the name Long Bow Lake to its present and inaccurate title, Long Bone Lake.

# XXI

Refuge manager Sam Hernández stopped pacing his office and came to rest his bulk on the edge of the desk now occupied by Tom Pérez. "Helluva mess," he said. "Goddamn mess."

"I'm stiff as a stiff, if you'll excuse the expression," said Tom, shoving a pile of papers aside and moving his neck from side to side. "These registration sheets aren't too much help. Only about half of the visitors seem to have signed. Besides, no murderer would sign a sheet and then run out to the marsh and kill someone."

Sam flexed his arms, stretching so that his brown uniform shirt detached itself, revealing an ample and hairy belly. "So, Tomás, maybe he didn't know he was going to murder anyone, and signed in like a good citizen. Of course, some never do sign. A lot of people are kind of nervous about putting their names on a government sheet—probably got a stack of parking tickets hidden away. Then we've got the jokers, mostly kids, signing Mickey Mouse, Davy Crockett, Darth Vader."

"You had two Frankensteins today," said Tom.

The screen door banged open and Alex walked in, his face drawn, his mouth hard, his clothes rumpled. He looked like a man who had lost a bout with a mangle.

"God, you look beat," said Tom.

Sam reached for his hat and started for the door. "I'll go along and check the refuge, or what's left of it."

Alex sank into a chair. "The parking lot is clearing out, so I suppose the police have just about wound up with the visitors."

Tom switched on the desk lamp. "Did you get your girl settled?"

"Sarah's not my girl, and just now she's no one's girl. The Ready Tour people turned up at the motel, and I've asked Jeff's aunts to keep an eye on her. Sensible types. Sarah wouldn't touch a sedative, so I've suggested a swim in the pool to keep off misery."

"Okay, I'll catch up with her later. We'll need a lot more data on Philip Lentz, and we have to check on Sarah's own movements when we get a better fix on the time of death."

"Come off that. No way." Alex's voice was rough. "Sarah came down to meet Philip, to spend her vacation with him."

"But where was she last evening? You had dinner with me. Did you see Sarah at the motel when you got back?"

"No. I knocked at her door, but she was asleep. She told me so this morning, and I believe her. Don't waste time on that line."

"People who don't answer may not be there to answer. Pull in your horns. We'll let it go for now. The body's gone to the morgue, and they'll do the autopsy later this evening. And, Alex, we'd like you to help out . . . not just the medical angle, but in general. I've got an okay from my boss. You knew Lentz, you can help with all those birds, and you know Sarah."

"Any ideas you have about my sneaking around Sarah, you can—"

"There you go again. Don't be so prickly. The boss remembers you from that drug study a few years back."

"Captain Nordstrom? I was an innocent medical student then."

"Contradiction in terms. There are no innocent medical students. We can certainly use you. The whole department is up to its balls in the border mess. Talk about drugs—we've got hard stuff coming in as regular as Ex-Lax. And that new crap, Celluwell. Jesus. I'll try and squeeze something out of the budget for you."

"Skip the money," said Alex. "I'll help out."

"Good. Now let's go over what we've got so far. The victim. I.D. by A. McKenzie, personal friend. An apparently healthy male, about one hundred forty pounds, five foot ten. His wallet is missing, so maybe robbery figures in. And what was his full name, his age?"

"Philip Beaufort Lentz, thirty-three. My age."

"And probable cause of death, strangulation?"

"Certainly looks like it, but I'll wait for the post. I suppose Philip might have tried to stop someone coming over the river."

"Possible. Maybe the guy panicked, strangled him, dragged him into the brush, and beat it. It's an easy enough solution." Tom lifted a ruler from the desk, walked over to the wall map of the refuge, and moved the ruler along the bends of the Rio Grande. "It's an open two-way valve, but mostly it works from south to north. They come from all over Mexico—to get a job, join their families, send money home."

"And drugs," said Alex.

"And drugs. The U.S. has the market, the cash; and Mexico, Central, South America, they have the stuff and the pipelines. But then we've got a whole bunch of characters here in Texas who find a refuge a handy place to do anything they've a mind to do. Maybe this Philip Lentz got caught in a dirty revolving door. Unless he was part of the scene and got what he deserved."

"Never. Not Philip Beaufort Lentz."

"Never say 'never.'" Tom sat down again. "Take a look at the things found on the body or thereabouts. Found so far, that is."

Alex ran his finger down the list. The clothes and the objects were those that any naturalist might have been expected to have on a field trip: pocketknife (secured to shorts with lanyard), pencil, wristwatch, two lens caps, checklist from Laguna Atascosa (filled in and dated March 15), trail map of Doña Clara, hiking shorts, shirt, undershorts, sneakers, socks (last two items under vegetation, or under body).

"Where," demanded Alex, "are Philip's binoculars?"

Tom picked up another sheet of paper and waved it in Alex's face. "No one goes birding without binoculars. I'm not that stupid. Look at this. Back down in the marsh reeds near Long Bone Lake we found this stuff: binoculars, Nikons, in a leather

case marked 'P. Lentz,' seven-by-thirty-five power; a folding canvas stool; a copy of *Birds of North America*, 'Lentz' on inside
cover; and one telescope set up on its tripod, all ready to go.
Without lens caps. The lens caps buttoned into his back pocket
fit nicely. I'd guess the whole telescope scene was arranged by our
junior birdman Jeff, who probably left his sticky prints all over
everything."

"I doubt if Jeff had anything to do with the murder. He just
stumbled on the body this morning—well after the fact. Philip
had been dead some time—well over eight hours, I'd say. Rigor
was well established, body temp down, facial mottling noticeable."

"I'm not thinking about boy stranglers yet, though Jeff could
have done it last evening on his solo. God knows there are plenty
of homicidal kids around." Tom shuffled his papers into neat piles
and began packing them into a folder. "Poor Philip Lentz. But
he wasn't throttled sitting down, because there's no sign of a
struggle, damage to the equipment, trampled vegetation, stuff like
that. As Jeff suggested, the scope and stool were probably
knocked over in that storm. The lab will let us know."

"But," said Alex, "the binoculars. Were they really in the
case?"

"Closed up tight. This Lentz was a tidy character. You
should see the things in his car, all stacked, folded, and filed. Sam
tells me that he checked the parking lot last night, but he didn't
spot Philip's Escort rental as not belonging, because it was parked
next to the cars of the University of Kansas biology team. Here's
the car list."

Alex studied it in silence. Besides the usual supply of clothing, toilet articles, a tennis racket, history textbooks, and student
papers, the objects included a Pentax camera, an address book, a
clutch of field guides, road maps, a plastic bag with a new nylon
strap and a repair ticket from the Camera Mart, Owings Mills,
Maryland, and a small knapsack.

Alex frowned. "The list looks okay, but I keep asking myself
why wasn't Philip wearing his binoculars? Birders are naked
without them."

"He was using his telescope, that's why. You can't look
through two things at once."

"But, Tom," protested Alex. "It doesn't work that way."

The door was flung open and Sam Hernández stumped in, a sheaf of papers and a pack of file cards held in one hand. These he tossed on the desk. "Here's the stuff from the picnic area. Your Sergeant Gleason just wrapped up the last interview. Not too bad, Tomás. Only thirty people in the refuge when we closed it off."

"Thanks, Sam," said Tom. "Only thirty we know about anyway. Besides, it's yesterday we should worry about, unless the murderer spent the night in the refuge or came back this morning. Alex here is going to do an assist, which will keep me off your back. He knew Lentz, and that's useful."

Sam threw himself heavily into a chair and began unlacing his boots. "Dirt, wet, and gunk," he grunted. "The marshes are big mud pies, and those rhinos of yours from Homicide are sure making it worse, Pérez. But we needed that rain—broke the dry spell and filled up the swamps." He kicked off his boots and wiggled his toes back and forth in their thick gray socks.

"Phew," said Tom. "Cover your feet. This room's too small."

Sam began pulling on an ancient pair of cowboy boots. "Closing the refuge is a damn pain. I've blocked off Bobcat Marsh and Long Bone Lake, but I'm opening all the other trails tomorrow. I've got six bird tours pushing at the gates, and God knows how many school groups and little old ladies in hiking boots. Not to mention," he added angrily, "the great American violence fan hankering for a cheap crime thrill."

Alex got to his feet abruptly. "This fan is going to get out. I'm going to the motel and check on Sarah, and then, gentlemen, I'm going to toss myself into the great gray-green greasy waters of the Vacation Villa swimming pool."

Sam rose. "Thanks for everything, Alex." He thumped his friend between the shoulder blades."

Alex winced. "Old hammer hand."

Tom closed his briefcase. "I'll follow you back, Alex. I'm going over the motel and take some statements. Damn lucky to find so many people who were at the refuge all under one roof. Old pussyfoot Carlos Allen will have hives when he sees me show up. Murder may not be his idea of publicity. *Buenas noches*, Sam. See you."

Together the two men walked down the path. The sun was low, and the air was soft with a hint of spice in it. Tom turned to Alex. "How about dinner? Bring Sarah, if she'll come, and we'll have a powwow about Philip afterwards—that is, if Doctor says okay. Then I hope I'll have the fortitude to take on those students. You can sit in and hold my pulse . . . or my temper. The high school crowd I can do without."

Alex stopped by his car. "I won't force Sarah on this. It's up to her. And did you know that the former headmistress of the school is down here with another old teacher? Probably staying at the same motel—Allen traps all the birders. The two of them run a bird tour now, and they can probably tell you about Philip —though with a negative bias, I'm sure. He helped them out of their jobs at the academy."

Tom nodded. "Quite a homecoming for Miss Morton's."

As Alex backed his car out of its place, he became aware of a swarm of men working over a blue Escort, which stood with its doors opened wide. All Philip's arrangements destroyed, his notebooks read, his maps unfolded, his luggage violated. With a rush of anger, Alex shoved his gearshift into first and kicked the accelerator so hard the car wheels spun and stones flew and rattled off the fender of a parked car.

Alex, driving far over the speed limit on the road to Boyden, thought of the enormity of Philip's death. Physicians are conditioned to a point past nausea to seeing the human body fall apart or become overgrown, but the Philips of the earth—strong, young, programmed for health, everything clicking away—it was intolerable. He remembered Philip playing tennis, driving down a ski run, his legs pumping up and down in response to the moguls and dips . . . Philip holding his viola under his chin and reminding fellow players that andante meant andante and to watch the time. He thought of Philip pushing a faltering girls' school into the twentieth century; Philip getting what he wanted —strength through planning. He saw him again, light hair, sunburned face, standing in a field watching a hawk soar, saw the grin of pleasure that showed the human hidden behind the efficiency machine. Then Philip as he'd found him this morning, his clothes sodden and mud-spattered, his hair wet and matted, his face and neck swollen, marked, disfigured, blooming like some blotched and ghastly tropical plant, the petechiae, the tongue blocking the open mouth, and, goddammit . . . Alex turned the Volvo too fast in to the motel, and spray from a puddle splashed on his windshield. He braked heavily. "God, I'll be killing someone myself next," he said furiously. He got out and walked slowly toward the motel entrance.

# XXII

For the entire morning and part of the afternoon, Miss Eleanor Lucas kept her pupils' noses, if not to a grindstone, at least to a bewildering series of unfamiliar trees, habitats, flowers, stamens, petals, pistils, and sepals. Concerning the unaccountable absence of her co-worker Philip Lentz, Miss Lucas was mute and refused all offers from the students to form search parties.

Finally released on their own recognizance, the girls moved to the tennis courts, where they passed an hour or so sunbathing and batting tennis balls at each other, so indeed it was almost a relief when Kate McMillan caught sight of their former headmistress and her associate coming toward them through the archway that divided the courts from the main section of the motel.

Mrs. Brent and Miss Fellows advanced across the grass, both wearing full-length terry-cloth robes. These, open at the front, revealed dark-patterned bathing dresses called by ladies' specialty shops "becoming to the mature figure," and by the academy girls, "absolutely freaky." As the former teachers approached their former students, both parties slid back into former roles. The teachers stepped more briskly, their white rubber bathing shoes squelching as they came, and the students rising, apparently all courteous attention. Kate McMillan, assuming the part of the poised college-bound senior, strode forward and extended a hand.

"Hello, Mrs. Brent. It's nice to see you again. Have you been trying out the pool? Hello, Miss Fellows. We miss you in European history. I heard you're both coming for graduation."

Mrs. Brent swept the group with a veteran eye. "How good

to see you, Kate. Your last year, isn't it? The best of all. And Susan, too. This must be your sister; you do look alike, and both as thin as pencils. We have been detained all afternoon at Doña Clara. Some unfortunate accident, I believe. The pool was indeed an anodyne. And here's Honoria Epstein and Dory Williams. How nice. Quite a reunion. Gracious, Honoria, I can certainly see a great deal of you in that bathing suit."

Kate, who seemed to have an early-warning system for approaching faculty, pointed to the archway, "Here's Miss Lucas."

"Oh, splendid," said Mrs. Brent. "We can go over next week's plans with her. You know, girls, that we will be taking you to Big Bend National Park on Friday in our new wagon."

The girls were making a common effort at enthusiasm when Eleanor Lucas walked deliberately up to the group and, without preliminaries, said in a peculiarly thick voice, "Doña Clara has been closed because of an accident. It's Philip Lentz. He's dead, and the police have left a message at the motel desk that a detective is coming over this evening, and he wants to question you girls after dinner . . . anything you know about Mr. Lentz." Here Miss Lucas paused, and then with more emphasis said, "Try not to let your imaginations run away with you. The police also want to talk to Mrs. Brent and Miss Fellows, and to me, tomorrow, or the next day." She turned from the silent group and walked away.

Mrs. Brent, impassive, drew a deep breath; Miss Fellows·bit her lip; the girls stood like statues, except for Dory Williams, who picked up her tennis racket and botany textbook and started for the motel. Kate McMillan spoke for her classmates.

"Jesus Christ Almighty," she said.


Alex stood on the edge of the pool. He thought, I'd like to go down into the water and keep going until I hit Cape Cod; and he imagined himself through some mysterious arrangement between the pool overflow and the Rio Grande delta released above Brownsville and carried on around the Gulf, swirling around the Florida Keys, on and out, finally surging into the cold and healing dark green currents of the North. He shook himself, flung up his hands, and smacked the water in a flat dive and, keeping his head down and his feet moving, made it to the deep end on one breath.

He came up, gasped, turned, dived to the bottom, pushed off on the rough cement, broke the surface with a rush of water, and became aware of a pair of bare feet planted by the side of the pool. Sarah looked down at him. She was muffled in a huge red, yellow, and black beach towel, and her wet hair clung to her head like a helmet.

"Hello, Alex."

"Hello, Sarah. Where did you get that towel?"

"It's a Mickey Mouse towel. Mrs. Goldsmith gave it to me; it belongs to her niece. The motel towels are too small. I keep having these shivering fits, but I'm not cold. I've done a lot of laps, but it hasn't helped much."

Alex pulled himself up beside her. "Come on, Sarah. Your friendly traveling physician prescribes tea or gin, followed by dinner. I suppose you never did get any lunch?"

Sarah wrapped herself more tightly in her towel. "I don't think I could have gotten any food past my front teeth. Today just goes on and on."

"Yes, I know," said Alex, "but it will end. Are you up to meeting Tom Pérez for dinner and talking to him afterwards?"

"I don't care much what I do. So why not?"

"Tom may seem a bit brusque at times, but he's concerned about the god-awful things that happen to people."

Sarah moved her big toe, tracing a wet circle. "I've got to ask something," she said in a low voice. "Did it take long? Philip dying, I mean. I can't remember what you said. Did it hurt a lot? I don't think Philip's ever been hurt—physically, anyway."

"Sarah, to be honest, I can only guess, but it looks like it was quick. An attack from behind. He probably never realized what was happening. Just a short struggle and then he would have lost consciousness. It was strangulation." He looked down at her. "I hope that doesn't make it worse."

"It couldn't be worse, could it . . . unless there'd been torture? But I guess I'm glad it was over soon. I couldn't bear to think of him lying hurt out in the rain in that marsh all night."

"Philip was dead before the rain. The ground under him was dry."

"And I'd hate to think that he knew, was aware, that he was going to die. He always made things work for him. He planned for emergencies, and—oh damn."

Together they walked through the garden toward the side entrance of the motel. Alex stopped at the door. "Sarah, if you want to go swimming again, will you use the buddy system? You know what the Red Cross says. Call me or one of Jeff's aunts."

"I can see right through that request. If you think I'm going to play Ophelia in the motel pool, forget it."

"But if you have—well, a sinking spell, will you get me? Use me as a backup system."

"Thank you for your interest and kindness, Alex, but I can take care of myself." And Sarah pulled her towel closer and departed.

# XXIII

Later that evening, settled at a small table in a room off the motel kitchen, the affairs of the late Philip Lentz were introduced by Tom, who had shown admirable restraint during dinner. He now turned to Sarah, who was poking a hole in a melting dish of ice cream.

"You told me, I think, that Philip was in charge of this school trip to Boyden?"

"Yes, Philip taught history, but he also gave a course in ornithology and did the weekend bird walks."

"Were you going to help out down here with the students?"

Sarah stirred her ice cream. "Perhaps. I knew most of the girls. But next week we were going off on our own. I'm not much of a bird-watcher, but Philip thought Texas would be so exciting that I'd be hooked."

"Do you know anyone from the school—anyone anywhere —who had strong feelings about Philip? One way or the other?"

"You mean to the point of murder?" asked Sarah sharply.

"Let's back up, Sarah," said Tom quietly. "I didn't mean that. How about anyone who resented Philip? Who didn't feel neutral about him? I'm not going to leap out of this room with handcuffs."

"I have no idea." Sarah looked over Tom's head at a large framed painting of a lone cowboy who pursued a dogie with a whirling rope against a livid sky.

"Don't push her," said Alex.

"He's not pushing me," said Sarah irritably. "I just don't know how to answer without getting into all sorts of irrelevant things like school politics. Why don't you ask the students about Philip's school relationships? I'm not there this year."

"I will," said Tom calmly, "in about ten minutes. But you know girls. They'll say half the school had a raging passion for Philip, and the other half was slipping arsenic in his coffee. They'll tell me that the entire faculty is sexually hung up or psychotic."

The smallest of smiles flickered across Sarah's face. "Yes, you're right. I'm sure they think either that I'm his scarlet mistress or too cold for him."

"Okay, then, Sarah. Which of these girls, if any, will give me something like a straight story?"

"Mostly you'll get a lot of pseudo-psychoanalytic garbage, but not from Dory Williams. She's the tall black student. She has sense and never lets herself get caught up in school fads and gossip. If she wants to talk, she's your best bet."

"How about Mrs. Brent and Miss Fellows? Recent amputees from Miss Morton's, I hear. I see they're at this motel. And then there's Eleanor Lucas."

"I told Alex on the way down here about Mrs. Brent and Miss Fellows and the big shake-up. And I think you'd better ask Miss Lucas about Miss Lucas." Sarah pushed herself away from the table. "That's it. That's really it."

Alex rose and reached for her arm, but Sarah moved away. "I'm going swimming now. Nine hundred laps. I don't want pills or sympathy. I'm just fine, so don't try and stop me. Thanks for the dinner, both of you. Good night." The door closed with a sharp click, leaving Alex standing shaking his head.

"Let her go, Alex. She's acting feisty, which is a good sign. You can look in on her later. Exercise might help her settle down. Now what's this about a shake-up?"

"Philip, the organization man," said Alex, and he proceeded to relate Sarah's story of the decapitation of the two teachers. "I would guess," he finished, "although Sarah didn't spell it out, that there must have been a hell of a lot of bitterness built up in those two ladies by the end of that last term. And Philip was the executioner."

"And Eleanor Lucas?" Tom pulled a file card from a folder. "Five years at the academy, teaches biology, tennis, fencing. I haven't talked to her yet, so I don't know much more than this, which I got when I called the school before dinner. She wasn't at the refuge this morning, but her name's on the registration sheet for Friday, along with Dory Williams."

"You're on your own with Lucas."

"Any useful biographical info on Sarah herself?"

"I've told you. She was one of those women in the background doing other things with other people—in this case, Philip. I gather that after college Sarah batted around, lived in Boston, then got that job at Miss Morton's. Now she's back in the Northeast teaching school and working on a master's. I can only add—and I feel like a gossip—that I've heard that some guy she lived with got himself killed in a car accident a few years ago. Maybe Sarah's defensive, hands-off manner may have to do with that. Or maybe not."

"So Philip's death might be a breaking point?"

"Two men in your life killed wouldn't do much for your mental health, do you think? I do worry about her, but she doesn't seem like the suicidal type."

"Arrange to keep an eye on her. And now let's have in those babes from Miss Muffet's."

"Ladies from the school for scandal. I can't wait." Alex sat down and poured himself another cup of coffee.


"Almost ten-thirty," groaned Tom, shifting his weight in the unyielding kitchen chair. "I feel like I've been swallowed whole. Let's get the last one in." Tom consulted is list. "It's Dory Williams."

Alex walked to the door. "Dory Williams, will you come in, please?" He extended his hand. "I'm Dr. McKenzie and this is Lieutenant Pérez, who wants to ask you some questions, the same ones he's asked everyone."

Dory walked in, a tall girl with her chin high. She was wearing the school uniform decreed for evening: blue skirt and high-necked white blouse. She sat down quietly and folded her hands in her lap.

"We appreciate your help, Dory," said Tom. "Now can you tell me what time you and Miss Lucas got to Doña Clara yesterday, what you did there, and, if possible, when you did it?"

Dory considered for a moment and then, without verbal side trips, described her arrival at the refuge with Eleanor Lucas at three o'clock, their splitting up at about four, her own hike in the opposite direction from Miss Lucas, down the western section of the Rio Vista Trail, and their meeting as arranged just before six thirty in the parking lot. Yes, Dory had an accurate watch. And then? Dory related how she and Miss Lucas returned directly to the motel, where after greeting the just arrived students, Miss Lucas said that she had a headache and was going to her room. She did not join them for dinner, nor had Dory seen her again that evening. Dory ate with the other students at a table reserved for the school group. And what of Philip Lentz? At no time, neither at the refuge nor at the motel, had Dory seen Mr. Lentz. In fact, at dinner they had all speculated about the absence of both teachers. After dinner Dory had left the others watching television and had gone to her room to study a new botany field guide. She did not leave her room again.

Taken closely through the events of Saturday morning, Dory's account did not differ from that of her classmates, so Tom returned to the botany teacher. When Miss Lucas finally turned up this morning, did she mention a headache as the reason for missing dinner last night? Or for coming late this morning? "Yes," said Dory.

"Does Miss Lucas have frequent headaches?"

Dory had heard that Miss Lucas had an occasional migraine.

Tom tapped his pencil, looked at the wall, and asked the windup question for the last time that night. "Dory, do you know anyone who disliked Mr. Lentz? Strongly disliked?"

"I suppose," said Dory calmly, "the faculty he got rid of didn't like him much. Especially Miss Fellows and Mrs. Brent."

"Anyone else?"

"Miss Lucas probably didn't like being ditched for Miss Deane."

"Oh?"

"I don't spend much time on who's making it and who isn't, but before Mr. Lentz came everyone seemed to think Miss Lucas was in line for Assistant Director of Studies. But Mr. Lentz began looking at Sarah Deane, and this year he was made the Acting Director and Miss Lucas wasn't made anything. I don't draw conclusions. Miss Lucas is a good biology teacher. That's all I ask."

Tom looked hard at Dory. "The other girls suggested that Miss Lucas knew Mr. Lentz before he came to Morton's. What about it?"

Dory shrugged her shoulders slightly. "Miss Lucas lived with Mr. Lentz before she came to the academy. Didn't the other students tell you? Of course, they're into psychology and analysis and forget the facts."

"Thank you very much, Dory," said Tom. "It's been very helpful talking to someone who isn't into psychology and analysis."

Dory stood up, nodded, smoothed her skirt, moved to the door, opened it, and noiselessly disappeared.

# SUNDAY, MARCH 17

## XXIV

The editor of the Sunday edition of the Boyden *Express,* faced with the rival claims of a Vice-Presidential trip to Houston, another oil spill in the Gulf, mayhem by motorcycle, or a body in a National Wildlife Refuge, gave front-page pride of place to the motorcycles—the remnants of which were, after all, still holed up in Dead Horse Arroyo.

Cheryl Cabot was disappointed, but her natural optimism allowed her to hope for a better spread in the Monday edition. Meanwhile, without actually lying, she managed to convey the idea to motel guests that Philip Lentz was a regular at Vacation Villa and that she could say a lot more if she felt like it.

"Like what?" asked Nina Goldsmith, who found murder more to her taste than birding.

"Like nothing, kiddo," said Cheryl. "I might have to be a witness or something. Witnesses don't talk about what they know."

"No," said Nina, "they get rubbed out."

Motel guests who had visited Doña Clara on Friday or Saturday passed the day in a hubbub of unfamiliar activity. Police cars buzzed between the refuge, the motel, and the Homicide Division, and an office for Lieutenant Pérez was created from a rather stuffy chamber behind the manager's office. This space, grandly called the Conference Room, was in reality a repository for seldom-used furniture, and here the police set up typewriters, recording equipment, tacked a large-scale map of Doña Clara to the wall, and began to take statements.

Philip Lentz—deceased—was the central fact of the investigative process. However, to only a few guests at the motel was his death of any real interest; to others his murder merely caused a detour in their plans for that Sunday.

To Enid Plummer, suffering from an arthritic knee, the change in plan brought relief. To Waldo Plummer, the murder meant the interruption of the tour schedule. "We will go to Alta Hollow Park instead. An afternoon trip. Nina Goldsmith, today you may sit with me on the bus."

Mrs. Brent's and Miss Fellows's past experience with the police had been limited to the old *Dragnet* series, and their whole knowledge of the minutiae of homicide investigations came from mystery novels. However, since both ladies were addicted to the English form of the genre, they found themselves rather at sea in the present instance. Instead of an urbane Old Harrovian from the C.I.D. and his assistant in a Burberry and bowler, they were privy to all the oddities of an American police case presided over by a Hispanic-American lieutenant with a satiric eye and a razor tongue. But Mrs. Brent, distressed as she was, had to admit that she was rather taken with Lieutenant Pérez. Miss Fellows, pale and silent, refused to accompany Mrs. Brent to church and kept a good deal to her room.

Mrs. Bailey and Mrs. Goldsmith found that homicide hit home, since, through their nephew Jeff, they were connected to the discovery of the body in the marsh. Lois Bailey reported that the boy had slept badly Saturday night; she had heard him heaving himself about on the cot set up off the room that she shared with Nina. Then, too, both women had been asked to keep an eye on Sarah Deane, and there she was going around like a shadow, swimming up and down the pool or standing in the middle of the garden staring at nothing. They had done their best with offers of restorative drinks and conversation, but Sarah was unresponsive, and their efforts had been reduced to those of discreet watchdogs. That nice Dr. McKenzie had taken her for a long hike in the morning, but she had come back looking worn and walking with her head down.

Major Foster expressed in the voice of a bullhorn both his desire to cooperate with "that mighty fine police department we've got here in Boyden" and his exasperation at the change in schedule. He did, however, on the short trip to Alta Hollow, locate a jacana stepping daintily in the middle of some water plants, so the day did not pass without a life bird being added to club members' lists.

Mrs. van Hoek found herself in a crisis of costume so that the respite afforded by murder was most welcome. She hadn't known that Texas could be so hot in March—she had a regular heat rash, and she was going to need a hair appointment soon. Those bird classes at the science museum had been rather fun—some amusing people had turned up and they had all gone out afterward for a drink. This tour—not a bit what she expected. They seemed to take this birding so very seriously, and there was no one along that she had really known before. Or heard of. Or wanted to see again. Those awful ragbag clothes. After all, outdoor things did not mean that one just gave up—style was perfectly possible. But today another statement was going to be taken, a longer one than those questions in the parking lot, which had hardly touched the surface. She would try to think if she hadn't seen something out of the ordinary—she rather thought she had. That lieutenant had quite an air, so decided a manner. And that attractive dark-haired doctor who seemed to be involved, perhaps he would sit in on the questioning.

Professor Axminster explained to any of the motel guests who would listen that a National Refuge being closed was yet another example of government interference, and that the Axminster Collection had not been built with federal funds, thank the dear Lord. . . .

Janice Axminster, in her dirndl looking like a bed pillow tied in the middle, alternated between arch little jokes at the expense of the Boyden police and bursts of annoyance that caused her to clench her pudgy hands. She and her husband made a series of contradictory statements to the police; after which both Axminsters departed for refuges unknown.

As Tom Pérez had predicted, the peace of Mr. Allen was overthrown, and the manager hustled about, soothing and informing, very much, as Mrs. Goldsmith remarked, in the manner of a mediator from the Middle East world of diplomacy.

By the end of Sunday, Sarah had set a new but unrecorded motel-pool lap record, Jeff Goldsmith had thrown up after dinner behind a flowering shrub, Mrs. Brent and Miss Fellows had had trays in their room, and, just before dark, the Axminsters had returned, looking smug.

# MONDAY, MARCH 18

## XXV

Restless since sunrise, Alex, shortly after six, had gone outside to the motel garden. There he found Jeff wandering about, lifting his binoculars in a weary way at a crowd of grackles that squeaked and rattled in the trees. Alex proposed a hike around the motel's perimeter, and Jeff, without noticeable enthusiasm, agreed.

Watching the boy at his side, Alex thought how young he was: the still-smooth cheeks, the mop of red hair growing down into the hollows of his neck, the thin arms and legs showing few signs of the developing musculature of the adolescent. But young or not, Alex thought, kids these days are amazingly sophisticated. No sexual kink or blood-and-gut event but hadn't turned up on the living-room screen or at the neighborhood cinema, to say nothing of the spread offered in the periodicals. Jeff could probably expound on transvestites, on the use of silicone in breast enlargement, and on getting high or being low, but the actual fact of a dead body at his feet must have shaken him up.

Alex nudged the boy. "There's a hummingbird by those flowers."

Jeff glanced over at the blossoms and sighed deeply.

"What's the matter, Jeff? Do you only look at the exotics?"

"Yeah. I mean, no. I guess I've got something on my mind."

"Is it the telescope that you found?"

"Yeah, that's one thing. You don't suppose the police think I wanted to steal it or something?"

"Don't worry about that, Jeff. But the telescope is one of the pieces of evidence in what's definitely a murder case. It belonged to the man you found. He was a schoolteacher and a naturalist."

"Someone murdered him bird-watching?" Jeff sounded incredulous.

"We don't know yet. The police are working on it."

"I know all about pathology and homicide," said Jeff slowly.

"But you never thought you'd walk right into a dead body —it only happens on TV. It really hits you, doesn't it? My first day in gross-anatomy class, I walked in and saw thirty cadavers in one room. I almost passed out. I'd never seen a body before— only rats and frogs in bottles. Anything else on your mind? I'm a good listener."

Jeff fingered his binoculars, turning them over and over, and then said, "I'm worried abut an identification problem. Do you make a lot of I.D. mistakes, Dr. McKenzie? Birds, I mean, not diseases."

"I make both kinds," said Alex cheerfully. "Even experts do. In medicine and ornithology. With birds, I misjudge the size, or the light gets in my eyes, or I forget to notice one crucial field mark. Then sometimes I see what I want to see."

"You mean a psychological mistake?"

"Sure. If I'm anxious to see a certain bird, then I can almost talk myself into it. That's why good field notes are important. It's a lot harder to fool yourself when it's all written down."

"So if I take good notes, I shouldn't make a mistake?"

"It's a lot harder that way, but still anyone can mess up an I.D."

"The Hamburg Club is stuffed with people who do."

"So, Jeff, why not give the beginners in your group some help and ease up on the runaway act? And Major Foster might just be able to show you a few things."

By the time the two had made their way back to the motel garden, the sun was already lighting up the courtyard, and a man was fishing about the swimming pool with a long-handled net. Beyond the pool, two women stood peering into the dark center of a large bottlebrush shrub.

"It's Aunt Lois and Aunt Connie," said Jeff. "But I don't suppose they really see anything in there." At that an undeniable bird shape whirred out of the bush and vanished in a brown blur.

"Oh, hello, Dr. McKenzie. We thought it might have been a chuck-will's-widow. It looked just like prune whip," said Lois Bailey, whose mind before meals usually produced edible figures of speech.

"That's a pretty good description," said Alex. "Jeff and I have been hiking around the motel to clear our brains. Now I've a favor to ask of you ladies. It's Sarah Deane. I wonder if there's any way she could be included in your trip today? I'm going to be tied up with the police, and I don't want Sarah here on her own. I'll speak to your club leader and Major Foster about it, if you'll say you'll keep an eye on her."

"Will she want to go with us?" asked Connie Goldsmith.

"I don't know, but after all, she can't spend all of the next twelve hours in the pool."

"Oh, the poor thing." said Lois Bailey.

At that moment the "poor thing" emerged from the door of

the terrace and marched resolutely toward them, the sureness of her step arguing against infirmity. She wore a fresh blue shirt, sleeves rolled high, and a pair of faded red cotton pants. Her short hair was brushed flat and her face had a scrubbed look. "I've decided to go hiking today," she announced.

Connie Goldsmith picked up her cue. "With us, I hope, Sarah. We need a new face. We're going to Laguna Atascosa. It's on the Gulf, and you can hike or look at birds. Nina's staying at the motel, thank heavens. They've got a play camp here for children."

Sarah looked with suspicion at Alex. "Have you been behaving like a doctor again? I'm perfectly okay."

"Sarah," said Alex mildly, "it's because you're perfectly okay that I think it would be a good idea for you to go along with the Ready Tour people. There's nothing you can do here."

Sarah hesitated. "I hate to leave. I feel stupid not helping."

"Honestly, we're just going over the ground—literally and figuratively," said Alex. "I'll look for you later in the afternoon. We'll do nine thousand laps."

"Gracious," said Mrs. Bailey, "I can hardly do six. Now let's all go in for breakfast. Those date muffins are heaven."

"Obesity," said Jeff, who had been standing listening, "can cause awful problems for middle-aged people."

"And younger-aged people have been put in solitary confinement for remarks like that," said Alex. "Ladies, after you."

# XXVI

After breakfast, Sarah returned to her room to pick up a hat and binoculars, and now she stood in the center of the room and studied herself in the long mirror that hung above the low motel chest of drawers. She saw some thin, pale stranger reflected, eyes charcoal smudges in a taut face. Like a drum skin, she thought, drawing her fingers across her cheeks. Behind her mirrored figure hung a large Audubon reproduction of the Carolina parakeets, handsome in its gold frame—extinct birds, like the passenger pigeon, and Sarah remembered her airplane fantasy about unsuccessful birds, and now Philip was unsuccessful, vanished, extinct. She stared in the mirror at the parakeets with their yellow-and-red faces and green-splashed feathers bending with big bills over dried leaves and cockleburs. They seemed grotesque, their postures awkward, unnatural. She saw that by accident the bathroom door with its tall mirror was angled to reflect the room mirror, so that the parakeets were repeated, static, unsympathetic avian forms in a hall of mirrors, and always in front of them stood this dark-haired meager figure, this stranger, alone, unimportant in a world of parakeets.

Suddenly, Sarah was overwhelmed by an ache from within so acute that she almost cried out. She wanted to go home, really home. Not to that garage apartment in Boston, but to the first one —that faded brick house that stood at the foot of the long spruce-lined driveway. Home. She walked in her mind away from the framed birds, down out of the mirrors, down her own driveway, through the gap in the box hedge and through the open front door, into the wide hall and then to the porch, where she could see the lake beyond, flat and blue, seeming to hang from the horizon. On the porch she saw her gray cat, Naomi, curled in a spot of sun next to the wicker swing, heard her mother practicing the piano in the living room, heard the whine of her father's table saw from the barn. Down she went, on down the slanting lawn past the white pines and balsam firs, down to the edge of the bank made orange with late June poppies, down the beach stairs, her towel around her hips, the sun hot on her bare shoulders, Sneezer, her black-and-white setter, wiggling down the stairs ahead of her, plume tail waving from side to side. Her brother Tony already on the beach in his red swimming trunks, heaping sand to make a mountain roadway for his Corgi cars. She felt the warm sand on the bottoms of her feet. . . .

A double knock on the motel door. "Sarah, are you ready?"

An overwhelming sense of loss swept Sarah. She stood bereft in the middle of the motel room staring into a mirror of parakeets. Home, house, vanished. Naomi was dead, run over. Sneezer was gone, shot by a deer hunter. The house sold, her father and mother moved from New Hampshire to a series of strange houses holding only guest rooms for grown and gone-away children. Tony in Vermont selling skis, her little brother over six feet tall with a black beard. Tears ran down her face and along her nose into her mouth, and she licked her lips and tasted salt.

"Sarah, are you in there? Shall I come in?" The doorknob turned, and Constance Goldsmith stepped into the room, binoculars around her neck, a green canvas hat on the back of her head. She saw Sarah standing motionless, her cheeks wet, her dark heavy lashes closing over her eyes.

"Would you like to rest here today? I'll stay with you. We could lie in the sun and swim and take it easy." Mrs. Goldsmith perched on the end of the unmade bed, her open face with its freckles and peeling nose crumpled with concern.

Sarah shook her head. "No, it's all right." She pulled a towel from the back of the chair and went into the bathroom. Mrs. Goldsmith could hear splashing water and then the gurgle of a toilet flushing. Sarah emerged, eyes red but open.

"No," she said. "I want to come. It'll keep one third of my brain busy."

"Birding is a good distraction," said Connie Goldsmith. "You can be as involved as you want. I'm not a fanatic, but it gets me out of the house, though I don't know if it's going to replace the movies."

Sarah looked up as if seeing her companion for the first time. I wanted to go home, she thought, and here's a mother ready-made.

"How's Jeff this morning, Mrs. Goldsmith?"

"Call me Connie, for heaven's sake. Jeff was upset for a while, but now he seems to be himself, which isn't always consoling. Do you really want to go? Major Foster says fine, and you'll certainly be a great improvement on Nina, who has absolutely had it with birds."

"I may feel the same way," said Sarah, reaching for her hat.

"Your binoculars?"

"Oh damn. These belong to Alex—mine are at home broken. But it's all right," she added, "Alex has two pairs. Let's go."

"Have you got your room key?" asked Connie Goldsmith, by which question confirming her role as a surrogate mother.

# XXVII

It was Mr. Allen's custom after breakfast to go directly to the front desk, the better to preside over the comings and goings of his guests. Now the manager fluttered over Alex McKenzie, who was established in an armchair waiting for Tom Pérez and trying to read the morning paper.

"I ask every day what is Texas coming to. Violence everywhere. Mr. Lentz, such a fine young man. He was here last year, you know, and I thought Friday that it was strange he hadn't checked in, but then some of our birders stay out quite late looking for owls. Those girls from Miss Morton's had to eat alone, and they were very noisy. Their teacher Miss Lucas had simply disappeared, but I suppose she was tired after her trip."

Alex looked up from his study of the weather chart. "Yes, Mr. Allen," he said.

". . . one of those border things or teenage drugs, I told Miss Cabot. One tries for balance." Here the manager tilted his small hands back and forth in illustration. "We walk a tightrope in this business. A little notoriety doesn't upset us—but murder, Dr. McKenzie!" Mr. Allen's hands did an aerial flip-flop.

Alex, aroused by the sound of his name, made assenting noises and refolded his newspaper closer about his head. Thus concealed, he missed the undulating approach of Cheryl Cabot, who was now on morning as well as afternoon duty. Cheryl sparkled. The dreary nature-oriented motel regime had been immeasurably leavened by murder, and with a view to increased lobby traffic, Cheryl had dressed herself in a slippery green garment that clung to her torso in pleasing invitation.

Mr. Allen regarded his handmaiden with an ill-humored eye. He was only too aware that the introduction of the police into the motel machinery had initiated new and provocative symptoms in Ms. Cabot.

"The police are here," announced Cheryl. "Dr. McKenzie, the lieutenant is in the Conference Room waiting for you."

"Thank you, Cheryl," said Mr. Allen. "Suppose you go and run off tonight's menus. The police will not wish to be disturbed."

Alex, who had taken happy root in an article on the Red Sox pitching staff, rose reluctantly and made his way to meet Tom. He found him, coat over a chair, sleeves rolled, sitting sideways at the end of a long table, his feet resting on the lower rung of a high chair.

"Anything I can get you, Lieutenant, or you, Doctor?" Cheryl lingered in the doorway.

Tom grinned. "It's Cheryl, isn't it? Yeah. How about some coffee and doughnuts?"

"Good God," said Alex as she left, "what a tourist attraction!"

"Oh, Cheryl's okay. Miss Boyden Beautyrest. She used to work at the Boyden Pizza House. A real favorite, that girl—what we call in the department a 'professional amateur.' The motel has her a bit boxed in, but I suppose there's usually an empty bed somewhere. So let's get on with crime. First, the autopsy. Just a preliminary report."

"Let me sit down and take a note or two." Alex settled himself at the table and helped himself to a pad of paper.

"We finished up around midnight. Death undoubtedly due to strangulation."

"Yes," said Alex. "That was fairly obvious."

"And he was strangled from behind by some sort of rope or a strap. The mark is deep and continuous around the front of the neck and breaks off in back into a series of irregular contusions."

"Someone's hands at their filthy work," said Alex.

"No doubt. We'll have some more data this morning."

"And time of death?"

"We're waiting on reports, but we can never fix it right on the nose. Detective stories always make it seem like a fine art. It isn't. Too many factors like heat and humidity. It's great if the victim's watch happens to break at the time of the attack, but today too many watches are shock-resistant. Lentz's was working fine."

Alex looked up in surprise. "They took his wallet and not his watch." He nodded. "Okay, I remember. The watch was on the list."

"This guy or these guys were in a hurry. That was a fast cover-up job with the leaves and the brush. The body was really quite visible; the feet completely exposed. So perhaps whoever it was just missed the watch because he had to get out of there pronto."

"So time of death—approximately?"

"We had a break with the rain. The ground under the body was dry. He was face down and the clothes on his back were soaked. The rain began sometime around ten, and it rained off and on until about four Saturday morning."

"Then he was killed before ten Friday evening?"

"Yes, and here's where you come in. How late can anyone watch birds through a telescope?"

"You can't get much more than a profile after the sun goes down, though it depends on the size of the optical field, how much light gets through, things like that."

"So Philip couldn't spot birds with his scope after dark?"

"Not possibly. And Philip was supercareful about equipment. He wouldn't have left it sitting there in the marsh."

"That's what I figure," said Tom. "Oh, thanks, Cheryl." He stood up and took hold of a tray laden with doughnuts, coffee cups, and a steaming pot. He poured out two cups and shoved one across to Alex. "I'm beginning to read some of what happened. I see Lentz sitting down at the scope, on his stool, putting the lens caps in his pocket—where we found them all buttoned down—and then along comes someone, and Philip gets up, leaves his equipment—scope, binoculars, book, stool—and never comes back."

"He gets murdered instead. But why and when?"

"And with what? The lab should come up with that soon. The 'when' is sometime, perhaps, that there was enough light to look through the scope and before it started to rain, but we can do a little better than that." Tom pulled out a sheet covered with penciled names. "We've got the Doña Clara registration sheets. Philip, like a conscientious visitor, signed in—three names after the Kansas biology team, which arrived after three-thirty Friday, according to Sam Hernández, who arranged camping permits for them. And Philip's name is four names ahead of the Cactus Wren ladies, who claim they got to the refuge a little before five. No verification on that. And, very interesting, they say they caught sight of someone like Lentz after five, but aren't sure, so we can't place our bets on that time yet."

"Then he was killed after three-thirty, perhaps after five," said Alex, "and if leaving the telescope and binoculars was connected with the murder, then we have, say, seven o'clock as the cut-off time. But hell, I don't know if that makes sense. He might have gotten up and gone after a bird or pursued an alien coming from the river, maybe met a friend, and then come back *after* dark for his telescope and was strangled then. You know, Tom, with that fair hair, the white shirt, someone might be able to remember him. Birders talk to each other."

"Only two sets of prints on the scope," said Tom. "Jeff's and Philip's. Some soil on the stool and the scope because the wind blew them over, but the lab says not enough to suggest a struggle; no scratches, no damage, no fibers from a stranger's clothing."

Alex, restless indoors on a bright day, got up and paced the length of the room and came to rest against a sideboard that now supported a typewriter and a telephone. "Where was he killed, Tom?"

"Not where he was found. The body was dragged from somewhere else, but with that rain, any track on the trail was washed out. He was dragged face up by a line or a belt fastened under his arms and then turned over. We found bruising and an indentation across the torso and a strip of soil on the front of the shirt. His sneakers and socks came off and were pushed under or near the body. He was wearing those hiking shorts with the button-down flap pockets, so he didn't leave a trail of objects."

The telephone jangled from the sideboard. Alex reached over and passed the instrument to Tom.

Tom crammed the receiver under his chin. "Pérez speaking."

Alex walked over and stood at the double window that overlooked a collection of natal plums edging the motel entrance. A shaft of sunlight full of suspended dust particles angled down from the top of the window. Alex put his palms flat against the glass and thought of himself hiking along a path by the Rio Grande—one of those bends where the water runs clear around little shaggy green islands. At his side, walking, her arms swinging loose . . . Alex began to whistle softly.

Tom dumped the receiver into place. "Alex, come to. What are you staring at? A chick going by?"

Alex turned from the window. "No," he said shortly.

"Well, don't give up, amigo. Texas is the land of opportunity."

"Not in the middle of a murder case, it isn't," returned Alex, irritated.

Tom stood, picked up his briefcase. "Anyway, we're off. They've got some news at the lab, and Joe said it was interesting. And you, Alex, have got some I.D. forms to sign. We called Lentz's married sister in Oregon, but she and the whole family are off on a ski trip."


The "splendid new forensic laboratory facility and mortuary," as it was described in the Chamber of Commerce brochure, was nothing more than the old police garage, gutted and refitted, but still remarkably like its original self. Alex was reading from a tablet inscribed to the memory of an early Boyden pathologist when Tom came briskly through a glass-paneled door at the end of the hall.

"This will open your eyes. Philip Lentz was strangled with a thin leather strap, black on one side, natural leather on the other —twisted together at the back of the neck. We've had microscopic identification and a prelim chem report. So, McKenzie, what does that say?"

"God," said Alex, staring at Tom.

"God, indeed. That sort of shoots the idea of some border crosser doing the job, doesn't it? Because I needn't tell you that this sort of strap is—as the lab report puts it—'commonly found on cameras, binoculars, and other similar equipment.' Now, you know that Mexicans sneaking in don't wade the river dressed up in cameras and binoculars. Possible, but very improbable. A change of socks, a few dollars or pesos, the address of Uncle Juán or Cousin Pedro—that's all."

"But," said Alex, "naturalists don't strangle each other."

"Who says? I'm going to eyeball all those folks who carry binocs and cameras. We'll start in with the visitors known to have been in the refuge on Friday and branch out if we have to."

"But why wasn't Philip killed with his own binocular strap?"

"Bonehead," said Tom. "His binocs were next to the telescope, safe and sound in their case. Only Philip's prints. Strap was a red nylon one."

"But that's what's so damn odd. I've said it before. Why wasn't Philip wearing his binoculars?"

"And I answered that he was sighting with his telescope."

Alex frowned. "No. That's wrong. That's been bugging me. You usually take a sighting first with binoculars and then zero in on the bird with the scope. It's quicker that way. Binoculars are easier to use to follow movement, and they have a wider field."

"Perhaps he had just that minute set up the scope."

"How was it focused?"

"We'll never know. No one noticed the setting when it was bagged for the lab, and besides, Jeff moved it, wiped it, and fooled around with the focus. But now, instead of sifting through the entire border area, we can look for some homicidal nature-lover. First we'll examine all the straps we can get our hands on."

"Good luck, Tom. Half the visitors that were in the refuge on Friday afternoon are probably in Borneo by now."

"We'll make do with what we have," said Tom stiffly. "You can help by telling me about camera and binocular straps. I haven't the time nor the money for such hobbies."

"You're looking for a leather strap, but a lot of people substitute a cloth or nylon strap. Easier on the neck."

"But the equipment is sold with a narrow leather strap?"

"The expensive stuff, yes. Sometimes nylon. Originally, almost all optical equipment came with a leather strap, but now the cheaper models come with plastic straps."

"Okay, now we have something to work with. I'll send some men right out to make a leather-strap collection. We can hand out a string replacement. Then we'll hot up the search for visitors who've left the area. Tour groups and school classes are easy to find; it's the singles and doubles that are a bitch."

"Do you know where all the Vacation Villa guests are today?"

"We're lucky. No one has checked out, and I've got the manager ready to call me on any escapees. Everyone's off on field trips, Brent and Fellows taking over the birding duties with the girls in place of Lentz. Only Eleanor Lucas left at the hotel, claiming to be unwell."

"Waiting for her strap to be examined."

"Yeah, I know. The murderer might have gotten rid of it. Never mind. We have to start somewhere. So, Alex, it's off to Bobcat Marsh. It's still closed off. Want to come out and give me the benefit of your diagnostic skills?"

"I never turn down fresh air," said Alex, making for the door. He paused and looked at Tom, who followed. "Goddammit," he said.

"*Por cierto,*" said Tom.

# XXVIII

Sarah, sitting next to the window on the Ready Tour bus, was to remember the trip out to Laguna Atascosa Wildlife Refuge as one more in a series of events at a remove from common experience. The bus traveled past dark green citrus groves and long fields punctuated by palm trees that stuck up in the sky like troops of attenuated dishmops. Then a ranch appeared, having on its ground a number of Brahman cattle, some standing about a waterwheel, others lying on the caked ochre soil, all reinforcing a sense of the foreign. As Sarah stared at the Brahmans, thinking what unearthly animals they were, all angles and bumps under the stretched hide, a flock of black-bellied ducks—creatures alien to Sarah's knowledge of ducks—rose suddenly from the far side of a feeding trough. She felt transported. Perhaps it was going to be one of those bus trips that turn into an expedition to heaven or hell or some cloud-filled waiting room where each traveler finds out some devastating moral truth about himself. But, thought Sarah, I don't think I'm ready for that.

As if in agreement, Eduardo, at the wheel of the bus, pulled into the Laguna parking lot, and the members of the tour began to gather themselves and their equipment. Sarah was swept off the bus with the others and directly into the way of a gray shaggy giant of a dog sitting upright on the path. The Hamburg group discreetly made its way around the animal, but Sarah paused and, seeing the heavy tail hit the ground, knelt down to the beast and was rewarded with a large paw and a forward tongue.

"You certainly are big," said Sarah. "Good boy."

Good boy responded by rearing and hurling himself at Sarah, knocking her backward and beginning in earnest the serious business of washing her face.

"You big goof," said Sarah. She rolled over and disengaged herself and stood up in a rumpled condition.

"Sarah, are you all right?" Lois Bailey hurried over. "I thought that dog was going to have you for lunch."

At the Visitor Information Booth, Sarah inquired about her new acquaintance, and the woman in charge responded with a pout of distaste. "Oh, him. He's been around for over two weeks because one of the staff keeps feeding him. Texas is just overrun with stray dogs. It's a shame, but we can't keep him here."

"But what are you going to do?"

"One of the staff is taking him to the animal shelter today. They'll probably put him to sleep. He's enormous, and he may not even be full grown. Who would feed an animal that size?"

"I would," said Sarah firmly.

"Sarah, we have to go." Constance Goldsmith pulled at Sarah's sleeve, but Sarah shook her off.

"When I get back," Sarah said to the woman, "I will take the dog with me. Can you see that he's ready? Please don't lose him. He has a home." Sarah marched after Mrs. Goldsmith and caught up with the tour members, who were boarding the bus. At the entrance Sarah found herself folded into an embrace with a well-packed bosom.

"It's Sarah from Corpus Christi. Oh, my dear, Mrs. Bailey has told me about your loss. My poor child, and all alone now in Texas."

Sarah endured another clasp while she tried to place her comforter. Yes, it was Iris, the one whose husband, Orwell, was dead, and who was making that yellow-and-brown crochet thing on the plane.

"Oh," said Sarah in comprehension.

"I know all about losing a loved one, and I want to share."

Sarah forced a smile and looked frantically around for her friends, who came forward like a pair of ministering middle-aged spirits and pushed her onto the bus and well to the rear. "It's Major Foster's sister. She'll be coming on some of the field trips," explained Lois Bailey. "Stick with us. We'll protect you."

The trip down the Paisano Trail was interesting only for the appearance of two policemen, who detained the group long enough to examine and measure certain straps and exchange some of them for a substitute length of string. The implications of this procedure were not lost on the group, and the remainder of the Laguna trip was a sober one. Sarah went about obediently raising and lowering her binoculars and seeing little. Once Major Foster's sister Iris pulled her aside, a plump hand grasping her elbow. "Have you gone to Jesus?" she whispered.

Sarah gave a little jump. "Gone where?"

"To Jesus, dearie. In time of trouble go right to Him."

Sarah detached her arm. "There hasn't been much time," she murmured. She drew herself up. "Thank you very much, but I think I see Mrs. Goldsmith looking for me." And Sarah escaped.

In her later memory, the single impressive sighting of the day, at least to Sarah, was the close view of a long, well-filled diamondback slowly looping across the sandy path of the Bayside Tour Road in front of Major Foster and Enid Plummer. The front members of the troop, like a trained corps de ballet, stopped in forward stride and, holding their positions, let the reptile pass. Then, after a moment of awed silence, they burst into chatter and movement. Sarah, at the sight of the slowly moving wedge-shaped head, knew that Laguna was not safe for stray dogs and began thinking about collars and leashes.

On returning to the Visitor Information Booth, Sarah found a young man holding the large dog by a rope. "He's part Irish wolfhound, isn't he?" she asked.

"More than half," said the man. "I've been calling him Patsy, after an Irish uncle of mine. I'd have taken him myself, but I'm renting. No dogs allowed."

"That's all right," said Sarah. "He's got me now. Down, Patsy. I said *down*. He does jump up," she said reproachfully.

"I haven't had time to train him, but he's not near as thin as he was." The man placed the rope in Sarah's hand.

To everyone's surprise but Sarah's, Patsy was made welcome. Major Foster and his sister regarded him indulgently, Jeff's aunts compared notes on the proper diet for a growing dog, and Mr. Plummer, whose interest in animals did not extend to the domestic varieties, did not dare rise against popular sentiment.

Patsy rode in triumph, sometimes parked next to Sarah and sometimes braced with his paws on the bus window, where he took great interest in the passing scene and especially in the Brahman cattle.

# XXIX

In the late afternoon, returning with Tom Pérez to the temporary motel police office after a lengthy visit to Doña Clara, Alex found that his temper, which had been simmering since the discovery of Philip's body, was about to boil over. The swinging of the investigation toward that loose fellowship of naturalists was almost intolerable. He stamped across the room to one of the windows, wrenched it open, and was immediately rewarded by seeing the gold curtains billow gently inward. He yanked them aside and tied each length into a huge knot.

"That's better. This damn air conditioning. It's like being in a bell jar."

"You're not usually such a sorehead," said Tom. "It's the case. It's turned and bit you. Bird-watchers don't strangle each other."

"I'm keeping an open mind," growled Alex. "Are you?" Without waiting for an answer, he dragged a chair over to the window, sat down, and took up a copy of *Modern Motel Management.*

But Tom had walked over to a folding table set up in the rear of the room. This was presided over by the same large policeman who had assisted in the parking-lot questioning at the refuge, and who was now laboring over a small pile of thin black straps heaped on a tray. Sergeant Theodore Cotton—widely known as "Tiger"—was wearing yellow plastic gloves and recording names from tags tied to each strap.

Tom regarded the collection with something less than satisfaction. "This all you've got, Cotton?" He poked the straps with the eraser end of a pencil. Sergeant Cotton, always glad of a break, looked up. "Yessir. That's all . . . all the ones that met the specifications." He smiled, a wide smile of brimming well-being.

Tiger Cotton was one of those engaging and often exasperating humans whose mental machinery runs undisturbed by the roils of daily life. Successive tours in divisions of armed robbery, assault, arson, and now homicide had left his countenance unlined and his optimism undimmed. The shadow of discontent appeared on the broad ruddy face only when he was sent indoors, as at present, to fester inside doing "office work."

"Didn't do too bad, Lieutenant. We got all the tours and four other parties—Laguna, Santa Ana, Brownsville, and Bentsen. Had a hard time findin' those butterfly people but got 'em too. Gleason and Ramirez did Doña Clara and Falcon Dam." Sergeant Cotton, with his large hands in their yellow gloves like animated bananas, began slipping each strap in a plastic bag and taping the top closed. He then grinned at Tom. "Finished with the straps. That's the last one bagged. What'll I do next?"

"Get them to the airport. We've got a plane waiting." Tom turned to Alex. "We haven't got lab facilities for this kind of job, so we fly the tough ones to Houston. Hold it, Cotton," said Tom as Tiger gave signs of violent forward propulsion. "On your way, pick up the tissue samples at our path lab. After the airport, get on out to the refuge and give a hand to the boys there. Tell Sam Hernández I'll stop in around five."

When the door had banged closed, Tom picked up the list over which the sergeant had toiled. "Not as many as I expected."

Alex joined Tom at the table. "I've just had another thought.

Straps also come on tape recorders. Lots of birders use them for birdcalls. And how about transistor radios?"

"Relax, *amigo*. The great Pérez has covered all that. We've collected every black leather strap which is approximately half an inch wide and sixteen or more inches long from everything we could find."

"May I see the list?"

"Sure. McKenzie heads the list. A born leader. You're down twice, both for binoculars. I gather Sarah's using a pair of yours."

Alex skimmed down the list: "Waldo and Enid Plummer, Mrs. Brent, Miss Fellows, one strap each from binoculars; Jeff Goldsmith, two straps, binocs and tape recorder; Lois Bailey, camera strap; Janice Axminster, one strap, camera; Eleanor Lucas, two straps, camera and lens case; U. of Kansas biology team, six straps, cameras and lens cases; Philip Lentz . . . Lentz!"

"His binoculars at the marsh site have a nylon strap, but the camera locked in his car has a black leather strap."

"Fascinating," said Alex. "The murderer locates Philip's locked rental car, breaks in, takes the strap, runs out to Bobcat Marsh, strangles Philip, zips back, replaces the strap . . . leaving no prints."

Tom ignored this flight of fancy. "We're probably looking for an older strap, one whose surface is cracked and friable. The fragments of leather in the neck crease were dry."

"I know that those glasses I gave to Sarah qualify," said Alex, "but it's insane to think that Sarah came all the way to Doña Clara to choke Philip when she could have done it much more conveniently in Maryland or Boston."

"Off my back, Alex. I don't think much of Sarah as a suspect. And now I'm going out to Doña Clara and try and wrap up that marsh job. If I don't, Sam is going to have my scalp for upsetting his animals. Then tonight, it's dinner with the Cactus Wren duo."

"Dinner-*cum*-questions?"

"Right. Gracious interrogation. That Chinese place out on Basswood Street. You and Sarah stop in around nine for coffee."

Alex rose and walked to the door. "As you know, Tomás, I came down here to do some work on Celluwell, but hell, there's been no time for anything like that."

"I know. Look, if I have a few minutes, I'll try and set up a session for you at Narcotics. Me, I have to stick to homicide."

"Never mind about today. I've had it for now. I think I'll see if Sarah's back from Laguna."

"She's back all right, and she's got company." Tom pointed out the window to a figure moving toward a side entrance.

"Good God, she's got a horse." Alex strode across the lobby and out onto the steps. "Sarah. Hey, there, Sarah!" he shouted.

Sarah stopped short, and a gray rough-haired giant pulled on its rope and lunged at Alex.

"What is it? Down, you beast." Alex pressed his hands on the paws that rested on his shoulders and turned his head away so that the tongue lapped his ear.

"He's called Patsy," said Sarah, tugging at the rope. "And he's fairly small—for his breed, I mean."

"It's a breed?" Alex moved adroitly out of range and extended a hand to be licked or eaten.

"He must be three-quarters Irish wolfhound. Aren't they the biggest of all?" Sarah succeeded in taking a reef in the rope, and Patsy backed up and sat on her feet. "Alex, you'll have to help me wash him. I think he has fleas. We can do it over by the tennis court where there's a hose. And you'd better put on your bathing suit because you'll probably get soaked."

"I probably will," said Alex grimly.

Alex straightened his back and held the hose against his legs, letting the stream of water mix with the grime and soap and dog hairs and run off into the grass. "I think I've transferred every flea directly to my own body," he said to Sarah, who was kneeling in the sun, vigorously applying Alex's towel to the dog's rough coat. "After all," Sarah had explained reasonably, "I've used up mine."

Alex looked down at the big dog's head with its coarse fur now fluffed on the long skull. He was rewarded with a rumbling noise from some interior recess; then the head lifted, the curved and hairy tail thumped, and a long tongue caressed Alex's wet feet.

"He's accepted you," said Sarah, applying the towel to Patsy's haunches. "He's still just a puppy, you know."

"Puppy, hell. But I'm flattered. Are you going to call the animal shelter?" asked Alex without much hope.

"Why would I do that?" Sarah looked up in surprise.

"For one thing, the owner might want his dog back."

"Alex, I told you. He's been at Laguna for over two weeks. He was starved when he showed up, but the people at the refuge were very good to him. There now," Sarah tenderly lifted and wiped a paw. "Now he's gorgeous. He can finish drying on the way to town."

"Are we going to town?"

"Of course. We have to buy dog food and a proper collar and leash, and then stop at a veterinarian's for his inoculations. It's almost five so we've got to hurry."

"He may have had his shots," said Alex.

"We don't know that," retorted Sarah, "and you as a doctor should be the first to see that he's properly immunized. Come on. Get your shirt and sneakers. We'll meet you out by the car."

Alex did not fail to notice that Sarah and her friendly beast had become "we." And, he added to himself, he and she will be tossed right out of the motel as soon as the manager finds out that she has a roommate.

Fifteen minutes later, the Volvo, its back seat apparently packed with a young mastodon, pulled away from the Boyden Pet Shop.

"Are you going to go on calling him Patsy?" asked Alex as he turned the car around and headed west out of Boyden.

"I know that 'Patsy' has some unfavorable connotations, but he's used to it, and besides, I found him the day after St. Patrick's Day."

"Couldn't we have found a vet closer to town?"

"The pet-store people said this one was the best with dogs. Nothing but the best for Patsy." Sarah reached behind her seat and scratched the dog gently behind the ears. "You know I've felt so awful. Poor Philip. I've found myself wanting to talk to someone . . . like my brother Tony. I miss Tony. If you only have one brother, and you've always worked things through together

. . . but now he has his own life and mine is pretty well messed up, and . . ." Sarah stumbled on incoherently, "So when we were washing Patsy, I felt that you almost took his place. A sort of honorary younger brother, if you don't mind."

Alex, who was five years Sarah's senior, rose to the occasion. "Thank you, Sarah. That's a compliment. I'll be glad to give you an ear or a brotherly shoulder anytime you want. Or"—he grimaced—"a strong hand with the leash."

"Slow down here. There's the sign for the vet. Well, I may need your shoulder sometime, but I'll try and get through this whole thing without making a fool of myself and falling apart."

Alex followed Sarah into the clinic reflecting that if it was so important these days to know exactly who one was, then he was fortunate. He saw himself fitted into Sarah's social hierarchy somewhere between her younger brother and a hybrid Irish wolfhound.

Driving back to the motel, Patsy, exhausted from ordeal by bath, collar, and veterinarian, slumbered noisily in the rear of the car, wedged between a case of dog food and a bag of kibble.

"We'll take the outer route—longer but no traffic," said Alex as he turned onto a small side road.

"The police came to Laguna today," said Sarah, her voice expressionless. "What's all this about binocular straps?"

Alex slowed the car. "Some of the lab's microscopic tests suggest that Philip was strangled by a narrow strap—"

"Like those on cameras and binoculars," finished Sarah.

"Yes, or from a tape recorder, transistor radio—a belt, perhaps."

"Then it's quite possible," continued Sarah, "that instead of it being some criminal, Philip was . . ." Sarah faltered, then her voice hardened. "Philip was strangled by some damn bird-watcher or photographer."

"Looking for the straps is just one route to follow. You can ask Tom about it tonight. He's asked us to stop at that Chinese place downtown. He's taking the Cactus Wren ladies there for dinner."

"Dinner and third degree, I suppose," said Sarah. "Why are you stopping here?"

"I think our friend might like to use a bush. He just licked the back of my neck."

"Oh, yes." Sarah's worried face smoothed. "I'll run ahead with him down the road." She jumped free of the car and, with Patsy in tow, disappeared around a bend in the road. Alex leaned over the back of the car and began rearranging the bag of kibble for Patsy's more perfect comfort. All at once he became aware of Sarah shouting at a distance. He turned to see her running toward him in full stride.

"Alex, Alex!" She stopped, gasping, the dog's leash wound around her legs. "I've been such an idiot."

"Take it easy." Alex reached for Patsy.

"Why didn't I think of it before? Alex, I was supposed to have binoculars—from Philip."

"I don't follow."

"Did the police find two pairs of binoculars with Philip's things?"

"Only the Nikons in their case. You mean he had another pair?"

"Yes. I think I told you on the way to Boyden. Philip knew mine were broken, so he was bringing a pair of his father's for me. With all that's happened, I forgot and so did you. His father's were old Bausch & Lomb ones. No case."

"Stop, Sarah. It fits. That's why Philip's own binocs were in their case. I told Tom that birders usually use binoculars and telescope together. He could have been using his father's—testing them out for you."

"Yes," said Sarah, her voice rising. "So they got him with his own binoculars, and all this strap-matching is a waste of time. It was simple, wasn't it? The straps were already around his neck."

"Hop in the car, and I'll stow Patsy. Don't jump to conclusions. The extra binoculars may have been stolen; his wallet was. The murderer may have missed the Nikons in the case. The grass is pretty tall there. And the telescope may have been left because it was too cumbersome to escape with."

"He probably choked Philip first with his father's binoculars and then stole them. I mean there they were. So handy," said Sarah, her face red, furious.

"We don't know, but we're sure as hell going to find out. Tom was going to be at Doña Clara late, so we'll go out and try and catch him. The police are damn well going to start dragging for a pair of Bausch & Lomb binoculars. With or without a strap."

# XXX

Arms folded across his chest, Tom Pérez stood in a supervisory posture in the smallest of the refuge equipment sheds. A naked light bulb hanging from the ceiling illuminated the Bobcat Marsh jetsam heaped on two picnic tables, and Tom regarded the unlovely collection with disgust. At the lieutenant's side, Sergeant Cotton labored, lifting dirt-caked and leaf-stuck objects from a wheelbarrow with a pair of forceps. The sergeant interspersed exclamations of interest and wonder with snatches of song.

"Don't know that I'd throw that sock away. Look, here's a ball-point—some rusted up, though. 'In a cavern, in a canyon, excavating for a mine.' This bottle's still got some rum in it. 'Dwelt a miner, forty-niner, and his daughter Clementine.' Here's another comb, must've found fifty. 'Ruby lips above the water, blowing bubbles soft and fine.' Regular lover's lane that marsh is. Here's another rubber."

"Christ," remarked Tom sourly, "if someone from outer space landed on Bobcat Marsh Trail, they'd think we spent all our time fornicating, defecating, and combing our hair."

" 'You are lost and gone forever, dreadful sorry, Clementine,' " warbled the sergeant, holding aloft a pair of mud-crusted underpants.

"Shut up, Cotton, and start tagging this crap."

"Have you found any Bausch & Lomb binoculars, Sergeant?" said a voice from the doorway.

Tom swung around, looked hard at Alex, and then at Sarah standing behind him. "I see Sarah still has her fuzzy friend. Cotton, march out and visit with Miss Deane and her new buddy.

Alex, you come in and tell me why I should be finding Bausch & Lomb binoculars."

Ten minutes later, Alex and Tom stepped out of the shed into the late-afternoon light. Sarah, perched on a pile of fencing, was gazing down the darkening service road.

"Where's Patsy?" asked Alex.

Sarah pointed. "Sergeant Cotton's taken him for a run down the road. Patsy liked him right off the bat."

Tom grinned. "They're made for each other. Come on, Sarah. Time you went back to the motel. I'm going to have to persuade Sam to keep the marsh and lake area closed a little longer. I hope you're not feeling bad because you didn't recollect those extra binoculars. Point is you did before Sam opened the marsh to the public. I'm one lousy detective for not checking out that camera-shop repair tag and the new nylon strap we found in Philip's car."

"But haven't you searched the whole marsh already?" asked Sarah.

"Yes, but now we'll have to get ourselves right down into Long Bone Lake. It'll be one hell of a job with all those weeds."

"Sam's going to have the environmentalists on his neck," said Alex.

"Don't I know it. Even so, I'll have to go ahead and set up for dragging, get a diver and some underwater lights. You don't have to hang around, Alex. Beat it back to town with Sarah, and I'll see you tonight at Chen Pao's. And here comes Peter Cottontail." Tom gestured at the road as Patsy and his escort pounded into sight.

"This dog sure is a winner," said Sergeant Cotton, his broad chest heaving. "I'd sure be glad to keep him at my place if that motel gives you any shit."

"Cotton," said Tom, "move off and get on with it."

"Sarah," asked Alex as they started toward the parking lot, "how in God's name are you going to get that beast . . ."

"His name is Patsy," said Sarah. "You should use it as often as possible in an encouraging voice. Positive reinforcement."

". . . get Patsy past the manager's nose?"

"I'll smuggle him in," said Sarah, pulling the dog into a struggling heel position. "If there's a fuss, I'll get out. Most of the Hamburg group liked him—even Iris what's-her-name."

"Here's the car. See if Patsy can get in without tearing up my road maps. And who is Iris what's-her-name?"

"Iris is the fat woman who sat next to me on the plane. I didn't really listen to her then, except I remember she thought chickadees were cute and had a brother who was a bird expert."

"And she turns up here?" Alex bounced the car over the Dike Road, eliciting guttural noises from the rear passenger.

"Yes. She turns out to be Major Foster's sister. Only on the plane she sounded like a real dodo about birds."

"To coin a phrase."

"Sorry. Anyway, she wasn't a dodo at Laguna, which struck me as odd. She made a couple of identifications that had the others stumped. She'd say something like 'That isn't a stilt sandpiper; look at the crown,' and then she'd simper and say, 'But I really don't know, I'm just guessing.' I didn't pay much attention to the birding today, but this contradiction began to hit me as I was sitting outside the shed waiting for you."

"The lady is a fake?"

"She may think that knowing too much isn't feminine. Some of that generation are so hung up that they hardly admit to knowing how to spell their own names—especially some Southern women."

Alex frowned and considered the implications of a stout housewife who knew more abut birds than she admitted. "How did Foster react to her?" he asked.

"Oh, he joked, implied she was a sort of lovable incompetent who made a good guess now and then. That's all."

"Did she recognize you?"

"Right away. She was briefed by Lois Bailey about what happened and got me aside and told me to go to Jesus."

Alex shook his head. "I can't see the major's sister as a sinister presence because she knows a stilt sandpiper when she sees it. You couldn't spend time with Foster and not know. But I'll mention it to Tom."

"Turn in here by the side door," said Sarah as they approached the lighted motel sign. "I don't actually want to flaunt Patsy at the front desk. And could you bring that bag of kibble and the dog-food cans to my room, Alex?"

Alex pulled into the side entrance and trod on the brake.

"Yes, memsahib, Missee Deane, chop-chop."

# XXXI

Tom Pérez looked at the disheveled table, the overturned wine-glasses, the crumpled napkins, the scattered chopsticks, and swore long and elaborately in Spanish, then topped it with a coda from his Anglo-Saxon repertoire. He reached across the table for the one partly filled wineglass still standing and took its contents in a swallow.

The dinner had seemed like a good idea and a change of pace. Tom considered himself a master of the interview disguised as a social event—the subject eased and drawn out deftly in a setting of comfort and good food. The technique was especially felicitous with persons at the periphery of an investigation who might have fragments of information that could light up the dark corners of a case.

Hence the Cactus Wren ladies. Elderly, unused to the harsh clasp of the law, in an appropriately domestic situation they could certainly be cosseted and nudged toward revealing whatever had not come out in the preliminary interviews. Tom didn't think they had much to tell, but they had known Philip Lentz, and at his behest had lost their jobs. That must have generated a nice pool of resentment which could be fished. And also the ladies could be counted on to supplement the information given by Sarah Deane and the Morton students.

So with the air of one planning a special treat, Tom had invited the two teachers to Chen Pao's. To keep it honest, he had mentioned that, as a matter of routine, he had to touch base with them again as persons who had known Mr. Lentz and had been in the Doña Clara area. But the dinner was really to be an outing, a chance to get away from motel meals. Mrs. Brent had accepted for both.

Tom had rushed home from the refuge, taken a two-minute shower, put on his best suit and his least frightening necktie, and, driving well over the speed limit, managed to pick up the ladies

at seven-thirty. Both women had made an effort, wearing costumes clearly labeled "suitable for dinner when traveling"—Mrs.
Brent neat in dark red with a black scroll trim and Miss Fellows
playing it safe in navy with white neck bands, which gave her
rather the look of being in holy orders.

Dinner had begun well. They had been settled in a softly lit
inglenook at the rear of the dining room where the ambience had
enough of the Orient to offer a contrast to Vacation Villa. Cock-
tails were ordered, and Tom led the conversation around to Eastern cooking, woks, egg rolls, and the meaning of "sub gum" as
a prefix.

After the excitement of ordering, and choosing chopsticks
instead of forks and knives, Tom had given his guests a quick
sketch of his own background: his father a second-generation
Texan, his mother, half-Mexican, half-Irish, who had celebrated
the mix by giving him Michael O'Brien as middle names.
Through the wonton-soup session, Tom had touched on his
friendship with Alex McKenzie, cemented one summer when
Alex had come to Boyden on a research project; and then he told
them of his night-school years at Boyden Community College
while working a beat as a patrolman.

Tom had next chivied the talk around to the ladies. Keeping
them on a loose line, he brought them into the tranquil waters of
their college days together at Wellesley: Miss Fellows, captain of
the hockey team, the classics prize for Mrs. Brent, Phi Beta Kappa
for both. Then graduate school, and finally their happy haven at
Miss Morton's. The passing decades—nobody knows the changes
we've seen—and then the arrival of Philip Lentz, whose name
was inserted into the stream by Tom between the last bites of a
dish called Yu-lang-chi. And then—all hell had broken out.

Miss Fellows went red and then pale. She choked on something half chewed; her eyes bulged; she clutched her napkin.
Tom, standing up, had been about to start Heimlich's Maneuver,
when she swallowed, gasped, and broke down. All over the place.
Philip Lentz was a murderer or just as bad. Her life so perfect
. . . the academy . . . the girls . . . watched them grow up . . . her
own room . . . new wallpaper. Her study, her civilization course,
her hockey team, undefeated last year. The girls who wrote to
her. The girls who forgot. Everything changed. Philip Lentz,

cruel, inhuman, a spy. What did a man know about the school? Gestapo. Ruthless. She had seen him at Doña Clara—yes, she had. It was dreadful. He would ruin Texas. Horrible, horrible man.

Tears ran down Miss Fellows's cheeks; her nose dripped; her face mottled. How could she start again? She was glad he was dead. Dead, dead, DEAD. Her hands worked; saliva appeared at the corners of her mouth and along her lips—lips still with the traces of lipstick applied in preparation for an evening out.

Mrs. Brent, who had been ineffectually thumping her friend's back and trying to snatch at her hands, was finally able to lead her hiccupping, stumbling, and gulping to the ladies' room. And Tom, now studying the wreckage of the dinner table, waved away an anxious waiter, who hovered uncertainly with a plate of fortune cookies, and swore long and hard.

An hour later, after a hasty telephone call to Alex, and after Miss Fellows had been taken back to the motel and assisted by Alex into bed, Tom slumped in the largest chair afforded by his motel office and listened with a scowl to the dinner music coming from an outdoor buffet being held in the garden. Well, he had blown that one. Instead of information he had gotten hysterics. Served him right for trying to put frills on an investigation. Of course, from one angle, hysteria itself was a fact worth examining. Never say die. Tom reached for the telephone and asked for Mrs. Brent.

Addie Brent, when she presented herself, was plainly done up. Her eyes were bruised, the lines around her mouth were set deep, and she looked every bit the age of retirement. She had taken off the red dress and wore a mongrel garment, part dressing gown, part polo coat, the color of a muddy river. She plumped down wearily on a chair.

"Everything's quiet. Midge—Miss Fellows—is resting. I'm only sorry that the whole thing burst on your head, Lieutenant. She's been holding it in for months."

"A lot of hate bottled up inside?"

"What do you expect, Lieutenant? Mr. Lentz is the reason that we are no longer part of Morton's Academy. Poor Midge. She thought of the whole thing as a sort of putsch." Mrs. Brent sighed deeply.

A tap sounded on the office door, and Tom lifted his head. "Come in. . . . Oh, it's you, Alex. Sit down. Mrs. Brent knows you're helping me. We're just talking about Miss Fellows's attachment to the school."

"You see," said Mrs. Brent, "Miss Fellows is extremely intelligent, but from a conventional social sphere where one does not make waves. Miss Morton's offered a respectable home in which she could function effectively. She's really a gentle soul. Upset only by real provocation. Mr. Lentz just came along and tossed her on the ash heap along with the rest of us. I doubt if he understood the enormity of what he was doing; the younger teachers were all on his side. You see, Lieutenant, we are so old hat."

"Old what, Mrs. Brent?"

"There, you see. 'Old hat,' Mr. Pérez, is an old-hat expression for a couple of has-beens. I've had a year to live with this, and, do you know, it was time we left."

"Are you serious, Mrs. Brent?" asked Alex.

"Indeed I am. I can't adapt to a generation that uses four-letter words with every breath. I'm sure they're good girls, but, as they would say, 'It's not our scene.' So I had the bird-tour idea —a new life for us both. We put our savings into the wagon and the advertising, and because our pension is very small, it means a great deal to have Cactus Wren Tours succeed. But you see, Midge has never gotten over the academy, which makes it hard for her to concentrate on business. I would say that she is—well, envenomed. And, of course, she's never been too comfortable with men. No brothers, no male cousins, no beaux, no admirers, so Miss Fellows—ironic name, is it not?—perhaps centered all her suspicions and fears about men in Mr. Lentz."

"Would you . . . was she considered . . ."

"Don't beat about the bush, Mr. Pérez. Miss Fellows has never been to my knowledge a homosexual. Nor do she and I have that sort of relationship. It may be hard for the twentieth century to believe, but for us, even though we live and work together, it is not so. Call her, if you wish a label, a neuter. Both of us now. Just a pair of neuters. So much more comfortable, I feel, at our age. But what sex has to do with this case is beyond me." Mrs. Brent, agitated, florid of face, emphasized her words with little bobs of the head.

Tom waited for the brief storm to subside and thought, She's high-strung, too. In his notebook he wrote: "Fellows—bad temper under pressure—upset by men—revenge motive?" He smiled encouragingly at Mrs. Brent. "Now, I see you've given us a statement saying that you might have seen Mr. Lentz late Friday afternoon. Miss Fellows seemed to think when she was all worked up this evening that she did see him. How about you? Are you any more sure?"

Mrs. Brent hesitated and then nodded. "Yes, thinking it over, I do believe we might have caught sight of him. Almost a hundred yards ahead of us on the Lupine Lake boardwalk—his fair hair, a white shirt, carrying a telescope on a tripod. He was walking faster than we were, and we lost sight of him."

"You didn't try to catch up and speak to him?" asked Tom.

"Oh, no. I knew how Midge felt. She dreaded meeting him."

"Forgive me, Mrs. Brent, if some of these questions are like those you've already answered. But you two ladies gave a joint statement on Saturday, which shouldn't have been allowed. So about the time you might have seen Philip Lentz?"

"It may have been around five-fifteen, because we were late coming to Doña Clara, and I looked at my watch as we drove into the parking lot, and it was just before five then."

"And when did you leave Doña Clara?"

"As it was getting dark. Perhaps six-thirty or so. We wished to locate an elf owl reported by the Dike Road."

"And you never saw Philip Lentz again after that first possible sighting?"

"No, I did not, and I'm sure Midge didn't either."

"You didn't stay together."

"Oh, no. As soon as we came to the end of the boardwalk, we separated. We were in a hurry to learn about as many trails as possible before we took any groups through. We had planned to register at the motel as guides."

"And now," said Tom, treading softly, "what trails did you cover until you rejoined Miss Fellows?"

"Oh dear, let me see. I wrote it all down in my field notebook."

"Here," said Tom, walking to the wall and detaching the map of Doña Clara, "trace your route as you remember it." He spread the map out before her and watched Mrs. Brent, after some pursing of lips, indicate her path across the boardwalk with Miss Fellows, glimpsing the possible Philip Lentz midway, then her separation from her friend and subsequent exploration south to Heron Pond, her return to the Lupine Lake Trail, where she was swept into the Hamburg Bird Club as it converged on the parking lot. She recalled an elderly gentlemen, Mr. Plummer, she believed, who had mistaken her for one of his own group.

"He began to lecture me on the field marks of the olive sparrow, and I had to disagree on several points. . . ."

"And when did you meet up with Miss Fellows again?"

"We had arranged to meet at the parking area at six-fifteen, and I arrived before she did. It must have been close to six-thirty."

Tom now led Mrs. Brent to the inevitable questions, and Alex wondered whether she would shrink from the direction in which Tom was leading her.

"Do you know which trails Miss Fellows took when she left you?"

"I suggested to Midge that she go back over the boardwalk to Dodder Circle. To avoid Mr. Lentz."

"Did you see her turn around and go that way?"

"No," said Mrs. Brent uncertainly. "I was in a hurry to be off."

"Did Miss Fellows seem upset, excited, when she rejoined you? Act in any way that attracted your attention?"

"Why no, I don't think so. She was very quiet, but that is not unusual. After all, we had both had a long tiring day and . . ." Mrs. Brent faltered, and her voice trailed off. She stared at Tom, and then shook her head in a repeated negative. "No, no. You cannot think that." She leaned toward Tom, her face fierce.

Tom took the map and pinned it back on the wall. Coming back to his chair, he touched Mrs. Brent's arm gently. "I must check everyone, you know. Routine police dirty work. Now what can you tell me about Sarah Deane?"

Mrs. Brent's clasped hands unfolded. "You can't divert me so easily. Midge might have a temper, but she would never do anything so terrible. Now I will answer your question about Sarah Deane. She is an imaginative girl, and we were sorry to lose her at the academy."

"I'm interested in her personal relationships. With Philip

Lentz or anyone else if you think it has a bearing on this case."

"I suppose you must probe in this distasteful way. Sarah Deane, I gather, had an unhappy period at the end of her undergraduate years. A fiancé killed. Nothing to do with Mr. Lentz, and I never inquired about it. Sarah has had an unhappy time. I suggest you leave her alone."

Tom shook his head. "I can't leave anyone alone, Mrs. Brent. Now, did you know that Sarah Deane came down to Boyden to meet Philip Lentz?"

"I had known that they were friends. However, I was not aware until I learned yesterday from one of the students of their planned trip that their friendship was such a close one."

"Did you see Miss Deane at any time at Doña Clara on Friday?"

"No, Lieutenant, I did not. Nor do I think Sarah is capable of violence. A student of mine, and a teacher, too? A girl I have known since she was fifteen?"

Tom, feeling about fifteen himself, made another note: "Brent—stubborn? blind? loyalty." "All right, Mrs. Brent," he said. "What about Eleanor Lucas and her relationship with Mr. Lentz? It's been suggested that she knew him pretty well before he came to your school."

"And I can imagine who has been doing the suggesting. Let me give you a caveat on listening to students who have had more psychology courses than are good for them. Miss Lucas came to us from the Wayboro School in Boston, and since Mr. Lentz had taught at the same school, it is obvious that they knew each other." Here Mrs. Brent stopped and studied the edge of the table.

Tom Pérez was weary of the slow extraction of information, some of which he already had intimations of, but he was patient.

"Please tell me more, Mrs. Brent."

"Miss Lucas is a modern young woman." Mrs. Brent made it sound like an infectious disease. "She is respected, efficient, and energetic. Her students do very well on the science achievement tests."

Tom sighed. "I'm not planning to hire a biology teacher, Mrs. Brent. And," he continued in a pleasant voice, "I think you've forgotten the question. What about Lucas and Philip? You don't want me to go back to those students and hear all about that anal and oral stuff again. My ears are still vibrating from my interview with them, and Dr. McKenzie here is completely corrupted. How about it, Mrs. Brent?"

Mrs. Brent folded her hands in her lap and said in a resigned voice, "Miss Lucas and Mr. Lentz lived together for some time. An apartment near the school. It was generally known and apparently not a problem for Wayboro. They have a young headmaster. In fact, nothing would have come of it if they had not been found together on school property by some children from the middle school. Mr. Lentz and Miss Lucas had been using an athletic field house for activities best confined to the bedroom."

"Ah," said Tom, "a moral risk for growing children."

" 'A blush into the cheek of the young person'," said Alex softly.

Mrs. Brent turned to Alex. "I suppose I should congratulate you on having read Dickens. No one does anymore."

"Right now," said Tom, "we're reading Eleanor Lucas and Philip Lentz. We left them making out in the field house. What happened?"

"I heard privately that Miss Lucas had been asked to leave. Mr. Lentz, ironically, was too valuable to lose, it seemed. Miss Lucas applied to Miss Morton's, and I agreed to give her a chance."

"Weren't you uneasy about letting Lentz into the same school with Miss Lucas only three years later?"

"Mr. Lentz was presented to us by the trustees, who obviously had heard nothing of the Wayboro affair."

"Okay," said Tom. "So Lentz moves in like a fox in a hen coop, begging your pardon, Mrs. Brent, and eats you up."

"Mr. Lentz did have the courtesy to break the news in advance, so that we could retire while still in, shall I say, 'a state of grace.' But Miss Fellows refused and had to be what they called 'terminated.' "

"Did Miss Lucas cheer Mr. Lentz on?"

"Very possibly, but I do not know whether the two returned to their old relationship. If they did, I did not hear of it. From what I observed," added Mrs. Brent tartly, "Mr. Lentz lost interest in Miss Lucas during the winter term and began to notice Sarah."

"So," said Alex, "we have Lucas, the woman scorned."

"But Sarah went back to Boston," said Tom. "The coast was clear."

"Except then," put in Alex, "she must have heard that Philip had invited Sarah to come to Boyden, making a threesome."

"It must have been difficult for Miss Lucas to face working with Mr. Lentz with Sarah looking on," said Mrs. Brent.

"Difficult isn't the word," said Tom. He saw that Mrs. Brent's weariness was minute by minute becoming more obvious. "Please go to bed now, Mrs. Brent. If none of this is useful, I will see that it's buried twenty feet under."

Mrs. Brent got to her feet with the difficulty of someone whose joints are stiff from long sitting. Alex stood up and, hand under her arm, helped her to the door.

"We can't have the Cactus Wren Tours under the weather, Mrs. Brent. You have the Morton girls for birding tomorrow, I hear. You'll need all your strength."

Mrs. Brent drew in a deep breath and seemed to retire within herself for new resources—which she found. She detached her arm, squared her shoulders, and stepped firmly to the door and turned. "Lieutenant Pérez and Dr. McKenzie, you will both probably look back on these past days as a period in which you have distressed a great many innocent people. I suggest," she added crisply, "that you, Dr. McKenzie, practice your profession, and you, Lieutenant, investigate the undoubted mess at your border. You will probably discover the murderer among those vagrants and hippies I see everywhere. Good night."

The door closed, and Mrs. Brent could be heard moving with a measured tread down the corridor.

Tom leaned back in his chair. "That female was wasted at a girls' school. Sit down, Alex, and let's do a recap. My chief agrees with Mrs. Brent. Wants me to drop a net over a few aliens, so you see I'll have to come up with some valid reasons for keeping this motel scene alive."

"I'm at your service. Your objective, sharp-eyed physician, who, I think"—here Alex reached down and scratched an ankle —"has caught a bundle of fleas from a friend's dog."

# XXXII

As Tom Pérez and Alex McKenzie prepared to sift through the accumulata of the case, the guests of Vacation Villa, after a gala buffet dinner, were settling in for the night.

The Plummers bedded down early, as did the Axministers, but Mrs. van Hoek sat propped in bed and worked on a list of suspects that included the more unacceptable members of her tour group. Heading the names was that obnoxious Jeff Goldsmith, and then Major Foster, who had not even accorded her the deference he paid to that frump Enid Plummer. But there were social possibilities that might be developed from the investigation. Dr. McKenzie was certainly one of the more promising guests at the motel. Perhaps her blood pressure needed checking—all this heat.

Mrs. Goldsmith triumphed over Mrs. Bailey in a late game of Scrabble by the judicious use of the word "zarf" on a double-word square, and in the next room Nina slept, and Jeff in his alcove scribbled in his field notebook and repeatedly consulted his guides.

As Alex had done before her, Sarah pushed open her window and shut down the air conditioning. The night was cool and a northwest wind blew softly. Sarah had fed and watered Patsy and seen him comfortably settled in the center of the second bed. He looked handsome, she thought, circled into a large gray ball on the green-and-white flowered counterpane.

Now Sarah lay in the dark and tried to fill her head with matter as close to mental Jell-o as she could conjure. An effort to dislodge the tormenting Danny Deever had resulted in poetry equally ill-freighted. Shakespeare had emerged in his darkest coat, talking of graves, of worms, and epitaphs; then other mournful numbers dragged their feet through her memory. An effort to switch to folk songs produced ballads of death by poison, dagger, battle, and water. ". . . and he drifted with the tide and sank into the Lowland, Lowland, Lowland, sank into the Lowland sea," sang Sarah's head. She needed something soothing, something gentle, something calm and certain, and then her brain began a slow and careful recitation, with emphasis on correct pronunciation, of the Prologue to *The Canterbury Tales*, which proved a successful soporific. By the time Sarah reached "wel nyne and twenty in a compaignye of sondry folk," she was asleep.

# XXXIII

Tom unfolded a chart made up of squares and lists. "Here's the mess as I see it. Doña Clara was crawling with people so busy looking at nature that they missed seeing Philip Lentz—all but the Cactus Wren ladies. I'm taking that five-fifteen sighting of him on Friday as a working time when he was still alive and seven as a possible time when he may have been dead—too dark to look through a scope. Ten o'clock that evening—rain time—is the definite *terminus ad quem*."

"Do you have a system for sorting these people out?" asked Alex.

"The Pérez system. I tried our cranky computer, but it kept coming up with you and Sarah. Okay, not funny. Anyway, I've got a hopper for capability, opportunity, and motive. Also for those who have some connection with Lentz and those who don't. Then we've the ones who can't be vouched for during the critical time period. Next we've got the illegal aliens we rounded up on Saturday afternoon. They're frightened and can't give a clear account of where they were on Friday afternoon. Last, we have those folks who hang their equipment on black half-inch straps. A real zoo."

"Go on, professor. I'm listening."

"Okay. Those with no connection with Lentz: the Ready Tour group, of course. They confirm each other except for Jeff and Major Foster. Jeff, we know, buzzed off to do his own thing, whatever that was, ran back, and was late for the parking-lot meeting set for six o'clock. So far, no one has been known to have seen Jeff. His straps, two of them, qualify, and he's not convincing about why he took off again on Saturday. Too many questions about Jeff. Give him a star."

"And then you have the jolly tour leader, Big Foster."

"Right. He stayed with his tour until just after four Friday when the group split, some for ice cream, some for birds. Foster told 'em he was going to scout around. Sam says this is what Big does, and he's always in and out of the refuge at all times of day. Foster says that when he left the tour he drove around the Auto Tour Road, stopped here and there, saw nothing of much interest until he spotted a couple of oddballs, those hook-billed kites outside of the Old Settlers Village just before six." Tom frowned at his chart. "He says about five-fifty. We know he was late—a few minutes, says Mrs. Goldsmith—for the parking lot, but he arrived before Jeff, to whom he gave suitable hell for going off. Put Jeff at getting there at about six-fifteen to six-twenty, and the major at six-fifteen or earlier."

"Did anyone see the major prowling around?"

"A friend from Boyden saw him around five driving his van past the Heron Bill Trail. So far, no one else claims him, but Sam reported seeing these kite birds at the lower end of Bobcat Marsh just before five. Sam says the birds flew off into some trees."

"So that shows Foster wasn't hallucinating kites."

"True, and it's not very far from the south part of the marsh to Settlers Village if you have wings, so that's a partial support for Big's statement. His binocular straps don't match up, but he gets a star for opportunity."

"And he's strong enough to strangle an army."

"Yes, but strangulation may depend more on technique than on power. Even a wiry little kid like Jeff could do it."

"And the others with no connection with Philip?"

"We've got some checked out, thanks to the registration sheet. I won't tell you about Mrs. Garcia's fourth grade, who saw nothing to frighten them, or the Boyden Boy Scouts, Troup 7, or other such."

"A policeman's lot . . ."

"You said it. Now here we have Mrs. High Society, who waggles her fanny at me and is surprised that I speak English. She guesses and wonders. Was it Jeff? Was it the major? I'd say she doesn't like kids and has it in for Foster because he hasn't been sucked into her charm pool."

"And the butterfly people?"

"The Axminsters. They're a pain because they don't seem to know where they were. Wife contradicts husband and husband says wife is forgetful, and their Saturday statements don't agree with their Sunday ones. Both a bit flaky, if you ask me, but they were *somewhere* in that refuge during the murder period. Mrs. Goldsmith saw two people off the trail with butterfly nets on Friday but can't remember where."

"And the waifs and strays who didn't sign the register?"

"We're searching and interrogating. All we can do. Now let's look at the Philip Lentz fan club. Mrs. Addie Brent to start. She signed in for self and Fellows around five, may have seen Lentz at five-fifteen, then split with Fellows. We've only her word that she stuck to the Heron Pond and Lupine trails. No one claims to have seen her, but you could lose a circus inside that jungle. We do have confirmation that she got tangled up with the Hamburg people around six. *Vide:* Mr. Plummer. So what's the score for Brent? Opportunity, yes. Motive, yes, yes. Dethroned after thirty-plus years. Impression: loyal, gutsy, out-of-date lady putting up a good front."

"I think she's on the up-and-up," said Alex.

"How about a little Old Testament revenge? Let's try it out. Saw P. Lentz sitting at his scope. Put on her gloves. Don't ladies like that always have gloves? Strangled P. Lentz with her, or his, binocular strap. Lugged him into the bushes. Now it's sounding unreal. Capability? Does she have the physical strength?"

Alex considered. "I can see her dragging the body, but I do not see her choking an alert, five-foot-ten-inch male, even if she took him by surprise. Unless she's a secret practitioner of thuggee."

"Which?"

"The Thugs were a secret Hindu sect that got its kicks from strangulation. Expert technique. Sacrifices to Kali. Not nice."

"Mrs. Brent may be a Thug, then. Nothing surprises me.

But I've written 'doubtful' next to capability. And now Margaret Fellows."

"Spinster of this parish."

"With all the rights pertaining thereto. Sort of sad," said Tom. "Today she'd be a liberated woman."

"But she's not; she's 'old hat,' remember? Brought up with the three R's. Rectitude, respectability, right thinking."

"And built like Tarzan. Happy at history, girls' hockey, and then—zap—enter Philip Lentz, and so I'm awarding Miss Fellows the distinguished motive medal. Plus stars for physical capability and opportunity. No one claims to have seen her between say five-twenty and six-thirty."

"Oh, come off it, Tom. I don't think either of those ladies strangled anyone. At dinner tonight—why, you just touched a nerve, and suddenly Fellows let it all out. She's certainly a bona fide neurotic, but—"

"And murder isn't committed by neurotics? You come off it, Alex. Stop trying to protect the WASP community."

"Then you stop trying to ignore those Hispanics that are all over the riverbanks. I know you have a tender spot and . . ."

Both men stared at each other.

"Christ, Tom, I'm sorry."

Tom ran his hands in a distracted way through his hair. "Hell, we're both tired. I didn't mean to bait you." He grinned. "I'm sure they're some law-abiding WASPs around somewhere. Relax, Alex. I'm sorry, too. You're right. I do have a tender spot for those poor bastards who think they'll find Beulah Land when they cross the Rio Grande. Go and look at one of the colonias in Cameron and Hidalgo counties. No water, shack of a casita with a privy out back, irrigation ditches for water, often contaminated by fecal waste. A Public Health nightmare. But because the people are illegal, nothing's done."

"I know it's a hell of a situation."

"Yeah, and as soon as there's a crime, everyone yells 'Mexicans,' and, oh man, when a nice clean-cut citizen like Philip Lentz gets his, the brass sits up and yells, 'Illegal aliens did it.'"

"But what *are* you going to do about the aliens you picked up?"

"The chief wants me to nail one and stop bothering the

tourist trade. You see, as long as I could show that Lentz was throttled by someone carrying a camera or binoculars or something like that, he let me bother the refuge crowd. But if Philip's binoc straps are guilty—hell, anyone could have done it."

"So back to the WASPs," said Alex. "I agree that Miss Fellows is a candidate. She was around and is built for the decathlon. But I don't see her premeditating murder—coming to Texas for the purpose."

"But the trip may have triggered the idea. She knew Lentz was going to be here."

"I'm no psychiatrist, but I think it's more likely that she kept her feelings repressed until she saw him ahead on the trail. Then she may, or may not, have blown her fuse or perhaps held it in and exploded at your dinner party."

"What if it happened at Doña Clara? She followed Lentz, because there he was, enemy number one, right in front of her. So how does it go? Piece of cake in that overgrown place. She tails Philip from the boardwalk, watches him go into the marsh, get set up, and—"

"Remember you said he wasn't strangled sitting at his scope. No mess, no broken bushes, no damage to anything."

"Just listen. Enter Fellows. Lentz looks around, gets up, goes over, says howdy do, good to see you, et cetera. Remember he's a polite guy, everyone says so. Doesn't feel guilty. Did what he had to do."

"And does she say, "Please stand still while I slip this strap around your neck.'? Hell, no. He'd struggle, protect himself. But, as you said, no signs of a fight—on the ground or on the body."

"I'll try again," said Tom. "Lentz gets up, chats it up, and then she points out something, or he does. He lifts his binoculars to look, she grabs them, twists them, and goodbye Philip. Do you like that better? Here, take off your belt. See, I swing the binoculars quick out of the way, twisting hard, and there you are. Out like a light. Fast."

"I'll try that on you sometime with real binoculars and see if it works," said Alex, rubbing his neck. "But I don't see Miss Fellows making time for those conversational stratagems. I see her out of rational control, on a sort of emotional automatic pilot. If she did it, that is."

"She's a front runner in my book. Next we have Eleanor Lucas, former lover girl given the boot by her school because of Lentz, and then by Lentz himself because of Sarah. What a motive! And opportunity, too. Lucas split with Dory Williams, went hiking by herself, and met Dory as planned well after six . . . almost six-thirty. The witching hour."

"Is Dory Williams accounted for?"

"Yes. Two witnesses for Dory. To go on. Could Lucas strangle Lentz? I think so, especially if she got the drop on him. She looks tough, teaches tennis and fencing. But not the impulsive type. That female acts like someone who thinks and plans."

"Appearances can be you know what," said Alex. "Don't write her off as the mechanical maiden. Does that finish us?"

"For tonight it does. I'll see Lucas tomorrow and look in on the Axminsters. Of course, we've got the Doña Clara staff, but Sam is absolutely reliable—I've known him for years—and the rest are accounted for. As for Sarah Deane . . . a doubtful starter."

"She'll be delighted to hear it," said Alex dryly. "Come on, it's past eleven." He stood up and stretched out a hand. "Forgive any hasty remarks. You're a good friend, Tomás."

# TUESDAY, MARCH 19

# XXXIV

Sarah came out of her bathroom, one towel tied about her hips, another in a turban around her head. She dropped on the bed beside Patsy and loosened the towel from her hair, letting it fall across her bare shoulders. On the wall mirror she saw herself and the parakeets reflected as before: her face, the large eyes, the wet hair sticking up in dark spikes—like a golliwog, she thought. The rest of her seemed so slight, so bodily negative, that the two white towels emerged as the most noticeable parts of her anatomy. She looked around the room trying to find something that would bring substance to this reflected nonentity, but the collection of motel furniture gave nothing back. The chairs, lamps, and tables were formed into imitation fascicles of bamboo finished in a glossy white paint with touches of lime green to suggest joints. This bamboo motif was repeated in the curtains and other furnishings. The room looked as if it had been shipped intact from a store window.

"You're the only real thing in here, Patsy," said Sarah aloud, moving her fingers softly around the dog's ears. "A motel is no place for a growing dog," she added.

"A place for everything and everything in its place." Sarah could her her Grandmother Douglas's precise voice. "And every person, Grandma?" Sarah had asked. She was thirteen and had been watching her grandmother's ruthless weeding of the tulip bed.

"Of course," her grandmother had answered. "Everyone has a place, but at first we may not know what that place is. Or what God has planned for us, dear. God will help us find our place, and then we must accept it and trust in Him." And was it Grandma's place just to stay on in that big house with two-thirds of the rooms shut up and go out only to visit Grandpa in the nursing home after church? Maybe that was it. St. Paul's-by-the-Sea had kept Grandma glued together. The glue was given out once a week by the rector, who reminded her to accept and trust and know her place. But Sarah didn't seem to have any of that adhesive material to keep her stuck together. Sarah stared again at the figure in the glass. I'll soon be able to see right through me, she said to herself. But at that moment, Patsy, driven by the simple fact of hunger and the need to lift his leg against one of the motel bushes, barked—a loud bark that tailed off into a fine baritone howl.

"Quiet, Patsy," said Sarah severely. And knowing your place is also knowing what is not your place, she added to herself, and she flung off her towels and began dressing rapidly. Then, raking her hair fiercely into place, she shoved her bare feet into a pair of moccasins and snapped on Patsy's leash.

"Come on, dog," she said. "We're going to blow this place."

✝   ✝   ✝

Sergeant Cotton stood massively in the middle of the Vacation Villa lobby. At the desk, Cheryl Cabot, switched to days as less of a threat to Mr. Allen's peace, tucked the telephone receiver between a soft chin and a plump shoulder and flipped a keyboard switch. She eyed the sergeant, blinked slowly, and ran her tongue over her lower lip. The sergeant, however, was gazing at a blackboard set up by the front door. Under the legend "Interesting Birds Seen in the Rio Grande Valley" appeared "Doña Clara, two hook-billed kites, Friday, March 15." Following the complete list was written in uncertain cursive "All birds are stupid."

But hook-billed kites or other rarities left the sergeant unmoved. Birds, real birds, to Tiger Cotton, who was born on the seacoast, meant a cormorant on a channel buoy holding its wings out to dry, or a crow calling from the edge of a wood. He thought of herring gulls and terns screaming as they followed the draggers and fishing boats into the harbor, while, across the lobby, Cheryl winked and smiled. If anyone had told Sergeant Cotton that he was homesick, he would have answered that such a thing was for goddamn sissies, but he responded to his feelings in much the same way as Sarah had—by going out.

"I'll be back," he called to Cheryl, who raised her painted brows and adjusted the slipping sleeve on her Mexican blouse.

"Piss on you, Mr. Sergeant Cotton," she observed to the empty lobby, and, as if in answer, the switchboad buzzed loudly. "Vacation Villa. . . . Hello, Dr. McKenzie. . . . No one's here now. Lieutenant Pérez hasn't come in yet, and Sergeant Cotton's just gone outside. . . . Yes, Doctor. You'll be in the breakfast room. Y'all have a nice day." Cheryl pushed down a switch and made a face. "And piss on you, too, Doctor," she said and craned her neck toward the terrace door, but Tiger Cotton had disappeared. However, Cheryl, like a patient spider, could wait in her web at the front desk, hopeful, calculating. Something usually turned up.

Sergeant Cotton, meanwhile, tramped toward the outer garden area where he collided with a bounding Patsy.

"Hello, there, old fellow." Tiger knelt and accepted a moist greeting. "Down, big boy. Hello, Miss Deane. Patsy's lookin' good."

Sarah felt suddenly cheered. Her projected flight from the

motel had had no focus, but bumping into something as solid as Tiger Cotton brought a sense of sturdy reality to her escape.

"Oh, Sergeant Cotton, I'm glad to see you. Are you on duty here?"

"No, Miss Deane. I'm just to give this report to Dr. McKenzie." The sergeant thumped his windbreaker pocket. "And meet Lieutenant Pérez. Then I guess I have to go out to Doña Clara and help drag that marsh. I didn't want to stay inside the motel because I felt cooped up all of a sudden."

"I know just what you mean." Sarah smiled, one displaced person to another. "The motel was closing in on me, too, and it's not right for Patsy either."

"No, Miss Deane. That big dog needs some open-air place."

"But what shall I do, Sergeant? Have you any good ideas?"

The sergeant looked down at Patsy, and then over beyond the roof of the motel. Another wave of nostalgia swept over him. "Take Patsy out to Alta Hollow State Park. That's where I'd go. It's got some big trees, and a lake and a campground, too. You could put up a tent."

"You're a genius," said Sarah. "I'll get my things and tell the desk. I can buy a tent because I've got a raft of traveler's checks, and I can rent a car later if I need it."

Tiger Cotton was caught by her enthusiasm. "Good for you, Miss Deane. Give me Patsy while you pack up, and I'll go and see if Dr. McKenzie's down yet. Then I could run you out to the park. There's a real good sporting store on the way and you could get your camp stuff."

A short while later, Sarah and Patsy found themselves turning out of the motel driveway in a police car complete with a two-way radio and other unfamiliar hardware. Behind the wire grille, like a captive felon, rode Patsy surrounded by his dog food and Sarah's luggage.

"I didn't bother Dr. McKenzie. He's just havin' breakfast," explained the sergeant cheerfully. A sense of guilt was not among his faults, and his imagination failed to present him with an enraged Tom Pérez. The same imagination did, however, operate in the arena of the human appetite, and the sergeant opened a cardboard box packed with hot pecan buns and handed Sarah a plastic cup of hot coffee. "Cheryl got 'em for me," he said. "I'll bet you forgot to eat."

Sarah munched on a bun and slipped small warm pieces to Patsy through the wire, and then Tiger Cotton braked hard and wheeled into a parking lot. "Here's the camp store. Just take your time and get what you need."

Sarah opened the car door, and, marveling at her new sense of freedom, walked with an almost buoyant step toward the store.

# XXXV

Looking back long afterward, Tom Pérez judged Tuesday, the third day following the discovery of the body of Philip Lentz, as one of the most discouraging in his career as a policeman. The day began badly and slid steadily downhill thereafter.

At six-thirty in the morning, Tom's supervisor, Captain Earl "Pork" Nordstrom, called up and blew up. "It's that goddamn Lentz case," he bellowed into the telephone.

"Goddammit, Pérez, Arthur Ready said you were harassin' the people of his tour group. Arthur said it was an obvious case of violence by one of those vagrants or wetbacks who are frightenin' the shit out of tourists. So, Pérez, if those lab reports are negative on those straps, you leave the Ready Tour alone. You're drivin' Big Foster up the wall. Now move it. Get your ass in gear."

Tom, called from the shower and wrapped in a tufted bedspread, stood in a puddle by the telephone table and responded, when he could fit in a word, with a subdued "Yes, sir," and "No, sir."

"And leave that refuge be," growled Captain Nordstrom. "That Audubon group and another of those goddamn environmental outfits called, and they'll keep on my back unless you stop messin' around with their pet swamps, so that draggin' operation you've got rigged up better be closed down today, d'ya hear? And listen, don't you go soft on those Mexicans you're holdin' because your name is Pérez."

Tom, loudly profane, returned to his shower and had just rubbed up a good lather when, on cue, the phone rang, and there was Olive Tassel, of the Boyden Audubon, who wanted information—now—on the continuing damage done by the police to the nesting areas around Bobcat Marsh. Tom, the soap drying on his shoulders, calmed Miss Tassel, rinsed himself, dressed, and went down for breakfast. There, heavy in the humid air, his mother's perfume, lily of the valley, competed for attention with frying eggs and bacon. Tom drank his orange juice and was about to get on with his eggs when the telephone rang again.

Mrs. Pérez shook her head sadly as she watched her son sitting stiffly in his kitchen chair, the egg sticking to his fork, nodding, saying "Yes, sir," and "No, sir." She slid his eggs back into the frying pan.

Tom slumped in his chair and handed his mother the telephone. "Jesus Christ, I didn't need that."

His mother waggled a spatula in his face. "And in this kitchen, Tomás Pérez, we don't have a foul mouth. Now eat a good breakfast."

"That was a message from the D.A.'s office. You know the Lentz case, Mama? Well, Lentz's brother-in-law from Oregon called in last night . . . wants action and a complete report. Seems he's an attorney. Sorry, Mama, no time for breakfast. Got to get to the office and then to the motel for interviews." Tom grabbed his briefcase, opened the door, and was well across the lawn when he heard the telephone ring.

He returned to the kitchen, where the lily of the valley and the humidity had become oppressive. Tom took the phone from his mother.

"Hey, Tom," said the voice. "Houston lab, Eric Nichols. Thought I'd catch you early. Listen, we've worked like devils on those damn straps of yours. This is only a prelim, but we're pretty sure that none of the leather particles from the tissue samples match the leather in any of your straps. I suppose that sends the ball back to you?"

"Right," said Tom grimly. "Shoot the report to me when you got a final. And thanks, Eric." Tom settled the phone carefully on its cradle. He inhaled, puffed out his cheeks, and then picked up his briefcase again. He met his mother's eyes. "Jesus Christ. Jesus H. Christ," he said loudly and went out, slamming the kitchen door.

# XXXVI

Alex selected two waffles from the breakfast buffet table and balanced a cup of coffee and half a grapefruit on a plate with the other hand. He searched the room, but Sarah was missing. He hoped she was sleeping late, beginning to relax. He looked about again and then walked over to a single figure sitting at a small table overlooking the garden.

"May I join you, Mrs. Brent, or do you like breakfast in peace?"

"Do sit down, Dr. McKenzie." Addie Brent moved dishes and notebooks aside. "I have never been a breakfast recluse, because my temper is at its best in the morning. It is at night that I sometimes forget myself—when I am tired. Or tried," she added firmly.

Alex smiled, realizing that he had just received an apology for last night's burst of temper. "Are the girls keeping you on the run, Mrs. Brent?" He cut a wedge of waffle and dipped it in syrup.

"The waffles are quite crisp," said Mrs. Brent with approval. "Yes, the girls do keep us moving. Some of them have very little interest in biology and become restless."

"You seem to have a real student, though, in Dory Williams."

"Yes, Dory is an exceptional girl. She came to the academy on a full scholarship from a university association. We have a fairly strong science department, and I do not think she has been disappointed in the instruction. A gifted child."

"She seems to have discovered another gifted child," said

Alex. "I heard Dory and Jeff Goldsmith arguing about nomenclature."

"Two such young people often find each other—never mind the age difference. Jeff is young, but his knowledge of birds is quite remarkable. Yesterday afternoon at the refuge I heard him question Major Foster's identification of the call of a varied bunting."

"How did the major take that?"

"He spluttered for a moment, but then said he was getting a little deaf and complimented Jeff on his sharp ears. But Major Foster doesn't make many mistakes. I've overhead him discuss the sightings with his group. And now, Dr. McKenzie, I must go and see how Midge is doing. She was quite done up after last night. Letting down the floodgates always takes its toll."

"You're not taking the girls for their morning bird tour?"

"Oh, yes, but since I wanted Midge to rest this morning, I've delayed our trip until eleven thirty. Miss Lucas will do two hours of botany here in the garden, and then Miss Fellows and I will take the girls to Doña Clara. We have permission to go right down to the river for a picnic and birding. We are rather hoping to see the green kingfisher. Miss Lucas will have the afternoon off, which, I believe, she needs because she seems so very much on edge." Mrs. Brent rose, inclined her head, gathered her belongings, and departed.

Alex sauntered out to the terrace, thinking that Sarah might now be up and exercising Patsy, but he found only Miss Lucas in a corner of the garden setting up a blackboard. Walking back to the building, he reflected that he had begun to look forward to checking up on Sarah at the beginning of the day, seeing that she had something to keep her mind, her time, occupied. Of course, Patsy seemed to be serving that purpose. Sarah could show affection, ease her desolation, by giving herself to a lost dog. But certainly, Alex told himself, there could be no harm in his looking in on Sarah even if she no longer needed his active support. He opened the door into the lobby and found Tom Pérez barking at Cheryl Cabot.

"So where did he go, Cheryl? A great big policeman just doesn't self-destruct."

Alex stepped forward. "What's up, Tomás?"

"I've lost Cotton. He's supposed to meet me here and get a briefing on the dragging operation. Did he give you the report?"

"What report?"

"Oh Christ, Alex, didn't Tiger give you the lab report? I sent him over with a copy as soon as I got to the office. All negative. Every damn strap. Now we'll have to come up with those Bausch & Lomb binocs or forget the whole idea. I can't keep that part of the refuge closed much longer. The eco freaks are after me."

"Don't you have Eleanor Lucas for an interview this morning?"

"Yeah, all this and Lucas, too. Okay, Cheryl my beauty, if Sergeant Cotton shows up, send him to find me. I'll be in the motel office for a while and then out at Doña Clara."

"Miss Lucas seems otherwise engaged," said Alex. "She's in the garden setting up a blackboard for a botany party. Miss Fellows is resting after last night's blowup, so Lucas is taking the girls."

"The hell she is. Let's go out and upset that blackboard."

The Morton students were scattered in a semicircle under a tree, botany texts open before them. Miss Lucas noted the male arrivals with a curt nod and returned to a chalk diagram. She spoke without looking at them. "You don't have to sneak around, Lieutenant. My appointment with you has just been postponed for two hours. Then you may have fifteen minutes. If," continued Miss Lucas in a voice of flint, "you don't like the plan, you may take me into custody, in which case I will sue you for false arrest. Susan Gorham, will you please list on the blackboard the types of vegetation found on a flood plain? You're going to be on one this afternoon at Doña Clara. Sit down, Lieutenant, and you, Doctor. You might learn something about the plants the police have been trampling down. If you won't join us, please go away. You're disturbing the class standing there. Pogo, while Susan is at the blackboard, you may describe the surface characteristics of the river areas."

Tom, smoldering, took Alex by the arm and, swearing low and fluently, led him back to the motel.

"I'm glad my Spanish is rusty," remarked Alex.

"Man," said Tom. "What a morning. And I haven't even

returned two calls from the Border Patrol. They've probably got half a dozen unidentified bodies for me to look at. But hell, the day's been so bad it's bound to improve."

In which hope the lieutenant could not have been more wrong.


The session with Miss Lucas added to the winter of Tom's discontent. Seated rigidly on the edge of a chair in Tom's motel office, she proved to be as forthcoming as the proverbial stone. How well had she known Philip Lentz? As well as most people. Period. For how long? She hadn't bothered to keep track. Period. Had Philip Lentz any acquaintance who might have wished him harm? She couldn't say. Was he disliked by anyone? Most people were disliked by someone, weren't they? Had she seen Philip Lentz on Friday afternoon at Doña Clara? No. Was she sure? She would not say no if she were not sure. Had she anything to add to the short statement taken by the police on Sunday? Certainly not; her statement was complete and accurate. Could she go now?"

Granite face, said Tom to himself. "Isn't it true," he persisted in a quiet voice, "that you lost your job at a Boston school because of improper behavior with Philip Lentz on the school grounds? Isn't it also true that you lived with Lentz some time before that, and also when Lentz came to the academy he dropped you in favor of Sarah Deane?"

"If you get your jollies from prurient gossip, Lieutenant, that's your business. If you don't like what I've told you, you know what you can do with it. And if you don't stop bothering the girls—who prefer murder to botany—I shall start raising hell. I think I'll start with the Boyden Chamber of Commerce." Miss Lucas rose and wheeled on Alex. "You, Dr. McKenzie, instead of sticking your lng nose in other people's lives, should look for someone really sick. Is Sarah Deane your only patient? Try Miss Fellows. She looks as if she could use your services." Miss Lucas stamped out of the room.

"Hell hath no wrath like a woman dumped for another woman," observed Alex.

"I'll bet her blood is all vinegar," said Tom. "She certainly curdles mine." He pulled a pad from a back pocket and made a note, breaking his pencil point in the act. "Come on, long nose, let's go out to the refuge. With my luck, the mayor ought to be out there."

"Busy, busy, busy," said Alex. "And swamp dragnet in the bargain, too. But, Tom, I'm damn glad those lab reports were negative."

"I don't see why," said Tom. He climbed into the car and barely waited until Alex was seated before he started the car, overaccelerating in first gear. "All it means is that a nature-lover didn't strangle Lentz with his own strap. But he could have used another and gotten rid of it, or Philip's own binoc strap." Tom did a wheelie into Route 77. "And now that g.d. Cotton is off somewhere. Will I ever blister his balls."

Tom turned south, and the lines of Texas palmettos on the left and right gave way to plowed fields on one side and dark rows of citrus trees on the other; then a rush of the sweet scent of the blossoming trees came in through the open car windows.

Alex saw Tom's hands tight on the steering wheel, his knuckles light under his tan. He looked at the strong rounded chin, the dark mustache, the fashionable razor-cut hair. Intelligent, handsome, ambitious, and just now as mad as a scorpion.

"This too shall pass," said Alex.

"Like a kidney stone, you mean, Doctor?" But Tom eased his grip on the wheel, and the car shot past Llano Grande Lake and pointed at Progreso. "Where's Sarah today?" he asked.

"Lord, I forgot to find out. The Ready Tour was going to the Brownsville dump, but I don't know about Sarah."

"The dump! Christ, what for? That's a real crap heap, and it's going over ninety today."

"Tom, you just don't know birders. The Mexican crow, which says 'khurrr and craw,' may be there eating garbage. So might the white-necked raven. Illegal aliens. They fly over the border."

"Well, I can't see Sarah going to broil at the dump just to see a crow that says 'khurrr.'"

"As a matter of fact, neither can I, but I'm not going to call the motel. She needs a day free of my playing guard dog—besides, she has one of her own now. I'll look in tonight."

Tom nodded, slowed to make the turn from the Military

Highway into Doña Clara, spun down the gravel road and into the parking lot.

"Son of a bitch!" he said.

In a group at the edge of the parking area confronting the hefty presence of Sam Hernández was Olive Tassel and a platoon of cohorts from the Boyden Audubon Chapter, and, with camera at the ready, a photographer from the Boyden *Express*.

# XXXVII

Lois Bailey and Constance Goldsmith were taking the day off. Big Foster had smiled when they announced their defection. "You ladies just get yourselves a pretty tan or the folks back home won't know you've been in Texas." Which was true, since birders habitually went about as ambulatory mummies, wrapped and sprayed.

Waldo Plummer had shaken his head and spoken of the uprecedented opportunity afforded by the Brownsville dump. "A chance to see a true Mexican species, *Corvus imparatus*. However, I shall be happy to keep an eye on young Jeffrey."

Young Jeffrey's aunts nodded and drifted away. Jeff's early distaste for tour groups appeared to be taking a more positive turn. He had begun to function as an unofficial assistant leader, pointing out easily missed field marks, setting up telescopes, and paying close attention to Major Foster's explications. So far the major was bearing up fairly well under Jeff's attentions, even listening to the boy's earnest entreaties that the whole tour skip next week's planned trip to the Edwards Plateau and go to the more exciting Big Bend National Park instead.

"I'm glad the pressure's on the major instead of us," said Lois as she unfolded a canvas chair in the shade of a chinaberry tree by the side of the swimming pool.

Connie Goldsmith agreed. She settled in her own chair and tipped a straw hat over her eyes. "How good it is to do nothing but sit and read and watch Nina doing her dives."

"Without having to jump off the board yourself," said Lois.

Nina stood at the end of the diving board, hands over her head, a small spherical figure in a red bathing suit. "I'll do a jack-knife. Look at me," she called.

The aunts waved, and then Lois Bailey pulled out a pile of postcards, and Constance Goldsmith opened to her place in a worn copy of *Emma*. For some twenty minutes there was peace, with the heat and a lazy breeze combining to give a sense of summer languor to the scene.

Mrs. Goldsmith had just arrived at that interesting point in *Emma* where Mr. Elton has seized Emma's hand in the carriage and Emma is saying, "This to *me!* You forget yourself; you take me for my friend . . ." when she became aware of two shadows beside her. She sighed and looked up to see Mrs. Brent and Miss Fellows standing before her in their ancient bathing attire.

Mrs. Brent beamed down at her. "I see you are reading *Emma*. One of my favorites. I read it every year, although Midge here does not agree with me about Miss Austen."

"I prefer Hardy, or George Eliot, or the Brontës, especially Charlotte," Miss Fellows observed in her deep voice.

Mrs. Goldsmith peered at Miss Fellows from under her straw hat. There seemed to be a sense of tranquillity and firmness about the woman that had been absent when she had seen her in the dining room or about the garden. She had remarked yesterday to Lois on what an unhappy face that big schoolteacher had, and that she never seemed to say anything unless prodded by Mrs. Brent.

"I agree with Charlotte Brontë's own assessment of Jane Austen," continued Miss Fellows. "Not enough passion."

What a surprising remark, thought Mrs. Goldsmith.

"Now, Midge," said Mrs. Brent, "we must take our dip quickly. We have the Morton girls for the rest of the day," she explained.

"And so we must be on our toes," added Miss Fellows, and the two teachers moved toward the pool.

"Good heavens, she's human. I mean the big one, that Miss Fellows," said Lois Bailey. "I've been thinking that she was just one more soured teacher, another Miss Lemonpuss."

"Sarah Deane told me that she'd been kicked out of her job

at Morton's Academy. She's probably very bitter. I'd be bitter too."

"Except this morning she's all serene. You know, it's amazing, Connie, how much you learn about each other if you're all doing the same thing and staying in the same place."

"A touch of murder may have helped," said Constance tartly. "The tie that binds."

"Or the bind that ties. Oh, hello, Mrs. Brent. That *was* a quick swim." This to the former headmistress, who had materialized beside her chair like a short wet genie.

"I just needed to cool off. Midge is going to give some diving pointers to your niece," said Mrs. Brent, rubbing her head vigorously with her towel so that her hair looked exactly like steel wool.

"How kind of Miss Fellows," murmured Constance Goldsmith.

"Midge has been very low this past year," said Mrs. Brent in her blunt way as she pulled up a folding chair. "Then last night she went to pieces at dinner. You see, we were being softened up by Lieutenant Pérez into revealing heavens knows what, but he got hysterics for his trouble. But I'm glad it happened and is over with. 'Catharsis' is probably the word. There are other modern terms, but I do think that we can always go safely back to the Greeks. Ah, here they come now. Nina seems a nice child. I hope you aren't forcing birds upon her. Let the interest come naturally. Are we off, Midge?"

"Nina," asked Lois Bailey, "have we forced birds on you?"

"Yes, you have," said Nina. "Birds are dumb. I'm going in and ask Cheryl to show me how to put on eyelashes."

"After this trip I may need a catharsis, too," said Mrs. Bailey. "Or perhaps just a cathartic."

Mrs. Goldsmith smiled and took up *Emma* again, and Mrs. Bailey returned to a postcard of the Alamo. The heat mounted, and the morning drowsed toward noon.

At eleven-thirty, Mrs. Brent and Miss Fellows, with picnic packs, telescopes, and binoculars, together with the five students, climbed into the blue Cactus Wren bus and departed for Doña Clara and the banks of the Rio Grande.

At one-fifteen, following the picnic lunch by a clear, fast-moving section of the river, the girls were given permission to explore along the banks and wade in the shallows.

Ten minutes later, Susan Gorham was crouching by a fallen branch of a willow tree and holding her sister's head. Nancy was vomiting.

Nearby, almost hidden by the roots of the willow and the brush growing around it, was the body of a man with a broken skull. At a short distance from his outstretched arm lay a pair of binoculars.

# XXXVIII

At about the time that Mrs. Brent and Miss Fellows were gathering their band for the trip to Doña Clara, Sarah Deane was kneeling in the middle of her new residence at Tent Site 137. The side vents were open, and now and then a small movement of air caused the tent fabric to breathe up and down, which, with the green light filtering through the roof, suggested some sort of undersea cavern.

Sarah searched about for her bathing suit, struggled into it, crawled, perspiring, out from under the nylon portico, and stood up and inspected her new domain. Very neat. Tents with external supports certainly gave one more room. Sarah then picked up her new plastic bucket, filled it with water from the tent-site faucet, and, raising it with difficulty, tipped the contents over her head. The water flooded over her body and ran down her legs and between her toes. Thus refreshed, she moved Patsy and his water dish to a place of shade under her newly strung string hammock and then hitched her wet body lengthwise into its folds. Finally, knees bent, hands laced behind her head, Sarah began to sort things out.

A muddle. Her whole life seemed to have been tending from muddle to muddle for a long time, and now she was at the center of a monster one. Philip, too. Mess and muddle. His life, which had been so carefully plotted . . . well, Philip had ended in the biggest mess of them all. It was all like that novel in which the characters, despite effort or intention, moved inexorably into a giant and fatal muddle . . . lives of purpose and will reduced to trifling nugatory gestures and journeys into oblivion.

And Pres, too. Smashed into a tree. Avoiding a dog. They had been going to buy a dog someday—after graduation, maybe. She remembered sitting next to Pres on the seat of his old pickup truck and telling him that they were both too haphazard, too sentimental, to arrange for a dog from a proper kennel. They would probably find one along the road someday. Which she had —five years later.

The curious thing was that Pres had lived for almost three hours after they brought him to the hospital. She had come just as they were wheeling him out of the emergency room, and the resident on the service had told her a lot of confusing things about vital signs and hemorrhage and perforation. They wheeled him into an emergency ICU and bent the rules to let Sarah stay next to the bed. Which was almost impossible with all those boxes with dials and the IV stands and the tubes and wires that went into Pres. "He can't last much longer." The resident had been perfectly straightforward. "No way we can get it all under control, and he's losing blood faster than we can get it in. No point in opening him, he's too busted up—he'd exsanguinate on the table." Sarah had never heard the word, and limpetlike, it attached itself to her vocabulary along with other horrors like "defenestrate" and "metastasize."

For a while Pres was quiet, his breathing fast and shallow, and then he opened his eyes and tried to grin. "Hi," he whispered. "I really blew it." Sarah poked her head in among the IV tubes and bent low. "Don't worry, Sarah," he said. "I can't feel a thing. Better living through chemistry," but the words ended in a gurgle and he seemed to choke. A nurse at the end of the bed adjusted the IV, and a man in a scrub suit felt for a pulse at the angle of Pres's throat.

The service had been full-dress Episcopal. Sarah had learned for the first time that his middle name was Marion. "This thy servant, Preston Marion Dodge," which was followed by some

Bach and then "though this body shall be destroyed, yet shall I see God."

And Philip, he was an Episcopalian, too, although he never seemed to work at it. Philip and Pres, two long-adrift sons of the church meeting up with the Book of Common Prayer again, much sooner than either could have guessed. Both names began with a P. What did that mean? Then there was Patsy. Should she change his name? Sarah dangled a hand over the hammock and touched the dog's head. But that was crazy. She couldn't start avoiding people—or dogs—because their names began with P as if she were a contaminant, a plague. P as in plague. *Pasteurella pestis.* Where had that name come from? A scrap left over from some mandatory lab course somewhere. But there were healthy people whose name began with P. There was Professor Parkinson and her dentist, Dr. Philo, and . . . was it first names or last? Stop it, Sarah ordered herself.

Besides, she had gravitated toward Philip because he represented a sort of security system. Not loose and impulsive like Pres. Philip wouldn't have driven into a tree to miss a dog. Perhaps this was a fault in Philip, but if Pres had known the alternative, he might have done it differently.

Only in his love for the natural world had Philip allowed for spontaneity. To see a bird he dropped his tennis racket, stopped his car by the side of the road, missed lunch. But around his interest in birds he had built one of his systems: notebooks, logs, checklists. Sarah closed her eyes and heard Philip explaining how you jotted down your observations in the field and . . . Suddenly, Sarah struggled to a sitting position. Of course. If the police wanted to know what Philip was doing on Friday afternoon, all they had to do was read Philip's field notebook. But the police must have done that. Alex, who knew the habits of birders, would have seen to it. But I'll ask Alex when I see him, Sarah told herself.

She lowered herself back into the hammock, and the movement set it swinging from side to side. She closed her eyes again, and this time memory was kind, and she heard her father's voice chanting, "Up and down, up and down," as he pushed Tony and Sarah together on the old swing that hung from the oak tree by the beach stairs.

# XXXIX

Tom Pérez at twelve-thirty was hungry and beleaguered. He had sent Alex into the fray to face the ire of Olive Tassel and her troops, and now he stood in the refuge office listening to Sam fulminate against further police advances into Bobcat Marsh.

"Wind it up today, Tom. I mean it. As it is, I'm going to have to close the east part of the marsh for a couple of weeks to let everything settle down. Refuges are for animals. To take refuge in, goddammit."

At which point Patrolman Juán Flores walked into the office and handed Tom a small plastic bag. "We find this, Lieutenant. Down in the marsh. Where the trees start. Lots of leaves in there."

"Sam, look here." Tom opened the bag on Sam's desk, revealing a muddy piece of paper covered with a handwritten list of names. "What are these? Some kind of code? 'Mexican sister, sleepy orange, white peacock, Texan crescentspot, Vesta, white M hairstreak' . . . what the hell? A drug-drop schedule, maybe? Sleepy orange!"

"Hey, let me see that." Sam bent over the paper. " 'Mexican silverspot, dingy purple wing—*E. monima*, Erna roadside skipper—*A. erna* '. . . Tom, you goddamn policeman. It's time you got to know more about Texas than the morgue and the forensic lab."

"Skip the lecture, Sam," said Tom testily. "These aren't drugs?"

"Butterflies, butterflies. We have lepidopterists in here sometimes. Hell, Professor Axminster's the only one I know of who's come through lately."

Tom opened his folder and examined the Axminster statements. "Both wife and hubby say they were everywhere—everywhere, that is, but at Bobcat Marsh, but they contradict each other all over the place. And we've got statements suggesting they were seen off the trails, in the bush, on Friday afternoon, and by the Observation Tower on Saturday. Husband claims to have been, quote, 'sighting and listing butterflies.' " Tom looked up. "Sighting butterflies?"

"That's what they should have been doing," said Sam, fuming. "I refused them a collector's permit this year."

"Okay, Flores, you can get back to work," said Tom. "Now, Sam, let's get this straight. The Axminsters didn't have a permit?"

"Nope. Wasn't just them. A lot of refuges down here are refusing permits. Trouble is, we don't know what's here. Some species may be almost extinct. We're identifying species and variants all the time. And goddammit, look at this list. *Anaea glycerium*, that's the crinkled leafwing and it's a stray. And dingy purple wing, that's rare, and my God, white M hairstreak . . . we just don't have records here for that one. Do you think this was just a want list? Or do they have 'em all papered and spread and pinned ready to sneak back to Idaho? They're the sort who make us refuse permits."

"But the professor thought he could cheat?"

"Guess so. He's getting near retirement, and maybe he wants to go out in a burst of glory. I hear he's the big biology enchilada at his school. They've got something called the Axminster Collection."

"Man," said Tom, "you wouldn't think he'd risk all that by rustling butterflies. Of course, he'd have gotten away with it except for the search party." Tom was silent for a moment, and then he asked almost reluctantly, "How do you think the professor would react if someone caught him stealing butterflies?"

"He'd be plenty upset. Federal property. Big stink in biology circles. Would louse him up at his college—pension canceled, maybe." Sam grunted and sat down heavily at his desk. "You'll be checking the handwriting on this list. If the stuff turns out to be the Axminsters', I'll heave the book at them. They're both old enough to know better. And, speaking of specimens," Sam gestured at the window, "here's a big one."

Tom twisted around to the window and then swore. "That bastard Cotton! Almost two hours late this morning. I gave him double hell and look, the idiot is smiling."

The screen door snapped open and Sergeant Cotton loomed. "Cotton, why aren't you out there with your head in the mud?"

Instead of answering, the sergeant placed a bundle gently on the desk. Even through its plastic cocoon, the outline of binoculars was unmistakable.

Tom went into action. "Get those to the lab, Cotton. Prints first, if possible, and I.D. marks. Then get the straps to Houston. Where were they found? Any brand name visible?"

"Too much mud on 'em to see a name. I was the one who found 'em," said Tiger Cotton. His smile widened. "I was near the edge of the marsh where the long grass leaves off and it starts goin' down deep, and I had my waders on and felt this lump with my toe."

"Did you mark the place, numbskull?"

"Yessir. With a buoy marker."

"Okay. Take off. Stay at the lab until you get some sort of I.D. and then take the strap—if it's the right type—to the airport. I'll have a plane waiting. And, Cotton, keep your nose clean, and I may forgive you someday."

"Sergeant Paul Bunyan," observed Sam as the door slammed shut.

"Sergeant Pain-in-the-Tail . . . but sometimes he does something right. Okay, Sam. You can have your marsh back. Let's hope those binocs are the ones. I'll tell Flores and the boys to take some pictures, get measurements, and rope off the buoy area, and then pack up and go home. How about joining Alex and me for lunch down at Papa Ortega's diner? My stomach needs help. No? Okay, stay here and eat your miserable sandwich, and I hope the next time I see you it will be out at the ball game."

Fifty minutes later, Tom pushed away the platter with the remains of Papa Ortega's Burrito Special and leaned back, a glass of iced coffee in his hand. "The day doesn't look as bad as it did," he said to Alex. "It's Papa's food, not the case. That's still a bitch, but maybe those binocs will shove it closer to the finish line. How do you favor the idea of a homicidal lepidopterist? Shall I fill you in on our new little complication?"

Alex listened to Tom's tale of the butterfly poachers and, at the same time from his seat facing the road, watched with increasing interest the approach of a squad car with lights flashing coming from the direction of Doña Clara. The car now swung into the front drive of the diner and came to a tilting stop. Alex drained his mug of beer. "I think," he said quietly, "that you must have just hit the complication jackpot."

Standing by the edge of the river, Alex and Tom watched the two men with the stretcher clamber awkwardly up the bank with their plastic-wrapped burden, their shoes slipping on the shifting sand and loose stones.

"Poor bastard," said Tom. "I wonder who he is? No wallet, no I.D. material. Just standing here bird-watching and then, wham, and it was all over."

"Yes, he must have died at once," said Alex, "if that smash on the head turns out to be the only injury. No wonder the Gorham girl threw up—half his skull caved in like that."

Tom opened his notebook. His sunburned face was streaked with sweat and dirt; the bottoms of his pants were rolled and wet, the result of shallow-water exploration. "Any idea how long he's been here?"

"Probably over fifteen hours, but leave that to the pathologist."

Sam Hernández, who had been in gloomy attendance throughout the afternoon, looked up. "I'll tell you this. There was no corpse here two days ago—on Sunday, that is. I had the University of Kansas biology team down here all day doing a grid study—flora, fauna, soil analysis, the whole bit. No way they could have missed this guy."

"When did they pack up?" asked Tom.

"About noon on Monday, no one reporting a body. Jeezus, Tom, besides closing the refuge again, I'll have sightseers. I mean one homicide isn't that big a deal. Anyone can have a murder, but this isn't Dallas or Houston. I can just see the TV news tonight," Sam went on bitterly, " 'Crazed killer loose in refuge.' Great shit!"

"Keep your ears on, Sam. No one's happy about this," said Tom.

Together the three men watched as the post-homicide rituals drew to a close: measurements, photographs, footprint casts. "Hundreds of footprints," complained Tom. "All those Morton girls blundering around."

Alex nodded. He had seen attempts at sand-dribble castles farther along at the water's edge.

"We'll rake through the whole area," said Tom. "See if we can find the weapon or stone that did it. Sam, I'll ask you to close the Rio Vista Trail and the Bobcat and Middle spurs down to the river and all along the banks here." Tom indicated the entire bend of the river with a wide sweep of his arm.

Sam scowled. "This is the number-one place for the green kingfisher, and sometimes we even get the ringed kingfisher. Goddammit, they don't need the police wading in their fishing spot."

"Sam, Sam, keep calm. I have no choice and neither do you. And the police can't louse things up more than some of those bird-watchers I've seen here with their whistles and tape recorders."

"Touché," said Alex. "You've hit a sore spot."

"Yeah," said Sam. "Some bird-watchers act like football players with a minute to play. What can I say? Do what you've got to do. I'll get the registration sheets for yesterday and today, though a fat lot of good it'll probably do."

The three men trudged in silence up the sandy path. Reaching his car, Tom turned to Sam. "Give me first crack at the Axminsters, will you? Then you can grind up their bones any way you want."

## XL

Alex, imperfectly restored after a shower, looked about for Sarah, and, applying to the front desk, was handed a folded piece of paper. This he opened and read: "Hi, Alex. Couldn't stand motel any longer. Need to think. Am going to camp at park near here—Hollow something. Sergeant Cotton is fixing it up. See he doesn't get into trouble. Come and see us. Patsy and Sarah."

Twenty minutes later, Alex pulled his car over on the grass next to Tent Site 137 and walked over to the hammock. Sarah in her yellow bathing suit lay asleep, her lips slightly open, her hair tousled, and an imprint of knots from the hammock showing along one arm. She looked fourteen again. No one should look so vulnerable, thought Alex, and he moved quietly back to his car, opened and closed the door, and stamped his feet. Patsy, previously obscured under the hammock, barked and strained at his rope. Sarah rolled over and sat up.

"Oh, hello, Alex. You found us. What time is it? I think I've been sleeping all day. How do you like my new house?"

Alec allowed himself to be shown the tent. He admired the stove, the mini ice chest, and accepted a paper cup of lemonade.

"The motel room was getting to me," said Sarah. "All those matching bedspreads and paper-wrapped glasses and toilets 'sealed for your protection.' This place has kids and dogs and peanut butter and flies and junk."

"I haven't said a word against it." Alex, mindful of ticks, sat down at the end of the picnic table. "You've been thinking?" he said.

Sarah nodded. "Circling and thinking. But I haven't really gotten past wondering whether I'm someone who causes things. I mean there was Pres, and then there was Philip."

"You mean that you might be a fatal friend?"

"It crossed my mind. A sort of ordaining. Sarah as fate. Who was the one that cut the thread? Atropos? You know that line about 'the malignancy of my fate perhaps distempers yours. . . .'?"

"No, I don't, and you read too much," said Alex, "and all out of context, probably. Listen, Sarah, when I was a resident, I once lost three patients in three days, and the next week three more. I began to wonder whether it was the disease or it was me. Was I an agent? Did I make things happen in threes? You know when you're sleepless, spaced-out, overworked, anything seems possible. We try so hard to explain things, to impose order on accident, to build systems on coincidence. Well, here's a quotation for you. 'The most ingenious method of becoming foolish is by a system.' That's from the Earl of Shaftesbury."

"It seems to me," said Sarah, "that up until Friday, Philip was pretty successful with system. Fortifications all around."

"Fortifications often have cracks. What did Philip tell you about his family, his mother and father?"

"Not much. They were from Virginia, an old family. Both dead now. Philip didn't talk about them much."

"With good reason. His mother was a longtime alcoholic. His father a gentleman loser. Harris-tweed shooting jackets, smelled of bay rum, bounced from job to job, and cried on Philip's shoulder about life's disappointments. Genus Old Southern Comfort. Both of them. Out of Faulkner by Tennessee Williams."

"Poor Philip," said Sarah. "Except that he seemed to have it all together."

"I agree. I'd guess he took up bird-watching to get away from them. I used to see his parents in action when they came up to the college, but Philip always stayed pretty much in control."

Sarah pushed her bare foot on the ground and set the hammock swinging. "So what have you been up to today? Sleuthing?"

Alex stood up and leaned against the tree that supported one end of the hammock. He looked down at Sarah. "I'm afraid it's been another of those bad days," he said soberly.

Sarah glanced quickly at his face. "Someone else is dead?"

Alex nodded. "Let's take Patsy for a walk down one of the trails, and I'll tell you about it."

When they came out at the end of the mile loop trail, Sarah was shaking her head in disbelief. "Two bird-watchers murdered at Doña Clara? Do you think some bird fiend is going around?"

"There's nothing to show a connection besides the location and the bird-watching angle, but, after all, bird-watching is the common denominator at Doña Clara."

Sarah came to a sudden halt. "Oh, Alex. Philip's notebook and his Doña Clara checklist. He wrote everything down, you know. What he'd seen and where and when. But I suppose the police know all that."

Alex stared at her. "No," he answered slowly. "I remember the list of things found with Philip and in his car. There was a

Laguna checklist in his pocket, but none from Doña Clara. And no field notebook. Come on, Sarah, put on some clothes, and I'll load Patsy in the car. We'll find Tom and clear this up."

As they turned out of the park entrance, Sarah said rather wistfully, "I hate to leave my camp so soon. I thought I'd found a little way station where I could sort things out, although I don't think I'm really designed to be a reflective person—creating myself by digesting my own liver, if you see what I mean."

Alex, who privately thought that this was a rather grisly route to self-knowledge, nodded his understanding.

"I think I've always bounced along, helping myself to other people's ideas. I mean when you can go around saying, 'My mind to me a kingdom is,' and 'The Soul selects her own Society,' or 'Do I dare to eat a peach?' . . . which I probably don't . . . well, why think?"

"If I may push in here," said Alex, "wasn't it Yeats who said something like 'nothing can be sole or whole that has not been rent'?"

"The well-read physician speaks again. I'm going to have to revise some of my preconceptions about doctors. Anyway, that's a good quote, although I'm not mad about pitching my mansion in a place of excrement. Couldn't he have just said 'mud'? Yes, I'm feeling 'rent'; but I hate opening wounds, or rents, so everyone can peer into my innards. I don't want to look in either. After Pres—and now Philip—it seemed safer to keep everything closed up, but now it's beginning to look like a cop-out. What I'm trying to say is that I've got to face what this Texas scene has turned into. A murder. And I'm not a pedestrian walking away with my head turned, but right there, front and center. Tom Pérez might even think that I killed Philip."

"Good Lord, no," said Alex too quickly.

"Oh?" said Sarah, enlightened. "Well, I suppose from Tom's view, I'm the 'girlfriend' in the case. Aren't half the murders done by girlfriends and boyfriends? But, suspect or not, I'll tell Tom about Philip's notebooks, and then I'll go back to my tent and start thinking again."

"Here's a humble suggestion. Try an approach which doesn't mean grabbing onto some literary metaphor. Start with yourself."

"It's hard to block old escape routes, but okay. I'll try and reconstruct all by myself the house of Sarah Douglas Deane."

"Douglas is my mother's middle name," said Alex, deciding to keep it light. "You may be my long-lost cousin from across the sea."

"That would be nice, although I said you could be a brother. Your choice, brother, cousin, whatever."

"Dr. Whatever at your service. Mysterious, sinister Dr. Whatever, whose body is entirely made from the parts of old laundry machines, but a mighty brain has he."

Sarah smiled. "That was a fine fancy flight."

"I'm always struck dumb by alliteration."

"I doubt that," said Sarah. And then she added with a sigh, "Oh Lord, we're almost there. The Homicide Division is downtown, isn't it?"

Tom was tracked down in a second-floor office at the end of a hall, sitting behind a stack of filing boxes. He had washed the dirt but not the weariness from his face. Despite an open window and a fan whirling from the ceiling, the air was musty and the room too warm. Tom did not seem surprised to see his visitors, merely lifting a hand and indicating two scarred wooden chairs. He nodded at the door. "Captain Nordstrom's been messing up the file cabinets because he's got a hunch, and it's a real winner."

At that, the door was wrenched open and the bulk of the chief of Homicide took center stage. "Pork" Nordstrom's person overlapped the confinements of belt, pants, and shirt. His face was florid, his eyes small, and his gray bristled head was as round as a muskmelon. He brandished a folder at Tom. "Got it, Pérez. Now you git to work on it."

"Captain Nordstrom, you remember Dr. McKenzie, who's been assisting me? And this is Miss Deane, who's also giving us a hand."

Captain Nordstrom acknowledged these civilities with a short nod and turned back on Tom. "Ah should've thought of it sooner. You, too, Pérez. Just went over the list of people staying at that motel. Statements from everybody concerned except—git this," Captain Nordstrom jerked a sausage finger at the folder. "No one got a real statement from those Boyden gay jokers, those homos. One paragraph. A summary. Shit, that's no statement."

"There was an executive meeting of the Texas Gay Alliance at the motel, with the Boyden branch acting as hosts," Tom explained to Alex and Sarah.

"Yeah," growled the captain. " 'Boyden Gays for Alternate Living,' it says here. Alternate bullshit. Ah say alter-nut living. Alter-nuts. Haw!" The captain gave a thick chortle. "Alter-nuts. Pretty damn good. Okay, Pérez, get on to it, ya hear? Pronto, Lieutenant. *Comprende? Rápido!* P.D.Q." And the captain was gone.

"I may have to fumigate," said Tom, rising, going to the door, and releasing the night lock. "I've tried to tell him that the Boyden gay conference people are accounted for. No lost, strays, or stolens. Nordstrom's a character . . . no, he's a caricature. He loves scapegoats. Eats 'em for dinner. Broiled Hispanic, fried black, roasted Jew, poached Indian, Catholic, Italian. You name it, he eats it."

"This is your boss?" asked Sarah, appalled.

"We coexist. He's a type that's on its way out. I hope."

"Like the shark?" suggested Sarah.

"He'll be eating someone else tomorrow," said Tom. "Very short attention span. So, you two, *qué pasa?* What brings you to my cage?"

Alex told Tom, and Sarah elaborated on Philip's note-taking habits when doing field work.

Tom listened and then pulled a paper from his hoard and ran his finger down the list. "No small, medium, or large notebook in or around the body or in the car. No Doña Clara checklist. Only one hardbound logbook with entries through Thursday. The only things marked missing were the wallet and the second pair of binoculars, which, by the way, are no longer missing. We had an I.D. from the lab. Bausch & Lomb seven by thirty-five, 'Lentz' stamped on them. We checked the Maryland camera store, too. They *had* repaired them."

"But," put in Sarah, "the field notebook and the checklist aren't things that would attract the ordinary thief or murderer. Wouldn't someone have to know the purpose of them, someone who knew about field biology? But whoever it was left the Laguna list because it wouldn't be pertinent, wouldn't be a threat."

"It seems to me," said Tom, "that the murderer simply

didn't want any sort of identification stuff around, so he took the wallet and the notebook and the checklist, but overlooked the Laguna list. That one was buttoned in Philip's back pocket. And the murderer must have left in one hell of a hurry, because he just dragged the body off, then got out. By the way, the path lab has given us a rough time fix for the murder. Lentz was killed between five and seven-thirty that evening. That fits with our estimate."

"I think Sarah might like to get back to her campground," said Alex, looking anxiously at her.

"Before you go," said Tom, "I'd like a response from both of you to a couple of things we found on the second body." Tom picked up a paper. "Most of the stuff is what you'd expect, well-worn clothes, some U.S., some Mexican manufacture; a plastic bag with wet sneakers, wet socks—these hidden under a bush; U.S. currency of five dollars and twenty-seven cents, a five-peso bill, a one-peso bill, seventy centavos; one Doña Clara checklist; one pair of binoculars, eye caps on eyepieces, but missing from large end—binocs, Japanese make, Bino-View."

"Bino-View! exclaimed Sarah. "Those are terrible. Real cheapies. I was going to buy some, but Philip stopped me."

"May I see that checklist, Tom?" asked Alex.

"It's a photostat. We're going over the original in the lab."

Alex studied the list in silence, then frowned and shook his head. "This is a very peculiar list."

"And so are they all peculiar," returned his friend. "Peculiar lists, peculiar people. Adults running around the countryside counting birds on little laundry lists."

"But this one right here is not only peculiar, it's abnormal, eccentric, idiosyncratic. A real oddball. Here, Sarah, you look."

"Okay, Doctor," said Tom. "I suppose you had better tell me as painlessly as possible about checklists."

Alex sat back to lecture while Sarah puzzled over the photostat. "A checklist, Tomás, is exactly that. A list of birds which might be found in a given area. It's based on birds that have been seen in that area by naturalists and ornithologists, and opposite the name of the bird is a blank space where the visitor will make a check when, and if, he sees the bird."

"Do they all look like this one?"

"More or less. They're usually narrow folders which fit into a pocket. Each wildlife area uses a slightly different format, but the essentials are the same. The lists follow the order used in most North American field guides, from loons and grebes on through to sparrows and longspurs."

"Sir Lancelot Longspur, no doubt."

"Shut up. Some checklists take in larger areas, like Texas or the Eastern U.S. The Doña Clara list, of course, gives only those birds that have been seen in that part of the Rio Grande Valley. Sarah, do you want to help out with this?"

"Well," said Sarah, "for strangers, or dumbheads like me, they usually label each bird as 'abundant,' 'common,' 'occasional,' 'uncommon,' 'rare,' or 'accidental' under columns marked 'summer,' 'spring,' 'fall,' and 'winter.' There, you see, Alex, I *have* learned something. So, if I see something fantastic . . ." Sarah paused, searching her brain for a fantastic bird. "If I see, say, a cockatoo, and if it's not even listed as accidental, then I have a problem, and I'd have to get confirmation—someone else seeing it—or take a photograph—to prove that it was really there. Then I'd have to write up every detail before anyone would listen to me, which no one would without proof. If I were an ornithologist, I might get permission to collect it, which is just a horrible euphemism for shoot it."

"And," said Alex, "if Sarah goes out tomorrow and sees a scissor-tailed flycatcher and looks it up on the Doña Clara checklist, she'll see that it's abundant in the spring, uncommon or absent in the summer, turns up as common in the fall, and disappears in the winter. March being counted as spring in south Texas, she'll know it's around, and and if she feels sure about the field marks, she'll check it off."

"How do you remember all that?" asked Sarah.

"It's a lot easier than learning sixty lines of *Paradise Lost*. Of course, Tom, the statistics aren't compiled really for the benefit of the occasional visitor. Naturalists, park and refuge personnel all keep tabs on species distribution and population changes as a way of knowing what's going on with the birds and their habitat —and our habitat, I should add. Every hurricane, freeze, oil spill, every new parking lot, construction project, every water-level change has its effect. Now if very few people report seeing scissor-tailed flycatchers this spring, we'll know something's haywire, or changed somewhere. There's a Blue List of declining species . . ."

"Hell, I'm having enough trouble with checklists, so spare me the blue ones," interrupted Tom testily. "And come to the point. I don't want to know about scissor-tailed anythings, rare or extinct."

"Patience, Tomás," said Alex. "Just remember that each list relates only to the area with which it's concerned, and on this Doña Clara list the birds which have a black line underneath are ones usually found in south Texas but not in the rest of North America. They're Mexican and Rio Grande specialties."

"You're driving me crazy," said Tom.

"For instance," said Alex, "these hook-billed kites that have Major Foster and Sam and the Hamburg Club in a lather have never been seen at Doña Clara and hence aren't named on the checklist."

"Okay. So now I've passed Checklist 101. Why is this one weird?"

"I'll bet Sarah can tell you, even if she is only a beginner."

Sarah ran her fingers down the names. "Well, he's only seen a few different birds, and the number he's seen is queer. Look, three least grebes listed as 'common' in the spring, but nineteen black-bellied ducks, which are 'occasional,' and six masked ducks, and they're marked 'rare.' Then forty-five chachalacas, which is okay, I guess, because they're all over, and then there's a circle filled in with his pencil next to the jacana—but a dark circle means 'nests locally.' Does the jacana nest at Doña Clara?"

"No," said Alex, "but go on. What else strikes you?"

"Not much. There are checks after roseate spoonbill, listed as 'rare,' gadwall 'common,' blue-winged teal and cinnamon teal both 'common,' and the last one is a swallow-tailed kite, which is marked rare.' "

"Okay. Tell the nice lieutenant what you make of it."

"He's seen quite a few birds marked rare, and only a few of the common ones. It's all out of balance."

"Right, and he's got numbers against some birds with the line underneath—the south Texas specialties—and only a check against the others. But the birds are crazy. Six masked ducks! I knock myself out trying to see one masked duck. And where are the bread-and-butter birds, the green jay, the ground dove, the kiskadee?"

"Maybe with cheap binoculars you see rare birds," said Tom.

"Only ten species? No one at Doña Clara sees only ten species."

"Unless you're killed trying to see number eleven."

"Okay, okay. But there are other things. Wet sneakers and wet socks, for instance."

"I did say that Mexicans don't wade over to bird-watch, but I could be wrong. Or maybe he's a U.S. citizen who wanted to cool his feet. We'll wait for the I.D."

"And those cheap Bino-View binocs with the ocular caps still on?"

"Someone buys them," said Tom sharply. "Poor guys can't afford the high-priced spread—Nikons, Bausch & Lomb. And, being poor, he takes care of his equipment, keeps his eyepieces covered."

"And where were his big lens caps?"

"In his pocket. So big deal. He was probably about to put them on or take them off when he got smashed on the head."

"Can you get me a copy of this checklist?" asked Alex wearily.

"I'll have it for you in the morning. Then you can turn it into a crossword puzzle or fold it into a paper dart."

"I'm quite good at puzzles," put in Sarah.

"Fine. Two can play. But don't come back and tell me it's some Egyptian code for a drug ring. I tried that with Sam this morning with a butterfly list, and he laughed me out of the county. Sleepy orange, white peacock. Now you know damn well that's a better name for a drug than a butterfly. So, back to the real world. We're doing the postmortem tonight at nine, Alex. Want to come back?"

Alex stood up. "Thanks, but no thanks. I'll get the details from you in the morning. Tonight I'm going to put checklists under my pillow and see what I dream about. Come on, Sarah.

We'll pick up some food and try out your new camp stove."

Tom lifted his head briefly. "Good night, children. Thanks for the seminar, and look out for overhead pigeons. That's a bird to watch."

# WEDNESDAY, MARCH 20

## ——————— XLI ———————

The autopsy report delivered to Tom's desk at nine-thirty the next morning revealed that the man found at the foot of the riverbank had been hit on the back of the head, and that death, instantaneous, resulted from massive cranial injuries. The instrument was probably a large brick, or two small ones, with portions of mortar adhering, particles of both materials having been found in the brain tissue and among bone fragments. The man was described as being approximately thirty-five years old, five feet seven inches, weighing one hundred fifty-three pounds. Time of death was set tentatively in the period of 4 P.M. to 8 P.M. on Monday. The facts of Mexican clothing, dark skin, dark hair, facial structure, all suggested someone of Mexican-Indian origin, and, of course, the damp socks and sneakers pointed to the probability of a recent trip across the Rio Grande.

"But it doesn't mean a damn thing," Chuck Kennedy, of the Personal Analysis lab, told Tom. "Hispanic Indians are all over the country, and those Bino-View binoculars are imported and sold all through the U.S. in large-volume chain stores. Only the victim's prints on them, and no decent prints on anything else. Sorry, Tom."

Tom tossed the report to Alex, who sat next to the desk. "You can see that he was not very tall, so that any of my favorites, except Jeff and Lucas—and she probably makes up in agility—

could have come down on him with a brick when he wasn't looking. Someone he may have known, been waiting for, and so wasn't on his guard."

"I still don't connect bird-watching with murder," said Alex in a discouraged voice.

"Yeah," said Tom. "Bird-watching is for Girl Scouts and deep-breathing wilderness types. Mr. and Mrs. Clean and Baby Clean in the great outdoors. Don't kid yourself. The killer can be that sweet little baby-sitter next door. Come on. Back to that motel."

Ten minutes later the two men were once more on their way to Vacation Villa to take up the burden of the investigation, now further cumbered by the second homicide. Tom, cutting deftly in and out of Boyden's downtown traffic, turned to Alex.

"You're slipping, amigo. There's one more question you should have asked about that autopsy report."

Alex considered. "I give up . . . unless it's that the murder was done with a brick, and bricks don't grow by the Rio Grande."

"That's it," said Tom, disappointed. "I thought only the keen brain of Detective Pérez had picked it up. You're right. No houses ever in that part of the border, so the brick may have come from Settlers Village. We're collecting samples of bricks and mortar. Looks like the murderer was thinking ahead. No one carries bricks in his pocket for comfort. I'm sending a wading party into the river in the murder area to try and recover the brick."

"Leaving no brick unturned?"

"You said it. And here we are again. Carlos Allen's tourist trap, and, oh God, those Morton girls again."

But Tom and Alex found that two murders had put a noticeable crimp in the students' imagination. The excitement generated by the death of Philip Lentz had turned into something like apprehension, and the girls added no frills to their descriptions of Tuesday's river picnic and its gruesome sequel. All were preternaturally serious and sometimes tearful. Nancy Gorham volunteered the information that her projected nurse's training had been abruptly canceled at the sight of her first corpse; Susan Gorham, however, had discovered a vocation in holding heads and mopping faces. So are careers discarded and born, thought Alex, sitting silent through the sessions.

Dory Williams remained true to first impressions. A calm and dispassionate observer, she had helped move the girls away from the area and, with Mrs. Brent, had sat guard at the site.

Kate McMillan related how she and Miss Fellows had gone for help, and finished by telling Tom and Alex how Miss Fellows had changed from the brooding silent woman of the first days of the Texas visit into the teacher of authority that Kate had known in the classroom. "When I first saw her down here, I thought she was on some sort of nervous-breakdown trip. She wasn't together at all," said Kate.

Tom had noticed it, too. "That Miss Fellows has been transformed," he observed to Alex after Kate and then Miss Fellows had made their statements. "What's gotten into her?"

"It's more like what's gotten out of her," said Alex. "Those bad vibes about Philip. And he's gone, too. Very therapeutic."

"I damn well wouldn't like to meet Miss Fellows with her hockey stick if I'd done her wrong."

For several moments Alex and Tom went over the Jekyll and Hyde potential of Miss Fellows.

"Like Lizzie Borden," said Tom.

"No," said Alex, "not the type."

"Neither was Lizzie. But, putting Fellows aside, how about Foster? Because I've just had a call from Mrs. High Society."

"Mrs. van Hoek?"

"Right on. She's sure it's the major. Has a hunch. Always gets hunches. Sure she saw someone, somewhere, on Monday. Was it the major, was it someone else? Wants to discuss it, perhaps at lunch. Won't I bring that attractive Dr. McKenzie?"

"Bullshit."

"Think about it. An older woman has so much to offer." Tom leered at his friend.

"Go to hell. But she's got a point. Foster goes everywhere."

"And so don't we all. You, me, Sam, Foster, and all the nature freaks that infest the refuge. I've also got forty-plus people known to be in the refuge Monday afternoon—my men are tracing them now. But right now the motel folk are my meat, so sit up, Doctor, it's time for the others to come in and confess."

But when put together, the statements from the motel guests who had been at Doña Clara on Monday revealed little beyond the fact that, given the possible time-of-death span from four until eight that evening, the opportunities to sneak down to the Rio Grande with a concealed brick were legion.

After the return from Laguna at four, it was showers and naps for the Plummers, a swim for Mrs. Goldsmith, birding at Doña Clara for Jeff, Lois Bailey, and others of the tour. The Morton girls, released by Miss Lucas, retired to the pool, except for Miss Lucas herself and Dory Williams, who were offered a lift to Doña Clara on the Ready Tour bus. Major Foster followed, as usual, in his van.

"And there we are again," grumbled Tom. "The same old circus. Brent and Fellows hit the refuge at four-thirty and then split up. The Axminsters were crawling around in the bushes, and—wouldn't you know?—Mrs. van Hoek is the only one who says she saw a man matching the description of the victim. Hell, she got it out of the newspapers. She'd see Dracula if she needed the attention."

"To repeat," said Alex, "people in refuges look at the birds and the bees, not at people carrying bricks."

"I've heard that before. I suppose you can vouch for Sarah?"

"Back off, Tom, and stow that idea. For good. I was with Sarah washing fleas and doing other good deeds. We had supper in my room and spent the time trying to disguise Patsy as a piece of furniture."

"All right. Consider Sarah as canceled as anything but a friend to stray animals. But that whole Monday Doña Clara scene is a washout. No suspect eliminated. Of course, I'm not counting Foster's fat sister, who isn't concerned. She says she was home at her brother's house all afternoon. And then I've got that goddamn Viennese buffet thing to figure out. Utter chaos from seven o'clock on."

Vacation Villa, to Tom's disgust, had put on one of its Heritage Buffets. Monday was a salute to Austria, and native costumes were encouraged. However, what with dinner served in a garden dimly lit with lanterns, and the mingling in the shadows of outside guests and regulars, no one seemed to be quite sure when they stopped drinking and began eating, or with whom they did these things.

"Did I see Major Foster?" repeated Waldo Plummer. "Yes, indeed, I must have. Such a large man. A lovely evening with the music of the country. *Eine kleine Nachtmusik,* to be sure. Köchel 525, you know." Tom did not know and moved on to Mrs. Goldsmith's statement suggesting that Major Foster's sister had come late. "I couldn't forget because she was stuffed into a sort of Heidi dress. But it was dark, so I can't tell about anyone else." Manager Allen recalled seeing Major Foster arriving with his sister just before eight, and Dory Williams reported that Miss Lucas had told her during the return bus trip that she might be getting another migraine. No one had seen Miss Lucas after she returned to the motel.

"But it's just more garbage," said Tom. "And I was really counting on good old Cheryl. She knows the regular guests by sight."

But Cheryl, who had been pressed into evening service, failed to have any really useful recollections. She thought she had seen Miss Fellows coming in by the service entrance . . . or was she going out? Cheryl couldn't say for sure, except that if it was Miss Fellows, why wasn't she using one of the guest entrances? What time was this? Cheryl thought maybe it was around six. Or was it? On the whole, it appeared that Cheryl's attention had centered on the trouble she had had during the evening in keeping her Austrian dress in order. "The neck kept opening, and those little strings came undone, and I couldn't lace the top part closed because I'm too big in front, you see. It was embarrassing, you wouldn't believe."

Alex could believe. There rose before him the not unwelcome picture of Cheryl's amplitude forcing her laced bodice to part. He mentally shook himself, noting privately that this came from being turned into Sarah's brother or cousin . . . into Dr. Whatever.

Back in Tom's office at Homicide, the two men sat down over a late lunch, and Tom, in an almost symbolic act, poured ketchup over his hamburger and French fries.

"Anyone could have murdered that man and then turned up to eat Wiener schnitzel, or could have left the buffet early, run over, made a pit stop to pick up the brick, gotten to the river, slammed the guy on the skull, and made it back in time to dance 'The Blue Danube.' I took Brent and Fellows out for dinner that evening, but for all I know, one or both could have joined me fresh from murder."

"Tom, don't force a connection between the murders."

"I'm not forcing, and I'm not neglecting," said Tom, flipping a call switch on his desk and picking up the telephone. "Yes," he said. "Okay, that's that. Thanks, Eric." He hung up and ran his fingers into his hair so that it stood up in black quills. "That's the Houston lab. Lentz was killed with his own binocs, the second pair. They had a tough time with all that mud, but everything matched. Come in, Cotton!" Tom yelled as a large shadow fell over the office door's glass panel and the frame shuddered from a strong whack.

"From our lab, Lieutenant." Sergeant Cotton held out a slip of paper.

Tom took it, tipped in his chair, read, and came upright with a jerk. "Interesting. Analysis of the stuff in the pockets of our second refuge victim shows that along with fluff and tobacco bits, a small amount of concentrated Celluwell was present. They suggest that it might have leaked from a package."

"Damn, that *is* interesting." Alex reached for the report. "Particularly because I've just had a report—forgot to tell you with all that went on yesterday—that Celluwell seems to be in short supply in the New England area. They think that some of it comes by way of the Everglades and some from over the Rio Grande."

"I don't know much about Celluwell," said Tom. "There's a lot of talk, but we police usually try to grab the hard stuff."

"It's called the new Laetrile . . . from tree bark, a subtropical species. It's causing plenty of misery, getting hopes up, making the medical profession look like rats for withholding it."

"My Aunt Rita tried it before she died. Cancer of the stomach. But she'd never tell anyone where she got it. My guess is that some little pharmacy setup which can't make ends meet legitimately is involved, and that the stuff is cut, prepared, and packaged at its final distribution point. Anyway, we've got a second murdered bird-watcher, who may have been dealing on the side. Right now we need an I.D. for the guy. We're checking with Missing Persons and the Mexican police."

"Have you got a copy of that crazy checklist for me? I have an idea, but it hasn't any shape yet."

"Right here waiting for you. And, Alex, I'm moving into high gear and going to give some of our refuge regulars the real workout down here at Homicide, not all comfortable at the motel. Eduardo, the bus driver, for one. I've been neglecting him. Then Foster. No connection with Lentz, but plenty footloose. And a word with sister fats."

"Which reminds me, Sarah says Foster's sister seems to know more about birds than she pretends."

"Christ, I'm not going to quiz the lady about her secret bird life. I just want a few slices of brother's background. Then I'm going to turn a screw on Professor and Madame Butterfly and give Jeff Goldsmith a nudge—I still don't think he's squaring with me. Next, I'll see Lucas, and then go to work on Fellows and Brent."

"Look, Tom, could you hold off on those last two? For humane reasons."

"Humane? Balls! What's humane about murder? I'm a policeman. I don't go in for 'warm interpersonal relations' between doctor and patient. It's a hell of a lot better for me to handle them than to let Pork Nordstrom start deviling them, or having him lean on some poor bastard whose name or color or sex life he doesn't like."

Alex saw his friend's face set like a cast. "Right, Tom. But do this. Put off the old ladies until last. Mrs. Brent is just catching her breath, and Miss Fellows is just getting a grip on her sanity."

"And I aim to see how good that grip is. If strangling Philip Lentz has given her peace of mind, I'm going to snatch it away." Tom sighed. "For you, I'll put the old girls at the end of Torquemada's list and see them tomorrow noon. Before lunch." He grinned. "Deep interrogation on an empty stomach. You can sit in, Alex, with brandy and Valium at the ready."

"Or sal volatile—more their style. Thanks, Tomás. Sarah is having the two of them for tea at her tent site this afternoon, and I said I'd drop by. Shall I warn them of what's coming?"

"No," said Tom. "I'll call them tonight. Be off. Go your way."

"But not rejoicing," said Alex, standing up.

# XLII

Sarah, having hitched a ride into town with a family going shopping, had gathered a presentable collection of tea-party food. She arranged gingersnaps and buttered whole-wheat bread on two tin plates and put a pan of water to boil on her alcohol stove. A glass jar of illicitly picked wildflowers completed the arrangements.

Now that the guests were almost upon her, she had a spasm of apprehension. She felt all the embarrassment of being identified as the girlfriend of the very person who had removed her guests from their jobs, and whose death now caused these ladies to be suspected of his murder. And another possible hazard: they might both come dripping with sympathy, and she wasn't sure she could handle that. I haven't seen them alone since it all happened, and everyone's acting as if I were almost a widow, she thought bitterly.

Just then the sound of an approaching motor brought Sarah to attention. The blue Cactus Wren wagon appeared down the road, slowed, turned in, and halted a few feet from the picnic table.

Sarah found that she need not have worried about unwelcome expressions of sympathy.

"Sarah, my dear." Mrs. Brent, a red bandanna rolled about her head, climbed briskly down from her perch in the driver's seat. "How very nice, and flowers, too. Redbud and bee-blossom. We have been looking forward to this. A pause in the day's occupation."

Miss Fellows came forth from the other side of the wagon. She was wearing olive-drab work pants and a cotton shirt of a military cut. She gave Sarah her hand. "This *is* a good idea. A respite from bird-watching." She glanced at the little stove. "And tea made with boiling water. The motel gives us lukewarm slop with a tea bag."

Sarah took the teachers on a tour of the tent site, and they applauded her domestic arrangements and patted Patsy. Miss Fellows called him a "big fellow" and laughed at her own joke. There was no attempt at hand holding and only one reference to recent events.

"We've all had a difficult year, Sarah," said Mrs. Brent as she added milk to her mug of tea. "But we must simply go on, must we not? Now *our* life has taken a turn for the better, and I am sure yours will. What splendid gingersnaps. They taste home-made."

Miss Fellows praised the tent and expressed interest in its support system. She crawled inside and came out announcing that she was going to discard her old Boy Scout model and go modern.

Sarah, like the others before her, was astounded. Miss Fellows seemed restored to cheer and ready to enter into the spirit of the party with her old vigor. The guests each had two cups of tea and devastated the bread and gingersnap supply. They talked about Sarah's first year at the academy, and how, as a New Girl, she had threatened a hunger strike because she missed her setter Sneezer. Thus teatime passed peacefully, and Sarah felt curiously at ease.

Alex arrived at the end of the second cup and was duly served. Sarah sat sidewise in her hammock and listened to Mrs. Brent raise the possibility of seeing Bell's vireo in the Rio Grande Valley.

"I know that it may have disappeared from the whole area, but I thought I heard a call which just might have been . . . you know, 'cheedle cheedle chee? cheedle cheedle chew!' "

Miss Fellows stoutly resisted the idea of Bell's vireo being anywhere in the vicinity, and Alex was called on to referee. Then the discussion moved on to the Canada warbler and whether it said, as Peterson noted, "Chip, chupety swee-ditchety," or, as Clark Beardslee had claimed, "Che wichety-wippy-che-witchy-wippy."

"Not 'che,' " said Miss Fellows. " 'Tche.' "

"But I haven't caught sight of these hook-billed kites," said Mrs. Brent, "and I am most anxious to. A life bird. Midge, here, thought perhaps she might have had a glimpse."

"Oh, yes?" said Alex.

"I'm not sure," said Miss Fellows. "Only a quick impression, so I have not reported them."

The low sun came in blurred patterns through the leaves of the willows and oak trees, and the shadows stretched softly across the picnic table. Patsy began to snore gently, and Sarah half listened to the talk and pushed the hammock back and forth with her feet.

She remembered when her mother had friends for tea. Those teapots and water jugs, the cream pitcher on little feet, the thin sandwiches rolled up with leaves sticking out at the ends, the shortbread with a design stamped on it, and . . .

The mood broke abruptly. A youth on a motorcycle shot through the tent area with a head-splitting roar, Patsy woke, barked, and began chewing on his flank, and Mrs. Brent and Miss Fellows stood up. "Thank you *so* much, Sarah . . . so *very* pleasant . . . *such* a good idea." They shook hands, mounted into their van, and were gone. Alex started to gather the tea things together, and his elbow knocked over the glass jar of flowers. Water spread in a puddle and began dripping onto the bench at the side.

Sarah, recalled from the protection of teatime and past memory, sat down suddenly at the picnic table and burst into tears.

The tears that had not come full flood when Sarah had faced herself in the motel mirror came now, and she cried as if it were the only thing she knew how to do. She cried for the spilled flowers, and for her brother Tony because he was away in Vermont, and she wept for Patsy because he had once been abandoned. She cried for Pres, and for Philip, and then for the man who was found yesterday, dead by the Rio Grande. And then she cried for herself.

Alex put a box of tissues by her head, which was now resting on her arms on the picnic table. For a while he let her have her tears, and then lifted her head gently and let it rest against his shoulder and blotted her streaked face with a piece of tissue. "All right, Sarah. It's getting dark. I'll help you wash up, and then, perhaps, you'll come back to the motel with me and take a room next to mine, or near Connie and Lois."

Sarah raised her head. "No," she said in a choked voice. "I feel better now. Please, I want to stay here."

"We'll see." Alex went into the tent, found a towel which he soaked under the water tap, folded it, and applied it to Sarah's eyes. She took it from him and rubbed her face vigorously.

"Dr. McKenzie, you must be hard up for patients."

"Get a jacket, Sarah. It's cooling off. You're my only patient just now, and you know how we doctors like to keep a practice going."

Sarah returned from the tent in her new safari-cloth jacket, now somewhat the worse for being rolled into her knapsack. She pushed her hands into the pockets, pulled out a narrow yellow folder, and looked at it, puzzled. "It's a Doña Clara checklist, but I haven't worn this jacket since the first day when I got off the plane."

"Let me see." Alex reached for the folder. "It's filled in—or, rather, partly filled in. Sarah, it's like that other oddball list, the one found on the second body. Not exactly, but almost. See, three masked ducks and a spoonbill. Where did you get this, anyway?"

"I don't know. Let me think." Sarah sat down at the picnic table and began to put the limp strands of bee-blossom and redbud back in the empty jar.

"Here, Sarah, I'll clean up. You try and remember about this list. You know, you really are something. Every step forward in this god-awful affair has come from a fact you've forgotten and then remembered. I've been fooling around with an idea, and if your list fits with the other one, we may be on to something hot."

"I must have picked it up somewhere." Sarah closed her eyes and then looked up at Alex. "Okay. I've got it. You know that Major Foster's sister sat next to me on the plane? Well, when she got up, this dropped down in the aisle. At least I suppose it was hers. I picked it up but never caught up with her, and so I forgot all about it." She made a face. "It's sort of a natural law. The more you hope you'll never see certain people again, the more you bump into them. She was on the Laguna trip, and I saw her at the motel. So far—knock on wood—she hasn't turned up here. I think," Sarah went on, "that having her around made Philip's death harder."

"I'm sorry. The world is full of well-intentioned intrusive bores. But no wonder you forgot about the list."

"Alex, I've been thinking about that other checklist too. If this one is like the other, maybe they're messages."

"Tom warned me about thinking I was about to crack a wildlife code."

"You know," persisted Sarah, "I wouldn't get bogged down in the bird angle. If there is a message, it may be based on just the numbers and letters. That's only an idea, probably because I'm not into birds the way you all are, and I'd hate to work on a puzzle based on species distribution. And now we've got the major's sister involved, but she's such a twit."

"What's that European bird, the great tit? Let's talk about it at dinner. Some genuine Spanish food that will make you breathe fire."

"Alex, that crying spell. I apologize."

"Don't. Time you had a good sob. Doctor knows best. Let's fix Patsy's dinner and then hit town."


That night, after the lantern light from the tent at Tent Site 137 had been put out, a red Volvo inched into an empty site some seventy yards away. The illumination from a nearby wash hut showed a dark figure lowering the back seat of the car and wrestling itself into a sleeping position.

# THURSDAY, MARCH 21

## XLIII

It was well past seven-thirty when Tom Pérez walked into his office bearing a Thermos of cocoa and a package of coffee cake. His mother had pressed these supplies on her son after giving him a vivid picture of Great-Uncle Alonzo's death from tuberculosis, apparently caused by neglecting breakfast.

With one hand wrapped around his mug of cocoa, Tom ran

over the notes from yesterday afternoon's round of interviews. The Ready Tour driver, Eduardo, had little to contribute. All his activities during the two periods under investigation had concerned transporting tour members, visiting with the refuge staff, and going to the men's room. Off duty, he was at home with a numerous family. Had he ever noticed anything out of the way? Anything that bothered him?

"That Major Foster, he never obey the rules."

"How is that, Eduardo?"

Eduardo shook his head. "The one-way part of the road. He never obey the sign. All the time in his van he go where he damn well like to go."

"And on last Friday, where did he like to go?"

"I don't know where he go," said Eduardo. "I sure know where he come from. I'm talking to my friend who works by headquarters, after we come back from the ice cream, and I see him come along the Auto Tour Road the wrong way. Sometime he going to get it right in the ass. Someone they come the right way, and they smash him good."

"Was he in a hurry?"

"The major, he always in a hurry. He look for new birds all the time and not the signs. Don't take me wrong," added Eduardo in a worried voice. "Major Foster, he's okay. Big joker."

Big Foster, who followed Eduardo in the questioning, roared with laughter. "Eduardo, that ol' guy is just a nervous Nellie. Sure, on that Auto Tour Road I go the wrong way. But only after the place is cleared out. Saves time. I usually let the tour groups go off on their own at the end of the day or get a shake or cone with Eduardo. Then I scout around and see if anything new has come in."

"Birds?" asked Tom.

"Sure, birds. That's where it's at, Pérez, that's where it's at."

"You were a few minutes late meeting the tour Friday afternoon."

"Yeah. Those hook-billed kites. Almost blew my mind. A real first for Doña Clara. Maybe they'll settle in and nest. . . ."

Tom cut short the kite speculation and asked Major Foster —Tom was punctilious in the use of what he was sure was a bogus title—whether he had seen any of the motel regulars in his travels around the refuge. But the major denied them all, as well as anyone resembling Philip Lentz, or the second victim, and gave an emphatic "no" to mysterious strangers with or without a brick. The major, taken on a biographical trip of his career as a salesman of hotel glass and china, and as a tour leader, had nothing more to show Pérez than ill-concealed impatience at the advancing clock.

Tom looked out his window and counted four pigeons on the window ledge and then turned quickly. "What do you know about Celluwell?"

"Cancer cure, some say," replied the major calmly, his fingers not pausing their drumming on the arm of his chair. "Don't know as I'd try it, but you can't blame folks for bein' interested."

Tom finally let him go, but as he reached the door, called him back. "This 'major' business, Foster. Are you a major in something?"

Big grinned, suddenly good-natured. "That's been eatin' you, hasn't it, Pérez? Thought I was just an ol' fraud. It's like this. Art Ready likes to use the title; looks good in the advertisin', and you see in the Korean War I was sure enough a major." Big leaned forward like an actor with a good exit line. "Not a major anymore." He strode to the door, opened it, and turned. "When I left the marines awhile back, I was plain Colonel Foster. Full chicken colonel. Still am. In the reserves. Y'all have a nice day, ya hear, Lieutenant."

Eleanor Lucas, ushered in on the heels of Big Foster, had nothing to add to her previous statements. She sat rigidly on the wooden office chair, her field boots flat on the floor, her hands held tightly together in her lap, and her blonde head held high. No, she had not seen any stranger killing or being killed on the banks of the Rio Grande, nor had she herself used a brick in an unlawful manner. On Monday night she had started a migraine and gone to her room and stayed there—that fake Austrian buffet she could do without. No, she had not had any dinner sent up to her room. "Have you ever had a migraine, Lieutenant?"

Probing for a weak link in Eleanor Lucas's chain mail, Tom was rewarded with grim silence. Asked sternly whether she had an attorney, she said that she intended to find one. "Goodbye, Lieutenant."

Hell, thought Tom, reviewing Wednesday's non-results. I'm trying to force something that isn't there. The phone on his desk gave an angry buzz, reminding him that although Wednesday was a blank, Thursday was another day and Mrs. Iris Meyer was on deck.

The major's sister had made an effort. Her upswept hair was newly turned to brass, and her turquoise suit was faultless, but it was the rake of her bow and the lines of her superstructure that invited wonder. Her inner supports were somehow fixed so that her bosom declined in a forty-five-degree angle from her chin, rounded off, and headed for her hips without the slightest hint of a waistline. It was amazing, thought Tom, what could be done with fat. Tall like her brother, certainly weighty, familiar with refuges and birds despite playing dumb —all this did not persuade Tom that Mrs. Meyer had a talent for murder. Shoplifting or blackmail, possibly. Or cheating at bingo. Tom, not yet aware of the second maverick checklist that Sarah had found, began his interrogation on a mild note.

But the questioning made heavy weather against a confused torrent of side subjects, and Tom listened with growing depression as Iris tacked erratically between Jesus and the Living Water; Sarah Deane and her Loss; her husband, Orwell, and his Lingering Illness; and her Dear Brother, the major. Her activities during the crucial time periods seem to have centered on citrus groves, shopping, and having dinner ready for her brother on Friday, and putting on her Austrian costume for Monday evening. For none of these times was there confirmation. Finally, Tom assisted her to rise, and, like a tug escorting an ocean vessel, got her to the door and out.

Johnny Shapiro, the office clerk, stopped him at the door. "Some people here come to see you," he announced. "An old man. He's talking up a storm out there. Name of Plummer. And a kid, and Dr. McKenzie. You got a call from the lab, too. Those brick pieces from that guy's head. They match the brick at Settlers Village."

"That settles that," said Tom. He grimaced. "I was afraid that ten minutes alone in my office was too good to be true. Okay, Johnny, when Professor Axminster and his wife show up for their ten-thirty slot, let 'em dangle out there for a while. I'd like them to get a feel for the place. And send McKenzie in first, will you?"

# XLIV

Professor Leo Axminster wrestled with his suitcase, pushing at protruding material and poking notebooks and netting in among folded shirts and pants. Into his wife's cosmetic case—innocent of cosmetics—he packed with trembling hands small cases of pinned and papered butterflies. These he swaddled with Vacation Villa towels and pillowcases. Then the professor sat on the edge of the unmade bed and looked at his watch. Just past ten. Janice must be running into a snag at the desk.

Unfortunately for the professor's plan, the ubiquitous Mr. Allen had gotten into the act, and Cheryl was at that moment executing a delaying maneuver with the Axminster credit card while the manager dialed the police. But Tom Pérez, busy with Major Foster's sister, had told Johnny Shapiro not to interrupt him short of an emergency. So Johnny took the message and put it on ice, and Janice, escaping at last from the manager's deliberately extended valedictory, bustled along to her room and assisted her mate in last-minute fastenings. When all was ready, she looked about the room and then opened her pouchlike handbag and slipped in two ceramic ashtrays with the motel crest, and, as an afterthought, added the Gideon Bible.

Twenty minutes later, the gray Land-Rover turned right out of Pharr and swung north on Route 281 and pointed at San Antonio.

# XLV

Unaware of the vanishing Axminsters, Tom greeted his friend. "It's Dr. McKenzie come to brighten my morning with Plummer and Kid Goldsmith. What's the idea? I'm seeing Jeff later anyway. Why Plummer? Protecting the rights of minors?"

"Easy, Tom. It's no joke." Alex sat down in the chair just vacated by Major Foster's sister and still warm from its contact with that impressive posterior. "Tom, I've got to force some more data from the bird world on you. It may be serious, so please listen."

"Don't preach, Alex," said Tom stiffly. "I'll hear anything you can say in fifteen minutes; then I've got the Axminsters."

Alex produced the second Doña Clara checklist and told Tom of Sarah's picking it up in the airplane aisle. "And, by God, it's as screwy as the one you found on the man by the river. It has to be a time-and-place code, and, I think, a ridiculously simple one."

"I thought I warned you off the code idea," said Tom.

"Only for a bit. I should have got on to it sooner, but I was hung up on the birds—the species themselves. Well, last night Sarah gave me the lead when she said to look at the numbers and letters. She's right. The list has nothing to do with birds."

"Okay, I'm ready. Go ahead and decode."

"Take the checklist from the body by the river. The underlined species indicate birds unique to south Texas. But forget the birds."

"Gladly," said Tom.

"The numbers next to the underlined species taken in sequence give you three, nineteen, six, forty-five, and then there's a circle penciled by jacana which I haven't figured out; it may mean P.M. rather than A.M. But we've got a date and a time. March 19 was the day the man was killed and six-forty-five is within the possible homicide period. Now take the birds with the check marks beside their names. The first letter of the species taken in order gives you R, G, B, C, and S."

"And what's that? A Rotary Club meeting?"

"Patience, Tomás. I had to fit the letters into the context of date, time, and place, and possibly into the drug scene. Well, C stood for Celluwell and cocaine or Chicago green—that's pot mixed with opium, or G for Golf Balls—those are barbiturates. Anyway there are probably a hundred street names for drugs that begin with the initial letters used on the checklist."

"Like Brown, which is Mexican heroin," broke in Tom, "or Bomber—that's a Texas reefer. You could go on forever."

"But I didn't. I began to work on the Doña Clara trail map, and bingo!"

"Bingo what?"

"Get your map. We're lucky because we can figure this out after the event. We know the man was killed by the Rio Grande, so the letter sequence can stand for Rio Grande, Bobcat Spur— taking Bob and Cat as two words probably to avoid confusion with some other trail. That's exactly where the body was found."

"And I can twist those letters around to mean a porno movie ad."

"Hold on. When I saw the second goofy list that Foster's sister dropped, I tried to see if it worked the same way, and lo and behold, see the numbers three, sixteen, three, twenty-seven. That's the date sister arrived in Boyden and the time her shuttle plane came into Harlingen from Corpus Christi. I checked with the airport this morning; it's a regular flight. She arrived in the afternoon, and the little circle is penciled in, so P.M. is a good guess on that mark."

"How about the letter sequence? I don't see any trails in Doña Clara fitting in," said Tom, frowning at the map.

"Not at Doña Clara, you don't. But sister didn't surface there. She turned up at L, A, R, T, B. That's Laguna Atascosa Ready Tour Bus. L for least grebe, A for American bittern, R for roseate spoonbill, T for turkey vulture, and B for black vulture. You begin the sequence with the first L starting at the top and then find the next initial letters in order as they occur on the Doña Clara list."

"But why not use a Laguna checklist if she's going there?"

"Unnecessarily complicated, although perhaps different refuge lists are used in rotation. But remember, birds as birds are irrelevant. Now I don't know how this all fits together. A Celluwell drop, maybe, with Mrs. All-American Widow Spider at the center."

"I'm speechless," said Tom. "But it all seems too easy once you get on to it. If you have."

"But it's beautiful. Who would look twice at a marked checklist with no one's name on it? They're as common as ticket stubs at a ball park. And I've been thinking about those Bino-View glasses. Hell, they could just be a cover. You suggested that the murdered man might be a bird-watcher with drugs as a sideline. How about a drug dealer with bird-watching on the side? Sarah was talking last night at dinner about not being able to read detective stories since Philip's murder, and she mentioned Jane Marple."

"Who in hell is she?"

"Jane Marple is one of Agatha Christie's detectives, an elderly female who snoops around with binoculars—to detect, or to be seen engaging in a legitimate activity while she snoops. Well, our guy wasn't detecting, but he may have used them as a cover for what he was really up to. No one looks twice at someone prowling around a refuge with binoculars—in fact, you look naked without them."

"Okay, Alex. I'll believe those lists are wacky, but I don't know that I'll buy the whole package yet. Let's put it together. This guy got his head smashed after bringing Celluwell over the border. With a brick, which, by the way, did come from Settlers Village. Say he was meeting someone because of this code message. Say the someone was in the refuge with a brick ready to clobber this guy for some reason. So where does Lentz fit in? Was he waiting for someone because of a funny checklist? Keep your hair on, Alex, that's a logical question. Well, I'll get Foster's sister in again and go back to her first baby shoes, and I'll scratch around in the major's backyard again. You know he's not a major?"

"A courtesy title, like Kentucky colonel?"

"Like a real colonel. In the marines yet. So he's not a fake

on that score. And now, amigo, what brings Jeff and Mr. Bird
Club here? Excuse me." Tom responded to the telephone buzzer.
"Yes, Cotton. . . . You have? . . . You're sure? . . . Has she been
to the morgue? All right, I'll cancel my eleven-thirty and see her
then. What's the name again? Thanks, Tiger." Tom hung up.

"We've got an I.D. for the second homicide. A Reynaldo
Sánchez from across Mexico way. His wife got hold of the Mexican police because he left home Monday morning and never came
back. Now I'll see Plummer and the kid, and I'll call and put off
the Cactus Wren ladies, which should make you happy."

Mr. Plummer, followed by Jeff, advanced into the room, his
expression animated. "So good of you, Lieutenant, to fit us in."

Tom indicated chairs. "Please sit down, sir. You, too, Jeff."

The problem, it seemed, was an ornithological one involving
the tricky business of verifying the presence of two pairs of rare
birds seen at Doña Clara on last Friday afternoon at almost the
same time.

"*Chondrohierax uncinatus aquilonis,* or in lay parlance, the
hook-billed kite," explained Mr. Plummer in a pleased voice,
"belongs to a large family of diurnal birds of prey. We are concerned here, Lieutenant, with a species with a noticeable hook on
its bill; a bird which can be found in several basic color patterns.
Now the adult . . ."

Alex, seeing desperation on Jeff's face and incomprehension
on Tom's, intervened. "Mr. Plummer, perhaps you would let me
summarize. Lieutenant Pérez is a layman, and you are too knowl-
edgeable for him."

Mr. Plummer subsided a bit reluctantly, Jeff and Tom
looked grateful, and Alex launched into a modified exposition.

"You see, Tom, the chance of four rare birds being seen at
almost the same time a short distance apart is very small. Possible
—anything's possible with birds—but not likely. First, we have
Sam reporting two of the kites at the south end of Bobcat Marsh
just before five on Friday. Now it gets interesting. Jeff left the
Lupine Lake Trail where he was supposed to stay with the others
of his club and took off down the Creosote Cut-off on up to the
Observation Tower, which overlooks Long Bone Lake and Bobcat Marsh—a detail he neglected to tell you about. From the
tower he looked at two hook-billed kites from five-forty until

five-forty-nine. Jeff says his watch keeps good time and that he always times the length of a sighting. Now, Major Foster reported two kites at Settlers Village about one minute afterward, and took his group the next day, Saturday, to try and see them there. Now do we have an explosion of hook-billed kites north of the border, or is something else going on?"

Tom fought a desire to kick his wastebasket across the room. Instead, he simply said in a repressed voice, "I don't know what this is leading to. Big Foster must know which bird is which."

"That's why we're here . . . to convince you that Jeff's sighting is just as valid as those of Sam and Foster. Remember, Sam spotted his kites just about where Jeff claims to have seen them, approximately an hour earlier."

"Birds fly," said Tom. "Even to Settlers Village."

"I've just said that Jeff saw them at the marsh and Foster at the village about one minute apart."

"Two big strong birds could probably make it to Brownsville in one minute," said Tom stubbornly.

At this impasse, Mr. Plummer interrupted and spoke, albeit without enthusiasm, of Jeff's work in the field with the Hamburg Club. "He does not always behave in social situations as one could wish"—here Jeff raised his eyes and darkly regarded the slowly revolving ceiling fan—"but I can vouch for his accuracy and attention to detail."

"What we're trying to say," said Alex, "is that . . ."

Tom looked up from a pad on which he had drawn a series of rudimentary pigeons with arrows through them. "What you're trying to say is that if Jeff is telling the truth, and if the chance of seeing two sets of rare birds at the same time in two different places is about zero, then Foster may have messed up his identification. Or he may be lying. Right?"

Alex nodded.

"And if he's lying, why? Why see birds you haven't seen? Prestige? Hell, he's got that already. He's a bird V.I.P."

Jeff, who had been unnaturally quiet, spoke. "Maybe Major Foster saw the kites, but not where he said. Maybe he got his locations mixed up."

"I'd guess," said Alex, "that Foster knows these refuges like his own face. He wouldn't make a mistake like that unless he wanted to. I'd love to challenge him on this in public."

For a moment there was silence, and then Jeff said, "About the time, the major always checks his watch because of the tour schedule."

"Jeff," said Alex, "have you told anyone besides Mr. Plummer and me about the kites you spotted from the tower on Friday?"

"I didn't want to."

"Why not?" said Tom sharply.

Jeff hesitated, troubled. "Well, because people would know I'd been near the murder place, and somebody stupid might think I did it."

"Were the kites why you ran off the next morning?" demanded Tom.

"Yes, sir," said Jeff in a low voice. "I just had to get loose on Saturday and see if I could find them again, because everyone was charging around the Settlers Village, and I couldn't see how a second pair of kites could have turned up there at almost the same time, even if Major Foster had said he'd seen them and—"

Tom broke in. "Okay, Jeff. Let's cut out the crap. Excuse me, Mr. Plummer. I want the truth, Jeff. Did you see anyone in the Bobcat Marsh area Friday afternoon? Hear anything? Did you see Philip Lentz murdered? Did you find the body Friday afternoon and then rediscover it for the police on Saturday morning? Answer me straight."

"No, Lieutenant. No way. I didn't see or hear anything. Not on the Auto Tour Road or from the tower. I never even got over to the Bobcat Marsh Trail on Friday. I just looked at the kites from the tower. I made a sketch and wrote down the details in my notebook. Remember, Dr. McKenzie, how I asked you about experts making I.D. mistakes on Monday when we were walking around the motel?"

"Yes," said Alex, "and I wish I'd known what you were driving at. You see, Tom, why Philip's notebook would be so handy. It might be confirmation for Jeff. Philip might have spotted the kites."

"We don't have it," said Tom. "We have Jeff's instead, for what it's worth. Okay, Jeff. Go on. Did you see anyone on the way back to join your group?"

"I was in a sweat to get back on time, so I don't think so."

"What the hell do you mean, 'don't think so'?"

"I looked behind me a couple of times, and once I thought I saw that big teacher, you know, that sort of tall ugly woman. She was way behind me."

"Damn," said Alex.

There followed the sort of pause described in literature as "pregnant." Tom fished forth a folder and made a deliberate entry, and then took up the thread of questioning as if there had not been an interruption. "Jeff, how come you're such an expert on south Texas birds? You must have different kinds back in New York."

Jeff looked at Tom with something like scorn. "Before you go to a strange place," he said slowly, as to a backward child, "you read up. You go through guides and checklists and listen to tapes of bird calls. Just now I'm studying up on Big Bend. I'm going to ask Major Foster and Mr. Ready if we can go there instead of . . ."

"Stop. Turn it off." Tom held up his hands. "I believe you. So you know Texas birds. Oh God, Johnny, what now?" This in response to a face in the doorway.

"Forgot about this." Johnny advanced and extended a note.

Tom scanned the paper and then pounded the desk, making two pencils jump. "Johnny, you've let them get away. Christ! Send out an all-points. And when someone picks up the professor and his missus, tell 'em to hold 'em by their balls and tits and get me on the horn. They're wanted for questioning in two homicides and for theft of federal property."

Tom turned back to his visitors. Mr. Plummer's face was a study in elderly disapproval, but Jeff was grinning. "Sorry, Mr. Plummer. We police are a little crude at times. It's the company we keep. Alex, I'll put this all in my little stove and cook it up. I'll do more. I'll put a tail on Foster's sister and, maybe, on Foster. And maybe not, because I don't see how I'm going to put the screws on Big about his bird identifications. He'd demolish me and Jeff. I'll have to have all of you, and Sam, too, sit in on a bird session. But if it's the kid's word against Foster's, you know who's going to win that one. Sam has a lot of respect for Foster. I've heard him say so. And now do you suppose anyone else is keeping their hook-billed kites a dark secret?"

Alex started. "Oh God . . . yes. When I was having tea at Sarah's campsite, Miss Fellows mentioned that she might just have seen the kites, but wasn't sure and so didn't report them."

"It wouldn't surprise me," said Tom, "to hear that there has been an invasion of these kites, and they're lining up to peck out the eyes of bird-watchers. Remember Hitchcock?"

# XLVI

Alex found Sarah seated on a fallen log behind her tent, filling her lantern. She shook her head as he approached.

"Alexander McKenzie, thank you very much for spending an uncomfortable night wedged in your car as my extra guard dog, but you needn't do it again tonight. Though," she added, "I hope you don't think I actually look on you as another Patsy."

"I can never come up to Patsy," said Alex firmly. "I know my place. And now I'll fill you in on the latest news. More birds. We're going to drive Tom out of his skull with them." And Alex told Sarah of the Axminster departure, and then of the conflict over the kite sightings, and of Jeff's seeing Miss Fellows Friday afternoon.

"What an awful mess," said Sarah. "None of it makes any sort of sense, and I'd say that Major Foster made a mistake and won't admit it. Pride, ego, hubris. I'll bet he's got lots of all those."

"So rise and shine, Sarah. I've got to go over to Narcotics and do some reading. Some new reports on Celluwell—a shipment's hit New Hampshire. I'll drop you at the motel because, Jane Marple, I'd like you to wander around, visit, and chat. The Hamburg Club has a free day, and some of the faithful may be about."

"With my notebook, binoculars, and loyal Irish wolf-hound?"

"That's the idea. Just take impressions, look for tidbits."


Sarah, walking up the motel driveway, found Jeff Goldsmith scanning the sky with his binoculars.

"Hello," he said. "It's a hawk flight—a kettle of broad-winged hawks. They're starting to migrate through."

"A kettle?" asked Sarah.

"Yeah. See them gliding in spirals." Jeff launched into an explanation of thermals, updrafts, buteos, and accipiters. "Boy," he finished, "I'd love to make it to Big Bend. Maybe some zone-tailed hawks will be there, even if it's too early for the Colima warbler."

"Stick with the tour, Jeff," said Sarah, "or you'll be shipped home in a cage."

"Major Foster said he's going there anyway, and a few of us could go with him. The others, like Mr. Plummer, could go on to the Edwards Plateau. Big Bend's got the Chisos Mountains, you know."

"Jeff, you can't turn the tour upside down. I'm sure it's a package deal with reservations made weeks ago."

"They can be unmade," said Jeff. "Adults just aren't flexible. I'm memorizing the common birds at Big Bend so I could help lead. Of course, we could head for Mexico and the rain forests," continued Jeff, undeflected by reason. "But I haven't studied up on the Mexican species . . . all those motmots and ant birds." He paused and then said unexpectedly, "Are you going to the program tonight? It's slides and stuff. The birds we've seen."

"No," said Sarah. "I hadn't planned on it."

"Mr. Plummer's doing snakes, and Mr. Ready's doing the Edwards Plateau, and I'm going to make a report. Dr. McKenzie would be interested. He knows quite a lot about the species down here."

"I don't know," said Sarah doubtfully, and then she remembered her role as observer. "All right, Jeff. I'll try and bring Alex." She looked up again at the sky and watched the wide-winged shapes spiral and rise, circle and drift down again. " 'Turning and turning in the widening gyre,'" she said. "'The falcon cannot hear the falconer; things fall apart . . .'"

"Broad-winged hawks aren't falcons," said Jeff. "They're buteos. That's a mistake a lot of people make. Look at the shape of the wings."

"Would you like to take Patsy for a run?" asked Sarah, vowing never again to waste a perfectly good quotation on such barren ground.

But Jeff was not to be diverted by a dog. "No, thanks. Patsy's okay, but some of us are going on the bus and have another look around Doña Clara. I don't need a day to pack up and relax in."

Sarah, rebuffed, walked toward the side entrance leading to the garden. Ahead she saw the Cactus Wren wagon loading its complement of Morton students. Mrs. Brent waved. "Sarah, we are just running over to the McAllen Sewer Ponds for shore birds. Won't you join us?"

Sarah declined with thanks and sauntered on to the garden, thinking that Miss Fellows, who had stood in the background, looked troubled, more as she had in the first days of the visit. It isn't an easy time for her, Sarah thought. She knows she's due for more questioning. Rounding the terrace wall, she came up against Eleanor Lucas, sitting in a canvas chair, a pile of workbooks at her feet, a red pencil in her hand.

Sarah halted. "Hello, Eleanor," she said tentatively.

Miss Lucas looked up. "Hello, Sarah. Looking for someone?"

"No, not really. Just visiting, giving Patsy a change of scene. Are you correcting papers?" she asked unnecessarily.

"Yes, the usual. The girls are getting half a credit for this trip, and I'm going to see that they earn it. They probably won't be getting a proper exam in ornithology, which they would have had if . . ."

Sarah took a breath and finished the sentence: ". . . if Philip had been here."

For a moment the name stood between them, and then Eleanor Lucas looked steadily at Sarah. "Yes, Philip would have seen to a proper written final." She paused and then said, "Things haven't worked out, have they, Sarah? For either of us."

"No," said Sarah. Miss Lucas was silent. "I'll leave you in

peace." Sarah took a step away and then stopped. "I'm sorry about everything, Eleanor." What a stupid remark, she told herself.

Eleanor Lucas lifted her shoulders slightly. "That's all right. It's the way things happen sometimes." She bent her head again over the workbook in her lap and made a slash with a red pencil.

Sarah took herself off. She heard her Grandmother Douglas's voice: "Least said, soonest mended." Well, perhaps, but Sarah doubted it. A crevasse separated the two women, with Philip Lentz at the bottom of it.

"Come on, Patsy," called Sarah. She broke into a run, and Patsy pulled ahead, making little half-stifled barks against his collar. At the other end of the garden she discovered Lois Bailey and Connie Goldsmith sitting in the shade of a tree.

"Hi, Sarah. How about lunch?" Mrs. Goldsmith put down her book. "Our last day here—for which I'm grateful. Enough is enough. The police have our addresses and where we'll be next week. Peace today. Nina's off playing with some children she met at the pool. How about you, Sarah? We'll miss you."

"Oh, I don't know about me. I think I'll take off with Patsy when I'm not needed here . . . which I'm really not."

"Peach cobbler for dessert today," said Lois Bailey with enthusiasm. "The whole scene is breaking up—all but the Morton girls, who are stuck here with their teachers, the two older women, because of finding that second body. First the butterfly couple disappeared, and today, I heard, Major Foster's sister left."

"She's gone?" Sarah's voice squeaked in surprise.

"Apparently." Mrs. Goldsmith did not sound as if she wished to linger on the subject. "She meant well, but what a bore. On and on about her husband and her hysterectomy."

"I've just remembered a telephone call I should make," said Sarah abruptly. "Could you please hold on to Patsy?" Sarah ran into the motel to the lobby telephone booth, reported Mrs. Meyer's departure to Johnny Shapiro, and returned to the terrace.

"She really had it for him bad," said Cheryl Cabot, who had watched Sarah from her overlook in the lobby.

"Who did?" asked Mr. Allen, who was writing Miracle Bird Tours into their room slots on Oriole Hall.

"She did. Sarah Deane. For Philip Lentz. She still looks all shook up."

"We seem to have survived the murders," said Mr. Allen with satisfaction. "Two bird tours due tomorrow, and the Axminster room is booked for the week. Only one day lost when they checked out early."

"And a few towels, pillowcases, and ashtrays," said Cheryl, who ate lunch with the housekeeper.

# XLVII

Tom Pérez endured a stormy session with Señora Sánchez, new-made widow of the second victim. Señora Sánchez had been incoherent with, alternately, grief and rage. It had been hard to tell which feeling would win out, but at the end of the interview Tom thought that rage had a small edge.

Señora Sánchez had not had the support expected of a husband. Jobs had been few and uncertain, yet there had been intermittent evidences of money: a new suit for himself, and a swing for the porch. But nothing coming her way, and with five children all needing shoes—the Holy Virgin knew that she tried to be patient, and he promised to be home Monday night and not stay away from home so long. She prayed for him, but he was up to no damn good, she was sure. And the TV set. He had brought it home proudly last week. But they had no electricity. She had put a flowerpot on it. He was a good man . . . no, he was a bad man. Bad to make her go to the police to find him, bad to make her come over the border to see him in the morgue. No, she didn't know why he crossed the river when he shouldn't have. Why did he get himself killed with five children at home? "Holy Mary, Mother of God, what will I do now?"

Tom could make sense of nothing beyond the fact that Señor Sánchez had been up to something—Celluwell?—that was paying off. In suits, porch swings, and TV sets anyhow. Tonight, said Tom to himself as he climbed the stairs back to his office, come hell or high water, I'll take in an early show. With a girl. That new Woody Allen at the drive-in. Screw homicide.

# XLVIII

Waldo Plummer, notes in hand, dinner napkin still tucked into his belt, made his way like the old war-horse he was directly to the lectern in the Rotary Room, where Arthur Ready quietly relieved him of his napkin. Mr. Plummer smiled upon Mr. Ready and beamed upon the rows of empty chairs.

"The identification of reptiles," he said to Mr. Ready, "is a neglected subject among laymen who, because of a negative gestalt, so often give a startle response. I shall set the scene with a sketch of the biotic provinces of Texas, focusing on the Tamaulipan and the Balconian—the environments where we have been and to which we go. I shall begin by asking, 'What is a snake?' "

Fifteen minutes later found the Rotary Room audience sitting up and taking notice of Mr. Plummer's slides. If the biotic provinces left them indifferent, the specific query "What is a pit viper?" shook them awake. Mr. Plummer had hit upon one of the great human truths: venomous snakes turn people on. Happy again at the lectern, he introduced the genus *Crotalus*, or the rattlesnake, and for once, as he swept from the timber rattlesnake (*C. horridus*), the rock rattlesnake (*C. lepidus*), to the western diamondback (*C. atrox*), he had his listeners on the ropes. The prairie rattlesnake, he assured them, thrives in many habitats, and the diamondback, which can grow to seventy-two inches, is fearless and aggressive, standing its ground and giving battle if disturbed.

These last facts caused stirrings among the audience, and even widened the eyes of the intrepid Cactus Wren leaders. Particularly alert were those from the Boyden community who had come to the motel under the impression that this was the night for tennis movies.

Then Arthur Ready, faithful to his name, rose in the middle of Mr. Plummer's exegesis of the neurotoxic venom of *Micrurus fulvius*, the eastern coral snake, shook Mr. Plummer's hand, and added that he doubted whether any member of his tour would ever see a coral snake.

Mr. Ready then took his audience through a photographic ramble of the Edwards Plateau and spoke temptingly of the pleasant climate, the spring-fed rivers, and of the possibility of an early-arriving golden-cheeked warbler.

Lois Bailey, filled with a banquet dinner of Chicken Rio Grande, slumbered, her head against a pillar at the side of the room; Mrs. Goldsmith yawned; and the rest of the audience watched or fidgeted according to the dictates of interest or comfort. However, there was a reviving rustle when Arthur Ready stepped down and Big Foster took the floor to wrap up the week's sightings and to present slides illustrating the several rarities seen: the Bahama duck at Laguna, the jacana at Alta Hollow, and the hook-billed kites at Doña Clara.

"Though we never did find them," Mrs. Bailey whispered.

Mrs. Goldsmith said that she'd never seen a more disagreeable expression than the one on that female kite, and Alex leaned over from his seat behind her and said, "Hence the expression 'hell-kite,' " and Sarah said, "Macbeth, Act IV," and Eduardo, doing double duty as projector operator, clicked the last slide into place. A white line of great egrets appeared, flying across an evening sky the color of watermelon with the legend "Ready to Tour" showing like a golden ribbon along the darkened bottom of the screen.

"Tacky," whispered Mrs. Goldsmith.

"Kitsch," said Sarah.

"But effective," said Alex.

"Hush," said Mrs. Bailey.

Major Foster stepped before the screen and called for lights and asked for questions. To the general annoyance, Mrs. van Hoek was on her feet, tossing a scarf with a practiced hand over her shoulder, and claiming in a throaty voice to have seen a northern beardless tyrannulet, "just outside the Doña Clara Refuge office."

"Good grief, what's that?" asked Mrs. Goldsmith.

"Hush," said Mrs. Bailey, "she's just showing off."

". . . a tan-gray bird," said Mrs. van Hoek, lifting her chin to improve her profile. "It said 'peee-yuk' and 'squeee-up,' just as the book said it did. I knew right away it was unusual."

The major was Deep South and gallant. "Ah would nevah contrahdict a lovely lady, but it is a very difficult bird to identify. Ah would not say y'all could not see it, but it might be one of those pesky *Empidonax* flycatchers, but Ah thank you."

Arthur Ready stood up and said, "And I, too, thank you for sharing, and now I see another hand. Yes, young man?"

Jeff Goldsmith got to his feet, holding open a small notebook. "Major Foster," he began, but his unreliable thirteen-year-old voice rose to a high tenor, and he had to swallow and begin again. "Major Foster, I want to report sighting two hook-billed kites on Friday afternoon at the eastern edge of Bobcat Marsh. I identified a male and a female, both adults. The light was adequate. I saw them from the Observation Tower at five-forty, and I watched for nine minutes. Then they took off and went into the woods." Jeff paused, panting.

"Oh Christ!" groaned Alex. "Wouldn't you know."

"Shhh," said Sarah. "I thought he might try something."

Big Foster smiled at the audience. "Well, now, Jeff boy, so that's where you went on Friday afternoon. Why haven't you mentioned this great discovery of yours before?"

"Because I knew you had reported two kites at the Settlers Village at about the same time, and I thought everyone would laugh if I said there were two more kites in the refuge."

"Why, Jeff, golly," said Major Foster with a chuckle. "We'll have to mark that bird as abundant on the checklist, won't we, Arthur?"

Jeff broke in. "I have a sketch in my field notebook, and I'd like to put the kites on the tour record."

"Jeff boy," said the major, "all these good folks are pretty anxious to get up and have their coffee and some of those brownies."

But Jeff held his ground. "The female," he said doggedly,

"was mostly darkish brown with reddish-brown stripes on her underparts and with a long hooked bill, and the male was gray-headed with the same bill, and when they flew, the tails were long and broad, and they were in the same plumage you reported your kites in, and—"

"Jeff," said the major, still smiling, "you can mark it on your own checklist, but we can't tinker with the official tour list. We'd need confirmation, a photograph, and now—"

Suddenly, Sarah was on her feet. "Major Foster, do you really think that there were four kites in the refuge at the same time?"

The major's temper was showing. "I don't think Jeff Goldsmith saw any kites. The boy just wanted to get into the act. Thank you, Miss Deane, and you, Jeffrey. You have contributed greatly to our meeting," said the major loudly.

But Sarah, her face flushed, held up her hand and faced an increasingly puzzled and restive audience. "Jeff is a very sharp birder, and he takes very good field notes." Sarah bit her lip, and then took a deep breath. "I confirm Jeff's kites; I was at the Bobcat March at five-forty-five on Friday. I took a picture of them."

Major Foster marched to the opposite wall, switched on the ceiling light, said "Thank you" in an even louder voice, and the audience rose and churned toward the waiting refreshment table at the back of the room.

Alex grabbed Sarah's arm. "What the hell . . . Sarah! For God's sake, what did you say that for? You weren't at the marsh Friday afternoon, you were at the motel. What are you trying to do?"

Sarah, still red in the face, smiled. "I got carried away. It was an ad lib. I thought Jeff needed a little support."

"Christ, save me from imaginative women . . . and from kids who can't leave bad enough alone. Come on, let's find Jeff." Alex strode off, followed by Sarah, and finally caught up with the boy in the lobby, a brownie in one hand, a glass of beer in the other.

"Someone lifted it for me," said Jeff, indicating the glass. "How did you like my report, Dr. McKenzie? You said at the police office you'd like someone to challenge Major Foster on his kites, and besides, I had to put my kites on the tour record."

"Jeff," said Alex ruefully, "sometimes silence is golden. Leave the police work to the police. Don't push your luck. Mr. Plummer and I believe in your kites. That's enough for now."

On the drive to the campground, Alex turned to Sarah and said, "Well, Madame Ad Lib, that was quite an evening at the theatre."

"Theatre of the Absurd, I think," said Sarah. "If the major's lying, he's doing a good job of it. Jeff and my little walk-on part didn't shake him much. Maybe we need an apparition, Banquo's ghost, or a headless horseman."

"Or it's as you said. He blew his identification and won't retract. Hell . . . or, more to the point, hell-kite."

"You don't suppose," said Sarah, "that the whole Arthur Ready thing is just a big front?"

"But the Ready Tours have a top reputation, and Tom ran a complete check on Foster; he came out clean and shining, plus he's a real live colonel in the Marine Corps reserve."

"Maybe that's why he didn't get rattled tonight. A colonel wouldn't have much trouble with a raw recruit like Jeff."

"And then there's sister lady . . ."

"Oh, Alex, she's gone off. I left word at Tom's office."

"She won't disappear. Tom has a tail on her." Alex turned the car and pulled in by the dim outline of Sarah's tent. "We'll just call tonight an unsuccessful happening. Hell, let's have it the Axminsters. The notorious butterfly murderers. I think the professor is an arrogant bastard, and his wife, under that little-girl dress she bounces around in, is all steel and teeth. I keep hoping to hear that a net has dropped over their heads, and that they've confessed to both murders and to the manufacture of Celluwell out of butterfly wings."

"And I think it's Major Foster's sister."

"Iris Meyer as the Godmother? I can't buy it."

"Bull," said Sarah succinctly. "I don't trust women who pat cheeks. Husband Orwell is probably some code name. And now it's bedtime, Alex. Good night, and you don't have to curl up in your car and play Red Cross Knight. I'm okay. Really. I've got Patsy, the poor wench's Grendel."

"I think you've got your stories mixed up, English teacher.

But all right. I'll pick you up for lunch at twelve. I've fixed it up with the ladies Goldsmith and Bailey. A last meeting."

That night Sarah lay on her sleeping bag pondering duplicate sets of hook-billed kites, and then irritably pushed them out of her mind. Kites, Major Foster, his sister, Jeff Goldsmith, the Axminsters, Miss Fellows, Eleanor Lucas . . . she was sick of the lot of them.

She pulled her pillow under her head and was about to turn over when, all at once, she had the sense of a form, a shadow, as if a cloud had passed over the tent . . . in the darkness a greater dark. Sarah lay, suddenly stiff, and then she heard a soft movement, a shuffle of footsteps on the sand near the entrance flap, and at the same instant, Patsy lifted his head and howled—a strangled, unearthly howl as if a hundred wolflike ancestors within him gave tongue. Sarah, perspiring, her hands clutching the edge of her sleeping bag, felt rather than saw the figure withdraw a space and stand still.

Somewhere far off down the path, a pauraque whistled and, as if in answer, a screech owl quavered.

And Patsy raised his head and howled again.

# FRIDAY, MARCH 22

## XLIX

Friday was, for many, a day of arrivals and departures, of alarms and excursions.

A few miles south of Dallas in a diner set on the edge of Waxahachie, Professor Axminster and his wife settled into their booth and ordered apple juice, eggs over easy with grits on the side, and Postum, for a shared life had brought them to shared tastes in breakfasts. From an open map the professor traced a route north through New Mexico and Colorado, but just as his pencil was crawling between the mountains in Durango, they were interrupted by two men in uniform who, combining breakfast with duty, had discovered the wanted Land-Rover parked at the nearby motel.

Professor Axminster looked up at the two men and bent again over the dissection of an egg yolk from its white collar.

"Mr. Axminster?" began the taller of the two men.

The professor transferred the egg yolk through the thicket of his beard into his mouth and chomped down.

"Mr. and Mrs. Axminster?" said the man.

"My dear," said the professor to his wife when he had swallowed his egg, "these men have something to say." He looked at the two. "You may sit down and join us for coffee—or, if you prefer as we do, Postum—and we will talk. Janice, these officers, if they are officers, will join us, and I will explain to them all about academic titles and the difference between 'doctor' and 'professor.' "

Twenty minutes later the Land-Rover, under close escort, drove up to the police station at Waxahachie, and the professor and his wife, followed by the two uniformed men, made their way through the door.

To the sergeant at the desk, the professor expressed, in tones of peevish irritation, his opinion of police systems that spent their time and treasure hounding visitors from other states.

"All right, Mr. Axminster," said the sergeant. "You and your wife can wait out in the hall while I do some telephoning to Boyden."

The Axminsters retreated to the hall, and a frosted glass door closed after them. Janice turned to her spouse and said in her natural voice, which was uncommonly like a whisper, "There's a door that goes out right next to the ladies' room."

Thus it was that shortly after their arrival at the police station, the professor and his lady were back in their Land-Rover turning onto a small road that headed northwest.

"What do you say, love," said Leo Axminster, "to leaving the Rover at a garage in Fort Worth and picking up a rental?"

"I think that's a real fine idea, Leo," said Janice as she spread her road atlas across her dirndl-covered knees.

# L

Back in Boyden, the morning was turning into the sort of humid overcast day that demands a change of wind and an opening of clouds for its relief. However, things went on as before at Vacation Villa, and the departure of one group merely signaled the coming of another. Mr. Allen, in turn, bade farewell and rubbed his palms together in anticipation.

The luggage of the Hamburg Bird Club had begun arriving in the lobby before breakfast and grew by heaps thereafter, antique honors going, hands down, to Waldo and Enid Plummer, who arrived with two suitcases made of some extinct amphibian and decorated with faded and tattered stickers of the Cunard Line.

In the corner of the lobby, Jeff Goldsmith was badgering his aunts. "Just look at this neat book. *Birds of the Big Bend National Park and Vicinity*. If you could talk to Mr. Ready about not spending a lot of time fooling around the Edwards Plateau . . ."

"Jeff, for heaven's sake, be quiet," said Constance Goldsmith.

"Major Foster's going west. Maybe I could go to Big Bend with him. Please, Aunt Connie. Please, Aunt Lois."

Lois Bailey turned on Jeff. "You, Jeff, are becoming one big pain in the neck. Major Foster has better things to do than escort you to Big Bend. Now forget it."

"Amen," said Alex, who had joined the group. "Listen, Jeff. The Edwards Plateau has bats. Caves with millions of Mexican free-tailed bats. Don't be narrow. Branch out."

"Hello, Dr. McKenzie," growled Jeff. "I don't like bats. They can suck your blood and give you rabies. I'll get my things now." And Jeff stamped off in the direction of his room.

"Oh dear," sighed Constance Goldsmith, looking after the

boy. She turned to Alex. "We're meeting you and Sarah for lunch?"

"Yes," said Alex. "The new Dandy's, east of McAllen. I hear you're doing the Edinburg farm country this morning. Now I have a question. Did anything strike you about last night?"

"You mean the lecture?" asked Mrs. Bailey. "I dozed through a lot of it . . . except those awful snake slides. But yes, I was surprised at Jeff going on about the kites. What nerve."

"Sarah was kind to stand up for him," put in Mrs. Goldsmith.

"How do you think Major Foster handled the questions?" persisted Alex.

"Well, I think he kept his temper pretty well," said Mrs. Goldsmith. "After all, Jeff almost suggested the major didn't know a kite when he saw it."

Alex gave it up. "See you both later." He strode out of the lobby to his car and headed for Tom's office.

# LI

A cardinal called in the oak tree above Sarah's tent: "what cheer? what cheer? cheer, cheer, twoo, twoo." Inside the tent everything seemed quite ordinary, and the idea of a nocturnal apparition seemed ridiculous. "Sarah Deane, chicken heart," said Sarah aloud, but she gave Patsy an appreciative thump.

Once outside, Sarah made her breakfast and then addressed herself to the emerging morning. It was increasingly evident to her that as an outdoor girl she was an utter fraud. I don't even know what kinds of trees these are, she said to herself with chagrin. Suddenly, she stood up and detached Patsy from his station by the hammock. "All right, dog," she said. "We're going for a nature walk."

Sarah's intention was a laudable one, but the human mind cannot be so easily diverted from its favorite subject of self. Sarah walked with Patsy and looked with a serious expression at the labels on pines and huisaches and catclaws, and listened to vireos and flycatchers, and thought about Philip Lentz and Sarah Deane. And so, wandering down the park's La Paloma Trail, she began examining a disturbing and growing sense of guilt. At first, it seemed tied to the shock of Philip's death, but then it detached itself and began to lead an uneasy life of its own and to call itself by its proper name.

Sarah asked herself, but why do I feel guilty? It's because I never had a chance to settle things. Are you, asked an ironic inner voice, saying that you never said goodbye? How trite, what a cop-out! You feel guilty, the voice reminded her as she stared without seeing at a prickly pear, for a damn good reason. You were using Philip as a prop, a crutch, until you felt better about Pres. But Philip was serious. He didn't play Ping-Pong with people. But you were going to lean on him, let him make you all safe and comfortable. Then you were going to ditch him, weren't you? I wouldn't do that, Sarah told herself. Want to bet? said the voice. "Oh hell," said Sarah aloud, and she kicked a lump of dirt out of her path.

She found now that she had walked full circle on the trail and was heading into the trailer and recreational-vehicle area. Sarah shortened Patsy's leash and entered into a tightly packed village of huge silver and cream-colored machines bright with awnings, lights, and hanging beach towels. Like gigantic carp come to spawn, they lay in semicircles attached to earth by long corrugated lines of blue, white, and green exterior viscera. Tiny plastic picket fences, plaster dwarfs, mushrooms, and flights of plaster ducks gave Sarah the sense of having wandered into a remote section of the Munchkin country and, feeling like a creature from another world, she guided Patsy back to her tent . . . from the Munchkin country to the Gilliken country . . . and beyond lay the Deadly Desert.

Sarah sat atop her picnic table and surveyed her kingdom. She remembered that Dorothy, if things weren't going right in Kansas, had only to sit with her dog Toto at a certain time of day and make a special sign, and Ozma, watching in the Emerald City, would touch her magic belt and, swoosh, Dorothy would be transported back to Oz. Oz, where no one died; Oz, a perpetual childhood with Ozma, the magic mother, presiding and rescuing you whenever a wicked witch or a tyrant king got uppity.

So, said Sarah to herself, I've gotten myself transported to Alta Hollow State Park, and I've got a magic dog and a magic tent and a magic stove and a magic toilet, and it's bloody well time I got out of Oz and back to Kansas—or at least to Boston.

Sarah, resolute, climbed off her picnic table and looked severely at her tent. In another week she would have to be back teaching and going to her seminars at Boston University. She saw that all her life she had believed, like Dorothy, that someone would turn up and do things for her, or with her, while she played at being the liberated woman. Her whole life had been made by protective screens, loving parents, Miss Morton's boarding school. And at college, when she was adrift for the first time, Pres had turned up and they had played house together. And when she lost Pres—why, there was Philip ready to take charge of her life. With a sickening rush, she recognized that part of her distress at Philip's death was because someone so orderly, so responsible, had had the temerity to get himself killed and leave her without the support to which she had become accustomed.

Oh, said Sarah's small voice, now we have it. Philip let *you* down . . . you, you . . . barnacle, hanging on to him while the poor guy thought you loved him. And you're so sorry for yourself. Shame. Oh, you are a monster. And look at Alex McKenzie, right on deck as doctor-nursemaid, so that great big Sarah can go on living in Oz. Sarah clutched her head. Why, right now she was probably planning deep inside her nasty barnacle self to have Alex available in Boston taking her about in his Volvo while she puttered around in graduate school and taught schoolchildren that it was better to turn into little fairy-tale addicts than little Gradgrinds. A dose of Gradgrindism would do her good. Men weren't playmates like Pres, or manager-fathers like Philip, or Red Cross Knights like Alex. They were semi-hairy omniverous bipeds and life was real and everyone should learn to walk on his own two feet through the mud—or excrement, as Alex had reminded her. Yeats was right.

I'll do a self-heal program, Sarah told herself, and she

remembered that long-ago exchange with Alex when she told him that self-healing was such a bother. "I'll do something useful," she said to Patsy. "The Peace Corps or Vista." And Sarah strode to her tent and began breaking camp.

## LII

Alex opened Tom Pérez's door and collided with the torso of Captain Nordstrom, who, magenta of face, pushed past and out.

"He's got a bad tooth," explained Tom. "It hasn't improved my morning briefing much. Can you do better?"

Alex sat down and shook his head. "Sorry. Our boy wonder took it on himself to face Big Foster after the lecture with that kite-sighting conflict, and Sarah got into the act. Amateur night. Nothing came of it. Foster hardly got warm under the collar."

"Jeff had better shut up or he's going to find himself playing hardball. Okay, Alex. We've done some work on Iris Meyer. As follows. She is indeed a widow. Husband died last year. Cancer. She visits Boyden often, stays with her brother at his house here, and joins birding tours from time to time. Refuge personnel think she's fairly sharp about birds—no beginner anyway—which confirms Sarah's impression. Never been seen to pull anything funny. On the contrary."

"The very model of a model major's sister."

"You said it. Goes to church, plays cribbage with the local ladies, and so forth. That's all, except"—Tom paused and passed a hand through his hair in his habitual gesture—"it may not mean a damn thing, but husband Orwell was a pharmacist. Sold out to a cousin four years ago. It's a chain, if you call five stores a chain. One in Nueces, one in Refugio, one in Webb, two in Victoria."

"And this cousin?" Alex leaned forward, interested.

"Larry Potts. Lives in Houston. A chiropractor who doesn't work at it. Orwell and Potts are clean—no records. Hell, Alex, this may just be more crap. Owning pharmacies isn't against the law."

"Smells like a lead, though."

"If there's any pattern to sister's trips to Boyden and Celluwell shipments to the Northeast, I'll pull her in so fast her girdle will pop. Did you know she's skipped town? But all's well. My spies say she's safe home in Corpus."

"Her life-style? Comfortable?"

"Nice house. Seems to live over what's presumed to be her income—charge accounts, church donations, but she tells everyone how generous her brother is. Here's the picture I'm trying not to believe: Iris Meyer toting raw Celluwell from Boyden to Cousin Potts, who has it cut, packaged, and sent out east, north, and west, where it dives under the counter and does one hell of a business."

Alex looked thoughtful. "We may have to swallow Foster as his sister's cover—chivalry, family style. He may have been shielding her for a long time, but now that she's added murder to her act, he isn't about to turn her in. Besides, he's an accessory. He may even help her, lie for her. Because if he doesn't, there goes his job, his tour-leading, which he obviously rejoices in. And somehow, somewhere, those damn kites fit into the picture."

"Can you see me," said Tom irritably, "going to Nordstrom and the D.A.'s office with a couple of oddball checklists and some mumbo jumbo about a kid who saw two Mexican birds that Foster claims to have seen somewhere else, and say I want to pull in Foster's sister? Hell, I'd be blown right into the Brownsville dump."

"Try saying you've two elderly teachers, a botany female with a grudge, or a pair of butterfly burglars."

Tom groaned. "It's a real freak show. And you'll be interested to hear that the Waxahachie police had their hooks into the Axminsters and let them slip. They're off and running."

"Bonnie and Clyde."

"What a waste of police energy and equipment. Hell, I'd like to drop the two of them—send them along to face Sam Hernández, who's waiting with open jaws—but they won't let me, behaving like big-time fugitives."

"Did you do another scan on Big Foster?"

"Very boring. Local schools, varsity football, university biology prize—no dummy. U. Texas at Austin. Korean War, marine commission, reserves. Makes me yawn."

"Police record?"

"Are you kidding? Not even for speeding. Has got one wife, two kids. Is an Elk, a Lion, and Mr. Birdman of Boyden. He's Major Good and Colonel Brave. Stop me if you've heard this."

"What about home life?" asked Alex. "Conspicuous consumer, trips to Vegas, collection of Nazi flags or hand grenades?"

"Nice house in Boyden. Very nice. Started out average size and grew wings."

"Like an angel?"

"Wings, patios, a pool, an office. On the expensive side of town. That posh-deluxe setting is the only thing that attracts my attention, but what the hell, he's been working at two jobs for a long time. Wins sales awards, so he must be good at the glass-china business, and he's Art Ready's favorite leader in these parts. One more thing. Foster's got quite a few bank accounts around, so I'm going to find out if there's any sort of pattern to his deposits that doesn't tie in with his salary picture."

Alex rose and wandered over to the window behind Tom's desk and saw a gray cloud of pigeons explode from the cornice above him and flutter to the sidewalk below. He watched as a small dog lifted its leg against the rear tire of a light-colored Cadillac and then trotted diagonally across the street and disappeared. Alex turned and faced Tom. "That's it. Your special assistant McKenzie can't hack it any longer. What's the point? I'm not helping Philip or Sarah. Or you."

"Oh hell, Alex, the crime business is probably like the medicine business. Up two steps, back three. Win some, lose some, screw some up."

"And I think I'd better stick to screwing up what I know best. I was supposed to be looking into Celluwell, and I've only been over to Narcotics once. Time to get on with my own work."

"Come off it. You've helped a lot—you and Sarah. That checklist code idea is pretty good, and even if we don't get a murderer out of it, the Foster lead isn't hopeless. We may throw him to the income-tax wolves, and we haven't finished with sister

Iris. Hell, you've helped me keep my wig on, and I may turn into a bird-watcher yet—or learn to love pigeons."

"Someday I'll take you out to a lake in the early morning, and let the birds and the ducks go past and you'll understand."

"Don't count on it. Once a cop . . ."

"And, Tom, if you've finished with Sarah, I can drive her to Corpus Christi, start her on the road home."

"Yes, I'm finished. Are you? Don't answer. Keep in touch, Alejandro. You know I have to follow up on those schoolteachers. If Fellows saw kites anywhere near the marsh—well, that's one more nail in her case."

Alex sighed. "I can't protect the Cactus Wren ladies. I'm just sorry for them. And I'm sorry for Eleanor Lucas, too. She looks so damned unhappy."

"Hey, almost forgot, Alex. I've got a piece of news on that score. We went back to some of the people who'd been in Doña Clara that Friday afternoon when Lentz was strangled, and one of the Troop 7 Boyden Boy Scouts identified a photo of Lucas as the woman who'd yelled at him for stepping on some kind of special plant and then gave him a lecture about destroying wild-flowers. The kid wrote the plant up in his logbook—he's trying for a nature merit badge—and he wrote down the time—five-twenty—and place. Nowhere near the Bobcat Marsh during the murder time period. And the kid followed Lucas all around the refuge at a safe distance and out to the parking lot at six-thirty where he met his troop. He'd gotten separated from them in the refuge."

"Why didn't the boy come out with all of this earlier?"

"Kid was afraid Lucas would report him for wrecking refuge plants and he wouldn't get his badge. So much for 'scout's honor.' "

"Well," said Alex, "that's one suspect off the books. Eleanor Lucas is probably guilty of wishing Philip dead, and then, when it happened, feeling even more guilty. No wonder she's been having headaches. So I'm off, Tomás. *Hasta luego.*"

"Wait, Alex, so you can exit laughing. Mrs. van Hoek, who always sounds like she's talking through a mink coat, called and said she was sure she'd seen Major Foster several places he shouldn't have been."

"Like the ladies' room?"

"I thanked her, and she said it was such fun knowing some-one in police work, and how was Dr. McKenzie?"

"He's in a flight pattern," and Alex closed the door behind him. In the outer office he stopped at a desk where Sergeant Cotton was groping through what looked like an unabridged dictionary.

"Hi, there, Tiger," said Alex. "How about lunch today if you can get a break? I'm picking up Sarah Deane at noon, so I can do the same for you. If Tom hassles you, I'll say you're my new patient. Suffering from severe malnutrition."

When the Volvo swept around the bend and stopped at Tent Site 137, Sarah was standing by the picnic table surrounded by her household goods, packaged, duffeled, and stuff-bagged. Patsy lay with his head athwart the sleeping-bag roll, eyes half closed, waiting. Alex eyed the collection, opened his mouth to speak, and then thought better of it. Sergeant Cotton was not so restrained.

"Miss Deane, are you givin' up the camping idea? I know it looks somethin' like rain, but don't let that scare you off."

Sarah said she was very glad to see him again, but that she thought that it was time she got going.

"Where?" asked the sergeant, concerned. "I'd sure hate to be losin' track of Patsy, here—and you, too."

Sarah slid a look at Alex, but he only waved her into the car and said, "We're off. Lunch and the greatest food show in Texas."

## LIII

The chain of Dandy's Cafeterias loops across the lower abdomen of Texas and presents a spread certain to rock the most ardent dieter off the wagon. This particular link is laid outside of

McAllen in one of those concrete cubes that make up the blight known as the shopping plaza. In consideration of Patsy's comfort, the Volvo was parked under a post-oak tree at the edge of the lot, and the three diners made for the end of the waiting line. Sarah, hurrying between the two men, thought only Sergeant Cotton could make Alex look small. Six feet seven inches and at least two hundred and thirty pounds amiably overlooked six feet.

After some few minutes of foot shuffling, the wonders of Dandy's came in view. Peering ahead, Sarah caught sight of rows of glass dishes sitting on an incline of shaved ice: puddings, tortes, tarts, meringues, bombes, floating islands—all flanked by batteries of fresh fruit. Dumbfounded, Sarah, Alex, and Tiger Cotton inched their way past salads, vegetables, and then joints, tongues, chops, ribs, carne picada, paella, things sauté and things flambé, all followed by schools of cooked fish on shoals of ice.

Sarah pushed her already loaded tray ahead and said, "It's the American dream gone haywire. Sixty chickens in every pot."

"Shove along, lady," said Alex. "Look at our friend Tiger."

The sergeant smiled a bit sheepishly. His tray was crowded with a host of saucers and dishes, all surrounding a molded casserole the size of a football. "I can't say no," he admitted.

Moving forward, Sarah made out across a forest of tables a waving hand attached to the person of Constance Goldsmith.

"We put two tables together," said that lady, making room for Sarah's tray, "but after seeing your lunch, Sergeant, we need three."

Sarah sat down and looked about her. It's a twentieth-century orgy, she thought, appalled, fascinated, as she watched the waitresses in their aprons and mobcaps, multiplied by the huge ceiling-to-floor mirrors, move about as if in some special choreographed feast ceremony, bowing over tables, cradling pitchers of ice water. "Is everything all right? Would you care for coffee? *Un coctel? Té? Con limón? Con crema? Otra servilleta?*"

For a while the luncheon party bent to its work, and then Sarah pushed a baked apple aside. "I never want to see food again."

"Right," said Alex. "Nothing by mouth for twenty-four hours. Has Jeff calmed down?" he asked Lois Bailey, who was beginning to look with disfavor on her curried shrimp.

"Jeff's in a real grump. No Big Bend. Just the same old tour with the two old dingbat aunties and sister Nina."

"Where's he sitting?"

"He was over there at that long table with the others. But I don't see him now. Maybe he's gone back for seconds."

"There he is," said Sergeant Cotton. "Out there by the rest rooms. I can see that yellow cap he wears."

Lois Bailey nodded, and then, seized by a sense that the time had come for parting formalities, smiled at Sarah and Alex. "If you go through Buffalo, Sarah—or you, Alex—do visit. We've got lots of birds at Niagara Falls."

"We had a smew once," said Mrs. Goldsmith.

Alex smiled and stood up. "I'm going to try and catch up with Jeff and have a word. Someone can have my shortcake."

The others sat at the table, probing their desserts in half-hearted exploration. The light was low, as it so often is—inexplicably—in restaurants in the daytime. Sarah looked in the long mirror opposite the table and could just make out Alex's head and shoulders as he wove his way back toward them through the maze of tables. Poor guy, she thought, it really hasn't been much of a vacation for him either, and then she realized with a twinge that this was the first time she had spared a thought for Alex alone.

Alex was pushing through the obstacles with something like urgency. "I can't find Jeff," he said, confronting them.

"Oh, he'll turn up," said Connie Goldsmith. "He's probably loading up on candy bars."

A waitress materialized at the table. "I have a note," she said. "It was left at the cashier's desk. For Mrs. Bailey and Mrs. Goldsmith. Table 125."

Lois Bailey read aloud from a single sheet of lined notebook paper with a message scrawled in pencil. "Dear Aunt Connie and Aunt Lois: I've got a chance to go west birding with a bird tour leader. I'll be O.K. and see you in Hamburg. Don't be mad. Love, Jeff. P.S. I'll be gone when you get this."

"Well, goddamn that boy!" Lois Bailey forgot herself for the first time on the trip. "After all we've said."

"I don't believe it." Mrs. Goldsmith snatched at the note. "Pulling this again. Running away three times."

Sergeant Cotton got to his feet. "I'll go on out to the parkin' lot and see if I can head him off."

"Oh, yes, thank you, Sergeant, and please hurry." Mrs. Goldsmith shook her head again. "I just don't believe it. We should have given him real hell the first time he sneaked off. What do we do now? And what tour leader? Texas is alive with tour leaders and tours."

"Has he got some money and his airline ticket?" asked Sarah.

"Yes," said Mrs. Goldsmith unhappily. "He said he was old enough to take care of his own things. Damn. Damn."

"May I see the note?" asked Alex. "Is this Jeff's handwriting?"

"It looks like it," said Mrs. Goldsmith. "And the paper looks like it came from his field notebook. But if he had this all planned, why did he tease us about going to Big Bend this morning? He must have met someone, a tour group, in the cafeteria."

"A tour group going to Big Bend, you mean," added Mrs. Goldsmith angrily. "That remark about going 'west' doesn't fool me."

Both ladies shook their heads sadly. They had thought that they could trust Jeff, that he had at the bottom the steadfastness that he had shown toward his scientific interests. "But what do you really know about another person's child?" asked Lois.

"Or even your own?" said Connie.

"We can't just sit here moaning," said Mrs. Bailey. "If Sergeant Cotton doesn't catch him, we should see about chasing him. I'll go and ask Mr. Ready what to do. He's in charge now. Jeff can't have gone far. The police could pick him up." She rose hurriedly and set off for the long table.

Sarah looked across the swarm of tables, saw Lois Bailey bending over Arthur Ready, saw Arthur Ready rise, napkin in hand. They both looked at the door, then at each other. It was a mime of shared distress and annoyance.

"Sarah," said Alex, "does all that gear of yours we loaded into my car mean that you're going somewhere?"

"I thought it was time that I faced up to things and started north. I was going to rent a car and head for Boston."

"All right," said Alex. "Here's Cotton coming back shaking his head. Hello, Tiger. No luck? Okay, I'm going to write a note to Tom. Will you call and read it to him, and if you can't get him on the phone, deliver it into his hand? Connie, will you ask Arthur Ready to call Tom's office and cooperate in putting together a list of bird tours or clubs heading west, and particularly to Big Bend? Also, any ornithologists or tour leaders who might be heading out that way? Then Tom can start tracking Jeff."

"Here's Mr. Ready coming now," said Sarah.

Alex repeated his request, and Arthur nodded, adding how unfortunate that Major Foster had already left for either El Paso or Big Bend itself. "We could have enlisted his help in the search, but I do not have his immediate schedule. He's meeting a group for me in El Paso but not until the end of next week. I believe he's expecting to make some business calls and perhaps do some independent field trips. If he calls in to the office, I'll tell him about young Goldsmith, whom, of course, he knows." Mr. Ready turned to the aunts and put on the paternal smile of a man used to wayward boys and distressed relatives. "Boys like your nephew land on their feet. I have a two-way radio in the bus, and so we'll keep in touch with Boyden, and with refuge and park personnel in west Texas."

Alex handed his note to Tiger Cotton. "Can you pick up a squad car to get back to Boyden?"

"Easy," said Tiger.

"Tell Tom I'll call him tonight and let him know what I'm doing and find out what's turned up from his end. . . . Jeff, I hope." Alex turned to Arthur Ready. "I was thinking of driving west today, perhaps around Big Bend, so I'll just take a look around for Jeff."

You were not thinking of any such thing, said Sarah to herself. She watched Alex say a few words to Jeff's aunts and saw the lines of tension smooth away from their faces. He's the physician calming the family, she thought.

Alex turned back to Sarah. "I'll drop you someplace where you can rent a car. Unless," he added, "you want to drive west with me. Come on, we can duck out the side door."

"Yes," called Sarah as they began to twist their way out of the dining room. "Yes, I mean I'm coming with you."

Sarah was dripping by the time they got to the car. More with some kind of ill-defined apprehension than heat, she realized, because the sky had clouded into a heavy gray and a cool wind was making the Texas flag snap at the top of its pole by the plaza entrance. She released Patsy from the back seat, ran him to a bush and back, and jumped him into the car.

"We're off," said Alex, starting the car and swinging it fast into the traffic while Sarah struggled with her seat belt.

"Are you really going west, to Big Bend? All the way? Looking for Jeff with some bird leader or in the middle of some bird tour?" asked Sarah, subsiding breathlessly in her seat.

"I certainly am, and you can open my map and chart a route to Big Bend, because I don't think Jeff would have run off for anything less than Big Bend; he had a fixation on it. Also, Sarah, keep an eye out for any vans or buses that suggest a bird tour. Look for the Audubon decal and bird-club stickers."

"You know, Alex, I don't see how Jeff—a boy his age—could have convinced some absolutely strange tour leader to take him along on a trip. Not without talking to Jeff's family. So what I think is that Jeff must be a stowaway in some bus, or that he somehow teased and teased Major Foster until the major gave in. Jeff could have told the major that his aunts had given him permission."

"Yes, I agree with all that . . . and also that Foster may be involved. I mentioned this in my note to Tom. So keep a lookout for the major's tan Dodge van while you're at it."

Sarah unfolded the road map of Texas. "You don't have much choice. Follow U.S. 83 along the border, past Laredo and north, then pick up U.S. 277 somewhere south of Crystal City."

"That's enough for now. I can't remember more than five numbers. Dandy's Cafeteria has gone to my head." And Alex cut in front of a truck, shot forward, and took the lead away from the surprised owner of a white Thunderbird.

## LIV

The ladies of the Cactus Wren Tours sat in the garden of Vacation Villa at a glass-topped table covered with maps and field guidebooks. Miss Fellows stared off into the distance, and Mrs. Brent lamented over the change in schedule.

"Such a shame to give up Big Bend. I can't think that the

police really need us. The girls are becoming bored. Perhaps we can get permission for an overnight to Aransas, because, as it is, we may run out of refuges, or patience . . . or both."

"I have an appointment to see Lieutenant Pérez again," said Miss Fellows in a detached voice. "On Saturday morning."

"And I have one on Monday," said Mrs. Brent. "It's just routine. Now what do you think of a joint field trip with the St. Agnes girls? I ran into their principal, Mother Mary Innocenta, on the trail yesterday, and she feels it would add zest to the studies of both groups."

"I'm having bad dreams, you know, Addie."

"Everyone has bad dreams from time to time, but that little breakdown did you a world of good. It's all behind you now. I wonder if we could manage a day trip to Falcon State Park?"

"Variations on the same dream," continued Miss Fellows in a faraway voice, "as if I were being drawn along without being in control of where I was going . . . or what I was doing. I found myself out of bed last night. Sleepwalking. I haven't done that in years. I suppose it's been waiting for me all along."

"You're sounding like one of those gothic novels, Midge. It's just nerves. I will buy some Ovaltine for you to take at bedtime. Now, I think that Miss Lucas should not insist on both an oral *and* a written examination in both botany and ornithology. One test—"

"I don't want to break down again," said Miss Fellows. "It's not fair to you, Addie, or to Cactus Wren Tours. Or, I suppose, to what they call the interests of justice. Because I've been thinking . . ."

"What in heaven's name are you talking about, Midge?" demanded Mrs. Brent, diverted at last from her scheduling problems.

"I've been hiding from what must have happened, and at night it comes out. Truth waits for you. It's always there if you look hard enough. Or it comes for you."

"Frankly, Midge, you do not sound entirely sane. Stop being Delphic and say what you mean, and I will help you deal with it. Don't let these investigations get to you. Every morning I brace myself against them. I fend them off. I master them."

"But they have gotten to me, and I'm afraid I'll lose my nerve when I see Lieutenant Pérez."

"But, Midge, I will stand by you." Mrs. Brent's voice was anxious. "I will come with you on Saturday."

"No, Addie, I've got to go alone. Lieutenant Pérez emphasized that. I know that I'm sounding melodramatic, and I've been telling myself that it will all go away, but that discussion about the kites last night fixed something in my mind. Oh, Addie, I envy you. You live in such a safe world, always some wheel you can put your shoulder to. I know I'm being trite, but you always make the best of all possible worlds. And thank you for being such a good friend. A friend in need."

"Now you sound like *Poor Richard's Almanack,*" said Mrs. Brent crossly. "Lieutenant Pérez doesn't know you the way I do, and he'll jump to some wild conclusion all because you've been having nightmares and have been upset this past year."

"I'm going off somewhere to be alone to try and think. Do what you want about the girls." And Miss Fellows rose from the table, settled her white canvas hat on her head, and walked off toward the end of the garden. Mrs. Brent, her hands holding tightly to her road atlas, watched her go with increasing distress and bewilderment.

# LV

Sarah watched the highway rise up, over, and down a long series of overpasses, the now familiar fields reaching out on each side with only the lines of Mexican palms giving them definition. Then these, too, fell behind, and the dark soil of the Valley changed to lighter rolling ground crossed by arroyos and patched here and there by low brush, mesquite, and juniper.

It was like those rides at world's fairs, Sarah thought, where you sit in a little car that draws you through different habitats. Barbed-wire fences appeared at the edge of fields, tall posts, and gates marking the entrances to ranches: The Rocking A, Rancho Benito, Rancho del Sol. Now came a verdant stretch with wildflowers coloring the side of the road, and here and there a Mexican cemetery, with its low white wall surrounding tiny white stones and little Madonnas in blue coats. Then ahead the road narrowed into two lanes, and small slatternly buildings began to crowd the highway, then fruit stands with net bags of oranges and grapefruit that hung from posts and spun as the heavy cattle, poultry, and vegetable trucks rumbled by. And now they crawled through Rio Grande City, past crumbling courtyards and houses with fallen balconies; then they sped forward, released from the town.

"Now we'll make time," said Alex. "On to Marathon and Big Bend. Can you stand driving through with only a few pit stops?"

Sarah looked over at Alex, saw his face tense, his hands clenched around the steering wheel. "You're worried, aren't you? It's not just Jeff running away, is it? It's that he might be with Major Foster."

"My thumbs have been pricking ever since we left McAllen. I just hope Jeff hasn't put himself into real trouble."

"But I thought we agreed that Major Foster wasn't bothered that much by Jeff's report, that the lecture scene didn't prove anything."

"Not to us, perhaps, but it may have proved to Foster that Jeff was dangerous. Pretend, just for the moment, that Foster is the murderer. If that's so, then Jeff may have been on the Observation Tower at a damn inconvenient time for Big, who was claiming to see kites at Settlers Village just then. Remember, someone's lying about those birds. Is it Foster, or is it Jeff?"

"Maybe it's just a matter of someone's watch not keeping time . . . or of someone wanting too hard to see rare birds."

"Yes, that's just as reasonable. But I wish I hadn't been the wise ass who gave Jeff the idea of challenging Foster. It won't be much consolation to Jeff if he is in hot water to know that Foster finally took his kite sighting seriously."

"I think you're jumping to conclusions. After all, I stood up at the lecture and said I'd taken a picture of the kites and that I confirmed Jeff's sighting. Major Foster hasn't tried to kidnap me." But then Sarah remembered the shadow over her tent and shivered.

Alex didn't notice. He shook his head. "No one said 'kidnap.' But Jeff's Big Bend obsession may mean that by hook or crook he's getting himself there, or that he made himself an awfully easy pickup for someone who was waiting for the opportunity."

"But none of this makes sense," Sarah objected. "We know that the major's sister is mixed into something with that crazy checklist, and that maybe the major is in with her. But if the two of them are behind the murders and the Celluwell thing, and if Jeff is a threat, why wouldn't they do Jeff in right away? Why take him on a trip west? Why to Big Bend, if that's where the major's going? Everyone knows that's just where Jeff wanted to go, so that's where he'll be looked for."

"But there was no chance to get hold of Jeff before this noon. He was with two guardian aunts and the tour group. Then, after Big had said goodbye to the Hamburg people, he may have found Jeff loose somewhere in that cafeteria madhouse. He could have pretended to Jeff that it was a legitimate trip, that he'd square it with the aunts."

"And it was easy because Jeff was so ripe for the picking."

"Right. And why would Big head for Big Bend? We don't know that he did, or that Jeff's with him. It's all guesswork and full of holes. But, first, Big was heading west anyway and the route to Big Bend, as you've noticed, runs along the border. That means that Mexico is available to escape to in case things get hot. Then, if I had to choose a Texas landscape in which to lose a body, I'd take Big Bend. Foster knows the area. He can take Jeff there, all eager, and dump him, say, in the Chisos Mountains, and then go about his business."

"And turn up in El Paso in time for his next tour?"

"Exactly, and when someone asks him, 'Have you seen Jeff Goldsmith,' he says, 'No, sir. Didn't he stay with that Hamburg group?'"

"But can't you convince Tom to get into the act? Fast."

"I suggested it in my note, but Tom still thinks bird-watchers are an arcane lot, and he might hesitate about alerting half of southwest Texas because of my crazy hunch."

"Well, I think it *is* crazy, and I don't like all this talk about a body. I'll bet you're wrong, and we'll find Jeff sitting in the middle of some Wonder Bird Tour driving everyone bananas with proper nomenclature. But," continued Sarah soberly, "the whole story can't have a happy ending. Two people are dead. That's one reason I wanted to head north, to get away, make a new start, and do something serious."

"I know you want to think things out, but, Sarah, don't let that new start turn into a sort of ashes-on-the-head routine . . . an emotional suttee."

"I just think I should face up to real life," retorted Sarah. "Suttee is for wives. I never thought of myself as Philip's wife."

"You're being literal. I think you feel a little guilty because you were never going to marry Philip, and you knew that Philip had settled on you for life. You were coasting along, getting better from Pres. Am I right?"

"No, you're not, and it's none of your goddamn business."

"Sorry." Alex didn't look at Sarah, but the speedometer crept past seventy. "You're right. It isn't."

They drove in silence. The sky seemed darker ahead, and Falcon Lake appeared at the top of the rises, a long dull slate-blue stretch. Barn swallows swooped over the road and under culverts, and a freight train went by, toy cars set against immense distances. Then Sarah saw a dead sheep caught on barbed wire at the edge of a field. It looked like a blanket of dirty wool with hooves unaccountably attached. A tear, and then another, slipped down her cheek, but she didn't dare move her hand to wipe them off. But Alex hadn't seen. He was reaching over, fiddling with the car radio, and rejecting a series of stations in which static and country music mixed egregiously.

Sarah made a quarter turn and regarded his profile, the dark hair loose over the forehead, the long thin lips held tightly together. With her eyes she traced around the chin and across the ears, large and flat to the skull.

"Are you measuring me for an executioner's hood?" said Alex.

"No," said Sarah. "I'm bracing to say I'm sorry. Forgive me. I'm a bitch."

"My fault," said Alex. "As you said, it's none of my god-damn business."

"If the truth pinches, put it on."

"Forget it, Sarah. Look, there's a hawk up ahead. Over the road."

"Don't divert me. I've read somewhere that Abraham Lincoln once said that if you've made a bad bargain, hug it all the tighter. I used to think he meant Mrs. Lincoln. Anyway, I don't agree, because that's what I was trying to do with Philip. Not that he was a bad bargain, but I was making one out of him. We didn't really belong together. You're right. I liked him for the wrong reasons. I was looking for someone to make the world safe for Sarah."

"I never wanted to force you into a corner on this. It's my bad temper, and the rain coming on, and being in a lather about Jeff. I took it out on you."

"Don't let me wiggle out of this. I've been furious with all the people who treated me like Philip's honorary widow, but I didn't tell myself that it was because I didn't deserve it. Sooner or later I would have made him miserable and upset his careful life."

"Well, Philip was difficult. He was obsessed by order because his whole growing up was disordered. He would have tried to pattern you, and you'd have struggled because you're a free spirit . . . well, fairly free. You have that solid rock behind you, family, house, home, to use as a springboard."

"And 'Home is where one starts from.' " But I think it's time that the free spirit came down to earth. That's why I broke camp."

"You're on your way down, but don't overdo it."

"Don't encourage me. I need a good dose of the salt mines."

"I'd hate to find you in sensible shoes and a navy beret going around as the district nurse."

"I'd thought of joining Vista or the Peace Corps."

"Fine, great, but not as a guilt reaction. I know I'm meddling again, but hell, Sarah, good English teachers are like gold. I'll bet you're a whiz. Someone has to tell the world what a predicate is and why D. H. Lawrence loved his mother."

"Shoemaker, stick to your last?"

"Something like that. Forgive, Sarah?"

"Yes, Alex. Dr. Whatever. And vice versa?"

The Volvo streaked past a Border Control checkpoint, a Tick Eradication Center, past fields of umber and ochre and chalk, past vultures sitting on fence posts, past slow-moving cattle.

Sarah began to sing very softly, " 'As I was a-walking the streets of Laredo . . .' " Her voice trailed off. "I used to love all those songs about lonesome cowboys and Old Paint, but the closest I ever got to the West was the Saturday-afternoon movie."

"On the way back, maybe, I'll take you to Horsehead Crossing over the Pecos River. The forty-niners used it, and the Goodnight-Loving Trail crossed it."

"There really was such a trail?"

"Of course, effete Easterner."

Sarah sang again, very low, " 'His hat was throw'd back and his spurs were a-jingle. . . .' " And Patsy lifted his head and howled.

And they drove north out of Laredo, turned west from Carrizo Springs and northwest at Eagle Pass and on to Del Rio. The land became increasingly harsh, interrupted only by thorny brush, grass, and rocky slopes, and Sarah thought of the ghosts of long-dead cowboys who had driven their herds through Texas toward Wyoming.

# LVI

Jeff Goldsmith sat hunched on the front seat of an International Scout, an auxiliary Ready Tour vehicle, the existence of which was unsuspected by Sarah and Alex. It was kept behind Arthur Ready's garage at his house in McAllen and used for off-the-road exploration.

Jeff was now feeling decidedly restive. At first, he had vigorously suppressed any disquiet that he felt on running away for the third time in one week. After all, this had been his last chance. When Major Foster had found him at the entrance of the cafeteria men's room, Jeff had begged the major to take him along. And the major had said yes. Just like that. Jeff had been so surprised that he almost couldn't answer. But then the major had said that they had to leave right away because they had to trade the van for the four-wheel-drive Scout at Mr. Ready's house and then make tracks, as it was a long drive.

"But," Jeff had protested, "I don't have my duffel bag . . . only my knapsack, and I've got to tell Aunt Lois and Aunt Connie."

"This is a man's trip, Jeff. I've got enough gear for both of us. I'll call the aunties tonight when we get to the park. Right now, I don't aim to waste time pesterin' your womenfolk about whether you've got an extra pair of clean underdrawers to take. You can send a note over to their table. I'll tell you what to say. We don't want to rile 'em up and have 'em start chasing us."

Later, settled in the Scout, Jeff had asked whether he should keep an eye out for interesting birds on the way, and the major had said in a sharp voice, "Now you just sit there on that seat and keep still, Jeff boy, so's I can concentrate on makin' time."

Time really did seem to be a matter of concern, for as mile after mile was racked up, the major remained unspeaking, leaning forward over the wheel, giving a sense of urgency to the trip. Jeff, his uneasiness growing, reminded the major about calling the aunts when they reached their lodge that night.

"Jeff boy, you let me worry about the ladies. You sound like you want to be holdin' on to their skirts like a big baby."

Jeff, mortified, did not bring up the subject again, and the major, one hand on the wheel, began fooling with the CB. Jeff was puzzled at his continued silence, because he'd always seemed to enjoy doing a lot of talking. He remembered the major's flow of chat and information on the tour trips: "Just you look at that yucca . . . Spanish for bayonet . . . we're a mite early for the bloom . . . look at those thorns . . . just like sewin' needles." Now the man's stillness seemed more and more unnatural, and the dark cloud-thickened sky ahead only increased Jeff's anxiety.

Almost sixty miles northwest of Eagle Pass, the driver heading for Big Bend must turn sharply west and follow U.S. 90 over the Pecos River and pass through the arid plains and slopes dotted with creosote, cacti, and other plants hostile to human flesh that characterize the Chihuahuan Desert. Towns are few: a feed station, a pair of gas pumps at a general store, a café with a Spanish name, a tiny cemetery—none encourages the traveler to linger.

At last, reaching Marathon, Big Foster turned the Scout in by a small food market. "Stay put, Jeff. None of that loose-foot stuff you're so partial to. I'll pick us up some supper."

Jeff stretched and wriggled unhappily. Why was he here? Why had he run off like this again? Back this morning, Big Bend had seemed so important, and he'd spent all that time studying the park field guide. Of course, his aunts had never said in so many exact words that he couldn't go, and he'd never promised them not to. Not really. But he supposed that what he'd done was a kind of cheating, and no one would trust him again. His parents would be told, and he'd be punished like some little kid. Like Nina. He'd be grounded for a year. Or maybe sent to one of those work farms for boys who got into trouble. Why had he asked to come anyway, and—and this was funny—why had Major Foster said yes? Because Major Foster had never acted as if he liked him that much. Of course, arguing last night about those kites hadn't helped. So the major made a mistake—Dr. McKenzie said experts did all the time. Why all the sweat about going to the police station with Mr. Plummer? In some weird way, it had to do with the major making a goof on his I.D. Or lying. And this *was* a murder case. Jeff remembered playing the game of Murder at home. Lights out, a scream, a body, a detective, and a murderer. Everyone telling the truth but the murderer. He lied.

Jeff was swept by a sudden urge to get out, get away. But how? Marathon was a small ranch town of wide streets. Beyond lay range land that extended unbroken until halted by the rise of rock layers that formed the Marathon Basin. Jeff could not imagine escape across such an expanse, nor a hiding place in such an unfurnished town. But he could look for a public telephone. Cautiously, he opened the car door and then saw Big Foster approaching with a box from which a carton of milk and a bunch of bananas protruded.

"Openin' the door for me, Jeff boy? Not thinkin' of goin'

somewhere? Or findin' a telephone? Told you I'd call the aunties tonight. I'll say you're fine. But maybe a tad homesick."

Jeff subsided into his seat. After all, the major had bought some food, so maybe everything was okay. But Jeff, with a sudden choking, realized that he'd never been so completely cut off from home and friends. I hope I'm not really homesick, he thought with disgust. Would that account for the way he was feeling? Better figure it out and not do anything dumb. Be the interested kid and watch Major Foster. Try to distract him, find out what he's thinking.

"I'm sure looking forward to the Chisos Mountains," said Jeff.

The major turned the Scout south, leaving the Glass Mountains behind them. "Are you?" he said ambiguously.

Jeff tried again. "There's a bird over on that fence post."

Major Foster slowed the Scout, looked, and accelerated. "That's a burrowing owl. I thought a whiz kid like you would know that."

"I don't know all the species around here. Thanks, sir."

The major made a derisive noise. "What are you playin' at, boy? Mr. Know It All gettin' modest? Okay, what's the species name for that owl? Quick! And a description. Speak up." It was a command.

"*Athene cunicularia* is a diurnal owl found in the plains, often nests in prairie-dog towns . . . bobs up and down, perches on fence posts or on the ground. . . . Sandy color and long legs make it different from other owls," Jeff recited in a monotone.

"Well, now, thank you, Jeff boy. Let's not play beginner. You're the expert, remember? You made that pretty clear last night, didn't you?"

Jeff saw that subtlety was called for. Don't be too polite, and get him talking. Jeff indicated the rising sweep of rock about him. "What are those mountains—the ones with the layers."

"Don't you know, bright boy?"

"No, honestly. I haven't studied geology yet."

"That's the Marathon Basin. Folks call it a window . . . lots of different strata exposed. You can see it from the side because of the way it's eroded." The major's natural garrulity, after too long a silence, came to the fore, and he delivered himself of a paragraph on the wonders of the Trans-Pecos region, while Jeff, seeing the western sun coming out through the somber clouds and the low backlighting of the mountain shapes, found the scene of such staggering strangeness that his attention was gathered away from his predicament and absorbed by the changing horizon.

# LVII

Thirty minutes later, in the following Volvo, Sarah, too, exclaimed over the formations of the Marathon Basin. "It's like those plastic layered cutouts they put in textbooks."

"Nature imitating a geology book?" asked Alex.

"Yes, a time machine display. It looks so old."

Sarah thought the Basin seemed to have been formed by some giant child who had been called away suddenly from his play with huge blocks and puzzle pieces and tumbled them into jagged heaps of raw sienna and burnt umber, leaving a skyline of illogical shapes.

"It's incredible. Alex, why doesn't everyone come here?"

"A lot do. But Big Bend's off the main track, one of the wildest parks in the country, and more like Mexico than anything north of the border. The river dips down into Chihuahua and Coahuila."

"Hence Big Bend?"

"Clever girl. And over seven hundred thousand acres total —a whole mountain range within the park, the Chisos Mountains."

"And we're trying to find one boy inside all that?"

"Yep," said Alex. "In gulches, canyons, resacas, windows, peaks, scarps, mesas, and lost mines. But we have to give it a try. And there are only so many campsites, so many hiking trails and roads. If Jeff is with Big Foster, remember that the major's knowledge of the park is probably no more than that of a leader who takes tours out on fairly well-traveled trails. And if Big is actually bent on homicide, I don't think he'd go too far off the marked paths. You can get terribly lost in a wilderness with Big Bend's topography. Besides, he'd have to have a plan for getting away fast. Of course, if Jeff's here with a real bird-tour leader, he should be fairly easy to pick up."

"But you'll start asking around for the major as well as Jeff?"

"Right away. If Foster's going to do something, he'll do it soon. Smart thirteen-year-old boys are hard to fool for long."

"Why not throw Jeff into a canyon the minute they hit the park?"

"That's possible. But by sundown the park will be filled with campers. Too many people around to risk being caught with a body in your arms. Best to keep a low profile and try and pass for a park visitor, wait for daylight, and then head up the mountains. If it is Foster, most likely he thinks he's gotten away free so far. No cops on his tail, no roadblocks. One problem: we don't have a detailed map. But I do have Jim Lane's *Birder's Guide.* Turn to the Big Bend section."

Sarah studied the booklet and presently said, "There are a lot of side roads called 'primitive' that lead to hiking areas, but only two possible tourist campsites: Rio Grande Village, by the river, and Chisos Basin, which is miles off in another direction. Alex, if it's Foster, won't he just pull off and hide under a rock?"

"You're often less conspicuous in a conventional place. If I were faking a birding trip with a boy, I'd skip the Chisos Basin campground. It's a saucer with everyone next to everyone else. Too cozy. And the upper Basin Lodge is too civilized. I'd go to Rio Village. It's large, with at least two camping areas and an overflow place. I'd get off at the end somewhere, away from people."

Sarah suddenly pointed. "Alex, look. There's a bus. Just ahead."

Alex shot the Volvo ahead and signaled with his hand, and a small bus filled with dark shapes pulled off the road. When Alex came back, he was shaking his head. "No Jeff. It's the Botteri Bird Tours from Austin. They'll watch out for Jeff, and for Foster, whom their leader knows—bit of luck there. They're going to the Chisos Basin, which is another reason for us to try Rio Grande

Village. And, bless the man, he gave me a trail map."

"I do wonder about bird tours," said Sarah as the Volvo bounced back onto the paved road. "Don't they take all the fun out of bird-watching—if bird-watching is fun."

"They work for a lot of people who wouldn't get away on their own—singles, students, older people, everyday good ladies like Connie Goldsmith and Lois Bailey. They learn something, maybe see more birds."

"But all that tape-playing, and crashing around, and calling 'pish, pish.' If I were a bird, I wouldn't nest with a bunch like that around. I'd become extinct—or accidental."

"Most bird tours are run by responsible people. Every use has a misuse," said Alex sententiously.

"And ornithologists—they experiment, put headphones on pigeons, paint the wings of redwing blackbirds, and shoot the rare birds."

"Photographing accidentals is much more common now, but study skins are needed. Accidentals don't have a chance to mate; they're out of their natural habitat. And ornithologists can show you how migration, reproduction work . . . what's happening to the nesting sites."

"Do not ask for whom the dead bird tolls? And the numbers game?"

"Okay, as long as people don't stampede to see a bird. Some birders get a kick out of counting. My life list is five hundred and eighty-five."

"I'm sitting next to a numbers man. You seemed so harmless."

"Dr. Whatever, in his mad drive to see seven hundred birds in one year, is now absconding with the hapless but toothsome Sarah Deane, whom he will place atop Emory Peak, the better to attract the ravenous and liver-eating Colima warbler."

Sarah allowed herself to smile and then rubbed her forehead in a worried gesture. "I suppose Emory Peak is another mountain to search?"

"Let's hope that Jeff and Foster stick to the most popular bird trails."

"And that the major's mania stops with birds," muttered Sarah.

# LVIII

Jeff hoped so, too. He had been studying Big Foster and had concluded that if the major had a weakness, it was, like Jeff's own, his unflagging interest in birds. He'd been able to cause the major's head to swivel and the car to slow by pointing out that owl, but he couldn't try it again with such a dud of a bird. Also, the time taken by the major to glance at the owl had hardly given Jeff the chance to leap out of the car and speed off into the countryside with no better cover than desert brush. He'd have to wait for the mountains, if that's where they were going. But Jeff had really only studied the more usual birds of the region and had almost neglected the accidentals. He indicated his copy of Wauer's *Birds of Big Bend*, sticking up from the top of his knapsack. "I should study up on the birds we might see," he said.

"Go to it, Jeff boy, you've got a little daylight left," said the major, sounding unnaturally agreeable.

He's watching me, thought Jeff. He opened the text to an illustration. "I wonder if I should study the birds of the Grassland?" The major made no reply. "Or," Jeff tried to sound offhand, "how about the birds of the Pinyon-Juniper-Oak, or the Cypress-Pine-Oak Woodlands?"

"I didn't think big shot needed a book," remarked the major. "You want to know where we're headin', but I don't aim to spoil the surprise. There's Panther Junction ahead—that's park headquarters. We'll pull over to this side road and give ourselves a break." Big guided the Scout down a sandy path. "They call this Mule Gap Arroyo . . . saw a lesser nighthawk last time I was here. We'll wait till dark. No point in havin' the rangers hassle us about where to stay."

For the short time the light lasted, Jeff scanned species records of the park and then sat in the increasing darkness watching the strange mountain shapes blend from blue to purple to darkest brown and then lose contour in the night sky. He had never felt so alone.

The major, who had been flexing his knees and rubbing the back of his neck, suddenly sat up. "What the hell?"

Jeff saw the outline of a bus, its high-beam lights leading the way, turn in to the path to the arroyo, and as the bus slowed, Major Foster's hand pushed hard on the top of Jeff's head, forcing him down on the seat of the Scout.

"Down on the floor and stay down, hear. I don't want trouble . . . you bein' a minor. Don't move or pull anything fancy, or I'll crack you one." The major paused. "That's a joke, boy, but I mean it." He reached over and pulled the Scout's headlights on so that they hit the windshield of the bus.

Jeff, without speaking, rolled to the floor, and Big Foster propelled himself out of the driver's seat and slammed the door. Jeff, in his huddled position, knees under his chin, head against the gearshift, considered. Big Foster's offer to crack him one had almost resolved his doubts. He had to get away . . . it was now or never. Jeff poked his head up, saw the bulk of Major Foster walking away from the Scout headlights, ducked down again, and opted for never . . . or not just yet.

The major, returned, was jovial. "Get up, boy. They're on their way. An acquaintance of mine. Botteri Bird Tours. They're lookin' for some runaway kid. Yellow cap, red hair, glasses. Looks about eleven or twelve."

Jeff was offended but did not answer.

"I said I'd keep an eye out for the kid. Seems there's this guy in a Volvo lookin' for him, not understandin' that the kid's on a private trip. Don't suppose it's young Dr. Hawkeye comin' all this way, do you? By golly, I'd sure hate to try and locate a person in Big Bend, especially if that person did not desire to be neighborly."

Jeff's continued silence seemed to affect the major, because he clapped the boy on the back. "Sorry I got hot under the collar back there. Hate to be bothered when I'm off on vacation. Besides, Jeff boy, you don't want to be dragged back to that tour group, do you?"

Jeff was all at once subject to some surprising emotions. One was the unexpected wish to see his aunts, and even Nina, and the other was a rising joy at the idea of Alex McKenzie somewhere in the park.

"Okay, Jeff," continued Big Foster, "in the interest of not havin' you taken away, your aunts havin' come all over lonesome for you, we'll just have you change your clothes. Open that knapsack and get undressed. Pronto."

Jeff unzipped his knapsack and produced a shirt, a cluster of dingy sweat socks, a wool sweater, and a pair of dilapidated sneakers rolled up in a pair of blue jeans, and under the major's flashlight, shivering in the cool night air, wiggled into the designated garments. Most reluctantly, he exchanged his hiking boots for the sneakers.

"That's right, boy. Those shorts were no good for hiking here. Ever get a cholla stuck in your flesh? That's a cactus comes out and jumps you. What else have you got? I'll take charge of your wallet. Don't want you losin' your money up here in the park. And those famous notebooks of yours. Thank you, boy."

Jeff sullenly handed over his wallet and notebooks to the major, who stowed them in his own duffel, snapped off the flashlight, and started the motor. "Not sure the sharpest thing you ever did, Jeff, was to spot those hook-billed kites when you did." The major shook his head with something like regret and pulled the Scout into a turn. "Nosiree, Jeff, you should've gone and had yourself an ice cream last Friday like your little sister did. Well, now, it's gettin' on, so I think we'll shoot right through Panther Junction and not bother the aunties with any telephone call."


Sometime later, Big Foster drove slowly past the Chisos Basin campground, announcing, "Filled up. Anyway, we don't want to be with a noisy bunch like that. There's a pull-off past the lodge that's mighty private. Have ourselves a bite to eat." Big down-shifted and after going past a group of lighted buildings—that's the lodge and store, thought Jeff, taking bearings—continued up the road, swerved abruptly, bumped hard for a short distance, turned again, and stopped.

"We'll make an early start. That's the time to see birds. Now get off into the bushes and go potty. I'll have a flashlight on you. And give me those tennis shoes. Barefoot is best for kids like you."

Jeff, red-faced, furious, made his way into the brush, hoping to avoid a cholla cactus—did they grow at this altitude? Later, after forcing a banana and a cup of milk on top of a bologna sandwich, he lay curled on the top of a blanket in the confined space of the rear of the Scout and tried to keep his enlarging panic from overwhelming his ability to think.

Obviously, he should try to get away during the night, but the major had run a clothesline around one door handle to the other and pulled it tight. "I don't aim to lose a boy in these mountains. Should've got a rope on you first time I saw you. Saved us both a barrel of trouble." Big then promised Jeff that he was a light sleeper and reminded him that he was still in possession of the boy's sneakers. "You can't get far without shoes, old buddy."

Like Alex and Sarah, Jeff began to appreciate the choice of Big Bend as a place in which to dispose of an inconvenient person. And I couldn't wait to get here, he reminded himself bitterly. If he could just get down to a phone and call his aunts and say 'I'm sorry, come and get me.' But even if he could climb past the major, who, lying propped up on a rolled jacket, more than filled the front seat, he'd only find himself hopelessly mixed up in the dark, an easy target for the major and his flashlight.

Then again, but stronger now, came a longing for the normal humdrum world which he had so energetically resisted. Now it would be a comfort to help Aunt Connie and Aunt Lois with their sparrow identifications or hit tennis balls with Nina. Dullsville became the desired home. And it was starting to rain. Jeff told himself that he mustn't be lulled by it, must stay awake and make a plan for the morning. But no sooner had he so resolved than, exhausted, he fell asleep, heavily without dreaming, only to be wakened in the dark of the early morning by Major Foster shaking him strenuously by the arm.

# LIX

It had been a discouraging evening. Sarah and Alex had put in two fruitless hours at Rio Grande Village knocking on van doors, peering into trailers, scratching at tent flaps, and interrupting cookouts. Later, when at last the Volvo had crawled into the Chisos Basin campground, they found it quiet, with almost all lights out. But the tour leader of the Botteri Tour, when aroused, threw a bombshell. Yes, he had found Major Foster, parked off the road about a mile before Panther Junction. He was alone—no boy. Said he was resting up after the drive from Boyden. Was he sure about no boy, demanded Alex. Well, he hadn't seen another head sticking up in the Scout, and he hadn't felt he could go over and search, Big Foster being a friend and all that.

"A Scout!" exclaimed Alex.

"Yeah, an International Scout. Light tan or light gray."

"Where was he headed?" broke in Sarah.

But the tour leader hadn't asked. Big had said something about checking the park for his next tour and had promised to watch for this kid; said he knew all about him and his habit of running off.

Alex led the way back to his car, spluttering. "My God, Sarah! Foster hasn't got Jeff. Maybe he never did. Just an asshole idea of mine. But Foster's changed cars. What does that mean?"

"I don't know," said Sarah, "but maybe the man didn't see Jeff because Jeff's been tied up in the back of the Scout. Dead or alive."

"Or, as you suggested, taken care of earlier."

"We'll have to go on looking," said Sarah wearily. "And it's going to rain. The air feels thick, like a curtain coming down."

Together, dispiritedly, they made their rounds of the campground, but replies to their inquiries were universally negative, and they drove up to the Chisos Mountain Lodge and found the parking lot full of empty cars, their owners presumably enjoying the greater luxury of lodge bed and board.

"Let's camp here on the grass," said Alex. "Can you start putting up your tent while I call Tom? We might as well try for a few hours' sleep. We can't do much in the dark, and I don't know of any side roads around here to search."

Sarah nodded and began tugging a somnolent Patsy from the car. "He'll sleep between us," she said.

Alex swallowed a reference to canine bundling boards and left for the telephone booth. When he returned, he found that Sarah had opened his sleeping bag along one side of the tent and that Patsy did indeed form a fur barrier. Sarah was already encased in her bag.

"I've made some sandwiches from my food box," she said. "And some lemonade. What did Tom say?"

"Said he thought we were absolutely loco, but he's sent out a description of Jeff to the Public Safety people, to the local police, and to the International Crossing staff. I've told him about the Scout, and he's getting the details to the park rangers here and to other wildlife areas, also to Texas-based tour groups. I suggested roadblocks and a helicopter search, and he said he'd think about it. He's talked to Lois Bailey and Connie Goldsmith, and they're mad as hell but not really apprehensive."

"If," said Sarah, "Major Foster is innocent and Jeff just pulled another fast one, when I see Jeff, I'll shake him until his bones clack."

"Violent Ms. Deane. What you'll do is burst into tears like the womanly creature you are and clasp him to your bosom."

"Male stereotyping. And he'd freak out if I did."

"Go to sleep. I'm going to prowl around the lodge, then go in and talk to anyone I can find. One more thing. Tom said to tell you that Eleanor Lucas is cleared, but that the case is still alive. He's got an appointment with Miss Fellows tomorrow and is going to bear down."

Sarah sat up straight. "Oh, the poor woman. Alex, do you think . . ."

"I don't think. Tonight my crystal ball is very cloudy, and Miss Fellows is very far away. I can only be in one place at a time.

and right now my heart's in the highlands, a-hunting Jeff Gold-smith."

"I wish we were in the Highlands. The stag at eve and everything all safe and purple and misty."

"It's going to be plenty misty soon. I just felt raindrops."

"Be careful, Alex."

"Cautious McKenzie. I haven't a heroic hair on my head."

And I haven't either, thought Sarah as Alex's steps faded, and she wondered whether she should call Alex back and tell him about her shadow visitor. But no, Alex had enough to worry about. She was going to take responsibility for herself now—or anyway share it with Patsy. Sarah smiled sleepily and let one arm fall across the dog's back.

# SATURDAY, MARCH 23

## LX

Jeff sat up, a flashlight in his face, aware of a dry mouth and glued eyelids. Big Foster, without speaking, passed him the remains of last night's sandwich supply, but Jeff shook his head.

"It's all you're going to get. Take some milk with it and it'll go down. I don't want you faintin' on the trail." Big thrust a dark-colored baseball cap over the top of the seat and clapped it on the boy's head. "Okay, we're off. The rain's stopped. Fasten on that knapsack of yours and put your binoculars around your neck." Big Foster pulled the boy from the Scout and produced a can of insect spray. "Don't want you attractin' bugs." He proceeded to cover Jeff with a fine spray, and then repeated the process with himself.

In the dark of early morning, Jeff was hardly aware of more than a black shape looming over him, but he took comfort from these attentions, for, he reasoned, if he's going to kill me right away, he wouldn't care if I got all bitten up first. He looked down at his feet in their socks. "I haven't got my boots."

"So you haven't, boy. Think I'll let you wear those tennis shoes, because your hikin' boots are goin' to keep your other clothes company." Here the indistinct form of the major busied itself with what appeared to be a bundle, then disappeared behind a boulder. Returning, he carefully scuffed the ground and took hold of Jeff's shoulder. "If I had time, I could get you broke right Okay. If any smart ass turns up, your name is Joe. Joey Foster and leave the answers to me. Just Dad and his boy on a field trip. Now, get a move on, up the trail. I'm right behind you."

The major gave Jeff a shove, and Jeff started forward, stumbling in the dark. He must remember the trail descriptions, the maps he had studied in his motel room . . . was it only two or three days ago? It was too dark to see any trail markers, but he seemed to be walking uphill, heading generally south, if that lightening in the sky meant the east. So they weren't going to the Window Trail, which he knew started from the upper Basin and went northwest downhill. What was left was the complex of trails leading to Emory Peak and Boot Canyon and the trails of the East Rim and the South Rim. Jeff remembered that the South Rim promised a drop from an escarpment of twenty-five hundred feet into a wilderness below.

They climbed, the trail continually reversing direction, and as the dawn grew into morning, the air became heavy and humid with a sullen sun indistinct in the sky. The worn-out soles of Jeff's sneakers were no proper shield for the rocks on the trail, the straps of his knapsack rubbed against his clavicle, and the woolen sweater tied around his waist felt like a heating pad. To these discomforts were added the sweat that trickled down his face and the cloud of tiny insects that swirled around his head, getting into his mouth and nostrils, apparently more attracted than repelled by his bath of insect lotion.

Major Foster, seemingly impervious to such irritations, walked easily, leaning into the pitch of the trail, and from time to time prodded Jeff with the end of a staff that he had cut for himself. Once or twice he allowed the boy to pause and take a swallow from the canteen of water which he carried.

On the whole, the major seemed as immune to the presence of birds as he did to the rigors of the hike. However, as they reached the higher altitudes, Jeff, anxious for his own reasons to continue to demonstrate expertise, suggested that the most interesting migrants would not make it to the higher part of the mountains until April. The major did not disagree and was later pleased to confirm Jeff's identification of a painted redstart. Big Foster's large face lit up, and he took out his notebook. "Don't usually see this one till later," he remarked.

But mostly, they trudged on and on, and Jeff saw the pinyons, firs, junipers, and oaks become small below him and new ones appear and rise before him. And now the length of the hike, the non-appearance of Boulder Meadow, the benign rise, all told him that they were traveling the South Rim Trail, and as they wound their way back and forth, Jeff began to see that the possibilities for getting rid of someone were perhaps more favorable on this expansive trail, with its wide spaces between dips and switchbacks, and the heavy tree growth blocking the view of the next part of the path.

Maybe it was a bird trip after all. Maybe Major Foster wanted to go off on a two-man expedition, get away from stupid bird clubs for a while. And maybe the major admired him, thought he was pretty smart for his age. Part of Jeff's mind accepted the solace of these ideas, but the objective part of it wished to test the the major further. Thus, during one of their infrequent stops, Jeff, sitting on a fallen log, brought up the kites.

"I really saw them at Bobcat Marsh," he said.

"And look where it's gotten you, Jeff boy."

Jeff chose not to pursue this remark and, instead, asked the major about the kites he had reported at the Settlers Village.

"Birds fly, Jeff. Or sometimes it's convenient to migrate them just a tad."

Nor was this the time to dispute the morality of falsifying sightings, and Jeff only asked, "Were you excited to see those kites, Major Foster, because you've seen lots of accidentals?"

"You never get tired of seein' a rare bird come along. And I wasn't the only character to get a charge out of those kites," the major continued in a reminiscent tone.

"Another character?"

"Some smart-ass bird-watcher sticking his nose where it didn't belong."

"You mean me?" asked Jeff, stoutly pursuing the subject. "Or Mr. Hernández? He saw the kites."

"Yep. Sam saw 'em, too. And you did. It was quite a day for kite-watching, Jeff boy."

"But this other guy, this character—was he in the marsh?" asked Jeff, hardly breathing.

"And that's none of your business, Jeff boy. None at all. But a pair of hook-billed kites can sure be a distraction. Someday I'll write it all up. In my memoirs." The major chuckled deeply. "On your feet, boy. Want me to show you a marine trick or two that keeps the troops marchin' along?"

"No, sir," said Jeff, standing up hurriedly.

"Then get the lead out of your young tail. Hay foot, straw foot, belly-full-of-bean-soup, left, left, I had a good home and I left . . ."

Jeff picked up his knapsack, and his memory gave him back a brush-covered horror lying just about thirty feet off the Bobcat Marsh Trail. He marched forward, left foot, right foot, left foot.

## LXI

As the first fan of light spread over the mountains east of the Basin behind Casa Grande Peak, Sarah and Alex, squatting in the semi-dark, held a conference over doughnuts and oranges. Sarah, having decided to ignore any possible hazard to herself, was in favor of splitting forces. She and Patsy, who might reveal unknown tracking abilities, would take one trail, Alex another.

Alex rejected this proposal. "Tom has alerted the park staff, and they'll be on the lookout. And I don't think you could handle Big Foster if he's feeling mean—even with Patsy's help. That isn't meant to be a male chauvinist put-down," he added. "Just practical."

Sarah agreed reluctantly. "All right. Which trail, then?"

"We'll flip a coin. But first let's spend a few minutes in the light seeing if we can find that Scout pulled off the road."

They were almost immediately successful. Some thousand yards past the upper road that led above the lodge, they followed a turn into a clump of pinyon and came upon a dirt-and-rain-streaked International Scout with the Ready Tour decal on the back window.

"Damn, it must have been here all night, right above us." Alex peered into the car, moving his flashlight about, and then circled, trying the doors. "Locked. It looks empty. Just some sandwich stuff, a milk carton, and a blanket."

"Shall we look around for footprints?" asked Sarah.

"No, let's hit the mountains. Finding the Scout is a real break; now we know Foster was in the Basin area."

"But," Sarah objected, "we don't know that Jeff was. Maybe the time we're going to spend tracking Big Foster should be spent looking for Jeff, who may be miles from here. There's no proof that Jeff's with Foster."

"No proof that he isn't. Look, Sarah, all the park rangers are looking for Jeff; no one's looking for Foster as a first priority. We can look for both at once. Let's follow my first hunch: that Foster would stay on the usual bird trails, maybe the one to Boot Springs. Now the South Rim is the long way round." Alex opened his map. "But there's another trail. I don't see any reason to take the scenic route. We'll go up the quick way. Boot Canyon Trail by way of Pinnacles Pass. A toughish climb, but we're a toughish team. Right?"

"You hope," said Sarah, looking over Alex's arm at the map.

"We'll push on as fast as we can. I'll fill a canteen, and you do the same. Take heart. We might just catch them. Foster may be in great shape, but he's over fifty and Jeff has short legs."

"And our strength is as the strength of ten because our legs are long?" Sarah filled her canteen, settled the strap over her shoulder, and strode off with Patsy ahead in the skirmishing position. Within a short time, the wide trail had narrowed to a single rock-lined slot that marched, by a series of acute hairpin turns, directly up the side of the mountain. The dull sun appeared over the mountaintops, streaking the canyon walls with muted colors of sand and rust, and from high above a canyon wren called, its crystal-thin descending notes sounding like falling mountain water.

Sarah, in the lead, was conscious of the need to appear a resolute hiker, but the stones under her boots slipped on the incline so that sometimes she seemed to be sliding down faster than she was climbing. By the beginning of the second hour, Patsy had ceased pulling against the leash, and Sarah could feel the knots in her thighs, the pounding in her chest, and a rasping dryness in her throat. Blast Alex, he was stamping along behind her like a tireless robot.

Just as she decided to lose face and stop, Alex called, "Whoa. God, Sarah! Do you run up Mount Washington on your day off?"

"I keep in shape," gasped Sarah, and, opening her canteen, she tilted the water in her mouth, then knelt and gave Patsy a drink from a salvaged cut-down milk-shake container.

"It's the stones," said Alex. "And the altitude. We should be getting over six thousand feet by now, and we're sea-level people."

Sarah looked above her and saw the rust-brown castle formations rising above the trail, and then far below she saw the narrow trail going back and forth like a whiplash. "What's so special about Big Bend? Besides the scenery, I mean. Birds, flowers, or"—she grimaced—"snakes?"

"All of the above," said Alex, who was engaged in searching out an elusive stone from the toe of his boot. "Just watch where you step."

"It's funny what you remember. I couldn't come up with the name of that special Big Bend warbler, but I could pass an exam on *Crotalus lepidus* and *Crotalus atrox*. I can hear Mr. Plummer now."

"To repeat," said Alex, shaking out a sock, "watch your hands and feet, look out for logs—the other side of. And remember, we must protect our wildlife."

"Certainly," said Sarah. "I wouldn't dream of disturbing *C. atrox* while he's taking his nap."

"Sometime," said Alex, standing up, "I'll give you my Colima warbler lecture, but now on your feet, Wonder Woman. Shall I go first? No? Well, take it easy, I'm getting on in years."

# LXII

At the same time that Alex was naming the Colima warbler to Sarah, Jeff, trudging up the South Rim Trail, was wondering if he could produce an early-arriving specimen of the same. Because, since he couldn't count on seeing a rare bird, he'd better invent one. He needed a bird like that Barrow's goldeneye that made Mr. Plummer wade right into the Niagara River with his shoes on as the duck disappeared around a bend. The painted redstart had been good enough for at least a two-minute delay— almost enough for a breakaway. Jeff thought wildly of trogons and smews, but no, he couldn't use a bird he'd never seen himself. What he needed was a real zinger that wouldn't bring his own credibility into question.

Jeff deliberately slowed his pace, and for the first time, the major, breathing noisily behind him, did not prod the boy with his stick. He's pretty old, Jeff reminded himself, and we've been climbing more than three hours. It had been too dark to look at his watch when they set out, but now the sun, a smoky yellow circle, hung well up in the sky. If he's going to get rid of me, he'll try it pretty soon, because he'll want to get out of here before dark, Jeff told himself. He couldn't leave a trail or blaze a tree, because the major pounded along too close for any improvisations. Then, quite suddenly, Jeff became aware of dropping into another habitat. He saw quaking aspens above the trail, a chaparral community of sumacs and dwarf oaks and desert ceonothus. They must be coming into Laguna Meadow. Jeff could not believe that he was going to be brought safely all the way from the Meadow to Boot Springs. Hikers would be appearing anytime now; already, far below, he'd caught glimpses of light-shirted figures winding their way up the trail.

With desperate resolve, Jeff forced himself to review the details of bird incidence in late March as described in Wauer's field guide. He must be ready to play a scene with the same confidence he'd shown when he stood up at that slide lecture. Okay. He began turning the pages of the guide in his mind, straining to remember the crucial details: "Catbird . . . there are two park records of this bird. . . . Brown thrasher . . . uncommon migrant. . . . Wood thrush . . . rare spring migrant. . . . Red-eyed vireo . . . rare spring visitor.

"Keep those legs going, Jeff boy." The major, recovering his wind, stuck the forked end of his staff into the small of Jeff's back.

# LXIII

On the Saturday morning that saw two parties taking separate trails to Boot Springs, Johnny Shapiro opened Tom Pérez's office door and announced in a cheerful voice, "That butterfly couple dropped off their Land-Rover in Fort Worth and got themselves a rental Chevy wagon. Shall we keep trackin'?"

"Yes," said Tom. "This refuge thing isn't cleaned up by a long shot. And, Johnny, send Cotton in. I hear him bumping around out there."

Tom opened a desk drawer, took out a crumpled pack of cigarettes, shook one out and stuck it into his mouth, paused, and then snatched it away and threw it angrily in the wastebasket.

"That'll save you a pack of trouble, Lieutenant," said Tiger Cotton, who appeared like Punjab over Tom's desk. "That's a joke," Tiger observed. "A pack of trouble. Get it? And I thought you quit smokin'. Somethin' eatin' you?"

"This job is eating me, so wipe the grin of your big face. I've got Captain Nordstrom rooting around in his pen next door, and those damn Axminsters, and a missing kid, and my crazy doctor friend off on a wild bat to Big Bend with Sarah Deane, and this morning I've got a neurotic history teacher coming in."

"Send me to Big Bend," said Tiger Cotton. "I'd sure like to

help out. I'll do anything. Anything not routine," he added hopefully.

"For once we agree, Tiger. I've decided to fly you out there. You'll hook up with the chopper boys and try and put some zip into that search. You'll work with the park staff, set up roadblocks, the whole bit. See if you can stop Alex McKenzie and Sarah from racking themselves up and killing Jeff Goldsmith by trying some damn fool citizen's arrest. And don't you go and fall off some damn cliff."

Tom remained staring at the office door long after Tiger Cotton had slammed it shut and departed on thunder feet. The morning sun, arriving in a filtered state through a dusty window, lay in muddy rectangles on the panel of the door and along the paint-chipped wall. Nothing seemed urgent, or really important. Tom reached a second time for the cigarette pack, and as he did so Johnny opened the door and bobbed his head. "Miss Fellows here now, boss."

Tom looked up, turned his gaze again to the wall, and let thirty seconds slip by. Then he nodded. "Okay, send her in and get me a stenographer." He pushed the cigarettes aside and closed his eyes.

The door opened and after a short interval was shut. Tom raised his head. "Come in and sit down, Miss Fellows."


Almost an hour and fifty minutes later, Tom escorted Miss Fellows to the outer office, and, in a voice that did little for his carefully nurtured reputation as "that tough cop from Homicide," said to Johnny, "Miss Fellows took a taxi here, so I'm driving her back to Vacation Villa. Will you make a note that I'm releasing her into the custody of Mrs. Brent? She understands that she'll be under the usual police surveillance. She'll be back tomorrow and look over her statement. Yes, I know it's Sunday, but I'll come in."

Johnny lifted his eyebrows, but Tom frowned and shook his head.

"Miss Fellows," said Tom, "one of the most interesting periods of American history to me has always been the Reconstruction period. Do you feel that if Lincoln had lived . . ." Here the outer door closed behind the lieutenant and the lady, leaving Johnny to wonder at his boss, who had just left to drive to her motel, in all amity, one of his chief murder suspects—one whose statement he was about to guide through the typing and copying process.

# LXIV

Jeff, plodding ahead of Major Foster, finished turning in his mind the pages of the Big Bend guide and now noted that they were well into Laguna Meadow—a fact confirmed at that very moment by the limestone under his feet. He looked at the opening slopes around them, and then, finally, brought it all together: the bird, the place, the time. He slowed his steps.

"Could I have another drink of water, please, Major Foster?"

The major grunted but swung the canteen over to the boy. Jeff drank, recapped it, then appeared to listen. He hung the canteen over one arm, lifted his binoculars, and scanned a patch of brush.

"Get a move on, boy," said the major. "I'll take that canteen."

"Listen, Major Foster. Over there. Do you hear that?"

"I said get those feet movin' "

"I think I can see it. Right over there. Now it's gone up that pine . . . out on the limb . . . on the right side."

"Okay, spit it out. What do you see?"

"A warbler, a Blackburnian. I'm almost sure. I see them at home, in New York State. Look along that branch. It's a male."

"We don't get Blackburnians in the park. Not anytime."

"One record. Rio Grande Village in 1970. That's what the guide says, but maybe there've been more since. Look, moving at the top of the tree now. Listen. He's calling again."

"You've got rare birds on the brain, boy. I can't hear it."

"It's that high ending. And see, the orange throat."

The major lifted his binoculars, and Jeff slipped the canteen over his head and pushed it under one arm.

The major lowered his binoculars. "Stand next to me, boy, while I find this warbler. Still can't hear it."

"He's quiet now, but he's back down on the lower branches. About four o'clock."

The major moved forward, binoculars at the ready.

Jeff raised his voice slightly. "There, there . . . he flew. That tree over there . . . two o'clock."

Big Foster advanced with a stealthy step, five yards, ten yards, fifteen, and raised his glasses again, and Jeff slung his own binoculars under the arm away from the canteen and took off.

Legs pumping, sneakers sliding on the stones of the trail, Jeff ran, and the major, swearing loudly, pounded the ground behind him.

Keep going, keep going! Jeff shouted to himself. I can't beat him on the flat or downhill, I can't run through brush. . . . I'll have to go up. The trail splits . . . where? Almost out of Laguna Meadow now . . . hit it for Boot Springs.

Jeff ran and slipped and ran, the binoculars and canteen banging wildly against him, the long-striding major fifty yards behind. Run, run, he repeated. Left foot, right foot, hay foot, straw foot, run, crack the whip, crack your neck, break your mother's back . . . one, two, three . . . on your mark . . . get set . . . run, run sheep, run.

# LXV

With muscles in torment, Sarah and Alex gained Pinnacles Pass and pressed on to Boot Springs. Here they collapsed near the cabin that announces to the hiker that he has arrived, drank copiously from their canteens, and panted.

Sarah examined Patsy for paw damage. "He's okay. The fur

acts like a bedroom slipper, but I may have to knit booties soon. Where now, Alex?"

"Keep going. Case the South Rim, then swing over to the East Rim."

"Here's lunch," announced Sarah, and, digging into a back pocket, she produced two molten candy bars and two small boxes of raisins.

"Wonder Woman strikes again. Water Patsy and we'll start. If we draw a blank on these next trails, I think we should head for the Basin and call Tom. Then get hold of the park staff."

Sarah got slowly to her feet. "I suppose hiking one trail at a time looking for a boy and a man in a mountain range is plain stupid. We need Rogers' Rangers or a commando team."

"Would you settle for a helicopter?"

Sarah lifted her head. High up, just visible over a ridge, she saw a small mechanical dragonfly coming closer, the dry tock-tock of the motor now clearly audible.

# LXVI

Big Foster was steady in the chase, and Jeff was losing ground. The knapsack was awkward, and here the trail got steeper. Another choice. Jeff saw again in his mind the configurations of the trails. Not the South Rim with that cliff. It had to be Boot Springs. With a tremendous effort, Jeff gained another twenty yards, saw Big falter, and used the time to pull his canteen and binoculars loose and take the knapsack and hurl it down the trail.

Jeff saw the major pause, reach for the pack and yank it out of the way, and come on again. For a few minutes, like a cinema in slow motion, the two continued uphill. Then Jeff, in a sudden panic, with a last backward look, grabbed his glasses from his nose, jammed them in his jeans pocket, and leaped over the side of the trail, took three giant bounding steps down the decline, stumbled, pitched forward, and like some badly wrapped package, with binoculars and canteen in orbit around him, rolled and bounced from pinyon to juniper to cactus to pine and vanished from sight.

At the edge of the trail where Jeff had taken his leave, Major Foster stood silent, chest heaving, sweat rolling down his face and neck. Then, in an almost anguished voice, he called the boy's name, repeated it, and stood silent again. Finally, he lifted his binoculars and searched the slope, stepped over the rim of the trail, hesitated, and climbed back. For a long while he looked down over the quiet expanse of tree canopy below the path and then turned, walked slowly down the trail, picked up Jeff's knapsack, hung it over his arm, and was gone.

# LXVII

This time Sarah was adamant. She and Alex stood on the outer curve of the South Rim trail, which, mimicking itself, bends in a deep loop, going one way to the east, and the other directly north to a junction with the Boot Springs trail.

"Patsy and I'll take the easy way back and you go another. There'll be hikers around now, and I can quiz them."

Alex finally agreed. "They've started searching," he said. "For someone anyway. I'll go along the Juniper Canyon Trail for a ways, then double back and check Boot Canyon Trail down to the Basin again."

"You don't think the major has outfoxed us and taken the long way up and the short way down?" asked Sarah. "Murphy's Law?"

But Alex only shrugged and departed, and Sarah and Patsy began the return trip, which proved undemanding and unproductive. She reached the bottom at dusk and found Alex, somewhat the worse for wear from his uncompromising descent, sitting by her tent.

"They've set up blocks at the roads out of the park and at Terlingua, Alpine, and Marathon. I've called Tom, but he's drawn a blank on all the tour groups he's checked. Said he may have a break in one of the murders tomorrow. Said we wouldn't like it."

"Miss Fellows?"

"He wouldn't say. But he's sent us a present."

"We could use one."

"Tom's air-freighted Tiger Cotton, who's helping with the helicopter search. They'll keep at it until it's completely dark."

"Hallelujah!" said Sarah. "That makes me feel better." She sat down on the ground and began loosening the laces of her boots. "I didn't see the Scout when I came down. I mean, I didn't look for it."

Alex took off, forcing his used-up leg muscles into a dogtrot. Sarah looked up expectantly as he walked wearily back.

"It's gone. No Scout, no Jeff, no Foster."

"Oh God, what now?"

"I'll tell the rangers to let the roadblocks know."

That evening, Sarah, Alex, and Tiger Cotton held a council of war. The Scout had been found, locked and empty, in an unoccupied end of the Rio Village campground.

Tiger Cotton suggested several picturesque ways of dealing with murderers, kidnappers, and runaway boys, and then said, "I've got a park Jeep, so I'll take another look into those dirt roads around that Rio Village."

Alex offered to stay in the Basin and walk a distance down the Window Trail by flashlight, and Sarah said that she would talk to the campers and lodge people again.

"We'll start sweepin' the canyons by chopper as soon as it's light," said Tiger. "And I'll meet you around eleven-thirty at this Laguna Meadow place unless somethin's turned up by then. We'll get the bastard."

"Hold off, Tiger," said Alex. "We're not sure Foster *is* a bastard."

"Hey, Doc, don't you go confusin' me. I work better when I'm huntin' rats, but I'll look for Jeff, too."

"I'll leave Patsy in the tent now," said Sarah. "He's had it."

"He's not the only one," said Alex, getting painfully to his feet.

# LXVIII

Jeff, too, thought he had had it. It was dark. What time was it anyway? How had he missed the whole day? He seemed to have been lying, everything hurting, huddled on his side for his whole life. Oh, yes, Major Foster. Where was he? Now he remembered. They'd been hiking up that long trail. But now, somehow, he was caught in the bottom of a sort of bush. I've fallen down, he thought, and clobbered myself. There was a cactus under one knee, and his cheek was held fast against a stone by something sticky. He tried to raise his head, the skin on his cheek pulling away like adhesive tape, but his shoulder gave a jerk of pain that made him dizzy. And one of his wrists was bent in a funny way. He felt around with his other hand and took a cautious inventory. There was an enormous bump on his head, with his hair all stiff and stuck together around it. And one ankle felt as if it had grown into a melon. He tried to sit, but a throbbing chorus combined against him, and he sank back on the dry leaves and stones. He was thirsty, very thirsty. Oh, yes, he'd taken the canteen because he was going to run away from Major Foster. Jeff fumbled about and found the canteen. Holding the stopper with his teeth, he unscrewed it with one hand. The water tasted great.

But now he was cold. Jeff pulled at his sweater and slowly struggled into it, easing the cuff over his injured wrist, and was about to sink back on the ground when he became aware of a small movement close by, almost imperceptible; then the faintest of rustles, the driest of scrapings among the dead leaves and twigs.

Jeff held his position on one elbow and then slowly let himself down as if were being lowered by a winch. There it was again, a sound as if the dry leaves were being softly crumpled and rubbed together, so faint that it might have been his own breath coming in a rasp. But he had a sense of something near, and, like Sarah, but with even greater accuracy, his mind presented him with a photocopy of Mr. Plummer's slide of *C. atrox* in all its puissance, and then in a series of footnotes appeared pit vipers of sand, rock, and canyon. Jeff, keeping absolutely still, tried to think of all the innocuous creatures of the night, but always he was brought back to the genus *Crotalus*. He remembered the pit viper's sensitivity to heat, and thought of tales of these reptiles seeking warmth in tents, sleeping bags, perhaps in the inviting curve of the recumbent human body.

He was not a boy given to imaginative effort, but now, frozen into position, he searched for some discipline to keep himself unmoving. Snakes, he knew, cannot hear—if this unseen presence was a snake; they respond to vibration, movement, as well as to heat, so he had to find some metaphor for stillness and hold to it.

He thought of a gang member encased in concrete at the bottom of a river, of a yogi who reduced his body functions to the threshold of death, of a quadriplegic who wrote on a typewriter by breathing through a straw. Then he recalled the Tutankhamen exhibit from a trip to New York. He would make himself into a mummy in layers of cloth. A mummy in a series of nested sarcophagi, bandaged, silent, not the slightest movement possible—not the rise of the chest, the contraction of the throat, or the flare of the nostrils taking in air, so, like the dead young king, he would not disturb the royal and sacred presence of the serpent.

# SUNDAY, MARCH 24

## LXIX

And so Jeff stayed until the morning sun lighted the sides of the canyons and the points of the firs. Then, slowly, he broke through his self-imposed catatonia and became aware of a throbbing ankle, a broken wrist, a stone under his shoulder. Without being able to help himself, he turned his head to the left, to the right, and saw a long gray-patterned rope undulating up the slope, through the dry leaves, making again the faintest of rustles as it went away.

For a while Jeff lay, aching, sore, exhausted by a night of rigidity, and then, sick and dizzy, propped himself up and drank from his canteen, which now sloshed in a hollow way. I should have something to signal with, he thought, in case a plane flies over. But what could he use? His binoculars seemed to have disappeared; his glasses were smashed in his pocket, and the canteen was a dull metal covered with flannel.

"Oh shit," Jeff said to the surrounding mountains. "I'm just going to die here, or get hypothermia, or starve or something." And, fatigue and fear overwhelming him, Jeff's slight body was shaken by dry convulsive sobs. Then, gradually, the boy's natural impatience began to stir. After all, he could still move around; he had one good left foot and one good right arm, didn't he? Suddenly, in a fury of frustration, Jeff tugged his sweater over his head and then pulled off his shirt. Holding one end of the shirt in his teeth, he began with his good hand to wrench and tear it into strips. Fortunately, the lightweight denim cloth was old and ripped easily, and it had long sleeves and tails. Then, after tossing his sneaker aside, he laboriously wrapped and bound his swollen ankle, in fact the whole foot, with enough material left—one sleeve and part of the neck and collar—to fashion a rudimentary sling for his wrist.

Sweating, head pounding from these exertions, Jeff looked up the incline. Yes, there were the marks of his fall, the disturbed soil, the broken branches. I'm going home, he thought. Right now. I'm going to crawl out of this stupid dumb park and never come back here in my whole life. He rolled over to his side, and with his good foot pushing and his good hand pulling at roots and stones, like some strange wounded animal, Jeff crept painfully and awkwardly up the slope. At last, panting, tasting the mixture of dust and dried blood and sweat as he bit his lip from the effort, he hitched himself over the rim of the trail and onto the stones and dirt of the path. And there, lying across the way, was the very staff—Jeff saw the forked top, the slash marks made by the major's wide-bladed knife—that the major had used to prod him forward up the trail. Jeff reached for it and, fighting vertigo and pain, dragged himself to a standing position. Okay, so far. He leaned on the stick and took a cautious hopping step. And another. And another.

And, as if it had been meant to happen all along, from the shadow by the lip of the trail, shooting out from his coils with the hard forward thrust of his triangular head, *Crotalus atrox* struck.

# LXX

Alex took hold of the bottom of Sarah's sleeping bag and shook it gently. "Come on, wake up. It's getting light."

Sarah groaned. "No, it isn't."

"Almost. Grab a bite to eat. We're leaving in ten minutes. In style. I arranged last night for us to ride the park horses to Laguna Meadow and go on foot from there."

"But I don't know how to ride," Sarah protested. She sat up yawning, her hair ruffled.

"You don't have to. The horse knows the way, and a park wrangler will look after us. You just look for lost boys, and I'll look for missing tour leaders. The man at the store said he'd take care of Patsy today."

It was not yet midmorning when Sarah and Alex dismounted and turned their horses over to the wrangler.

"I've got muscles in my legs that no anatomy book has ever described," said Alex, taking a bowlegged step forward.

"I think I'm a natural-born rider," said Sarah. "I didn't fall off. What trails should we take?"

"As I see it," said Alex, unfolding his map, "what with the helicopter search, and the park rangers looking systematically, we're just extra help, but the more searchers the better. Let's go for Boot Springs and branch from there."

"No, Alex. Two lookers in two different places are better. I'll do Boot Springs, and you start another way. No . . . don't argue, please."

"Seriously, Sarah . . ."

"Seriously, Alex. I mean it. Look, I can whistle. Through two fingers." Here Sarah gave a brief ear-cracking demonstration that caused the horses to shy away from their handler. "Tony taught me," she explained. "If anything looks peculiar, I'll whistle."

"And at the sound of the whistle, I'll come flying over a canyon or two and get there," said Alex sarcastically.

"We're wasting time," said Sarah sternly. "I'll meet you back here at eleven-thirty—that's when Tiger said he'd meet us —and we can plan what to do next."

Alex nodded. "All right, Sarah. You win. Put your bandanna on your head. It's going to be hot today."

"Yes, Doctor." And Sarah walked quickly away lest Alex change his mind and insist on coming with her.

It was odd, Sarah thought as she trudged toward the Boot Springs turn-off, that Alex had given in so easily. See, she told herself, if you sound responsible and are firm, you're treated that way. But all the same she felt quite alone. No rangers in sight, no hikers either, but then, it was early. I miss Patsy, she thought. She began to walk faster, and from time to time, as she climbed along the trail, she stopped and called Jeff by name, and, now and then, as if to mock her voice, some unknown bird called loudly from the surrounding trees.

And I still don't know a sparrow from a blue jay, Sarah told herself as she clambered up a particularly steep rise of the trail. Philip would be so disappointed, and at the thought of Philip, she caught her breath and halted. Philip had never seemed so far away as here in these alien mountains. Sarah looked about her, blinking into the sun. It was quiet now—only her own audible breath, coming rather fast, and a faint, indeterminate whisper in the trees behind her. But then, just then—why, there was a bird she knew. A catbird. That mewing sound. At least I know a catbird. That's a start. A crow, a sea gull, a robin, and a catbird. But that's because I know cats . . . not much credit there. It certainly sounded unhappy, such an unhealthy, pathetic little mew. Or was it a mew? Sarah began to climb again, rapidly now, perspiring in the hot sun. Again she stopped. There it was. Not a catbird, and not a cat. It was someone crying, whimpering like a hurt animal. Sarah broke into a run. "Jeff, Jeff!" she shouted.

The mewing sounded just above her head so the trail must turn back someplace. Sarah pushed herself up the path, now stumbling on a loose stone, now pausing to listen. Here was the turn, and there he was, just ahead, a boy sprawled along the trail like some discarded puppet, his arms flung out, his head face down in the dirt.

"Jeff, is that you, Jeff?" Sarah called. And as she ran forward, she saw that one of the outstretched hands held a stick, and at the far end of the stick, caught in its fork, was the gray-patterned wedge-shaped head of a snake pressed against the side of the trail while the snake's body looped and twisted over the stick.

"Jeff, Jeff, oh my God!"

And Jeff, raising his head, turned slightly to look back over his shoulder, and in doing so he released the pressure on the fork, and the snake shook itself free.

Sarah, in a sudden unthinking spasm of movement, ran forward, and, with the sense that the triangular head was now erect, rearing back on its coils, grasped Jeff by his ankles, and in a series of jerks, hauled him backward while the boy screamed in anguish. But then, with one final tug, Sarah lost her balance, let go of the boy's feet, and tumbled over backward.

"Don't move, Jeff."

Jeff moaned. "Everything hurts. My ankle. It bit me."

"I said don't move," said Sarah through her teeth.

For a while they lay, rigid, in the sunlit trough of the path, and then Jeff whispered, "It's going away."

"Be quiet. Don't move," Sarah repeated.

"It's going right away. Off the trail." The boy lifted his head. "I can see it going. I'm so sick."

Sarah reared herself up and crawled cautiously over to Jeff. "It bit you on the ankle?"

"My leg, my bad ankle," said Jeff, tears rolling down his cheek, his breath coming in short choking sounds.

"Stay still, Jeff. I'm going to whistle for Alex. I said I would if there was trouble." And Sarah sat back on her heels, put her second and fourth fingers into her mouth, inhaled, and the whistle split the air. And again. And again.

She turned back to Jeff. "Have you got a knife?"

The boy closed his eyes. "My glasses are broken. In my pocket. You could use them," he said thickly. "But don't cut me. Please don't cut me. I'm not sure you're supposed to do that anymore."

Oh Lord, thought Sarah, why haven't I ever taken a first-aid course? Do you make a horizontal cut? Or is it vertical one? Above the fang puncture? Or on it? And—here she shuddered—do I have to suck the venom out? Well, she'd better do something fast. Jeff looked terrible, with that dried blood all over his head, and his color awful, and his skin cold.

Sarah bent over Jeff's ankle and slowly and uncertainly began unwrapping the lengths of torn cloth, and then, below the trail, she heard sounds of running. "Help!" Sarah cried. "Help! Please, help!"

"Okay, Sarah," called a voice. "Hang on."

Sarah had just time to wonder how on earth Alex had made it to the Boot Springs trail so fast when he was there, kneeling by her side, supporting Jeff's leg with one hand, and with his other, gently unrolling the cloth from the boy's ankle.

A short time later, just before eleven-thirty, the pilot of a search and rescue helicopter, with Tiger Cotton as crew, came in low over Laguna for the rendezvous with Sarah and Alex. Forty-five minutes later, Jeff Goldsmith, with Alex in attendance—his medical bag at last justifying its trip from Boston—was transferred to a larger Jet Ranger at Panther Junction, which took off for El Paso and the hospital.

As Alex said to Sarah later, back in Boyden, "Jeff was damn lucky, and you were quite a heroine."

"Lucky!" Sarah exclaimed. "Lucky to have been taken to Big Bend with Big Foster, lucky to fall down a mountain and get bitten by a rattlesnake! And I'm no heroine. I ran right up to Jeff, and he turned and let the snake loose."

"But you pulled him out of the way. Jeff told me. You looked the dragon right in the eye."

"If I had, I would have fainted. But I didn't really get Jeff out of range . . . and that's funny. Why did the snake just go away? I thought diamondbacks stood their ground. That's what Mr. Plummer said."

"Mr. Plummer also said that western diamondbacks can't survive long out in the hot sun. Snakes have no internal thermostats—they die from overheating. That snake was probably going off to a cooler place. But I'll say it again. Jeff *was* lucky. That rattler hit him on the bandaged ankle, barely punctured the skin, and the cloth wrapping acted as a tourniquet, which slowed up the lymph flow. Not much tissue destruction, no circulatory collapse. Oh, sure, Jeff was in rough shape, and he'll be sick for a while, but he was as sick from his other injuries, from fright and shock, as from the snake bite."

"Oh, poor Jeff. But how did he happen to have the rattler pinned by that stick? I didn't have a chance to ask."

"Luck again. Jeff found the stick the major had dropped in his retreat and was using it as a crutch when the snake struck. Jeff, in a very natural reaction, backed away from the snake, then turned the stick around and got the head caught in the fork end. Told me in the hospital he'd seen it done on some zoo TV series. But he had trouble keeping his balance with that bad foot, started to get dizzy and faint, and somehow managed to lower himself on the ground keeping pressure on the stick. He seems to think you got there almost immediately and whistled for me."

"And quick treatment is half the battle in snakebites?"

"Absolutely. That and antivenin, which fortunately the rangers keep on hand. Jeff's going to be fine, and with a new respect for mountains and pit vipers. As for running off, he's full of remorse."

"Which will probably last until Jeff sees another rare bird. And now, Alex, I want the truth. You didn't go off by yourself on some other trail. You followed me to Boot Springs, didn't you? At a safe distance. That's why you got to Jeff so fast."

"I don't think I'll answer that question."

# TUESDAY, MARCH 26

## LXXI

Sarah leaned her elbows on a picnic table in Alta Hollow State Park and watched as Tom tidied the remains of the lunch and then produced three oranges from a paper bag.

Tom took an orange, plunged his thumbs into its top, and split it apart in a single thrust. He confronted his two companions. "Okay, Dr. Watson and Mrs. Holmes, fill in the holes. I've only skimmed over Jeff's statement from the hospital."

"You kick off," said Alex, "and tell us why Miss Fellows confessed that she could have murdered Philip. That seems senseless."

"Not senseless. Interesting." Tom conveyed a section of orange into his mouth. "But I think I'll keep you on the hook. You talk first. Assuming for the time being that Foster is the man we want, tell me how Jeff got away from him. That couldn't have been easy."

"Jeff used strategy," said Alex. "He knew that rare birds were Big's weakness. Jeff's too, of course. And sadly, I gather, Philip's."

"Philip's? How's that?"

"I'm patching together some things Foster told Jeff, but it may be that Philip, sitting at his scope in Bobcat Marsh, overheard Big wheeling and dealing with that poor devil Reynaldo Sánchez, who later got banged on the head for being a witness to Philip's murder. We'll never know whether Philip tried to interfere, or whether he spotted the kites and, when they flew, stood up to track them. Couldn't help himself. Maybe the major put on a good act, talked ornithology with him, pointed out some bird—the kites coming back, perhaps. Who knows? Anyway, Philip probably looked up, and Foster took hold of Philip's binocular straps, and that was that."

"But," said Tom, "Big and Sánchez would have been speaking in Spanish. Could Philip understand them? And if he could, wouldn't he have been on guard if he heard a drug drop being arranged?"

"Spanish was Philip's minor in college. As for being on guard, Philip was foremost an ace bird-watcher. Even if he'd found himself in the middle of the O.K. Corral, he'd jump to see an unusual bird."

Sarah remembered Philip stopping cold in the middle of a tennis match. "Oh hell," she said.

"So," said Alex, "Foster must have taken the field notebook and the Doña Clara checklist in case Philip had written up the kites or jotted down something about the Celluwell traffic, then grabbed the wallet to suggest robbery."

"He was in a hurry," said Tom. "He had to meet that tour at the parking lot, so he didn't look around, just dragged the body into the bush, took off and drove the van wrong way on the Auto Tour Road, and met his group a little late, but ahead of Jeff, because, of course, Foster had wheels and—oh Christ! Am I class A stupid!"

"You've remembered something?"

"Goddamn it, yes. Eduardo gave it to me, but because he said Foster did it all the time, I didn't pay attention. Listen. Big driving north and east on the Auto Tour Road makes sense *only* if he came from Bobcat Marsh, or an eastern trail because that would be the quickest route."

"But," broke in Alex, "going by way of Bobcat Marsh isn't the quickest way from Settlers Village, where Big claimed he'd seen the kites. If he'd really been at the village, he'd have come directly to the parking lot from the turn-around."

"I should have my tail kicked for missing that one," said Tom, "but why in God's name did Big go and say he'd seen the kites in the village? That was asking for trouble. Why not shut up about them?"

"Tom, after all this," said Alex, "you still haven't climbed inside the infernal mind of the bird-watcher. The rare bird— that's it. Big could no more forget those kites than you could forget a Mafia boss in downtown Boyden. All Big had to do was move them a bit to the east. But then to have anyone in the marsh see the kites or the murder—or both—became a real threat to Big. So enter Jeff Goldsmith, announcing at the lecture that he'd been on the Observation Tower spotting kites, and enter fathead McKenzie, who put the idea into the boy's head. Foster was probably frightened into deciding he had to take care of Jeff. And Sarah, too. She played star witness. It's a wonder he didn't take after her and her so-called 'photograph.' "

"Maybe he did," said Sarah, and at long last told the two men about the shadow over the tent on the night of the lecture. Alex began to exclaim, but Sarah cut him short. "My own fault. I got carried away. And that shadow could have just as well been some drunk camper looking for his own tent. I was in a mood for apparitions. Anyway, Patsy howled like a banshee, and it went away."

"Good for Patsy," said Tom. "But Big must have been running scared, because he should have known that Sam and all the local bird bigwigs would have backed him against some out-of-state kid."

"And the major would have made mincemeat out of me," said Sarah.

"Okay," said Tom. "I see how Foster might have distracted Philip with the kites, but did Jeff use the same trick? See kites?"

"Jeff was too smart for that," said Alex. "Those birds had had it. It had to be a bird that would stop Foster cold."

"And Jeff had a secret weapon," put in Sarah. "He knew his birds."

"Right," said Alex. "He'd studied the species that have turned up at Big Bend and finally decided to go for a common eastern warbler, one he'd seen many times, but would be accidental at Big Bend. He chose a Blackburnian male because it's a striking bird, face pattern, orange throat. Big would know that Jeff couldn't miss on that one. And here's the touch of genius. Jeff had noticed on field trips that the major was a bit deaf and missed the high notes on bird calls. Now, the Blackburnian has one of the highest and thinnest songs going, with an ending that climbs out of the range of anyone with hearing trouble."

"So the major couldn't tell that Jeff was faking it?"

"Correct. Foster probably hasn't been able to hear a Blackburnian in years. Well, it worked. Except that the major wasn't so easy to shake, and Jeff got desperate and leaped over the trail. Over and down. He doesn't remember the actual jump too well, but he must have bounced like a soccer ball. As I told Sarah, all in all, he's just damn lucky."

"But Foster didn't chase Jeff down the hill?"

"Apparently not, or failed in the attempt. He must have been pretty well wiped out by then. He probably took the fastest route straight down, picked up the Scout, and got the hell out. To Rio Grande Village and Mexico, swimming and wading."

Tom nodded. "I've had a report that a bundle of Jeff's clothes and his knapsack were found by the riverbank. Foster may have wanted to suggest that Jeff ran away over the border. It might have worked if Jeff had been killed and left in the mountains."

"So," said Sarah bitterly, "Major Foster is probably living it up in Puerto Vallarta by now."

"We're waiting for him," said Tom. "He won't disappear forever, but it may take that long to get up a case against him."

"What do you mean?" said Sarah, staring.

"Just that. It's one thing to put together a nice neat story, everything fitting—the Lentz murder, the Sánchez murder, the boy witness, the Celluwell deals, even Philip's field notebook that we found at Foster's house."

"What did you say?" Alex half rose in his seat in surprise.

"Sit down, keep cool. We found the notebook all snug and warm hiding in a mess of bird magazines. So now guess what's written under the heading of Friday, March 15, Doña Clara, Bobcat Marsh at five-thirty?"

"Hook-billed kites!" Alex and Sarah exclaimed together.

Tom grinned. "Wrong. Green heron, mockingbird, and a rough-winged swallow plus a couple of flycatcher birds."

Sarah groaned. "He might not have had time to write them up."

"Take heart, children," said Tom. "There's the beginning of a sketch of a mean-looking hawk thing that Sam tells me might be this kite."

"But even so," put in Alex, "it isn't hard evidence, is it? Big could have picked the notebook up and been nervous about turning it in to the police—murdered man's property and all that."

"But why keep it at all?" asked Sarah. "No, don't tell me. Bird-watchers don't throw away bird data. But, Tom, are you saying that you can't catch him on Philip's murder?" Sarah began opening her orange in angry little tugs.

"Hell, I'd hate to work a jury over with what we've got: a conflict in sighting a pair of rare birds, taking the long way round to the parking lot, Philip's notebook, plus Jeff's recollections of some vague hints Foster gave out in Big Bend. Juries aren't crazy about high-I.Q. superkids."

"But how about Foster's abduction of Jeff?" demanded Sarah, red with indignation.

"It was no abduction," Alex broke in. "We'll never know what Big would have done about Jeff if the boy hadn't fallen right in his lap at the cafeteria."

"Anyway," said Tom, "the defense will note that Jeff went of his own free will. He wasn't misused, he wasn't really threatened. No deadly weapons waved in his face. No demand for ransom, no using him as a hostage or a shield. He was fed, bedded down, and taken for a bird hike. Precautions were taken to see that he didn't run away, because Jeff was always taking off. Jeff and Foster go on a hike, Jeff falls, slips, or tries to get away—whatever. Note: all injuries suffered being the result of the boy's own actions. Foster tries to find the boy, can't, panics, goes off to Mexico. Defense rests. What's Foster guilty of?"

"Plenty!" said Sarah.

"Nope. Defense says Foster is guilty of leaving the scene of an accident and failing to inform the authorities. Felt he couldn't face the aunties. Great remorse, very contrite. Throws self on the mercy of the court, and—"

"And I may throw up," said Sarah.

"And the Sánchez murder?" asked Alex, seeing an impasse.

"Again no hard evidence except the funny checklist, and that's only a circumstantial link to Big's sister. The brick—we picked it up in the river—was washed clean. We'd have to prove that Foster or his sister knew Sánchez, had dealings with him."

Sarah spread her orange pieces out like a ruined flower and shook her head over and over. "But the Celluwell lead?" she asked.

"That *was* a good lead," said Tom, looking more cheerful. "Narcotics paid a visit to cousin pharmacist, and found—"

"Celluwell!" broke in Sarah.

"Right on. Found some in bulk, some in capsules. Same color scheme used in a well-known arthritis compound. Clever."

"And Iris Meyer?" asked Sarah. "Is she the Queen Pin?"

"Linchpin is more like it. She helped hold the operation together, and thanks to that checklist code, we've an idea how it worked. The raw Celluwell came in from Mexico and points south. Sanchez and others like him picked it up and brought it across. Each time Sánchez came over he was given, or picked up at the checklist distribution box, a coded list giving the time and place of the next meeting or pickup. Perhaps these were slipped in halfway down the stack of lists, or tucked under a stone. Not hazardous, because—as you said, Alex—who'd look twice at a marked checklist? We assume that Foster left the coded lists at various refuges in turn."

"But what exactly did the major's sister do?" asked Sarah.

"I think," said Tom, "that Foster sent her instructions on when to come to Boyden for a pickup, and then she'd carry the stuff back to Corpus Christi. We've got her under surveillance because we'd like a lead to other dealers. But I'm not casting widow lady as the mastermind in all this."

"Try simple mind," said Alex. "Iris Meyer likes comfort, good things, and loves her brother. She wouldn't object if Big wanted her to do some silly errands, deliver a few 'business' packages. She'd live her own life and be grateful for those cash presents from Foster. I see her as a connection, but a fairly empty-headed one."

"Yes," said Sarah, "and she wasn't supposed to know too much about birds, because that would attract attention. But, being much too talkative for her own good, she blew it."

Alex, restless as usual, got up from the picnic table and jogged twice around it, and then leaned over and swept the orange peels into the paper bag. "Now," he said, confronting

Tom, "stop playing games and tell us about Miss Fellows. What the devil did she tell you?"

"No hysterics this time," said Tom. "Pretty calm and collected. But she's got me going in circles. You make the diagnosis. I had her in to see me Saturday, and, as she tells it, it sounds like a case of self-hypnosis. Says she *did* see Philip Lentz ahead on the trail on Friday, and then, after she'd split from Mrs. Brent, she followed the path in the direction she'd seen him disappear and then spotted him up ahead. Remember, I speculated that she might have blown her fuse at the sight of him? All that hate boiling up."

"Reluctantly, I do remember." said Alex.

"Well, she can't quite recall what happened. Believes she was, in her words, 'possessed,' 'out of control.' She saw him disappear into the Bobcat Marsh area, and thinks she stood for a while staring at the entrance to the trail, and then went and hid in a thicket off the path and stayed there . . . or didn't. Can't remember. Has a recollection of two unusual birds overhead— those goddamn kites, probably. Says she must have walked farther on the trail then, but when she 'came to' it was getting dark and there was no one around. She looked at her watch and was amazed to see that she'd lost a big piece of time, that it was past six. She hurried back, making good time—the field hockey coach in action—and was glimpsed, as we know, by Jeff. This blank spell didn't bother her at first. She was upset by her job loss and all that. Then, at the Chinese dinner, my question about Philip detonated a lot of repressed stuff."

"And then," said Sarah, "she felt better, a lot more together."

"Right. But later," continued Tom, "she began to wonder about that time gap. Where had she gone, what had she done? She'd begun walking in her sleep, which frightened her. She began to think that she might actually have killed the man whom she hated, whom she wished dead, and then blocked it out. I put a policeman on to watch her and released her into the custody of Mrs. Brent. Told everyone to stay put and keep cool."

"But you have her confession?" asked Sarah, incredulous.

"Yes, and it's burning a hole in my desk. She signed it Sunday. I can't trash it. A confession of wanting to murder Philip

Lentz and having the time and place in which to do it."

"Tom, it's worthless," said Alex, sitting down again. "The fact that she can't remember isn't evidence. I'd say Miss Fellows just stood rooted. Couldn't go on, couldn't go back. So for a while she took herself out of herself."

"If you say so. It's out of my line, but she's agreed to have a polygraph test tomorrow and try a hypnosis session. I'd be mighty glad to cut her loose from the case and concentrate on Foster."

"What about the Axminsters?" asked Alex. "All set free?"

"No way. They've been nailed in Santa Fe and are coming back to face Sam Hernández. Not exactly willingly, but it was suggested that we'd be getting in touch with his Idaho college if they didn't." Tom turned to Sarah. "What about it? Are you going to stay here camping or head north? Seriously, I know you've had a hell of a rough time."

"Thanks, Tom. It's been a stinker. Yes, I'm on my way, day after tomorrow. Alex is driving me to Corpus Christi. I'll pick up a car and camp on the way home. Patsy is an A-1 camper."

"Camp Spirit, in fact," said Alex. "And I have two thoughts for you, Tom. First, your boss was right. It *was* a border problem, and a drug one, and an illegal alien got into the act."

"Not for long, poor guy," said Tom.

"And second, your favorite lady-fair was right, and you didn't listen. Mrs. van Hoek kept telling you it might be Foster."

"Christ, so she did. How did that fluff brain arrive at that?"

"Because, Tomás, she's the only member of the tour group who doesn't know a bird from a cow. She's a people-watcher. Everyone was so busy on the crucial days looking for birds that they would have missed a massacre. Not so van Hoek. Some of those cute little guesses may have value in court if you could ever pin her down to a coherent statement. Never mind, Tom. She'll enjoy working with you. Didn't she think police work was 'rather fun'?"

"Go to hell, Alex."

"And didn't she think it was quite remarkable that you'd risen so far above your ethnic background? Okay . . . peace," said Alex, ducking a paper bag full of orange peels flung violently at his head.

# THURSDAY, MARCH 28

## LXXII

Just after nine o'clock in the morning, thirteen days after her arrival in Texas, Sarah broke camp for the second time and, with Patsy in tow, climbed into the Volvo and settled back in her seat. Alex started the engine, guided the car around Boyden, and pointed it toward Harlingen and north. Sarah did not look back.

"I wish the whole horrible thing were finished," she said.

"The mills of the gods grind exceeding slow," said Alex, "and the mills of the justice system sometimes hardly grind at all."

"Nor exceeding fine," said Sarah.

"But I have news that will cheer you. Miss Fellows got through her polygraph and hypnosis session in good shape. Not guilty."

"That sounds hopeful. For the mills of justice."

"Polygraphs and information given under hypnosis may not be admissible evidence, but a D.A. won't want to push a case with both against him. I'd say Miss Fellows is safe."

"And sane?" asked Sarah in a worried voice.

"I think so. The storm is over, and helping run Cactus Wren Tours shouldn't put too much pressure on her. Mrs. Brent is a supportive person—a positive natural force."

"Well, that's good."

"One more thing. Mrs. Reynaldo Sánchez has identified a photograph of Big Foster as someone who came to her house once upon a time, which is a link Tom's been looking for, and also he's found that Foster seems to have some irregular bank deposit habits that call for a closer look."

"Well, good again," said Sarah. "But you're staying down in Boyden?"

"I've got a solid week of work ahead on that Celluwell project."

"Then I shouldn't have let you drive me to Corpus Christi."

"It's all right. I'm going to see three patients there who've been dosing themselves with the stuff. They've been hospitalized, and I've a chance to get some clinical data, run some tests. We still don't know much about Celluwell, except any real benefits seem to be in the mind of the beholder—or the patient." Alex glanced up at the huge sign announcing Kingsville. "*Déjà vu,*" he said.

Sarah nodded. It was like a home movie run backward, she thought: the wide fields, the windmills, the wildflowers, now in greater profusion, because, she remembered, it was almost April.

After a while, Sarah pointed to a hawk, wings outstretched, drifting motionless across the sky. "I'm beginning to see a little of what Philip . . . of what other people see. And I used to be so bored. But Philip could sit and watch a hawk soar, watch swallows fly, and let time go all to hell. It was sort of an extra, an excess in him. A grace. One of the best things about Philip."

"And how about Big Foster? He was a bird-watcher."

"In him it was something evil."

"But Foster didn't traffic in Celluwell and commit murder because he was a bird-watcher. He used birding as a front, all right, but his interest in birds was genuine, and he liked to show it off."

"I hate to allow any good in a bad package," said Sarah.

"Yes, I agree that Major Foster is a pretty rotten human. Not just murder, but making money out of someone's sickness, someone's hope of getting better." Alex was silent for a moment, and then he said, "One thing puzzles me. Even if he was exhausted, why didn't Big follow Jeff down that bank and finish him? Jeff didn't fall that far—one of the rangers checked the place where he went off the trail. Anyway, Big didn't have to be a mountain climber to come after the boy. And, despite Tom's doubts about the case, Jeff was the one person who could say that Foster was lying about his whereabouts at the time of Philip's murder. Jeff dead was no threat . . . just an accident."

"Maybe the major thought that Jeff would die of injuries, or exposure. Never be found."

"Too much vegetation breaking his fall, not letting him tumble too far, and too many hikers coming to Boot Springs to take such a chance. No, Sarah, I'm unwillingly coming to the conclusion that Foster simply let the boy go after he'd jumped over the trail. And allowing Jeff to stay alive as far as Laguna Meadow suggests, just maybe, that he was putting off zero hour, and when it came time for the kill, he couldn't do it. Perhaps he almost admired the boy, his interest in birds, his skill. Who knows? Not that a killer and a drug dealer is redeemed, but—well, it's a puzzle."

They drove in silence, watching the road unroll before them through Kingsville, and on into Nueces County, and there was Robstown again and the road turning east to the airport, and here were the squares and rectangles of Corpus Christi hanging and shimmering like a mirage ahead of them.

"I have something for the Camp Spirit." Alex reached with one hand into a pocket and produced a small enamel medal. "For Patsy's collar. It's San Roque, the patron saint of dogs. I found it in a Boyden shop. Special thanks to Grendel."

"I'll fasten it on right away," said Sarah. "That's a fine goodbye present."

"Not goodbye," said Alex. "Keep in touch, Sarah." He didn't look at her. "We'll both be in Boston, you know. I won't take you out on any field trips. Not unless you say so."

"I think I'll skip birds for a while."

"A concert sometime? Or spring skiing? We could drive to Concord for Patriots' Day and show Patsy a man riding a horse. I don't think he saw any in Texas. How about it, Sarah? Do you think you might need a brother or a cousin sometime? Remember, we might be cousins. Distant ones."

"Here's the airport turn-off," said Sarah, reaching for her knapsack. "Could you drop me at the rental-car place, please, Alex?"

"You haven't answered my question."

"To be in touch?"

"To keep in touch. As an English teacher might say, there's difference."

Sarah looked ahead at the outlines of Corpus Christi, and in her mind she traveled to Houston, around New Orleans, through the Florida Panhandle, to Georgia, the Carolinas, and on and on, all the way to the Mass. Turnpike, and perhaps north and on to Grandmother Douglas in her closed-up house.

"A place for everything and everything in its place," she said aloud.

"Which means?"

"I don't know. Not Oz. Not the district nurse."

"Shall I find you running a home for lost dogs?"

"That's an idea. Yes, I'll be . . . no, I'll keep in touch." Sarah smiled up at him, and for a moment rested her hand lightly on his arm. "Sooner, perhaps later. You know that bit about 'neither love nor lamentation; no song but silence.'"

"And whose line is that?"

"Antigone's."

"No, you don't, Sarah. You're being absolute and using quotations to prop yourself up. You can stand by yourself. You're ready, I think, but don't overcorrect. Accommodate. Do your mourning and then let the past go. Forgive me for sounding like an old family physician and . . . oh hell."

"Here we are," said Sarah. "If you'll stop by the door and hold Patsy for me, I'll run in and sign for the car. I've made a reservation."

Alex watched the thin, dark-haired figure make her way toward the office door—the faded red cotton slacks, the creased safari jacket hanging loose from her shoulders, her large leather purse slung over her arm.

This time Sarah didn't protest against Alex's efforts as a baggage handler. Silently he transferred the duffel, the tent, the lantern, the sack of dog food to the rear of Sarah's car and arranged them to leave a space for Patsy. Sarah pulled the dog into the car and climbed into the driver's seat.

Alex stood outside looking down at the top of Sarah's head. "All set? Well . . . goodbye, Sarah."

Sarah looked up. "Goodbye. And thank you, Alex, Dr. Whatever, my cousin and the old family physician. For everything. I mean it. Someday I'll pick up the telephone and say 'Come over, please, and take Patsy on a hike, a mountain climb.'"

"And you, too?"

"Yes, and me too."

Alex nodded, as if satisfied, and then reached in the window and ran a finger softly down her cheek. "Take care now. You and Patsy." He straightened suddenly, turned, and walked away.

By the time Sarah had turned out of the rental-car parking lot, the red Volvo had moved out to the exit and been swallowed into the double line of traffic.

"But still the question is," Sarah said to Patsy as the dog circled about and settled himself in the back of the car, "just what is our proper place?"

And she pulled the car into the right-hand lane, turned away from the airport, and headed north.